GRAND  EMPIRE

Clearly the bourgeois world order did not suddenly emerge overnight after a thousand years of feudalism. Fate had repeatedly to lend a hand before the fledgling finally found its feet. France, which in the conflict between the contending forces found itself fighting on the main front, achieved a break-through in its Revolution of 1789. However, the final outcome was still uncertain and the forces of conservatism gathered for a major counter-offensive. It fell to General Bonaparte to parry the blow.

He dragged the world into the 19th century. His regime had various facets, including some extremely dubious ones. Napoleon turned out to be not the upholder of freedom but its destroyer, not the Republic's guardian angel but its executioner, not the defender of the Revolution's mother country but Europe's biggest land-grabber. Yet at the same time he pushed open one door after another on the Continent, helped to eradicate the prevailing rulers and to prepare the soil ready for the new seed to take root.

In France a quite peculiar form of society took shape: an unprecedented and unique transitional society in which conventional contradictions interbred with newly emerging ones.

They did not merely ruffle the political surface, they cut deep into the everyday lives of the people. In both town and country customs—the good as well as the bad ones—were subjected to a partly gradual and partly abrupt process of change.

New institutions and a new style—the Empire—arose. Some soon faded again and sank into oblivion. Others went on to survive, in more or less the same form, up to the present day.

To speak of an "age of Napoleon" would be to overstate the role of a single individual, however ostentatiously he may have demonstrated his prowess. Nevertheless, the concept of a "Napoleonic era", with all its positive and negative traits, did impress itself upon the minds of most contemporary observers, albeit with varying and even contrasting reactions. Recalling this period may not only be of some use, it may also provide some pleasure.

Both the author and the publishers would like to thank Dr. Harald Brost, Dr. Manfred Lemmer, Professor Hans Wussing and, in particular, Dr. Heinz Helmert for their valuable collaboration at various stages. The pictorial section, compiled by Dr. Claude Keisch, not only serves to complement and illustrate the historian's account, it is also a study in its own right of artistic developments during this period.

Statue de l'Empereur.

WALTER MARKOV

GRAND EMPIRE

*Virtue and Vice
in the Napoleonic Era*

Presentation of Illustrations

Claude Keisch

HIPPOCRENE BOOKS
NEW YORK, N.Y.

Endpapers and title link:

Medals commemorating the campaign of 1805.
Etchings from the work: *Napoléon à la Grande Armée.*
Paris, no date (*c.* 1810).

Half-title:

Initial N with laurel and snake representing eternity.
Woodcut by Horace Vernet.
From: P. M. Laurent de l'Ardèche, *Histoire de*
l'Empereur Napoléon. Paris, 1839/40.

Frontispiece:

Statue of Napoleon on the Vendôme Column.
Etching from the work: *Napoléon à la Grande Armée.*
Paris, no date (*c.* 1810).

Contents page:

Allegory on Napoleon's achievements.
Woodcut by Auguste Raffet. From Jacques de Norvins,
Histoire de Napoléon. Paris, 1839.

Translated from the German
by Peter Underwood

Copyright © 1990
by Edition Leipzig
ALL RIGHTS RESERVED
First published in the
United States 1990 by
Hippocrene Books, Inc.
171 Madison Avenue
New York, N. Y. 10016
Design: Volker Küster
Map: Matthias Weis
Total production:
Druckerei Fortschritt Erfurt
Manufactured in the
German Democratic Republic

ISBN 0-87052-716-9

CONTENTS

A WHIRLWIND
OF WORLD HISTORY
1789–1815

Maria Theresa and Francis I, Stephen, with their eleven children. Painting by Martin van Mytens, c. 1750. Kunsthistorisches Museum, Vienna.

Government follows property:
the fact that the first is determined by the second
was noted way back in 1656 in Harrington's Utopia *Oceana*.

The Ancien Régime

The seven to eight hundred million people who inhabited our planet towards the end of the 18th century differed from one another, as at any other epoch, in their external appearance, life style and mode of thinking, their language and religion, and in their customs and institutions. Yet amazingly enough the vast majority of them who already belonged to nation-states lived in societies which, despite all their local peculiarities, were based on a broadly similar economic system. As yet it bore no name; only later did it become to be termed feudal.

In Asia and Europe the origins of feudal society stretched far back into the past. It was transplanted to America much later. At times these societies influenced each other, but by and large they developed in accordance with their own laws of motion—sometimes in a convergent and sometimes in a divergent direction. Once the voyages of discovery of the 15th and 16th centuries had placed western Europe at the centre of a new network of relations and communications, the emergence of a world market signalled the growing integration of previously separate strands of development on a global scale.

Changes in the social structure, which were at first sporadic, coincided with the growing power of merchant capital and its penetration into the sphere of production. A beneficial combination of internal and external circumstances paved the way, at first in the Netherlands and then in England, not just for the accumulation of wealth but for a new, "capitalist" dynamic in commodity exchange and production. Victorious revolutions in the 16th and 17th centuries extended this economic power to the political sphere. British emigrants carried the ideal of a bourgeois polity to North America which, casting off its colonial fetters, declared itself a Republic in 1776.

In many parts of Europe monarchs "by divine right" were likewise at pains to improve the functioning of their states, if only to generate more wealth to meet the ever growing costs of maintaining their army and court. They showed that they were determined to give short shrift to aristocratic dissent or to irksome attempts by corporate assemblies to participate in government, but they were careful to avoid undermining the base of that pyramid of power whose apex they formed. Minor reforms in the mode of governing were the most that a sovereign would contemplate.

For centuries the main pillar of the social edifice had been the relationship between the lord of the manor and the peasants.

The ploughman was the archetypal beast of burden of this primarily agrarian society. His position varied from country to country and from county to county. There were hereditary, adscriptive and tributary serfs and also some free peasants with considerable holdings, but a much larger number were smallholders, tenant farmers, sharecroppers and poor landless labourers. In addition to paying oppressive taxes and duties to the Crown and clergy, they were burdened by assorted obligations towards the manorial lord or squire who, in addition, was the embodiment of local authority, the arbiter and enforcer of law and, as often as not, their own personal master. The countless rights which he exclusively enjoyed through a whole host of legal claims left the peasant, after performing his compulsory labour for the lord, with only a half or even a third of the fruits of his toil, which in years of poor harvest did not suffice to save his usually large family from starving.

Hardly any lords still lived with armed retinues in castles perched on rocky ledges, ready to suppress rebellious vassals. This task was now normally undertaken by units of the gendarmerie or the professional standing army which one ruler after another set up. The nobility began to build more comfortable residences for themselves where in the summer months they indulged in the fashionable pleasures of rural life, principally in the form of hunting and shooting, country outings and garden fêtes, open-air theatre and firework displays. They made music in their Rococo salons, played cards and read Richardson, Metastasio or Voltaire, took snuff and drank hot chocolate, coffee or tea. The ladies adorned their towering wigs with flowers of the potato plant—which was highly praised by the agronomist Parmentier—while their male counterparts concealed their natural hair beneath a white-powdered bagwig.

The peasant and his lord lived in close physical proximity, often separated only by the grounds of the estate, but they moved in two irreconcilable and mutually exclusive worlds. In the one arrogance was coupled with contempt and in the

other ingrained obsequiousness with unbridled hatred. Relations between the two verged between a tacit truce and an undeclared state of war. The towns were developing into a third social force. Especially in the ports and seats of princely power, as centres of industrial and intellectual activity, the medieval burgesses had evolved into the bourgeoisie as a class. It emerged from the working strata: small traders, guild craftsmen, factory workers, day labourers and servants. They represented a potential shock force. While economically the towns were bursting at the seams they were also openly challenging the educational and ideological monopoly of feudal-minded theologians, of whatever confession, and were calling on the individual to boldly begin to think for himself. The economic boom was accompanied by the emergence of a school of thought of Dutch and English origin which transcended national boundaries. Its acolytes called themselves *philosophes* or *lumières*, rationalists or *illuminati*. Their aim of the redemption of mankind, which was writ large on their banners, was somewhat over-ambitious. However, it was indeed the historic mission of the young bourgeois intelligentsia to tear down the ideological ramparts which were protecting the decaying social system against the onslaught of the new order. It politicized the philosophers, often against their wishes, and compelled them to attack feudalism using criticism as their weapon, which would one day evolve into a criticism of weapons.

But where was this likely to happen first?

At the age of sixty Klopstock, the author of the *Messiah*, set to verse his hope that the German nation be allowed to enjoy its birthright as the cradle of the Reformation. Yet this proved a pious wish, for "Germany" was basically a moral concept of the nascent national literature which bore as little resemblance to reality as did the Holy Roman Empire, which Voltaire derisively declared was neither holy, nor Roman, nor an empire. From some three hundred principalities two major powers emerged which vied bitterly with one another for pre-eminence: the Austria of the Habsburgs with territorial claims far beyond the Imperial borders, and the Prussia of the Hohenzollerns, which showed similar expansionist tendencies in the East at the expense of Poland. The Habsburgs, basking in the glory of the Imperial dignity, enjoyed great prestige as Europe's most senior ruling dynasty. On the other hand they faced all manner of difficulties in seeking to fuse their scattered possessions—consisting of their patrimonial Austrian domains, Bohemia and Hungary, Belgium and Lombardy (plus Galicia from 1772)—into a unitary state and national market in keeping with the norms of the century. Maria Theresa (1740–1780) made some progress in the desired direction. However, the more radical measures of Joseph II (1780–1790) aroused considerable opposition, particularly in Hungary and Belgium which, after the emperor had launched into an ambitious war against the Turks in 1788, broke out into open revolt and frustrated his programme of reform in its most advanced areas—such as the general abolition of serfdom. Nevertheless, "Josephism" did not vanish without a trace. The Vienna of the prolific writer Joseph von Sonnenfels carved out a respected place for itself within European Enlightenment and at the same time gave birth to an incipient national Austrian consciousness. Haydn and Mozart laid the basis for its world renown as a city of music. The at times creative unrest unleashed by Josephism inspired a movement towards national rebirth among the nations of the Austrian Empire. It found support among officialdom, the bourgeoisie, the enlightened nobility and even the peasantry. Some individuals were ready to disregard the limits despotically imposed by the emperor and to take the idea of revolution seriously. Prussia's development was more linear. Between 1740 and 1763 the militarized state was catapulted into the ranks of the major powers by means of three wars fought by Frederick II. The philosopher-king, who inside and outside his country was both admired and detested, proved to be a much tougher exponent of *Realpolitik* than was suggested by the 18-year-old deserter, the man of letters ensconced in Rheinsberg Castle or later the host of roundtable discussions at Sanssouci palace. However, he ruled over a country whose sources of wealth, even after the seizure of Silesia, were considerably inferior to those of other countries. Although the king encouraged bourgeois industriousness and the entrepreneurial spirit he did not touch the privileges of the Junkers east of the Elbe or their big landed estates. He considered that only the aristocracy, with its "sense of honour", was capable of bearing responsibility in a country whose political strength was its oversized army, reckoned to be the most powerful in the world. Most observers failed to notice that it was resting on its laurels and rigidifying. Although "Old Herod" (as the Empress Catherine II was wont to call him) tried to draw a few limited

The stone monuments on Easter Island as discovered by James Cook's expedition. Engraving by Robert Benard. From: James Cook, *Voyage dans l'hémisphère austral* (. . .), Vol. II. Paris, 1773.

Immanuel Kant. Aquatint by an unknown artist, c. 1800.

[1] MIRABEAU, H., COMTE DE: *Histoire secrète de la cour de Berlin* (1789).

lessons from the American War of Independence, his successors relied completely on the enduring myth of the invincible Potsdam garrison.

Containing such individuals as the architect Knobelsdorff and such philosophers and scholars as Christian Wolff in Halle, Kant in Königsberg or Nicolai and Moses Mendelssohn in Berlin, Prussia was scarcely "the most slavish land in Europe", as Lessing once referred to it. Nevertheless, the parade-ground atmosphere and the sense of blind obedience stifled any libertarian stirrings which threatened to emerge from the seclusion of the study or the salon into the open. Lampoons were no longer simply ignored, and gibes against religion, which Frederick the Great had tolerated with malicious glee as a harmless way of letting off steam, were soon once again regarded as offensive and suspicious by the obscurantists who came to hold sway at court after Frederick's death in 1786 and of whom even Kant fell foul. The rulers kept such a firm hold on their subjects that they did not need fear any explosion. Even Mirabeau on a voyage through the country was forced to ask himself how such a land would stand up to a real test of endurance.[1] Would the firm tread of its grenadiers suffice to withstand the tide of revolution, from wherever it came?

Of course, the Vienna Hofburg and the Berlin palace, Schönbrunn and Potsdam were not the whole story. There was another Germany: in Göttingen and Tübingen, in Hamburg and Leipzig, the Germany of such *illuminati* as Weishaupt and Knigge, of Goethe and Schiller. Here the vigorous young German bourgeoisie, excluded from the political sphere, sought refuge from the constricting atmosphere of the Empire's patchwork of states. They opened up new vistas to international learning, and attained new heights in the fields of literature and music which, almost out of pity, were left open to them. For they were paid for with powerlessness in that arena in which the struggle to determine the secular shape of human society was inevitably decided.

While Prussia was busy effecting an appreciable shift in the balance of international forces, the same was even more true of Russia, which from the reign of Peter the Great onwards had thrown open the door to Europe. The enormous Russian Empire which, though sparsely populated, stretched via Siberia to the Pacific Ocean, achieved unchallenged supremacy in the East. It drove the Swedes out of Estonia and Livonia and the Turks from the northern shores of the Black Sea. It strengthened its influence in Poland and secured a voice in European diplomacy which

Catherine II (1762–1796), the "Semiramis of the North", used vigorously and nearly always with success.

Russia was handicapped by its reliance on an antiquated system of serfdom which prevented

Medal struck to commemorate the unveiling of Falconet's equestrian statue of Peter the Great in St. Petersburg in 1782. Engraving by J. C. Krüger after Berolini.

Left:
The royal cake. A satirical allegory on the first partition of Poland in 1772. Engraving by Noël Lemire after Jean-Michel Moreau le Jeune.

Page 13:
Earthquake. Coloured engraving by Johann Michael Voltz, c. 1810.

[1] Guiseppe Verdi used these events as the basis for his opera *Un Ballo in Maschera* (1859).
[2] HÖLDERLIN, J. C. F.: *Hyperion oder der Eremit in Griechenland* (1797–1799).

the economic forces from developing more freely. The powerful uprising of peasants and Cossacks under Emelyan Pugachev in 1773 showed that this was dragging the country into a deep crisis. Although it gave much food for thought to liberalminded nobles, among whom such men as Novikov and Radishchev openly expressed their support, the empress thought that the risk involved in even a gradual emancipation of the peasants was just too great. So although Catherine's multifaceted and well thought-out legislation increased the efficiency of the late medieval state apparatus, it merely put off the real problem and did nothing to curtail the tsar's absolute autocracy. The forces of conservatism thus in Russia probably found their strongest and most resolute ally when the tide of social change swept over Europe.

The question of reform was quite another matter in countries which, for a variety of reasons, were in decline.

The Ottoman Empire under Sultan Selim III (1789–1807) made only half-hearted attempts. These were confined to reforming the army, which began to seem increasingly necessary after Turkey had sunk from its position of a feared conqueror under the symbol of the crescent to that of a prize coveted by its neighbours, whom it fended off only with difficulty—once through French protection and another time with British help.

The elective monarchy of Poland, torn by incessant factional strife, was exposed to the benevolence (and more often the malevolence) of its predatory neighbours who carved it up in 1772 and thereafter constantly threatened to repeat the operation. Hence fusing the Polish nation into a strong state around a reformed constitution was a pressing task. The Four Year Diet (Sejm; 1787 to 1791) attempted this but kept the downtrodden peasantry excluded from its *natio polonica*. It thereby divorced itself from the only force which would have enabled it to defend itself and its achievements when the invasion came and the "noble" but isolated Poles, despite putting up a desperate resistance, succumbed to superior force.

The collapse of Swedish hegemony in the Baltic during the long Northern War (1700–1721) undermined the monarchy's position. For the next fifty years the country was in effect ruled by the

Estates until Gustavus III regained absolute power for the Crown by his coup d'état of 1772. However, since leading ranks of the nobility opposed such a detrimental redistribution of power[1] Gustavus made concessions to the bourgeoisie and the peasantry, who outside Sweden enjoyed corporate representation only in Iceland. This did much to loosen the feudal structure and made possible a relatively painless transition to a bourgeois monarchy after 1809.

That this "Scandinavian road" was not the result of a freak and unique combination of individuals was shown even more graphically by the example of Denmark at the end of its "golden age". The precipitate reforms of Struensee, an upstart Prussian pastor's son, physician and royal favourite, ended with his execution by quartering in 1773— the details of which titillated the ladies throughout Europe. Yet only twelve years later the traditionalists were a spent force, and in 1788 Denmark carried out the first systematic liberation of the peasants in Europe.

The readiness to travel new roads was also evident in the Mediterranean where the Greeks rose against Ottoman rule during a Russo-Turkish

war (1768–1774) from which they at least managed to secure freedom of movement for their shipping.[2] It was also evident in dismembered Italy for which the century promised to bring both a slow recovery of its economy, which had stagnated ever since the major maritime routes had shifted, as well as stimulating a debate among its scholars: Giambattista Vico, the "father of sociology", the economist Genovesi and Filangieri, the historian Muratori and Beccaria (1737–1794), the much-translated champion of a more humanitarian penal code, nor should we forget such itinerant adventurers as Cagliostro or Casanova. Smaller princely courts spared by war vied with each other to establish the best possible provincial régime: Florence, Parma and Naples, whence first minister Tanucci also provided assistance to the Spanish reformers when in 1759 King Charles III exchanged his throne for the weightier crown in Madrid.

Following the papacy of the erudite Benedict XIV (1740–1758), even the Vatican was unable to remain totally immune from the winds of change, and in 1773 Clement XIV issued the papal bull *Dominus ac Redemptor* which suppressed the

Das Erdbeben.

Der Congreß erklärt die 13 vereinigten
Staaten von Nord America für in.
Dependent. am 4ten July 1776.

Declaration of the independence of the United
States of America by the Congress in 1776.
Engraving by Daniel Chodowiecki. From:
Historisch-genealogischer Kalender 1784.

Stroll along the ramparts of Paris. Engraving by
Pierre-François Courtois after Augustin de Saint-
Aubin, *c.* 1760.

Sint ut sunt, aut non sint:
  They should be as they are, or not be
was the message of the strict Dominican pope.

Jesuits, whom he thought incapable of adapting
to the new times.

This followed earlier actions by Catholic courts
which refused to tolerate any longer a quasi-reli-
gious and reputedly immensely wealthy state
within a state. The Jansenists and proponents of a
national church, excommunicated by the papal
bull *Unigenitus* of 1713, launched an offensive
against the Ultramontanists. Another victim of
the Spanish ban in 1767 was the legendary Jesuit-
ical state under the Guaraní of Paraguay. Minister Pombal, undaunted by the upheavals caused by
the Lisbon earthquake of 1755, acted particularly
brutally in his expulsion of the Jesuits from Portugal and Brazil. However, after his downfall
(1777) and the death of Charles III (1788) a coun-
tertrend was set in train on the Iberian peninsula
and the Inquisition once again reared its head,
until Napoleon came along and chopped it off.

It is more difficult to gauge the extent to which the
non-European world was involved in the tumul-
tuous world changes of the century. The starting
point of bourgeois emancipation from feudalism
lay in Europe. Countries on other continents made
only an indirect contribution. They paid with their
blood for the primitive accumulation of capital
from which they themselves would not benefit.
The British East India Company's subjugation of
India, which went hand in hand with the decline
of the Mogul Empire, drew the attention of European scholars to Sanskrit and the wisdom it incorporated. Ornate chinoiseries delighted Western
noble ladies and gentlemen; Rococo art made use
of them as graceful stylistic elements. Meanwhile
European manufacturers succeeded in discovering the secret of making porcelain—at first in
Meissen. The China of the Mandarins was recognized as an exotic major power, whose long-lived
Emperor K'ien-lung could afford to refuse permission for foreign legations to be set up in his
capital Peking. In 1793 he politely but firmly sent
the disappointed Lord Macartney packing. No
country had yet tried to penetrate Japan's self-imposed isolation, either through the use of force or
persuasion, and risk a confrontation with the land
of the Tokugawa shoguns. Yet the nations of Asia,
and still less of Africa, did not involve themselves
directly in the revolutionary crisis which was
looming in western Europe, nor in the trials of
strength which preceded and accompanied it; nor

would they feel its impact for a very long time to
come. It was a different situation in America
where, apart from a few inaccessible enclaves, the
colonial rule had destroyed the existing Indian
structures or superimposed its own on them. This
did not mean that a ready-made civilization was
simply shipped overseas. The colonial societies
developed rather out of the synthesis of the im-
migrants' traditional beliefs and their reaction to
the prevailing conditions. New practical criteria
supplemented those they had brought with them
from home. Nevertheless, the network of social
ties between the settlers and their native countries
was never served. To this extent the conflicts and
debates in Europe always had an influence on
America and vice versa. The American rebels' declaration in 1776 that all men are born free and
remain so had a wide and varied response. Although its promulgators, with regard to their
negro slaves, did not uphold it themselves it
created a precedent that was too readily acclaimed
by the downtrodden for sovereigns to acquire a
taste for it. The names of volunteers who fought
under George Washington were later to recur in
the revolutionary annals of Europe: Lafayette
and Saint-Simon from France, the Englishman
Tom Paine and the Pole Kościuszko.

In England the unaccustomed defeat caused dis-
quiet for another reason. In the light of Adam
Smith's enunciation of the interplay of supply and
demand in *The Wealth of Nations* (1776), the
oligarchy started wondering whether new methods were needed to spread the tentacles of English maritime trade around the globe to enable
them to act from a position of strength, to profit-
ably re-define "freedom" as the dual freedom of
movement of both capital and labour, and to
transfigure the practical consequences of industrial society in the philanthropic manner of the
Quaker William Wilberforce (1759–1833).

England's bourgeois radicals were in the middle
of such discussions as their country celebrated the
centenary of its Glorious Revolution in 1788—the
same year in which a tiny penal colony became
the germ-cell of an Anglo-Saxon Australia. There
was plenty going on, and what had been achieved
in the interim was pretty impressive. At the
expense of the peasant and the craftsman the
preconditions had been created for England to
become the "workshop of the world", symbolized
by the centrifugal governor which James Watt

patented in 1784. The national pride of the island race deemed it self-evident that progress should be a preserve of the British. The fact that in the birthplace of parliamentarism only one in a hundred Englishmen had the right to vote (or that even less made use of it) did not bother them overmuch. After all, had not the Glorious Revolution of 1688 come about as a sensible balance of interests between the Whig and Tory elites, thereby sparing the disruptive and fickle masses the bother of venturing in ignorance into the political arena? Did progress, that aptly coined term of the century, signify continuity and nothing more? The latter was interrupted by the real movement of history in that country in which the fundamental contradiction of the epoch between the adherents and opponents of feudalism had caused the biggest build-up of pressure: in France.

Revolution

France seemed the strongest link in the feudal world order, a system that permeated every sphere of its society. It was the birthplace of Frankish feudality, which set the example for the rest of western Europe. Its knights, urban communes, scholastic erudition and Gothic art came nearest to the medieval ideal of Western Christendom. During its evolution from a corporative state into an absolute monarchy France developed institutions which were eagerly copied elsewhere.

In the 18th century it led Europe in terms of population, agricultural yields and handicraft production. It also led the way in the spread of manufacturing, in commerce and the processing of precious metals, in tax revenue, in the sophisti-

cation of its administration and the size of its standing army. From the court at Versailles, and more especially from the intellectual melting pot which was Paris, the French way of life with its positive and negative aspects set the tone for the whole of the continent.

Yet though it was the envy of many, France was beset with profound contradictions. Objective observers identified the fundamental problem as being the discrepancy between the *pays réel* and the *pays légal*. They meant that the balance of power and legal relations, the institutions and constraints of the state, all based on special privileges for the nobility and clergy, no longer corresponded to social needs and potentialities.

In order to remedy the situation many of the "philosophers" set their sights on change, called by some a "revolution". They had a vague idea of the aim but were uncertain how to achieve it. They did not, however, envisage it as open class confrontation, let alone a mass armed uprising, but rather as a thorough-going reform which a sovereign, advised by enlightened men and enjoying the broad support of the nation, would implement according to the dictates of reason. Only such a figure, they thought, would be capable of overcoming the resistance of dyed-in-the-wool conservatives by virtue of his authority without unleashing general chaos. They clung to the illusion of an "enlightened" absolutism, the historic task of which they saw as the peaceful transition from a decrepit form of government to a more modern one, which in this case boiled, down to a compromise between the prestige of the nobility and the importance of the bourgeoisie.

In 1761 Voltaire had enjoined the "philosophers" to "serve the human race not with words but with deeds". They were quick to initiate an unending debate and to propagate slogans which were taken up by the masses in town and countryside because, and insofar as, they accorded with the reality of their lives.

D'Alembert, however, urged caution. Jean-Jacques Rousseau, a watchmaker's son from Geneva, was the first to cross the Rubicon. In his *Contrat Social* (1762) he outlined a theoretical programme for a democratic system, the egalitarian call of which went way beyond even the long-range objective of the bourgeoisie. The ideas of the Enlightenment were brought together in the *Encyclopédie* (1751–1772), conceived by D'Alembert and Diderot, before the social crisis had yet surfaced. Their brilliant pioneering effort laid the foundations which enabled a united Third Estate to claim to constitute the sovereign French nation.

Some contemporaries felt the earth quaking beneath their feet and sounded the alarm:

Well, the play that we have shown you,
    which you now criticize,
Reflects the lot of our good people,
    as seen through my own eyes.
If pressed more, they will rebel.
    What will happen then no one can tell . . .
(Beaumarchais: *Le Mariage de Figaro*, 1784)

Nor could the proponents of the Enlightenment predict the outcome. They too were stunned and overwhelmed by an eruption of passions more violent than they could ever have imagined. Primeval forces now determined the course of events.

"Two hostile nations coexisted on French soil. This was about the only link that connected them, though it did not unite them. One of these nations consisted of the humiliated and oppressed masses; the other of the nobility which, despite accounting for scarcely one Frenchman in sixty, regarded themselves as exclusively constituting the French nation."

This observation made in 1796 by Fantin Desodoards, one of the first interpreters of the events of 1789, pointed to the underlying weakness of the corporate state, namely its exclusion of all the non-privileged—from day-labourers to owners of vast fortunes—from the national decision-making process. Nowhere else had social confrontation reached such an advanced stage as in France. Nowhere else was the ruling class in such dire straits. Nowhere else was there a middle class fitted and soon determined to lead the opposition, that had experienced such an increase in economic, moral and ideological influence. Nowhere else did a social crisis mobilize in a comparable manner all sections of the population for an assault on the crumbling strongholds of despotism. The oppressed were no longer willing, and their oppressors no longer able, to continue in the old way.

Bourbon rule threatened to collapse under its mounting debts. Since the burden borne by the *menu peuple* was already so great that, as even the tax collectors admitted, they could not pay more, the government had no option, if it wanted to avoid the unforeseeable consequences of national bankruptcy, but to start taxing those who had hitherto been exempt. The revolt of the nobility against the attempted reforms of despairing ministers led in turn to the rapid collapse of authority throughout the country, while the bourgeoisie, courted now by both camps, began to recognize that it held the balance of power.

Clutching at straws, the Crown gave in to pressure to recall the States General, which had been in abeyance since 1614. This would at least gain time, appease the clamouring creditors and shift responsibility from the executive to a more broadly based motley assembly. Meanwhile the election campaign developed a dynamic of its

Jean-Jacques Rousseau. Below the medallion bearing his portrait is the tomb of the philosopher in Ermenonville. Engraving by an unknown artist.

Voltaire's room at Ferney. Lithograph by Charles-Philibert de Lasteyrie.

Everywhere I perceive the seeds of a revolution which is inexorably approaching but which, unfortunately, I shall not live long enough to witness. The French always arrive late, but they do get there in the end . . . and it will be a grand spectacle when it happens.
Voltaire to Chavelin, 1764.

Indisputably philosophy opened the door to and paved the way for the current revolution. Yet words alone are insufficient. Deeds are required. Thus to whom do we owe our liberty if not to the mobilized masses?
Marat in the *Ami du peuple* of November 10, 1789.

own. The private quarrel between the old and the up-and-coming ruling classes was now joined by the mass of the people, who had to date taken no part in the debate between the social élites.

The electoral system provided an opportunity to make King Louis XVI (1774–1792) aware of various evils and abuses. It acted like a spark to a powder keg, for the urban and rural masses were already seething since they were in a much more desperate plight even than normal. For years France had been suffering from the effects of economic stagnation which in 1788 resulted in mass unemployment in the industrial centres and was accompanied by a crop failure that sent the price of bread soaring way out of reach of the needy. The spectre of famine stalked the land. It ruined and uprooted the poor peasants and sent them begging in droves throughout the countryside, while in the towns and cities it led to looting and rioting.

Nor surprisingly the daily problem of finding something to eat and the disturbances, which reached their peak during the election period, were reflected in the political altercations and found their way into the *cahiers de doléance*. A groundswell of enthusiasm developed in which people recognized what they wanted as they had never done before in an electoral campaign—and would rarely do thereafter. It was as if the floodgates had been opened. Hundreds of thousands of people gave vent to their innermost cares and woes by putting pen to paper or by getting persons who were more articulate to do so on their behalf. At the same time a tremendous rise in the self-awareness and self-respect of ordinary people was reflected in demands, often bluntly expressed, to the state and the seignorial lords. They mandated their elected representatives accordingly but were not content to patiently await the outcome. Often the electors formed committees which remained in being in order to see how things were going and to keep an eye on their deputies. These were embryonic forms of new, bourgeois organs of power.

Calls that were too radical were doctored, not by the government but by the propertied and educated classes who headed the Third Estate. They were able to do so because the elections were held in stages, with the *cahiers* being "composited" at each higher level. It was not difficult for skilful editors, most of whom were trained lawyers, to eliminate unwelcome demands. The same process of sifting applied to the deputies themselves with the result that not a single peasant, let alone worker, got as far as the States General.

Even so, the Third Estate that appeared in Versailles in May 1789, uniformly bourgeois in composition but with a sprinkling of aristocratic and clerical sympathizers, presented a sufficiently frightening spectacle to the ruling caste. Avoiding the trap of voting by estate (which would have meant being outvoted by two to one), it defied the court, government and privileged stratum—and won the day. It abolished the absolute monarchy at a stroke by transforming the States General into a National Constituent Assembly and thereby claimed sovereignty for itself.

The court, realizing it had badly misjudged the balance of forces, retaliated. It dismissed the conciliatory Finance Minister Necker and called on the army to deal with the insubordinate assembly. Just as the days of the young Constituent Assembly seemed numbered, the city of Paris rose in its defence. On July 14, 1789 the Bastille was stormed and the tables turned. Shrinking back from a protracted civil war whose outcome was uncertain, Louis XVI yielded and decided to bide his time. Paris set the signal for a series of municipal revolutions in the provinces. The peasants, losing patience with the tug-of-war at Versailles from which they had so far gained nothing, were now all the more determined to ensure that the grandiose promises were kept and so took things into their own hands. In the reflection of burning châteaux, manorial rule died an ignominious death in the countryside, while during the melodramatic night of August 4 the National Assembly salvaged what it could by means of a legislative act lest the assault on feudalism should be extended to bourgeois property.

As Marat rightly observed, the struggle of the urban and rural masses had achieved "liberty", albeit a liberty whose main beneficiaries were not the masses, whose struggle had brought it about, but rather the leading bourgeois stratum which rose to power in the wake of the great upheaval.

The first President of the United States of America rightly predicted that the "patriots of 1789" had a long and arduous road ahead of them. The newly established journal *Révolutions de Paris* likewise warned in its second issue (July 25): "The whole of Europe is watching you. It is up to you to show the nations of the world how to use the fruits of victory after banishing the tyrants. Victory is not everything. One must also learn the relevant lessons."

Chambre de Voltaire à Ferney.

The whole of Europe was indeed watching, but the reactions of the spectators varied. On the one hand the crowned heads and their paladins were aghast with horror. They hastily discarded their "enlightened" trappings and, sinking their differences, closed ranks in face of the "hydra of anarchy".

European intellectuals, on the other hand, saw the revolution as realizing the ideas of the Enlightenment and, agreeing to "abandon their self-imposed immaturity" (Immanuel Kant), added their many voices to Washington's jubilation.

In his *Brief von Paris* of August 26, 1789 Campe, the author of a German-language edition of *Robinson Crusoe*, called "this transformation of the French state the greatest and most general blessing that Providence has bestowed on mankind since Luther's religious reforms". And many ordinary people, in Germany as elsewhere, felt the same.

On the same day the Constituent Assembly, following the American example, adopted a declaration of human and civil rights whose seventeen articles prefigured the guiding principles of the constitution (which in the event was not completed until 1791): the legitimation of bourgeois society within a bourgeois state which rapidly acquired the outlines of a parliamentary constitutional monarchy.

The Assembly beavered away under continuous mass pressure and put an end to the *ancien régime*. The confusing multiplicity of provinces, gouvernements, intendatures and other feudal administrative areas were replaced by the more manageable division of the country into eighty-three départements, each of which was named after its geographical features. Social burdens, which Merlin de Douai succinctly summarized as a *complexum feudale*, were amortized, albeit haltingly, inconsistently and above all unevenly: arbitrary rule and *lettres de cachet*, compulsory labour and ground rent, internal customs barriers and guild restrictions. Access and promotion to all public offices on the basis of ability, local and regional self-administration, uniformity in the dispensation of justice, freedom of the press, the suppression of the estates and their privileges, the complete abolition of the nobility and the secularization of the Church changed the face of France fundamentally.

In spite of all its shortcomings and limitations this bourgeois form of liberty and equality, though proportionate to the level of wealth, represented for that time a huge and almost unbelievable advance. Many of the institutions, surviving and adjusting flexibly to all the vicissitudes, have lasted to the present day.

Wherever it seemed expedient the new bourgeois ruling class sinned without compunction against their own principles as laid down in the Declaration of Human Rights. Thus the remunerative slave trade in the colonies remained intact in the interests of the sugar plantation owners, who had close ties with merchant capital. Yet even in France itself only the propertied counted as real shareholders in the great national undertaking; the Abbé Sieyès, fresh from addressing his proudest electoral catechism yet to the Third Estate, took this literally. Ignoring the objections of the few democrats, the authors of the constitution had the audacity to separate the people, according to the amount of taxes they paid, into active and passive citizens and to debar the latter both from voting and from serving in the newly created National Guard, thereby shrewdly disarming them politically whilst at the same time wresting from them the weapons which they had carried since the storming of the Bastille and the peasant insurgency. Even so the people lived, breathed, spoke, wrote and sang more freely than before. They were less regimented and harrassed. In the countryside they probably now also ate better than before, particularly as they were helped along by two good harvests in 1789 and 1790.

In the capital itself, however, there was little sign of a similar improvement in everyday life. In the first flush of excitement the Parisians had no doubt pitched their expectations too high. Instead, as an international centre of the luxury trades, the city suffered from the collapse and flight of its aristocratic clientèle. There were shortages, and servants found themselves jobless. In view of the uncertain situation, financiers stopped investing; building came to a virtual standstill, and capital flowed into speculative ventures. The assignat, the paper money which was circulating in excessive quantities, aroused mistrust among savers, and prices rose. With great foresight Marat—in the 8th issue of his *Ami du Peuple*—was the first to recognize the potential for a new "Caesar": "The tyrants are gone, yet the effects of tyranny remain. . . . The workshops are empty, the factories abandoned, trade is stagnating and the finances are in a sorry mess. . . . The enemies of liberty will make you, the people, tire of your independence; they will teach you to yearn for a return to slavery and to seek order, peace and plenty under the aegis of a strong ruler."

Each man is born equal and free
with a claim to rights aglore.
He can choose what to do or to be
if he only obeys the law.
No more defiant obstruction,
attempts to plot or to steal:
From now on social distinction
must be based on the common weal!
Music-hall song based on the text of the Rights of Man and the Citizen of 1789.

The revolution, which has been effected in France is of so wonderful a nature, that the mind can hardly realize the fact . . . but I fear, though it has gone triumphantly through the first paroxysm, it is not the last it has to encounter before matters are finally settled. In a word, the revolution is of too great magnitude to be effected in so short a space, and with the loss of so little blood.
George Washington to Gouverneur Morris, October 13, 1789.

A second National Assembly, called the Legislative, succeeded the Constituent in October 1791 and came under increasing pressure from counter-revolutionary forces abroad who were threatening to intervene. This caused the Legislative to panic: in April 1792 it urged Louis XVI to declare a preventive war on Austria to which the king, hoping for a French defeat, willingly agreed. This added new difficulties to the old ones. The debacle of the disorganized army, which was further weakened by the desertion of aristocratic officers, was followed by an invasion by the Prussians and Austrians in an attempt to rescue the king. Instead it cost him the throne: on August 10 the people of Paris stormed the Tuileries. The domestic French conflict at last became internationalized. To cope with this new challenge the nation clamoured for the proclamation of a Republic.

The Republic

The 10th of August 1792 was hardly the "second revolution" which it appeared to be to impartial onlookers at the time, but it did represent a highly significant shift from a big bourgeois-liberal phase to one which at least purported to be democratic. The passive citizens returned to the political stage and gave a very hard time to the preachers of moderation who fancied they were already home and dry. The revolutionary Paris Commune formed by the insurrectionists made up for the Legislative's weaknesses with its own decisiveness. The Legislative decreed its own premature dissolution and convoked a National Convention on the basis of equal and universal suffrage for all men over twenty-one years of age in order to draw up a Republican constitution. Before it broke up it awarded, in an act of cosmopolitan impartiality in September 1792, honorary French citizenship to a number of "writers who have undermined the foundations of tyranny and opened up the path to freedom". These included Washington, Tom Paine, Priestley, Wilberforce, Kościuszko, Pestalozzi, Cloots, Campe, Klopstock and Schiller.
Meanwhile a Parisian reader of the *Hamburgischer unparteiischer Correspondent* (No. 137, 1792) complained: "We must now kowtow to the

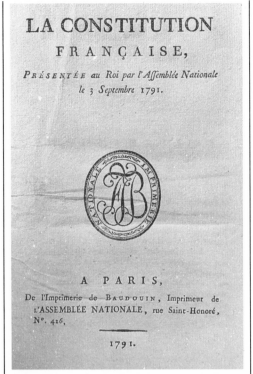

Title page of the first edition of the French Constitution of September 3, 1791. Staatsarchiv Weimar.

Assignat with a value of 50 livres, engraved by Antoine-François Tardieu after Nicolas Marie Gatteaux.

France has freed herself. This was the most sublime deed this century, a truly Olympian feat...
Comb through the annals of history and see if you can find anything that remotely compares therewith.
Klopstock, "Kennet euch selbst", 1789.

most cruel despotism, and this is called freedom! They vandalize artistic treasures and stain them with the blood of our citizens, and soon people will be asking what happened to the old France whose inhabitants were once famed for their amiability."
Initially the wanton acts of destruction were limited to the demolition of royal statues, emblems and memorial slabs. Blood also flowed: that of Swiss mercenaries who had been guarding the Tuileries for the king, and that of prisoners who, it was feared, would try to break out as the Prussians approached. Atrocities accompanied these "September massacres", which left an indelible impression on French memories. Thomas Jefferson, future president of the United States and far removed from being an iconoclastic terrorist, was able, despite his extreme misgivings, to properly assess these events in his letter to W. Short on January 3, 1793. He wrote that it was necessary to use the power of the people, a force which, while not as blind as bombs and bullets, was nevertheless fickle. But the liberty of the whole world depended on the outcome of the struggle, and the great goal was achieved with the shedding of hardly any blood. He added that though his heart bled for the victims he would rather the whole world were laid waste than that the revolution should be defeated.
It was not defeated. The Convention which met on September 20, 1792 proved itself, after many tests, worthy of the task. Unlike the ruling Gironde group the Montagne (the Mountain), a political faction inspired by the Jacobin Club, soon realized that the war which would decide the fate of the Republic could only be successfully waged as a people's war, and that this necessitated an honest alliance with the sans-culottes, the urban and rural masses.
The Gironde, allergic to any violation of property, centred its entire attention on maintaining the new relations of ownership—to the detriment of national security—so as to keep the door closed to all those below. It imagined it was safe after its troops checked the feared Prussian military machine at Valmy on September 20, 1792, after which Goethe reputedly uttered the phrase which still adorns the simple monument to victory:

This place and this day mark the beginning of a new era in the history of the world.

The volunteers fighting under the tricolour swelled with pride on hearing the Marseillaise and were transformed into fearless soldiers of the Revolution. The political and military leaders, on the other hand, failed right across the board. The Gironde's vacillation in the trial of the king, who was finally executed on January 21, 1793, was held against them. In March, as the northern front collapsed and Belgium, which the French had conquered, was lost again, the royalist peasants of the Vendée rebelled and overran whole départements with their "white terror". And in April Dumouriez, the Gironde's most renowned general, followed General Lafayette's example after the storming of the Tuileries and defected to the enemy.

The Gironde, who saw themselves as the moderate centre of the bourgeoisie, had no intention of pressing the revolution any further. Instead they put Marat on trial. The latter, however, was acquitted and reiterated his brutally clear message: "Liberty must be founded on force, and the moment has now come to establish the despotism of liberty in order to crush the despotism of kings."

Under such circumstances it is amazing how the Gironde managed to hang on for over two more months. Their fall could be prevented neither by declarations of loyalty from the helpless provinces, where they had their strongholds, nor by legislative concessions. It became generally recognized that they must be ousted in favour of a government based on the people as a whole.

On June 2, 1793 tens of thousands of National Guardsmen in Paris surrounded the Convention and forced it to arrest the leaders of the Gironde.

The way was now clear for the Mountain. The non-aligned centre in the Convention, derisely referred to as the "Plain" or "Swamp", came to terms with the new Montagnard leadership following the elimination of the Gironde. But how and by what means was the country to be governed?

"Following a revolution"—said Marx—"every provisional state formation requires a dictatorship, and a vigorous one at that." In the summer of 1793 the state formation was indeed provisional enough. The value of money had dropped to a quarter of what it had been. In addition to the civil war in the Vendée a "federalist revolt" against the "dictatorship of Paris" had flared up,

instigated by escaped Girondists. Two thirds of the départements rejected the violent change of government, the majority only verbally but some resorted to arms, and it took months to reconquer Marseilles, Bordeaux, Lyons (in October) and Toulon (in December). Corsica was lost for years to Pasquale Paoli and his English protectors. Marat was felled by an assassin's knife.

However, the army rallied to the flag and defended the front for the next three critical months, after which the revived military efforts gradually began to pay off. The mass mobilization (*levée en masse*) of August 1793 was sorely needed: for by now the Republic had to cross swords with four major powers. Austria and Prussia were joined by Bourbon Spain and—more importantly—by Great Britain, which ruled the seas.

During these probationary three months the Mountain, its support based on the high moral prestige of the Jacobin Club and its network of affiliated societies scattered around the country, relied more on the pikes of the sans-culottes than on a state apparatus of vacillating loyalty beset with legal scruples which was clearly in need of reform. Nor did the "Jacobin Constitution" of June 24, 1793 give it much assistance. This fine Rousseauesque proclamation of revolutionary democracy remained a mere declaration of intent, to be implemented when a glorious peace should be won within the "natural frontiers" along the Alps and the Rhine. Saint-Just, like Robespierre, argued that it could not be introduced amid the chaos of war and civil war: No freedom for the enemies of freedom, no democracy for the enemies of democracy!

The masses propelled the Convention forwards. On September 4 and 5 the people of Paris rose again—but this time peaceably, for the National Assembly avoided an unnecessary confrontation and bowed to popular will. It decreed a "general maximum" to safeguard the basic daily essentials and put the terror on the agenda. On October 10 it declared the government to be "revolutionary", i.e. not tied to any constitution, "until peace is restored". On December 4 it gave this revolutionary government (*gouvernement révolutionnaire*) a statutory framework.

This Jacobin state was meant as a temporary arrangement which no one dreamed of making permanent. It saw itself as the general staff of the "besieged fortress of France" and was empow-

ered by an enabling law. Its policy of terror (*la terreur*) corresponded to the state of emergency which is usually declared in times of war. In this, initially at least, it knew it had the support of the masses. Its core, grouped around Robespierre, lived off the respect which the Jacobin leader, who was known as the Incorruptible by friend and foe alike, enjoyed nationwide. But his plan of concentrating all the patriotic forces could only succeed if he managed to gather round him not only the common people but also the bourgeois supporters of the revolution. The defeat of both internal and external counter-revolution once and for all was their common denominator. There was a readiness to accept sacrifices in the process—though in various forms and to varying degrees. The need for rigorous central control—from armaments to the economy and to theatre programmes—was accepted, however grudgingly. The art of government consisted in maintaining a balance between the interests of the bourgeoisie and those of the sans-culottes. Spontaneous initiatives from below which were detrimental to reasons of state, such as the violent de-Christianization campaign which threatened to plunge the countryside into a highly superfluous religious war, were skilfully blocked by the Convention. This kind of compromise seemed both necessary and possible. Yet as soon as the Hébertist ultraleftists or Dantonist "Indulgents" grew more powerful and looked likely to oust the Robespierrist centre, the terror struck back mercilessly. "In the Convention," Robespierre was to say in June 1794, "there can be only two parties: the good and the bad." And he despatched the latter to the scaffold.

The Jacobin state was organized from top to bottom. It rejected notions of "direct democracy" harboured by the sans-culottes: the nation's sovereignty was looked after by the people's representatives in the Convention, which in theory ruled as a whole. In fact real power was exercised by the Committee of Public Safety (*Comité de Salut public*) and—less and less—by the Committee of General Security, the "Ministry of Terror". The Revolutionary Tribunal was guided by the various committees. The six-men Provisional Executive Committee, which had functioned as the executive since the overthrow of the monarchy, was dissolved; its tasks were transferred to legislative commissions.

Self-administration in the cantons, districts and départements was limited and subjected to the control of salaried revolutionary committees, government officials and "representatives on mission". All elections were halted for the duration of the war; elected bodies were altered through self-purging or, even more frequently, through imposed purges and supplemented by new appointments.

Such a state formation had not been prefigured by Rousseau and indeed was in no way premeditated. Although the Jacobins—and in particular the Robespierrists—acknowledged certain principles, they basically acted in accordance with the daily exigences. "The force of circumstance," Saint-Just freely admitted, "may lead to unforeseen results."

In the process the peasants achieved one of their main aims: all seignorial rights which had not yet been redeemed were transferred to them without compensation and any concomitant debts and arrears cancelled. Title deeds and documents which might be used as the basis for later claims

were to be destroyed, and common land could be parcelled up and sold on request. Another immense boost to the land fund was promised by the Ventôse laws of March 1794 which expropriated some 200,000 "suspects". However, the Montagnard bourgeoisie, who were disinclined to transfer land to smallholders, managed to delay and thus thwart their implementation.

Wage workers had less cause for satisfaction. Public subsidies and food rationing guaranteed the basic necessities at moderate prices, and arms production plus the conscription of men born in seven consecutive years soaked up the unemployed. Yet insistent demands for wage rises and stoppages in support thereof met with indignation from the revolutionary government, which immediately suppressed them.

In the wake of a successful attempt by the negro slaves of St. Domingue (today Haiti) led by Toussaint L'Ouverture to liberate themselves, slavery was abolished in all French colonies.

The stock exchange was closed down; joint-stock and trading companies went into liquidation.

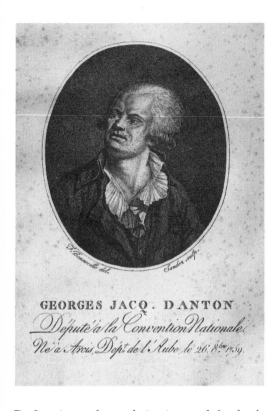

GEORGES JACQ. DANTON
Député à la Convention Nationale.
Né à Arcis, Dépt de l'Aube le 26:8bre 1759.

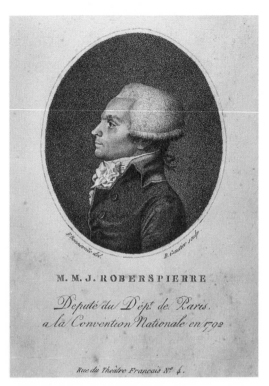

M. M. J. ROBERSPIERRE
Député du Dépt. de Paris.
à la Convention Nationale en 1792.

Rue du Theatre Français N°. 4.

Profiteering and speculation incurred the death penalty. However, major transgressors who managed to line their pockets in a "patriotic" manner were largely immune.

The Jacobins also turned their attentions to the cultural sphere. The academies and the Sorbonne in Paris, where the "old spirit" continued to hold sway, were forced to close their doors. On the other hand the Convention did all it could to promote practice-based scientific and technical research and established the principle (but without earmarking the necessary funds) of general and compulsory schooling within the framework of a system of free national education. To its credit it also introduced the metric system of measurement. The Republican calendar which came into being in 1793 remained in force for only a dozen years, but a number of the poetic names given to the months of the year were to go down in history in conjunction with specific political events.

The revolutionary government had largely achieved its immediate aim of warding off military encirclement—but at a price. A single will ruled, and nobody could evade its pressure.

The populace was no longer asked its opinion; passive followers were what the government now desired. People did not even impart their secrets to their diaries. The surviving newspapers acted little differently: meetings, petitions and despatches from the front reported without comment, occasional dutiful outpourings of praise, a few titbits of insipid gossip plus a section for culture in which the odd veiled allusion might sometimes be concealed.

Initially the government's staffing policy took into account the need for a reliable mass base of support. Continual purges removed "aristocrats" and the "rich" from public bodies and authorities. Cobblers, tailors and their ilk were promoted. Even the Jacobin Club itself, hitherto a solidly middle class preserve, broadened its base through the admission of plebeian elements. From the spring of 1794 there were signs of a sea-change: the relaxation of economic controls, the compulsory drafting of labour to work in the fields and the harassment of suspected leftwingers.

In a society structured along bourgeois lines, however democratic it might be, verdicts of the Committee of Public Safety in cases of arbitration obviously tended in the final analysis to favour the propertied. An aggravating factor, however, was that Robespierre became increasingly unsure of himself once splits began to appear even within the ranks of the revolutionary government.

Gunners, set your cannons roaring
  and show bravery divine.
Send our noble message pouring
  into the midst of those swine!
Riouffe, "Song of the Grenadiers, a Lesson for the Austrians", 1792.

The Revolution is a war being waged by Liberty on its enemies. The Constitution is the régime of victorious and peaceable Liberty.
Robespierre

Ah, here we go, here we go, here we go,
  let the aristocrats hang from on high!
Ah, here we go, here we go, here we go,
  let the aristos dangle in the sky!
And we'll take a spade as we pass
  to belt once more each noble arse.
"Ça ira", revolutionary anthem, 1790.

I. L. K. Grimm

W. Grimm.

~ 1797 ~

"The Revolution is frozen," Saint-Just confessed, and the Incorruptible allowed himself to be disarmed by the social contradictions which were just then coming to an explosive head. Too well aware of the bourgeoisie's historic task to tie himself too closely to the sans-culottes, he was at the same time much too sensitive to the needs of the ordinary people to find favour among the bourgeoisie after having done for them the dirty and difficult job of routing their enemies. His insecurity led to numerous mistakes. The "cult of the Supreme Being", as a gesture of metaphysical communion, was inconsistent with an institutionalized reign of terror on earth.

As the head of state Robespierre felt the need to help the people forward to a form of faith which, while sparing deeply ingrained habits, would nevertheless consolidate Republican customs.

The Guillotine. Drawing done by Jacob and Wilhelm Grimm as children from a print. Watercolour, 1797. Staatliche Schlösser und Gärten Homburg vor der Höhe.

Marie-Antoinette on the way to the scaffold. Drawing by Jacques-Louis David, 1793. His critics accused him of habitually sketching the condemned as they were being carted away to their death. Musée du Louvre, Paris.

Portrait de marie Antoinette reine de france conduite au Supplice ; dessiné à la plume par David Spectateur du Convoi, & Placé sur la fenetre avec la citoyenne jullien epouse du representant jullien, à qui je tiens cette piece.

Thus on May 7, 1794 he sought to define an ideological consensus for the nation: "Amorality is the basis of despotism, just as virtue is the essence of the Republic. Command in a manner that we are triumphant, but whatever else be sure to hurl vice back into the void! . . . In the eyes of the legislator everything which is useful to mankind and good in practice is the truth." He then concluded: "The notion of the Supreme Being is a continuous appeal to justice; it is thus both social and Republican."

The new cult was inaugurated on June 8, a fine summer's day, by means of a "festival of the Supreme Being and Nature". Although even his friends had misgivings and long-standing Convention members scoffed at the procession, organized by David, with its draught oxen with gilt horns, it was nevertheless very impressive. Mallet Dupan from Switzerland, an enemy of the Jacobins, was not far from the mark when he wrote: "People seriously believed that Robespierre had set about closing over the abyss of the Revolution." He failed to achieve his purpose once this misunderstanding was cleared up.

The dilemma of the olive branch versus the executioner's axe was compressed into the space of three days. Whereas the festival had seemed to signal an end to all the tribulations in harmonious accord, a law followed immediately afterwards—on June 10 (22 Prairial)—which gave rise to the nightmarish prospect that the terror was about to start all over again: it might be just one final "purge", but there was no foreseeable end in sight. Article 7 tersely proclaimed: "The punishment for all offences on which it is the Revolutionary Tribunal's prerogative to pass sentence, is death." The Law of Prairial—above and beyond all the moralizing and juggling with figures—was a mistake. The guillotine would never be able to unmask and deal with every dissident. So it had to be selective. But who exactly would be its victims: only the "suspects" (whether already in jail or not), the supporters of the old régime who had slipped through the legal net, the lukewarm and feeble patriots? Or was the triumvirate of Robespierre, Saint-Just and Couthon bent on yet another purge of the Convention?

When the full extent of the split emerged into the open Robespierre discovered that neither the Convention nor the Committee of Public Safety would any longer allow themselves to be held in

check by the pronouncements from the dais of the Jacobin Club. He realized too late that he had become a burden for those who had profiteered from the Revolution. Sulking, he withdrew from the Convention and the Committee of Public Safety, preferring to place his trust in his tribune within the Club in the erroneous assumption that his critics would beg him to come back.

As he voluntarily abandoned these two fields of struggle to his adversaries neither they nor he grasped the full significance of the news that had just reached Paris: at Fleurus on June 26 the result of the summer campaign had been largely settled by the defeat of the main Austrian force.

The outcome of the battle was not directly responsible for the disintegration of the revolutionary government. It did, however, alter the general political climate. Barère was by no means the victim of an hallucination when he anxiously warned the Convention on July 15 to keep a close eye on certain persons who toasted the health of the Republic with the words: "Our armies are everywhere victorious! It only remains for us to make peace, to live in harmony together and to put an end to the terrible revolutionary government."

The public prosecutors meeting in camera at the Paris Law Court, January 1790. Engraving.

"Un petit souper à la Parisienne—or—A family of sans-culottes refreshing after the fatigues of the day." Coloured etching by James Gillray, 1792. This caricature of the September massacres in Paris depicts the sans-culottes as monstrous cannibals.

The revolutionary calendar, which began on September 22, the day the Republic was officially founded:

Vendémiaire	—	*Month of Wine*
Brumaire	—	*Month of Mist*
Frimaire	—	*Month of Frost*
Nivôse	—	*Month of Snow*
Pluviôse	—	*Month of Rain*
Ventôse	—	*Month of Wind*
Germinal	—	*Month of Germination*
Floréal	—	*Month of Blossom*
Prairial	—	*Month of Meadows*
Messidor	—	*Month of Harvest*
Thermidor	—	*Month of Heat*
Fructidor	—	*Month of Fruit*

Twelve days later, on 9 Thermidor, the conspirators struck within the Convention. On July 28 the badly wounded Robespierre, along with Saint-Just, Couthon and nineteen of their supporters, were executed. Amid the thousands of cheering onlookers not a single voice expressed sympathy. The working people remained on the sidelines whither the Jacobin leaders had earlier relegated them. Of necessity the revolutionary government had been based on diverse and even contradictory social groups. Even the Jacobins, who formed its centre of gravity, did not represent any single class and were still less a disciplined class party. They were unable to erect the framework of their social edifice on firm foundations. Their rule ended simultaneously with the deaths of Robespierre and his comrades-in-arms. The humanitarian and egalitarian republic which—in spite of everything—had always remained their ultimate ideal turned out to be a sublime pipe dream. Even so, the signal importance of their pioneering effort cannot be denied. To have helped to achieve what was then feasible in the struggle against feudalism in a revolutionary manner, fearlessly, irrevocably and irreversibly will for ever remain the historic accomplishment of the Jacobins in tandem with the people.

Liberty or Law and Order

In the immediate aftermath of Thermidor it was of course impossible to foresee that the reaction against the Revolution which followed the rupture of its democratic axis would eventually usher in the Empire. Notwithstanding this, every observer described the event as a turning point.

In public Robespierre's overthrow was unanimously welcomed, including by Babeuf, though he pointed out that the Declaration of Rights, however imperfect, was a noble act despite having been inspired by Robespierre. His advice was to cherish the end result but to forget its originator.

It was, clearly, not quite such a simple matter as this. The "swamp" had made the repeal of the Law of Prairial and the release of numerous suspects a precondition of its support for the coup. Consequently Public Prosecutor Fouquier-Tinville was jailed and later executed. The revolutionary committees were replaced by cantonal and district committees, the leadership of which devolved in the main to "obedient" citizens. The Paris Commune was dissolved and the Jacobin Club closed down.

There was no lack of attempts to unite the left around a common platform. Babeuf, who was beginning to appreciate the way the land lay, proclaimed his allegiance to the Thermidorians; in future, he said, he also would recognize only two parties, that of the "golden million" and that of the other twenty-four millions. The first, he added, was aiming for a bourgeois and aristocratic republic while the second, believing it had been responsible for securing the republic, sought to make it as popular-based and democratic as possible. However, the attempt to rekindle a mass movement failed. The press and the streets were controlled by moderates of all hues. Armed gangs, the core of which were formed by the *jeunesse dorée* ("gilded youth"), took to attacking the patriots.

Outwardly a striking change overcame everyday life. Jacobin austerity was replaced by eccentric fashion crazes and an ostentatious zest for life. Exclusive balls were held which could be attended only by those who could claim a victim of the guillotine among their close relatives. Parliamentarians and the new rich rubbed shoulders with the old financial establishment and former notables, who had managed to flee, in the boudoirs of refined courtesans over whom Teresa Cabarrus, now Madame Tallien and known as "Our dear Lady Thermidor", and Josephine, widow of the executed General Beauharnais, winsomely presided.

Social welfare had no place in such a society. The abolition of the "maximum" gave a carte blanche to the profiteers. By April 1795 the assignat had fallen to eight and by July to a mere three per cent of its nominal value. Half a pound of bread per day could be obtained with ration cards or bought on the market for fifty times as much. It was no wonder that the blessings of the "liberated" economy seemed like a godsend to purchasers of nationalized property, army contractors, importers, farming magnates and speculators. The masses began to grow restive, for starvation plus the simultaneous persecution of proven revolutionaries—including dead ones whose corpses were removed from the Panthéon—indicated an organized plot. "We have no bread and are on the verge of regretting that we sacrificed so much for the Revolution," declared the faubourgs Saint-Marceau and Saint-Jacques on March 17 in the year 1795.

On the 31st the Quinze-Vingts Section demanded a freely elected commune, the reinstatement of the popular societies and the constitution of 1793; this was the signal for the Germinal rising which broke out on April 1.

It showed up all the weaknesses of a mass movement whose leaders had either been decimated or else were stuck behind bars, and which had neither a unified leadership nor a clear objective. It was followed by intensified repression which merely served to highlight the interrelationship between economic and political motives. This was the last straw for the Sections. A leaflet provided their stormy meetings with the slogan "bread and the constitution of 1793" under which the eastern part of Paris erupted for the second time on May 20 (1 Prairial in the Year III).

This time the Convention reeled under the assault. Yet once again there was little more than a verbal exchange of insults and promises. At the end of the second day the insurrectionists, their lungs and emotions exhausted, contented themselves with a part-payment on paper and a fraternal kiss from the president of the Convention for their spokesman.

Just how much this was worth they discovered two days later. For the first time since 1789 the government moved regular troops into Paris. Together with National Guard units loyal to the Convention they sealed off Saint-Antoine, the centre of the Prairial uprising, and on May 23 forced the rebels to surrender.

The Parisian sans-culottes never recovered from this defeat. After the Jacobins had quit the scene the working people, left to their own devices, were not in a position to wrest political—let alone social—democracy from the bourgeoisie. Provoked at a time when their privations defied the imagination, they marched into their last battle armed with the courage derived from desperation. Conquered and broken, they were sent packing by the Thermidorians.

The "rabble rousers" were dealt with severely. Thousands were disarmed and dozens executed. The last Montagnards, who had defended the demands of the rebels in the Convention, died stoically by their own hand. In the provinces thugs broke into the prisons and massacred any revolutionaries they found there; elsewhere Jacobins were executed "by court order". The Convention did not approve such over-zealousness, but nor did it seek to check these acts of vengeance, for it was in its own interests to eradicate the popular forces before it presented its own constitution. In this respect it had a few aces up its sleeve. The army had survived the Ninth of Thermidor intact. In 1795 the Rhine front (with the exception of Mainz) was firmly in French hands; Belgium had been annexed and a sister republic set up in the Netherlands. In April Prussia, more concerned with gaining territory in Poland than with a costly show of feudal class solidarity in the West, made its peace with France in Basle; war-weary Spain followed suit. In July a royalist landing force was destroyed at Quiberon in Brittany; the bursting of this bubble put an end to the hopes of both overt and covert agitators of being able to pressurize the Thermidorians into amending the constitution of the Year III so that it resembled more the first, monarchist constitution of 1791.

The new constitution which emerged after lengthy deliberations on August 22, 1795 was an undisguised expression of the class interests of the republican bourgeoisie. Universal suffrage was reduced to a limited franchise, and though all tax payers (but only these) retained the right to

Allegory on the annexation of the left bank of the Rhine by France. Etching by Friedrich Cöntgen after Müller, 1801. Resting beneath the palm of victory is the figure of the Republic. Beside her Minerva, the goddess of wisdom, holds the contract of reunion in her hand and points to the god of the Rhine, whose rudder bears the inscription "Freedom of Trade". The obelisk, a symbol of immortality, lists the names of the generals and statesmen concerned.

Page 28:
General Bonaparte before a battlefield. Mezzotint engraving by Pierre Charles Coqueret after Hilaire le Dru.

This is how the young Marx saw it:
Under the government of the Directory, bourgeois society [. . .] broke out in powerful streams of life. A storm and stress of commercial enterprise, a passion for enrichment, the exuberance of the new bourgeois life, whose first self-enjoyment is pert, light-hearted, frivolous and intoxicating; a real enlightenment of the land of France [. . .] which, by the first feverish efforts of the numerous new owners, had become the object of all-round cultivation; the first moves of industry that had now become free—these were some of the signs of life of the newly emerged bourgeois society.
The Holy Family.

vote in the primary assemblies, the 30,000 electors who chose the deputies to the Legislative Assembly had to prove they were property owners with substantial incomes. The fathers of the constitution—once bitten, twice shy—wanted to avoid the danger both of another intervention by the masses into the political arena as well as of a dictatorship, either by the Assembly or an individual. Hence they built in safeguards such as annual partial elections, though these merely made their institutions all the more vulnerable.

Well aware of the discontent among the masses, the Convention deprived them of their last independent organs by means of a decree of August 23: the clubs and popular societies. However, still nervous about the outcome of the elections, the Convention resorted to a ruse: it laid down that two thirds of those elected must be drawn from its own ranks. This would preserve, for the time being at least, the dominant position of the moderate republican centre in the Legislative Assembly in spite of the expected loss of votes. Whilst around one million votes were polled in favour of the constitution and only 50,000 against, the supplementary decree was rejected by almost one third of the electorate, including by every Parisian Section bar one.

Without delay the royalists set about winning over the hoodwinked voters by means of a demagogic campaign against the government. They persuaded seven Sections to declare an uprising on October 3. The military commander of Paris, Menou (the "Victor of Prairial"), surreptitiously abetted a coordinating committee of the 20,000 insurgents, who occupied the greater part of Paris. However, the Convention clearly had no intention of bowing out in such an inglorious fashion. It revoked the order to disarm the "terrorists", set up defence battalions consisting of reliable patriots and entrusted the operational command to officers who had earlier been weeded out as suspected Jacobins. On October 5 (13 Vendémiaire in the Year IV) a brigadier general of artillery brought in from outside by the name of Napoleone Buonaparte ruthlessly mowed down a mob advancing on the Convention, many of whom were acting in the laudable but erroneous belief that they were fighting for a proper electoral democracy. On November 3, 1795 the five Directors—Barras, La Revellière, Letourneur, Reubell and Carnot—were able to take over executive power unopposed. But the soldier who had made Vendémiaire possible had also begun his prestigious career.

Barras—in succession a count, a "terrorist" and a Thermidorian—led the Directory for four years; he was not a great man, but proved to have no scruples whatsoever in his choice of methods. The government indicated its intentions in a declaration on November 5, 1795: "To replace the chaos inseparable from revolution with social order . . . to actively combat royalism . . . to firmly suppress all agitators; to stifle any vengeful impulse. To institute concord and to restore peace . . . to revive industry and commerce . . . to re-establish plenty and public credit." The revolutionary convulsions

Josephine Bonaparte. Drawing by Jean-Baptiste Isabey, 1798.

Page 30:
Vow of the 1,500 Republicans at Montenesimo. Their readiness to defend the redoubt of Montenesimo under General Rampon helped Napoleon to win the Battle of Montenotte against the Austrians on April 12, 1796. Etching by Joseph Anton Koch, 1797. Whilst in Strasbourg the Tyrolese painter, who lived in Italy, was for a time a Jacobin and long continued to sympathize with the Revolution. At the centre of the oath-swearing ceremony—the modern appearance of which is idealized by a single antique helmet—Bonaparte can be seen next to the general with the flag.

I will lead you to the most fertile plains in the world. Rich provinces and great cities will fall into your hands. Here you will reap honour, martial glory and riches.
Bonaparte

[1] REBMANN, G.F.: *Holland und Frankreich in Briefen* (1796). Berlin, 1981.
[2] GODECHOT, J.: *La vie quotidienne en France sous le Directoire*. Paris, 1977.

were consigned to oblivion but the benefits accruing therefrom were to be utilized and defended.

At the height of inflation, when even beggars turned their noses up at low-denomination notes, speculators acquired nationalized property for next to nothing. The consumer, however, had to pay 150 francs for a loaf of bread after the subsidized daily ration was reduced to a derisory 75 grammes. In the spring of 1796 the hardships facing ordinary people exceeded even those of 1795.[1]

The Directory was well aware of the shaky foundations on which it rested. To counterbalance the polished demagoguery of the right Barras gave the rather tame leftwing press more leeway and eased the restraints on political associations. One of these, the "Panthéon Club", soon drew many democratic adherents, in particular men who, like Babeuf, had regained their freedom as the result of a general amnesty.

At the behest of Barras, the adroit Fouché acted as go-between in an effort to get the democrats to accept the Directory as the lesser evil. Napoleon's future minister of police, however, cut no ice with his old friend Babeuf. The "tribune of the people" rejected the idea of a united front of all republicans as class collaboration. "We are gathering around us all the democrats and proletarians, concepts which unquestionably have a clear and unmistakable meaning. Our tenets are pure democracy plus irreproachable and unadulterated equality." He published the *Manifeste de Plébéiens*, an outline of the future society he envisaged, to whet the people's appetite for true and perfect equality. And Babeuf, who significantly now referred to himself as "Gracchus", was determined to start building the new society at once.[2]

In response the Directory ordered the arrest of Babeuf, who now went underground. Whilst the government was instructing the newly appointed commander in chief of the Army of the Interior, General Buonaparte, to close down the Panthéon Club, Babeuf and Filippo Buonarroti from Tuscany, once a family friend of the Buonapartes in Ajaccio, Corsica, formed the conspiratorial Society of Equals, the first communistic party of action in history. It attracted revolutionaries from all sections of the left with the objective of overthrowing the government. The strategy of the "Equals" did not seek to involve the masses.

Their intention was to rule without a national assembly by means of a minority of impeccable revolutionaries until they had founded their utopia of a national "community of goods".

However, on May 10, 1796 the "tribune of the people" and his fellow comrades were captured. They were taken to distant Vendôme where, after a deliberately protracted show trial, Babeuf and Darthé were executed on May 27, 1797.

The Babouvists could not complain about lack of publicity. Following the discovery of their conspiracy the gazettes were falling over themselves to write about them. Along with Buonarroti, who got off with a life sentence, Babeuf not only digested the lesson of Thermidor, namely that bourgeois and communist ends were ultimately incompatible, but also acted accordingly. Even after his inevitable failure he never lost his conviction that a second, more far-reaching revolution was bound to occur. He has gone down in history as one of its most celebrated precursors. For the Directory, on the other hand, Babeuf's conspiracy was merely an embarrassing incident. Public interest soon faded in face of the turn which French military fortunes took from 1796 to 1797. Consequently, the name of the man who stole the Directory's scene was not Babeuf but Napoleon Buonaparte. As a protegé of the powerful Barras after having got him out of trouble during Vendémiaire, the 27 year-old little Corsican rapidly rose to prominence. Having in the previous autumn been promoted to divisional general in March 1796 he acquired both the "loveliest little bum in the world", meaning Josephine Beauharnais, as his wife and the confused Italian theatre of war as a testing ground for his military prowess. On taking over command he dropped the Italianate "u" from his name and refired the army's morale, which due to the Directors' stinginess was sagging, by promising it the rich spoils of Lombardy.

The ensuing campaign left friend and foe alike awestruck. What was conceived in Paris as an attempt to relieve the struggling main forces in southern Germany ended up routing not only the King of Sardinia and Piedmont but also the Papal States and Austria as well. The names of the battles became immortalized in military history, and in the geography of Paris: Lodi, Arcole, Rivoli. The infantrymen of the army fighting in Italy marched from one triumph to another, lived prodigally from the captured booty and in addition

filled the government's constantly empty coffers back home with barrels full of gold. A military commander emerged who, without paying too much heed to his orders, had the unparallelled knack of being able to translate revolutionary conditions into success on the battlefield while taking calculated risks into the bargain.

In March 1797 this Italian army advancing at breakneck speed, was already approaching the Semmering Pass and thus threatening the Imperial capital Vienna. On April 18 the nervous Austrians, not knowing that Bonaparte's reserves were exhausted, signed the preliminaries of Leoben, which put an end to the First Coalition against the French Republic. The Directory had no alternative but to rubber-stamp the unau-

thorized actions of its high-handed general. Sergeant Petitbon, for one, was still convinced this was all to the good of the Revolution: "In its last campaign the Italian army was forced to fight against a most belligerent nation which refused to acknowledge our country's independence; however, we were led by a man of genius who ensured that our courage proved invincible. He has shown that despotism's efforts are all in vain when directed against a people which has torn off its chains, and that the determination of the tyrant is inferior to that of free men."

Director Carnot still endeavoured, despite occasional doubts as to the loyalty of his high-flying general, to believe in the latter's basic goodness; but his letters to him already contained an openly

Entry of the French into Milan on 25 Floréal of the Year IV. Etching by Jean Duplessi-Bertaux and Maquelier after Carle Vernet.

The Feast of Virgil in Mantua on 24 Vendémiaire of the Year VI. Etching by Georges Malbeste and Claude Niquet after Carle Vernet.

From the work: *Campagnes des Français sous le Consulat et sous l'Empire*. Paris, 1806.

beseeching tone. Napoleon, who was holding court at Montebello palace in the Milanese, heard his plea but preferred to trust to his lucky star.

In 1797 the problem of famine and external danger receded, but the Directory was still unable to win over the electorate; in April it lost its majority in the Legislative Assembly. The new elite still had to learn how to rule inconspicuously, and they were slow learners to begin with. They paid the penalty for ignoring, either on purpose or out of incompetence, the multifarious subversive activities of monarchist agencies.

The authors of the constitution were the first to tamper with it so that, whilst infringing the parliamentary rules which they themselves had laid down, they could maintain their artificial majority. Deeming it inadvisable to reintroduce the masses into the fray they turned to the army. Their first coup of 18 Fructidor V (September 4, 1797) went off without a hitch only because Hoche and Napoleon, the two popular national heroes, believed it was in their interests to support the free state against a possible restoration.

The second Directory (of 18 Fructidor) continued its "democratic" path. It also lost the elections of 1798, this time ceding more votes to the left than to the right, and so promptly launched a second, smaller coup on 22 Floréal VI (May 11, 1798) which broke the Legislative Assembly's truculence through another reshuffle of its membership. The executive consolidated its dominance over the two chambers, while a ray of hope temporarily brightened up the horizon: the end of inflation and a return to a metal currency, the introduction of a state pension (though all at the cost of cancelling two thirds of the public debt, to the detriment of savers but to the state's advantage), the first reliable national census, an industrial exhibition in Paris and some useful municipal legislation.

The economic situation remained the weak spot: doubts about the durability of the peace settlement prevented its consolidation. For a bourgeoisie in power the idea of curbing consumption or even the search for profits was no longer a serious possibility. It sought to off-load its liabilities onto the conquered territories. After the Peace of

Campo Formio had been signed with Austria in October 1797 this option seemed promising. However, as soon as the acquisitions looked like being lost again the Directors had to shift the burden back onto the shoulders of the French tax payers, so that the economic problem again took on a political dimension. They did not survive the Second Coalition War.

Both sides were to blame for its outbreak. The Directory incurred responsibility through its aggressive policy of trying to squeeze every last drop out of the configuration of forces in Switzerland and Italy. Rather than aiming at a federation of liberated nations, which had been the ideal of the Jacobins and sans-culottes, the Directory preferred to subjugate or annexe other nations, collect booty and advance its military bases: a "Helvetic", a "Roman" and a "Parthenopean" sister republic were set up in the process.

For its part British diplomacy was battling for pre-eminence with a fellow capitalist rival. Britain's mistrust grew when the Directory gave its blessing to Bonaparte's plan to occupy Turkish-held Egypt and from there to undermine England's position in the Mediterranean and in India. The fact that some people in Paris were quite relieved to know that the energetic general was at a safe distance was regarded as a purely internal French affair.

Bonaparte took a gamble: if Nelson's fleet happened to come across the expedition that put to sea in May 1798 all would be lost. Luckily for him Nelson looked in the wrong place. After quickly capturing Malta and dispossessing the Order of the Knights of St. John, Bonaparte landed at Alexandria and defeated the Mameluke horsemen at Giza, where he told his troops: "From the summit of these pyramids forty centuries look down upon you." However, the British admiral discovered the French fleet at Aboukir and destroyed it, thereby stranding the "liberator of Egypt". India seemed more unattainable than ever as the French ally Tipu Sahib, Sultan of Mysore, was killed during the siege of his capital Seringapatam. Meanwhile Bonaparte rattled the chains of oriental feudalism, gave encouragement to Egyptologists, had an obelisk brought to the Seine and promoted the Pharaonic style. He rode on a camel, flirted with a soldier's wife, read Goethe's *The Sorrows of Werther* and judiciously praised the prophet Mohammed. Yet when he

moved against the Turks in Syria the British navy seized his artillery at sea. The eight assaults on the fortified town of Acre armed with nothing but hand weapons were a farcical fiasco and ended in an ignominious withdrawal. The English were just as pleased to see the back of him as his own superiors, and Commodore Sir Sydney Smith obligingly sent him newspapers from Europe. The Directory had gone too far, having deported the pope and occupied Naples. When its oriental policy also drove the tsar over to the side of Turkey and England, Austria granted the Russian troops free passage to Italy, to which the Directory responded on March 12, 1799 with a declaration of war: the reluctance of the potentates to accept the Revolution as an accomplished fact drove the five Directors in Paris, who were hardly straining at the leash, to take defensive action. The nation was in rebellious mood. As soon as the setbacks began to come in thick and fast and the guerilla war in the Vendée flared up again, the demand for a revolutionary prosecution of the war made itself heard.

In the elections of March/April 1799 two thirds of the government's candidates were rejected. At the same time Jacobins won votes from the monarchists, and the bulk of the Thermidorians, in the face of the first defeats, moved closer to them. This new left of centre majority went onto the attack against the Directory. The Legislative Assembly exacted its revenge for being emasculated during Floréal VI. It voted Sieyès onto the Directory, and Barras (as per usual) threw in his lot with the winning side. A third coup d'état on 30 Prairial VII (June 18, 1799), this time a parliamentary one carried out by the Legislative Assembly, completely disarmed the Directory. Bonaparte's brother Lucien dramatically proclaimed: "The Legislative Assembly has regained the foremost position in the state which is its due!" At this hour of great peril "democrats of 1793" took over the reins: Fouché, Cambacérès, Robert Lindet and Bernadotte. The legislators gave the active Jacobin minority its head. A levy of young men aged between twenty and twenty-five was mobilized and sent into battle, a forced loan was imposed on the wealthy and a law of hostages to combat banditry was passed. On the anniversary of the storming of the Bastille General Jourdan proposed a toast to the resurrection of the pikes.

The Apotheosis of General Hoche. This satire on the state funeral of the young Republican general is composed so as to resemble a picture of the Last Judgement. Hoche is enthroned on a rainbow above the Vendée (where he had fought the royalist rebels) and is surrounded by infernal monsters who represent the Revolution. In place of a Christian halo a noose hangs above his head, and instead of the lyre of Apollo his fingers strum a guillotine. The divine tablets at the top of the picture bear blasphemous inscriptions. The revolutionary is here depicted as the Antichrist. Coloured etching by James Gillray, January, 1798.

Such are the French! By turns constitutional with the court, moderate with Brissot, Jacobinic under Robespierre, with André Dumont Thermidorian and royalist, as a few extreme demagogues have become. These are the principles of this flock of sheep which is composed of a majority of the rentiers, of the present civil servants, advocates, agents and bourgeois for whom the return to the old order of things is a kind of resurrection—and whose permanent belief is that the opinion of the nation, state welfare, trade and industry (which are all at risk from incessant reaction) can all be sacrificed as long as their soup is nice and hot and no one demands taxes from them.
Hoche to Debelle, February 14, 1797.

A thousand projects are ascribed to you, each more absurd than the other. People refuse to believe that someone who has achieved such great things could content himself with living as an ordinary citizen. For my part I would say that only a Bonaparte who has rejoined the ranks of the ordinary citizens can demonstrate the true greatness of Bonaparte the general.
Carnot to Bonaparte, August 17, 1797.

The Apotheosis of HOCHE.

General Kleber attends to the wounded after the Battle of Heliopolis. Lithograph by Pierre-Roch Vigneron.

The recourse to so many methods of the Year II frightened the bourgeois notables and caused them, as soon as the position at the front had eased up a little, to part company again with their sinister confederates. On August 10 Sieyès warned of people "who, intoxicated by their provocative actions, squeeze dry the wells of social wealth, ruin public credit, bring trade to a halt and paralyze all work". On the 13th Fouché closed down the democratic "Club du Manège"; the lack of protests clearly showed that the Jacobins, unsupported by the people, had been unable to mobilize the masses anew.

They were also defeated in the Council of the Five Hundred, the Legislative Assembly's second chamber. When Jourdan proposed on September 13, 1799 that, in view of a possible Anglo-Russian landing in Holland, a state of emergency should be declared, Lucien Bonaparte argued in an uproarious debate that it would be better to expand the Directory's constitutional powers than to allow themselves to be swept along by the revolutionary tide.

Jourdan's motion was defeated by 245 votes to 171, but the bourgeoisie's desire to reinforce the government could no longer keep the water-logged Directory afloat. Thoroughly corrupt as it was, it had neither the power nor the prestige to push through a credible strategy of its own between the two feared extremes, and besides, new elections were due in the spring of 1800. Whether the monarchists or the Jacobins actually won them, depending on the particular swing of the political pendulum, the five continued to walk a tightrope, and the call for constitutional change spread.

In the early summer Sieyès started searching for a long-term solution that would be to his own advantage. He needed to find a suitable general. Hoche had met an early death in 1797, Joubert was killed during the defeat by Suvorov at Novi on 15 August 1799, and Bernadotte had no power base; the hesitant Moreau came into the reckoning but did not feel up to the job. Meanwhile Bonaparte, having got wind that things were coming to a head, abruptly abandoned his short-lived escapade on the Nile and on October 9 unexpectedly landed at Saint-Raphael near Fréjus. Back in Paris through the good offices of Talleyrand, the other key figure behind the scenes, he fitted perfectly into the plotters' plans. After weighing up the balance of forces the general,

It is not a matter of making an example but of exterminating incorrigible satellites of tyranny.
Couthon on the introduction of the Decree of Prairial.

I feel myself called to combat crime, not to preside over it. The time when upright citizens can serve their country with impunity is still a long way off. As long as the horde of rogues have the upper hand, the defenders of Liberty will remain outlawed.
Robespierre's last speech in the Convention, July 26, 1794.

In determining those matters which are termed constitutional we could not have taken a more favourable step than the separation of powers (into the Directory and the two councils of the Legislative Assembly—the Author). *In reality the constitutional organization of the French people is nothing more than a rough draft.*
Bonaparte to Talleyrand, September 19, 1797.

The "First Consul, Citizen Bonaparte", elected for ten years and thereafter eligible for re-election (Article 39), promulgates the laws in accordance with Article 41.
At his discretion he appoints and dismisses the members of the Council of State, the ministers, envoys and other representatives abroad, the members of the public administration and the government representatives at the law courts.

who was far too ambitious to share power with the Bourbons, put himself forward for the highest office in the Republic, the political institutions of which he had long regarded with scepticism.

The preparations were financed by army contractors worried about their money. The conspirators' propaganda coupled the widespread yearning for peace with, on the one hand, the failure of the constitution and, on the other, the bourgeoisie's fear of egalitarian terrorism. Bonaparte found a ready-made slogan waiting for him: Neither courtiers nor red bonnets!

Blunders committed during the execution of this fourth and last coup of 18 and 19 Brumaire (November 9/10, 1799) were rectified by the intervention of troops loyal to Bonaparte. Following strong initial resistance and the ejection of sixty-two "troublemakers", both chambers of the Legislative Assembly yielded and declared the Directory dissolved. Even Barras, who had been involved right up to the end, was this time left out in the cold. Pending the new, fourth constitution responsibility for running state affairs was entrusted to an executive consisting of three provisional Consuls—Bonaparte, Roger Ducos and Sieyès.

A poster appeared in Paris: "France desires something great and of lasting value. Instability has brought her to her knees; she now appeals for stability. She does not want a monarchy; this has been outlawed. But she does expect uniformity in the actions of the authorities charged with implementing the laws. She desires a free and independent Legislative Assembly . . . she wishes to be represented by peaceable conservatives and not by turbulent reformers; she wishes at last to reap the reward of ten years of sacrifice." And the *Moniteur* (on November 14) was not alone in accepting the self-avowed bourgeois character of the last paragraph. Bonaparte, if we are to believe Miot de Melito, expressed himself in similar vein: "We have ended the story of the revolution. Now we must begin its real history and see to what use its principles can be put."

Consulate and Empire

Bonaparte was not simply hoisted to power. He intervened himself as soon as he perceived that a serious political force was waiting only for him to give the go-ahead, nor did he let himself be dictated to subsequently by the stagers of the coup. Thus if some Brumairiens were hoping that, having enticed the fiery war horse into the unfamiliar arena of politics, they would be able to tamely lead him by the nose, they were in for a big surprise. Bonaparte personally tailored the ninety-five short and deliberately vague and vacuous articles of the "Constitution of the Year VIII" to suit himself.

Having no need of a mentor he got rid of Sieyès, who proposed to fob him off with titles and lavish endowments. As his fellow consuls he carefully chose two men of the second rank from either side of the political divide: the regicide Cambacérès and the conservative Lebrun. Their status was that of capable assistants. In all government affairs except those which Article 41 reserved for the First Consul, the other two consuls served in an advisory capacity. They signed the minutes of the meetings in order to prove they had been present and, if they so wished, could "enter their own opinions therein, whereupon the decision of the First Consul suffices".

To counterbalance the omission of human rights the document contained instructions for the exercise of French civil rights. Of the three chambers—the Senate, the Legislative Body and the Tribunate—none had any real say; Bonaparte worked principally with the Council of State, which he himself appointed.

On December 15, 1799 the Consuls made the text public, together with an appeal which likewise bore the general's trademark. Its concluding sentence proclaimed with military brevity: "Citizens, the Revolution is established upon the principles which began it; it is ended."

The new constitution came into force on Christmas Day. The idea of subsequently organizing a plebiscite paid off beyond all expectations. It was approved by three million votes in favour to 1,562 against, including that of Carnot.

Bonaparte adopted a benevolent air, promising good government for good citizens—a far cry from the barrack-room mentality. It was his deeply held view that the bayonet could be used for almost anything—except as a seat! Indeed, no military faction ever emerged, although this did not mean that he would ever consent to share power.

His programme had the benefit of simplicity: the spirit of discord, in its myriad guises, must be eliminated. He claimed to be all things to all men.

With the exception of a few envious notables, to whom he extended a conciliatory hand, he was able to rely on the army, which saw him not only as a genius on the battlefield but also as the guarantor of its influence within society and the state as a whole. For him the rank-and-file troops were the backbone of the army, but he by no means despised the "top brass". His ability to determine the essence of the matter and to unerringly identify his own interests was not restricted to military affairs; it stood him in equally good stead as a legislator and head of state. He allowed those who helped him to benefit thereby. The delegation of political rights in return for the granting of material advantages: this was his offer, which he reinforced by carefully ensuring that no possible pressure group ever accumulated in its hands the instruments of power. Independent thought had no place in a system that was to function like clockwork, strictly according to the rules and telling people what to think, even though the reins were occasionally slackened and plenty of distractions were organized. Nor did Bonaparte have much time for mental gymnastics, for while he was well read he was not well educated and could be easily disconcerted by nimble-minded speakers or writers.

Mindful of his own youthful indiscretions, he issued a general pardon to those who collaborated with him for theirs (regardless of whether they had erred to the right or to the left): to the deserter Lafayette and the organizer Carnot, to the constitutional monarchist Talleyrand and the terrorist Fouché, the Girondin François de Neufchateau and the Montagnard Jeanbon Saint-André, to the pederast Cambacérès and the punctilious Caulaincourt. He felt happier embracing émigrés than Jacobins, having once himself been one.

The obtaining situation explains why the Brumairiens were more or less handed victory on a plate and why the Consulate—which was conceived as

Portrait of Sieyès. Engraving in stipple technique by Ludwig Buchhorn after Bréa.

The political balance. ("Caught between two stools, landing on its arse".) A caricature of the Directory. Etching.

When a nation embarks on the road to conquest, wrote Captain Simon,
it is imperative that the military spirit dominates the other spheres.
Vérités et idées d'un militaire, 1799.

[1] THIRY, J.: *La Machine infernale.* Paris, 1952.

a temporary expedient—progressed with so little trouble after overcoming quite considerable initial opposition.

The Thermidorians had provided social pre-eminence and undiminished political power to an educated and property-owning bourgeoisie bent on conserving their gains, which were reinforced by the Directory. Yet the sudden squalls of 1799 showed that the womb from which the Revolution had issued was still fertile. If one were to believe the claims of the *Moniteur* of November 10, 1799 nothing could be taken for granted: neither liberty nor property nor the constitution which guaranteed both. After a decade of turbulence and reckless speculation the business community was looking to invest in the recuperated economy of a rationally run state. The question of who actually ran it was secondary. The peasants, opposed to the reintroduction of feudal obligations and tithes, were happy with any government that permitted them to till the liberated land without interference or a heavy tax burden.

The vehicle which enabled the First Consul to shine was an army that still contained within its ranks many of the conscripts of the 1793/94 classes and thus felt a greater sense of obligation towards the nation than the mass of vegetating backwoodsmen. Many revolutionaries who found it hard to follow the twists and turns of Thermidor, Prairial, Vendémiaire and finally the "golden mean" of the (often disunited) Directors saw it as the last refuge.

However, as the vision of an egalitarian republic began to fade they transferred their allegiance to military leaders who offered them prospects of advancement. Then was it not they who, commanding their troops in distant camps, embodied the true, the victorious, the great nation? Stripped of its humanitarian content, patriotism degenerated into chauvinistic conceit, the search for adventure plus the pursuit of plunder and martial glory.

Thus it was that, notwithstanding all the preventive measures, Bonaparte's hour now came. He made the most of it and rang in the 19th century with a plethora of new creations, many of which have survived to the present day.

On January 18, 1800 the Bank of France—the unassailable fortress of finance capital—was founded. On February 17 followed a law which reorganized regional and local administration.

By means of a concordat, which was the upshot of a prolonged tug-of-war, Church and state buried the hatchet. The judiciary was integrated into the state apparatus and hence the free election of judges was done away with. As a crystal-clear expression of real, capitalist relations of production and property, the *Code civil* of 1804 (renamed the *Code Napoléon* in 1807) became the model statute book for the whole epoch.

On the other hand, attempts to put the economy back on an even keel in a similar spirit of generosity did not quite come off. Although a simplified tax system ensured that revenue was collected more rapidly there continued to be a budget deficit year after year, and First Consul Bonaparte, though never a spendthrift in either his public or his private life (indeed, he systematically amassed a personal fortune), as Emperor Napoleon was still obliged to borrow heavily. The exigences of war left little room for drastic economizing. Although the rising value of the consolidated government bond indicated that confidence in the future of the Republic was returning, this sensitive reflector of public opinion never reached its nominal value.

Financial considerations were not the only nor even the main reason why Bonaparte sought peace with the enemy without the country as well as the one within. He knew that the French people were as heartily sick of the endless bloodletting as of the sudden changes in political direction and that they wanted him to use his military expertise not to blaze a new trail of glory but to break the enemy's will to wage war. In donning the mantle of peacemaker he could not wish for a more striking confirmation of his claim to be the patriarch of *la patrie.*

Obviously, it took two to make peace, though actually the new master in the Tuileries was not, on the whole, treated too badly by the press abroad. His skill as a general was acknowledged, while his exotic exploits on the Nile gave fresh nourishment to the image. Since the Second Coalition War had ground to a halt by the end of 1799 and Tsar Paul I, embittered by Austria's equivocations, had dropped out of the alliance and even looked set to change sides, Vienna and London both viewed the campaign of 1800 with some apprehension.

Despite being in a tight spot Bonaparte postponed action beyond the customary winter break in hostilities, nor did he then take over command of the more important German theatre but contented himself instead with the familiar Italian front. Relying on the element of surprise, he crossed the Alps via the snow-covered Great St. Bernard Pass, intending to attack the enemy from behind and thus settle the affair at one fell swoop. In fact, he came within an inch of defeat at Marengo on June 14, 1800: only the belated arrival of General Desaix, who was fatally wounded in the battle, snatched a magnificent victory from the jaws of defeat. The strategic aim was attained: the Austrians evacuated Italy in disarray, and after rapidly winding up the campaign Bonaparte was able to return to the reins of power in Paris, a hotbed of intrigue which, in view of the uncertainty of the situation, he deemed it inadvisable to abandon for too long.

The fact that this time Moreau in Germany also acquitted himself creditably and even drove the enemy out of Bavaria brought the end of the hostilities that bit nearer. The Viennese court had had enough. But before it settled with Bonaparte in the Treaty of Lunéville (1801) the counter-revolutionary forces had already tested their new secret weapon: assassination. No English lord needed to dirty his hands, for enough royalist Frenchmen were available.

On Christmas Eve in the year 1800, the first anniversary of the new constitution, Haydn's oratorio *The Creation* had its French première at the Théâtre des Arts, the Paris opera house. Bonaparte, who liked to present himself to the applauding audience on such occasions, was late arriving. In his absence the building was shaken after the first few bars of the music by a terrific bang. Soon afterwards the First Consul, outraged but uninjured, appeared in his box with the words: "The swine have just tried to blow me up!", acknowledged the ovations from the relieved audience and signalled to the orchestra to resume playing.[1]

The subsequent investigation was extremely lengthy. It confirmed yet again that there is no such thing as the perfect crime.

Cadoudal, the implacable leader of the Chouans, had slipped back from his refuge in England. He had sent his best men to Paris with ample funds. They succeeded in constructing a primitive but highly effective "infernal machine"—a home-

made bomb consisting of a strong barrel filled with gunpowder and stones—which they then loaded onto a horse and cart and parked in the narrow Rue Saint Nicaise through which Bonaparte's carriage was bound to pass. The first conspirator's job was to signal as soon as it turned into the street from the Place du Carousel, while the second had to make sure the fuse burned down in six to seven seconds. An unfortunate girl who happened to be passing by was persuaded to hold the nag's reins for a moment in return for the "princely" sum of 15 sous.

Bonaparte was delayed. He was exhausted and would have preferred to remain at home. To please Josephine he agreed to go after all, but amid all the toing and froing the minutes ticked away. His personal coachman César, who by this time had knocked back the odd drink or two, thus drove at full pelt to make up for lost time. So he raced the carriage from the Tuileries through the gap between the houses and the parked wagon at a full gallop instead of carefully threading his way past as the plotters had expected. The coach was already taking the next corner when the bomb went off with a deafening roar, tearing people to shreds, causing walls to collapse and rocking the entire neighbourhood.

Due to a palaver about how Josephine could show off her new Egyptian shawl to best effect, the second coach containing the ladies had not yet set off and was undamaged apart from its shattered windows. Had it been on time it would undoubtedly have been blown to smithereens.

Bonaparte was convinced that anarchists and inveterate terrorists were out to get him: the Jacobins, in defence of whom he had written the *Souper de Beaucaire* in August 1793, for whom his artillery had put down the revolt in Toulon in December 1793, from whom he had received the rank of general which made possible his triumph in Vendémiaire 1795, and from whose ranks the most courageous of his "grognards" had come. Like many another, he had sacrificed his youthful ideals on the altar of success and naturally assumed that the Jacobins would never be able to forgive his treachery. He thus saw himself compelled to mercilessly pursue former comrades-in-arms who took exception to his conversion to the "new realities". It seemed to be a question of either him or them. And only a short time before, a few leftist hotheads had indeed conspired against him—Ceracchi, Aréna, Topino-Lebrun—though they were unable to carry out their plan as Fouché's police beat them to it.

In fact the infernal machine bore quite a different trademark. Did the First Consul really believe it was the work of Jacobins or did he merely want to make people think so in order to use the occasion and the widespread outrage it provoked to put paid to that particular spectre once and for all? The latter is more likely, for despite being proved innocent Jacobins, members of the Sections and Babouvists—both famous and unknown—were

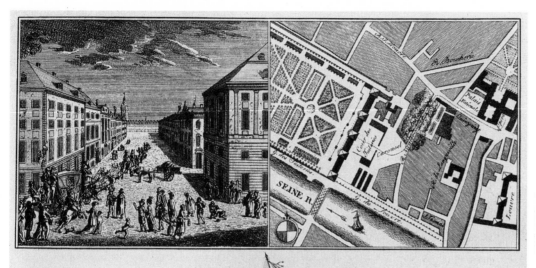

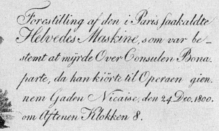

Vorstellung der sogenannten Pariser Höllen-Maschine, welche bestimt war, dem Ober-Consul Bonaparte, als er den 24 Dec.1800. Abends um 8 Uhr durch die Straße Nicaise, nach der Oper fuhr, ums Leben zu bringen

Forestilling af den i Paris saakaldte Helvedes Maskine, som var bestemt at myrde Over-Consulen Bonaparte, da han kiörte til Operaen gien, nem Gaden Nicaise, den 24 Dec.1800. om Aftenen Klokken 8.

"Representation of the so-called Parisian infernal machine, the aim of which was to kill First Consul Bonaparte." Engraving by an unknown artist, c. 1800.

Page 40:
The First Consul on horseback with his officers at a parade in the courtyard of the Tuileries Palace in the Year X (Revue du Décadi). Engraving by Louis Pauquet and Joseph Mécou after Jean-Baptiste Isabey and Carle Vernet.

nevertheless deported to Cayenne and the Seychelles whence the majority were never to return.

Fouché unravelled the threads of the plot and unearthed an altogether different nest of vipers. He discovered that the real front lay between the revolution and the counter-revolution, though this cost him his ministerial post for a time.[1]

Without doubt Bonaparte initially aroused hopes as well as fears both on the left and on the right: it seemed that all sides were keen to woo him. "Louis XVIII", previously Comte de Provence, who on the death of the Dauphin ("Louis XVII") in 1795 claimed the throne in succession to his executed brother Louis XVI, wrote to Bonaparte on February 20, 1800, completely misjudging the situation: "Whatever impression your conduct may inspire, Sir, men such as yourself never give cause for concern. You have taken on high office, and I am most indebted to you. You know better than anyone that strength and power are needed to make a great nation happy. Save France from her own frenzy, and you will have fulfilled my dearest wish. Give her back her king, and future generations will extol your memory. You will always be so indispensable to the State that, whatever position within it I might offer you, I would never be able to fully repay the debt owed to you by my forbears and myself."

Since the First Consul failed to respond, the offer was repeated after Marengo. This time, on September 7, he did reply, politely but in the negative. With this the exchange was broken off. The Bourbons had to abandon their hopes of using him as a compliant instrument of restoration, and it was three months later that their massive bomb exploded. Thereafter, as far as they were concerned, Bonaparte stood irrevocably on the other side of the barricades.

And what of France's rivals?

Austria needed time to get over its defeat. After the Peace of Lunéville it had to agree to Bonaparte settling Italian and Helvetic affairs as he saw fit, swallowing up in the process the whole of Piedmont whose king had fled to Sardinia. France had a big say in the process of indemnification of the feudal German rulers for the loss of their possessions on the left bank of the Rhine by means of ecclesiastical lands, imperial states and free cities on the right bank, which culminated in

[1] Ministère de la Police générale. Rapport aux Consuls de la République sur les auteurs de l'attentat du 3 nivôse. Paris, le 11 pluviôse an IX (signé, Fouché). Paris, 1801.

the *Reichsdeputationshauptschluss* of 1803. By giving preferential treatment to the larger southern German principalities it paved the way for business contacts with them. The overgenerous compensation given to Prussia reinforced the latter's policy of neutrality inaugurated by the Treaty of Basle. On the other hand the Habsburgs, retaining only their allodial Austrian possessions, lost their last leverage within the Holy Roman Empire with the extinction of the congeries of smaller states.

The feeble Spanish Bourbons, induced by the "prince of peace" Godoy to avoid conflict with their explosive neighbour on the other side of the Pyrenees at all costs, made do with maintaining their deferential relationship towards the French Republic which they had adopted during the Directory.

Following the assassination of Paul I in 1801 Russia dashed all hopes of an east-west alliance and a possible joint Indian campaign. But at least his successor Alexander I did not pick up the gauntlet again, while Turkey, which had got itself embroiled in European affairs over Egypt, happily made peace with Paris after the uninvited French "liberators" had left.

Their empty coffers obliged the European powers to put off the settling of outstanding scores till later. This was not intended to grant any guarantees to the Consulate or still less to signify their reconciliation with the republican principle—even though Bonaparte, if he would only curb his expansionist appetite, was still preferable to Robespierre and the danger that the spark of anarchy might spread across the frontier.

The decision lay with England, the unassailable island. Opinions among its rulers, in keeping with parliamentary pluralism, varied. The pros and cons of a prolonged maritime and overseas war without a continental army were considered. Burke took to prophesying doom and gloom. On the other hand Charles James Fox, along with others, did not hesitate to stigmatize his country's approach as unlawful interference in internal French affairs. Finally a peace lobby asserted itself under Whig pressure and resolved to seek a compromise: this was expressed in the Peace of Amiens of February 25, 1802.

For Bonaparte this was a red-letter day: for the first time in ten years the guns were silent. He, a soldier, had achieved peace for France. Never

Napoleon enthroned. This most solemn of all the representations of the emperor alludes to older paintings of God and Christ sitting in judgement upon the world. Painting by Jean-Auguste-Dominique Ingres, 1806.
Oil on canvas, Hôtel des Invalides, Paris.

Battle of Austerlitz. Engraving by Jean Bosq after Carle Vernet, 1806.

"It is not the enmity but the friendship of France that is truly terrible.
Her intercourse, her example, the spread of her doctrines are the most dreadful of her arms."
Burke

had he been so popular among the people. This time official assistance was hardly necessary in the ensuing plebiscite which secured three million votes from the grateful electorate to make him "Consul for life".

The form which the French state was to take was thus already anticipated in 1802. Henceforth the addition of the missing crowning glory seemed more a question of choosing the most suitable packaging and the right moment. Yet would not the world's most enlightened nation regard the founding of a new dynasty, as the culmination of their Revolution, as a crass anachronism?

The people whom this affected most saw things quite differently. For the royalist hawks the Republic was a provisional arrangement capable of rectification, the duration of which could and would be curtailed by internal dissensions. But a highly successful, bourgeois monarchy under the tricolour, once accepted and sanctioned by international law, might well prove an even more inexorable obstacle to the restoration of the *ancien régime*. It was therefore tempting to lop off the head of the one and only contender, particularly as His Britannic Majesty was prepared to shell out a fortune to this end, as the following events were soon to show.

The peaceful respite was short-lived. By May 1803 the two sides were at war again. They were equally to blame since they both tried to avoid honouring those parts of the treaty that were not to their liking. Neither side trusted its villainous counterpart an inch—and with good reason. Their interpretations of the treaty were likewise at variance. The English cabinet's understanding of the agreement was that it imposed limits which the First Consul was not permitted to overstep, whereas he thought it gave him freedom of action in all areas and matters that were of no concern to the English. John Bull had no interest in a peace which would elbow him out of Europe and cut him off from the many irons he had in the continental fire. He would rather prefer to resort to arms.

For Bonaparte this was a setback. The olive branch he had been holding lost its credibility. Now he had to start all over again and cut his losses. He sold Louisiana to the United States to prevent it falling into British hands and he abandoned St. Domingue (Haiti), for the subjugation of which he had dispatched an army corps.

Not even his ignominious revocation of the Jacobin decree on manumission and the death in a French dungeon of Toussaint L'Ouverture (1743–1803), the great leader of the slave revolt, could save the colony for France. The war would have to be fought out in Europe.

Bonaparte toyed with the idea of invading England, but for this he would need to gain control of the Channel for at least a brief period. For the French fleet, which was barely half as powerful as the British Navy, this was like trying to square the circle. Pending the elaboration of a suitable stratagem he contented himself with assembling an invasion force in a camp at Boulogne, which at least achieved the desired effect of unnerving the enemy.

In August 1803 Cadoudal once again crossed the Channel on an undercover mission financed by the English. Other groups made their way from the camp of royalist agents and saboteurs at Romsey to be joined by yet others from Brittany. The plan was that a total of 50 to 60 Chouans should meet up in Paris where, disguised as hussars, they were to seize Bonaparte during a military parade and, if he resisted, kill him. Neither Cadoudal nor his backers made any bones about the fact that their venture amounted to an assassination attempt.

The conspiracy was much bigger in scope than the bomb plot of 1800. General Pichegru, who had been deported as a royalist back in 1797, had likewise secretly re-entered the country from England on a secret mission and told Moreau what was afoot. Being a Republican, the latter declined to participate but, out of hostility towards Bonaparte, kept quiet and decided to await the outcome. "Spontaneous" uprisings were to break out simultaneously in Brittany, the Vendée and eastern France, all orchestrated by the British agent Drake in Munich. A royal prince was then to arrive in Paris to give the signal to attack and, in the ensuing general confusion, set up a regency.

Details of this mammoth conspiracy, which took months to prepare, inevitably leaked out. In March 1804 the police easily rounded up Cadoudal's suicide squad and put them safely behind bars before the prince in question, whose

identity was not known, had arrived. As a result of vague innuendoes the finger of suspicion was pointed at the Duc d'Enghien. He was one of the leading military figures among the émigrés and had settled at Ettenheim in Baden near the French border whence he sometimes slipped across to Strasbourg. In violation of Baden's sovereignty he was kidnapped one night, court-martialled for treasonably taking up arms against France and executed. Both Fouché and Talleyrand had urged that such "resolute action" be taken.

Bonaparte allowed Moreau to emigrate to the United States and was even ready to pardon Cadoudal, but the latter refused unless the lives of his followers were spared as well. It was one thing for one "hero" to pardon another one, but not to extend it to faithful peasants! Pichegru spared his judges the trouble of pronouncing sentence: he was found dead in his prison cell, either due to his own hand or that of his fellow comrades. The execution of d'Enghien, a Bourbon, was intended as a demonstrative burning of bridges, and was understood as such. Every well-bred European was suitably shocked at this caddish act, but they swallowed the bitter pill: even blue blood was no protection against folly.

The thwarted plot fitted in neatly with the First Consul's secret ambitions. His own advisers now forcefully urged him to put his position as head of state on a firmer basis. An hereditary monarchy, argued the Brumairiens, would settle once and for all the vexed question of the succession and would be the most likely way to discourage would-be killers from seeking to abruptly terminate the life of Bonaparte and hence also of the Republic, which was totally geared towards his person. There was nothing to prevent the French *Res publica*, like its Roman precursor, from being ruled by an emperor—who was, moreover, already at hand—as a firm bulwark against both internal disorder and external attack.

Was a Jacobin lieutenant to wield the imperial sceptre, an empire to arise under the red, white and blue of the tricolour?

The imperial dignity which emerged, having no connection with the previous dynasty of the Capetian kings, was able to couple its novel nature with the claim to hegemony in Europe. The semi-official propaganda found it easy to refute all objections that did not pertain to reasons of state. On December 2, 1804, in the cathedral of Notre Dame, Napoleon I crowned himself in the presence of the pope, who added his pontifical benediction. The crown at least was genuine, whereas in the rush other regal insignia had to be represented by theatrical props. The concomitant constitution of the Year XII was approved by three and a half million votes to three thousand.

The Empire, born—with a helping hand—of pragmatic considerations, was the logical pinnacle of Bonaparte's career. He was, however, unable to banish his mother Laetitia's misgivings concerning his meteoric rise to the top: "Pourvu que cela dure" ("let's hope your luck holds"), cautioned the old lady who did not even attend the coronation extravaganza. David had to resort to poetic licence to include Madame Mère in his painting.

As for Napoleon himself, was he really much more than one of the last condottieri, a man who in the international hurly-burly managed to grab a crown for himself? Many saw him as the guarantee that they could enjoy and augment the rewards they had reaped, by fair means or foul, during the Revolution. Perhaps Madame de Staël was not far wrong in describing him as not so much a Robespierre, more a "Danton on horseback". Others regarded him as a guard-dog which was keeping the Bourbons at bay. An emperor of the bourgeoisie, the army and the peasantry, working tirelessly and well-versed in statecraft: could one really ask for more? For democracy, after all the experiences France had had in that respect? Anyway, the Republic continued to exist formally, at least for the time being. In his congratulatory message François de Neufchateau audibly emphasized the fact twice. The Empire did not signify a breach with the Consulate. Nevertheless, this aping of monarchical appearances began to spread. Fouché and a few others may have been able to slow down the process a little, but they could not check it altogether, to the chagrin of liberal ideologues and the delight of the royalist camp. Furthermore, in order to gain the indispensable hallowed air of tradition, the system required a Europe fashioned in the image of France. "Military conquest is the only thing that can keep me in power," confessed Napoleon. He found no escape from this predicament, and was to some extent telling the truth when later on St. Helena he complained that he had never been free to make his own decisions but that these had always been forced upon him by the pressure of events.

His adversaries were obliged to gear themselves up for war as long as the Emperor of the French was still not sated. For his part Napoleon could only fend them off by marching forward against the *ancien régime* of Europe. Had he tried a conciliatory approach of any kind in 1804, none of the major powers would have followed him in good faith.

In 1805 England resumed and extended the war. The broad outlines of Napoleon's invasion plans were now discernible. In February he hoped, by means of complex fleet manoeuvres designed to lure the English Navy away from the Channel, to be able to fix an approximate date in early summer. He did not have a detailed plan, preferring to rely, as always, on inspiration at the critical moment. England spared no effort to preempt the venture before it got off the ground. Even before the projected invasion it had put together a Third Coalition with Russia and Austria.

It was not clear what prompted the two continental powers to join the alliance just at this moment. It was not solely the size of the subsidies offered. No doubt they hoped Prussia would also join and so reckoned that the chances of success were high—a logical presumption with four countries ranged against one.

Napoleon had a better understanding of the importance of the time factor. Seizing the initiative he broke camp at Boulogne and flung himself into his first German campaign. It was his most brilliant yet. Without waiting for the arrival of the Russian force, the Austrians revealed their intentions.

Napoleon attacked at Elchingen and forced them to capitulate at Ulm. The way to the Austrian capital now lay free. Vienna opened its gates to him and on the anniversary of his coronation—on December 2, 1805—the emperor crushed the combined enemy at Austerlitz in Moravia. Francis II withdrew from the war as suddenly as he had entered it.

In the Peace of Pressburg he ceded Venetia to the "Kingdom of Italy" and the Tyrol to Bavaria. The Confederation of the Rhine, which was formed by German princes under French pressure, asked Napoleon to become "protector". Francis was left with no alternative but to give up his title of Emperor of the Holy Roman Empire, which consequently perished from atrophy in 1806, and to confine himself to Austria.

Napoleon's success on *terra firma* was, however, tempered by a major setback at sea. On October 21, 1805 the indefatigable Nelson trapped and destroyed a Franco-Spanish fleet soon after it had left Cádiz.

The great admiral was killed in the battle and the French retaliated by occupying Naples, which had joined the Coalition. Yet Trafalgar not only rendered England invulnerable, it also closed the Seven Seas to France. For the next hundred years Britannia would rule the waves. This more than offset Austerlitz, even if this was not realized at the time.

Meanwhile the war continued on land. Napoleon tempted Prussia with the offer of Hanover, which actually belonged not to him but to the King of England, and the Prussian monarch seemed to swallow the bait. However, the exit of Austria and the proliferation of the Rhine Confederation made him doubt whether he could sustain his neutrality. Suddenly Prussia began receiving peremptory instructions from Paris which were tantamount to orders. In a fateful overestimation of its military heritage Prussia joined Russia, England and Sweden in a Fourth Coalition. This time the French were, if anything, even quicker off the mark than in the previous year against Austria.

They caught the Prussians unawares while they were still marshalling their forces, and on October 14, 1806 annihilated them in the confused double battle of Jena and Auerstedt. In headlong retreat, the Prussian army disintegrated and important fortresses, including Magdeburg, capitulated in the panic that followed. The court sought refuge on tsarist territory. Meanwhile the French advanced to the Vistula and were given a rapturous welcome by Polish patriots in Warsaw.

The "big two" were still at large. From Berlin, in November 1806, Napoleon declared his "continental blockade" against England, thereby resorting to a tactic which had been previously used by the Convention to hit Britain where it hurt most, i.e. by squeezing its commercial profits. This time England would be in real trouble if the emperor managed to impose his will on the whole of Europe. It was, however, a sword which cut both ways. Even the French satellite states were reluctant to fall into line, for such a boycott would mean cutting off their nose to spite their face.

Entry of the French into Berlin on October 27, 1806. Etching after Jacques Swebach. From the work: *Campagnes des Français sous le Consulat et sous l'Empire.* Paris, 1806.

Pages 46/47:
Gallery and porch at the entrance to Notre Dame cathedral. This ceremonial structure with neo-Gothic elements was erected for the Imperial coronation ceremony. This portrayal shows Napoleon being welcomed by the Archbishop of Paris amid the strains of martial music.

The interior of Notre Dame cathedral during the coronation ceremony.

Engravings after Charles Percier and Pierre Fontaine.
From the work: *Sacre et couronnement de Napoléon, Empereur des Français et Roi d'Italie.* Paris, 1807.

We need a king because I am a property-owner; a king who has a crown because I have a position. Hence in order to put an end to the revolution we need a king in its image who derives his rights from our own.
Champagny to d'Antraigues, August 21, 1801.

Once again it was Carnot who dissented with dignity:
The rule of one man neither guarantees stability and order, nor is it the proper reward for a citizen who restored political freedom to entrust him with sacrificing this selfsame freedom.

NISMES AIX TOULON ORLEANS TOURS BESANÇON

The Russians also made their presence felt.
In February 1807, contrary to military etiquette,
General Bennigsen prised Napoleon out of his
winter quarters in East Prussia and fought a
bloody but indecisive battle against him at Eylau.
The emperor just managed to fend it off, but it
was a warning of things to come. Not until the
spring was he able to wipe the slate clean and then
to scatter the tenacious but ponderously moving
enemy at Friedland on June 14.

Then came a touch of melodrama: the tsar, the
master of the East, and the emperor, the ruler of
the West, met on a raft on the Niemen. They concluded a treaty not just of peace but also of
friendship. If they joined forces London would be
left out in the cold, and there would be sufficient
spoils left over for each side to be able to extend its
sphere of influence. By the Treaty of Tilsit Alexander agreed to the dismemberment of his
erstwhile ally Prussia but left him Silesia. For his
part Napoleon opted not to restore Poland in full
and made do instead with the creation of the
"Grand Duchy of Warsaw" which he gave to the
King of Saxony, now a member of the Confederation of the Rhine.

He was mistaken if he thought Alexander's
change of heart was due to his own powers of persuasion. The tsar had long had a high opinion of
Napoleon's talents, but this was not at issue. He
was motivated rather by the sober consideration
that under the prevailing circumstances his country would have to bear the brunt of the struggle if
it continued while his reserves would be used up
in the interests of England, which was sitting
pretty. He saw no reason to run around in circles,
and discovered besides that a Franco-Russian armistice would benefit him more than his French
counterpart.

Napoleon's biggest shortcoming was his tendency to underestimate his opponents and to pay
too little attention to their motives. Nevertheless
Tilsit was his acme. This was unequivocally confirmed by the rise in the value of government
bonds. A new term was coined for the new politi-

cal reality: *le Grand Empire*—a vast expanse of territory stretching well beyond the confines of France which harked back to Charlemagne's day. Its predominance kept its junior partner pegged down in the East and permitted it to try and bankrupt its archenemy, England.

Napoleon had won his first military and diplomatic encounters as emperor. He had picked off his three continental rivals one by one and thereby dealt with two more Coalitions. His brothers were now kings—Joseph in Naples, Louis in Holland and Jérôme in Westphalia—while his stepson Eugène Beauharnais was viceroy in Milan. His uncle Fesch now sported a cardinal's hat, and if in Tuscany some simple member of the Buonaparte family declined out of humility to swap his village priest's post for an episcopal see it was his own fault.

But what could the conqueror offer the peoples—both the French and the many others—in order to bend them to his will or even persuade them to take a fancy to his new order? As the 19th century got underway, would the Grand Empire prove to be a social school of learning?

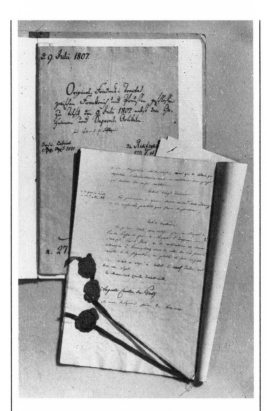

The Treaty of Tilsit signed between France and Prussia on July 9, 1807. Napoleon dictated the terms after making peace with Alexander I of Russia: Prussia lost half of its territory to the Grand Duchy of Warsaw and the Kingdom of Westphalia and had to agree to reparations and to the stationing of French troops. Staatsarchiv Merseburg.

[1] The event was recorded by Goya in his painting "Tres de Mayo".

All Europe in Erfurt

The year following Tilsit was marked by a flurry of diplomatic activity. A new balance of forces emerged which, being volatile, permitted all kinds of undertones but no provocative fanfares. The cordial understanding between Napoleon and Alexander was put to the test. This necessitated a delicate touch and a bit of give-and-take with no loss of face—and if possible at someone else's expense. The two rulers pursued their separate aims but took care not to tread on each other's toes.

In February 1808 the tsar moved against the Swedes, and the French emperor, in accordance with their agreement, gave Alexander his backing. He was happy to see Sweden punished for its involvement in the Fourth Coalition, but the Baltic lay outside his field of vision. He had a problem of his own in the Orient. In May 1807, while he was still at war with Russia, a friendship treaty was signed with the Kajar shah of Persia, and General Gardanne was despatched to Teheran. Meanwhile General Sebastiani badgered the Turkish sultan incessantly, promising him the moon, until in December 1806, much to England's annoyance, he let himself be inveigled into declaring war on Russia.

A chance occurrence then got him off the hook without his needing to renege: in May 1807 Sultan Selim III, the first Turkish reformer, was overthrown. This could not have happened at a more propitious moment. It was an easy matter for Napoleon to show France's goodwill by mediating an armistice. This held until March 1809, allowing sufficient time to drop the Turkish alliance and to revive the Indian project of 1800. The plan was to march overland to India and there, together with the Russians, to teach the British a lesson they would not forget.

The tsar courteously assented to this fanciful scheme. He was also agreeable to the precondition, which foresaw the partitioning of the European part of the Ottoman Empire. The experts busied themselves with redrawing the map until they came across a stumbling block: Napoleon refused with uncompromising stubbornness to cede Constantinople and the Straits to Russia. He found the prospect of yet another Mediterranean power intolerable. He believed the tsar of all the Russias should be satisfied with the two Balkan states, Moldavia and Wallachia, although Russia would thereby incur the lasting wrath of Austria.

Napoleon was not worsted. He was able to gain compensation within "his" hemisphere and wanted to conclude this before his next personal encounter with the tsar, at which their respective spheres of influence were to be settled once and for all. If he could present a fait accompli while Alexander was still tied up with the Persians and Turks it would give him a tactical advantage. However, the timing went awry.

The principal, and loudly proclaimed, overall aim of French policy was to bring England to its knees by seizing the European ports and thus blocking its trading markets. France's annexation of Tuscany and occupation of the Papal States could be explained, if not justified, in these terms, and, at a pinch, so could the forcible partitioning of Portugal by France and Spain. Yet this refused to yield any perceptible benefit to France, which had come to expect it, and conquest by the pen provided glory neither for the emperor nor for his grenadiers. At the same time the systematic weakening of the pope's temporal power raised the question of whether the Catholic world would take the pontiff's relegation to the status of Napoleon's court and private chaplain, a virtual lackey in his own house, lying down. Moreover, France's unbridled expansion across the Apennine peninsula aroused a pan-Italian national consciousness. It was awakened with great hopes by the Italian Jacobins, only to be painfully disappointed. At this stage the protests were still sporadic and purely intellectual in nature, unable to influence the real struggle. Nevertheless they began to take shape in the guise of the Carbonari—the secret society of the "charcoal burners", so called because the conspirators blackened their faces. Little did they suspect that one day their society would achieve world fame as the initiator of a democratic struggle for liberty.

The expedition to Portugal set in train a series of disasters. It was child's play for Napoleon to occupy Oporto and Lisbon, to seize the English depots there and to force the court to flee to the Portuguese colony of Brazil. But right from the start Napoleon had an ulterior motive when he got Spain to agree to the stationing of French troops on Spanish territory to secure his long line of communications to Portugal. Despite their wretched obsequiousness the Bourbons in Madrid, precisely because they were Bourbons, represented in the long term an intolerable historical handicap for Napoleon. He also considered them unreliable. In the case of Crown Prince Ferdinand he was right. So when a quarrel broke out between King Charles IV and his son, he sprang the trap. In April 1808 he summoned the pair of them to the French border town of Bayonne to settle the dispute and compelled both father and son, separately, to renounce their claims to the throne. An uprising in Madrid on May 2, though at once ruthlessly suppressed by Murat,[1] gave him just the lever he needed.

Having seen to this, Napoleon offered the Spanish crown on May 10 to his brother Joseph, who since 1806 had been King of Naples, which was now transferred to Napoleon's brother-in-law Murat. On June 20 the new monarch arrived in Madrid while the French troops stationed in the country provided military cover for the bloodless operation by simply veering south from their route to Portugal.

However, things did not go according to plan. The Spanish people rose, and the royal army refused to obey the new sovereign who had been foisted on it. *Juntas*—provisional organs of power—were formed; on June 6 the one in Seville even formally declared war on France. Others, backed by partisans, went onto the attack without such formalities, and King Joseph fled from his precarious capital after only ten days. The rashly overstretched French forces were faced with a confrontation for which they were not prepared. Napoleon found himself in an embarrassing position. He had earlier asked for another meeting with the tsar, who had agreed. The complications in Spain dragged on, and a fullblooded campaign was now imminent. This altered Napoleon's priorities and made it impossible to put off the tsar any longer. There was no question of cancelling the meeting, for the encounter was now more imperative than ever, but it was the tsar who now had the better hand as he set off on the long trip to Erfurt.

Napoleon's negotiating position worsened from day to day. The news from the front was appalling. On July 22, 1808 Dupont was encircled at Bailén and surrendered. On August 1 an English expeditionary corps landed in Portugal. It was led by Arthur Wellesley, the future Duke of Wellington. On the 30th, by the Convention of Cintra, he forced General Junot to evacuate the country. The rest of the French troops withdrew behind the Ebro in anticipation of Napoleon's arrival to take over command personally.

The emperor, however, was still busy harassing his important guest in the delightful autumnal setting of Thuringia and trying hard not to let his nervousness show. For his rendezvous with Alexander he had summoned a veritable congress of European royalty, and hardly any of their divine majesties ventured to decline the charmingly presented invitation. Although the role assigned to them was merely that of high-ranking onlookers, they too were interested in hearing what the tsar had to say. Besides, failure to attend might mean a missed opportunity. So it was that on September 30 Talma and Madame Raucourt of the Comédie-Française performed Racine's *Britannicus*, a play replete with contemporary references, before literally an audience of kings, even if most of them were kings only by the grace of Napoleon.

Without question Napoleon, who in the French enclave of Erfurt acted as host, was determined to spare no expense in order to impress his guests by bringing along an entire Parisian theatre. The staging of Voltaire's *Oedipus* gave the tsar an opportunity, on hearing the line "The friendship of a great man is a gift of the gods", to rise from his seat and demonstratively embrace Napoleon. Nor was the compliment purely an act of courtesy. He was genuinely impressed by Bonaparte's greatness. Whether his great friend would soon become his greatest enemy was a question which lay in the inscrutable lap of the gods. It was not answered at Erfurt.

There were two main points on the agenda. Firstly, agreement on the question of the Straits, and secondly the reaffirmation and renewal of the alliance in a somewhat loose form. Nothing came of the first point. Both sides kept their cards close to their chest. They simply avoided defining their standpoint in detail. Nor was there any urgent need for such precision: Russia's road to the Hagia Sophia in Constantinople would be a long and slippery one, so why should France tie its hands at this stage?

On the other hand the alliance was renewed in the form of a convention. It was couched in general terms and was likewise careful to avoid exacerbating the real problem areas. Napoleon sought to persuade the tsar to exercise a moderating influence on Austria, which began rearming. Alexander complied with his wish, and cautioned the Habsburgs against doing anything rash. But might not the Viennese court construe this to mean that Russia thought the time was not yet ripe for mooting a change of course? Anyway, the Archduke Charles, who was present at Erfurt and whom Napoleon respected as a capable soldier, continued apace his reform of the army in view of France's increasing difficulties in Spain and the expectation of an explosion in Germany. He guessed that when it came to the crunch Napoleon would find Alexander to be a half-hearted, if not treacherous, ally.

As for the tsar, he was mainly interested in discovering how strongly the French emperor would resist appeals for the restoration of Greater Poland. This was a very sensitive area indeed for Russia, for the Polish nobility claimed not just Polish territory but also Lithuania, White Russia and the Ukraine, where they also owned estates. The tsar did not want to contribute to a (likely) Austrian defeat as a result of which the victor would unite Galicia with the Grand Duchy of Warsaw and thereby establish a bulwark against Russia. For his part Napoleon wished to forfeit neither Polish sympathies, which secured him a sizeable army contingent, nor of course those of Russia. Consequently he promised faithfully to resolutely oppose all the fanciful schemes of the Polish patriots but did nothing to bring home to his admirers there the impossibility of such ventures in blunt and plain terms. Actually the truth behind this charade was simple: yes to Cracow but a strict no to Lemberg. He restrained them nevertheless, since even he could not foretell just how long the need to pander to Russia's obvious susceptibilities would continue to be more important than having a well-fortified outpost in the East.

Napoleon quickly dropped his fleeting idea of reducing the size of Prussia even further via the confiscation of Silesia as the tsar showed no enthusiasm. Nor was he able to eliminate another source of friction: Russian laxity in implementing the boycott of English ships and goods. It was only natural that the tsar should do no more than the bare minimum, otherwise he would be acting against his own interests. With England fighting for its economic survival it was the weaker mer-

The victory fountain on the Place du Châtelet in Paris, 1807, sculpted by Louis-Simon Boizot. Etching by an unknown artist.

Charles Maurice de Talleyrand-Périgord. Engraving by Auguste Boucher-Desnoyers after François Gérard.

Sire, what will you do here? It is up to you to save Europe, and you will only manage this by standing up to Napoleon. The people of France are civilized, their ruler is not.
Talleyrand to Alexander I.

[1] TARLÉ, E. V.: *Talleyrand.* Leipzig, 1972.
[2] FISCHER, A.: *Goethe und Napoleon,* 2nd edition. Frauenfeld, 1900;
REDSLOB, E.: *Goethes Begegnung mit Napoleon.* Baden-Baden, 1954.

cantile power Russia which now, for the first time, largely determined the terms of trade. Hence the tsar was inundated with pleas from commercial importers and agricultural exporters to temper justice with mercy and to turn a blind eye to double entry book-keeping.

Added to these economic considerations was a more far-reaching political one. Unlike France, Russia had nothing to gain from an English collapse. It was not averse to curbing England's arrogance or putting an end to its omnipresence, but the total obliteration of England would have placed Russia completely at Napoleon's mercy. Even Mikhail Speranski (1772–1839), the highly talented priest's son who had gained the tsar's absolute confidence and who would soon become the most influential minister at St. Petersburg, counselled against such a course. His stay in Erfurt strengthened his determination to hold the "French line". He became one of its most fervent proponents because he hoped it would encourage a climate of open-mindedness conducive to the introduction of internal reforms and a constitution in the spirit of the Enlightenment—but without dismantling absolutism. Yet he had no intention of delimiting his country's foreign policy options to this end. The tsar and the emperor had little to show for their meeting in Erfurt. This may explain why Napoleon was so out of sorts as he departed from the Thuringian town on October 14. He left in the knowledge that he could undertake his Spanish campaign, into which he rode from Paris two weeks later, without the need to look constantly over his shoulder. But this was the only thing of which he could be certain.

Apart from the obvious reasons for his reserve, the tsar also had another, secret motive.

On September 27 the first top-level talk took place. There was nothing unusual in the fact that the next day Talleyrand, as Napoleon's senior diplomat and adviser, met the tsar in the salon of the Princess of Thurn and Taxis (her family monopolized the postal service for generations) where he supplemented the views expressed by his master—who was still a dilettante in matters of diplomacy—with a few confidential remarks of his own on French foreign policy. What was so extraordinary was that he used the occasion to openly tip Alexander off. In addition to flattering the tsar he also disclosed to him the weak points in Napoleon's negotiating strategy.

Talleyrand's "advice", which he gave for the first, but not the last, time in Erfurt, brought him bounties from both St. Petersburg and Vienna alike.

He was confident that what he had to offer was well worth the recompense. But as much as the extravagant Talleyrand loved money, this was not the reason for his treachery. It was rather that his sixth sense had already told him that Napoleon had reached the summit of his success, so with the carefree amorality of which this last surviving aristocrat on the revolutionary merry-go-round was a past master, he took the next logical step. He had been the most vociferous advocate of intervention in Spain, but as soon as the plan misfired he became the first rat to leave the (still buoyant) ship.[1]

Alexander would perhaps have been less eager to receive encouragement from the protean French diplomat of ill repute had he not realized that Talleyrand would hardly have chanced his arm in this way unless he had noticed real signs of flagging enthusiasm and confidence in France. The fall in value of the state bonds after the Spanish setback indicated that the well-heeled bourgeoisie, of all people, were now worried lest their post-revolutionary gains should evaporate. Talleyrand was neither their leader nor their spokesman, but his volte-face—not the first nor the last in his long life—signalled that great changes were afoot.

And it was precisely this which made him so useful to Europe's conservative monarchs, not just as a source of information but also as an eavesdropper and barometer of internal French developments.

Goethe would not hear of any pessimism. This is one reason why the famous German poet and privy councillor at the court of Weimar has so often been accused of grovelling towards his superiors. And it is true that he was one of the first to view the Revolution more with misgivings than with euphoria. Filled with aversion towards a sans-culottism which he even detected in literature, he saw the victor of 18 Brumaire as someone who had put the world to rights again. He thought it simply ludicrous to insist on pedigree in the face of one of the truly great men of history, a man who epitomized the claim of Dr. Faustus, to wit "The mark made by my life's span will persist for countless ages".

Whether or not in his heart of hearts Goethe related the boast to himself, something extraordinary and incredible transpired in Erfurt and Weimar: the two great men actually met each other.

Was not this the *real* summit meeting, which due to its unique importance deserved to go down in the annals of history, even though no one properly recorded their tête-à-tête?

It was Napoleon's wont to have celebrities presented to him during his travels on whom he then kept a file. He considered this more useful than the custom of patting children's heads in which other potentates indulged. He briefed himself beforehand about the individual in question and prepared thoroughly for the interview so as not to put his foot in it. For instance, he had read Goethe's *The Sorrows of Werther*, albeit in translation, whereas Wieland, another eminent German poet based in Weimar, was an unknown quantity to him.

On October 1 Goethe was invited to a reception and on the next day to an audience. They were far from agreeing on every point. Thus the doyen of German writers rejected the suggestion made by Napoleon that he write a Roman drama. However, the two contrasting characters were attracted to one another.

Both men considered their meeting a signal event despite the fact that the one was the bestower of an accolade and the other the recipient. They met again at a banquet in Weimar where they resumed their conversation while the tsar disported himself on the dance floor. It is unlikely that their thoughts strayed back to a similar encounter fifty years earlier at Sans-souci palace between Voltaire and Frederick II, two men whom they both admired. The times had changed completely, and the respective allocation of power and intellect was rather different. And who of all men could tell whether the hand of fortune might not intervene once again?[2]

Goethe never went as far as Hegel, who called Napoleon the "apogee of the world", but nevertheless when he heard of the emperor's death he imagined the Almighty challenging the Devil: "If you dare to touch this mortal, then haul him through your hellish portal."

The "little corporal" had at least achieved this much at Erfurt. And it was not such a mean achievement either.

Napoleon and his contemporaries. This fictitious
assembly of prominent figures includes scholars
as well as politicians. Lithograph by Martin
Lavigne after a work by Victor Adam composed in
historical retrospect.

Napoleon of Goethe:
"Voilà un homme!"

Goethe of Napoleon:
*"One could well say of him that he lived in a
state of perpetual inspiration."*

Changing Fortunes

Napoleon had to act quickly to clear up the situation in Spain before the winter set in. He employed his tried-and-tested tactic of massed artillery fire followed by an attack in the centre with superior forces, smashing everything that stood in the way, then occupation of the enemy's capital and the dictation of peace terms. On November 5, 1808 he took over command in Victoria, and by December 4 he had forced Madrid to capitulate. He decreed the abolition of feudal privileges and of the Inquisition, ordered his generals to drive the English troops back to La Coruña and from there back to their ships, and assumed the rest would be a routine task for the experienced regiments which he left behind on the peninsula when he returned to Paris in January 1809 to face the Austrians.

The decision had been forced on him. The Archduke Charles confidently built on the start given him by his military preparations and on the infectious influence of the Austrians' daring. Without formally declaring war he went over to the offensive. On March 8 he issued a patriotic appeal to the army, on the 27th a call to the Germans to shake off the yoke of foreign rule. On April 8 the Austrians moved into Bavaria, a member of the Confederation of the Rhine, and on the 12th accepted an English subsidy which sealed the Fifth Coalition.

Indubitably it was Spain's resistance which gave rise to this call to arms. One of the most conservative courts in Europe made so bold as to incite the subjects of other sovereigns to rebel. Napoleon replied in kind by calling on the Hungarians to resume their existence as an independent nation, which meant severing the link with Vienna and booting out the Habsburgs. After forming a new "Grande Armée" from the units stationed within the Rhine Confederation reinforced by new recruits, he launched his campaign from Donauwörth on April 17 and on May 10 entered Schönbrunn. Vienna surrendered without a fight four days later. Joseph Haydn, the composer of the anthem "God preserve and protect our good Emperor Francis"—to whose dulcet tones Napoleon had listened eight years previously on the evening the "infernal machine" exploded—was given a French guard of honour for his house. Unfortu-

nately he died in the occupied city on the last day of the month.

"These are not the same Austrians as before," the victor observed with amazement, but an even bigger surprise lay in store for him. As he tried to cross the Danube in haste, a second spring flood came to the aid of the defenders and on May 22 the bloody battle of Aspern-Essling was lost. Whether due to a freak of nature or not, the defeat ended a run of success which had encouraged the emperor to become arrogant and to underrate the enemy. Scarcely six months earlier, as he confronted the defile of Somosierra in Spain, he had superciliously remarked: "Impossible? For me there is no such word!" Not until July 7 at Wagram did he make amends. Afterwards he agreed to an armistice and, after some hesitation, to the Peace of Schönbrunn. The Austrian emperor forfeited almost one sixth of his subjects and the entire Adriatic coast, and was now cut off from Italy.

Napoleon had successfully dealt with another challenge from his most tenacious adversary. He was the uncontested overlord of a vast empire. Although unhappy at the expansion of the Grand Duchy of Warsaw, the tsar kept to his agreement. And on the other side the Prussians, thanks to Russian counselling, did not budge. An English expeditionary force, badly led and decimated by fever, landed on the Dutch island of Walcheren in the Scheldt estuary but had to retreat. Austria was fast heading for bankruptcy, and its new foreign minister, the nimble-minded Rhinelander Clemens von Metternich, needed to pull out all the stops to get his country back into the fray—not, for the time being, as an enemy of Napoleon but as his ally.

The ace which Metternich produced in 1810 was Marie Louise, and he played the role of the discreet matchmaker impeccably. He knew from experience of the French emperor's striving to marry into European royalty so as to give a firm dynastic basis to the claims of his longed-for heir. Since the prospect of such an untoward union had aroused definite misgivings at the Russian court and the tsar—amid all manner of prevarications—avoided proffering his sister's hand to Napoleon, the place of honour in the Imperial boudoir at the Tuileries was free to be filled by a Habsburg. She was of ancient lineage and a pleasant and attractive young person into the bar-

Metternich. Lithograph after Friedrich (called Franz) Lieder and Alois von Saar.

If, following the Battle of Aspern, the Austrians had moved up three times as many reinforcements as the French Emperor, which they were in a position to do, the lull prior to the Battle of Wagram would have served them well. Since they did not do so, the time was wasted, and they would have done better to exploit Napoleon's disadvantageous situation in order to capitalize on the consequences of the Battle of Aspern.
Clausewitz

Fouché voted for the execution of Louis XVI. The more the Emperor departs from the principles of the Revolution, the more he will seek to eliminate those who are regarded as its instigators.
S. de Girardin in *Journal et Souvenirs.*

gain. Napoleon, who had already taken the precaution of divorcing Josephine, did not take long to choose the Emperor Francis as his new father-in-law. When in 1811 his son was duly born—and immediately proclaimed "King of Rome"—he was confident that he had founded a new dynasty.

No doubt he envisaged this as entailing bourgeois advance under a strong hereditary crown which, while eliminating the feudal and the democratic element, would firmly fuse together conservative and liberal forces. But the retreat was unmistakeable. The abolition in 1807 of the Tribunate, set up in 1799, was mourned by no one, and the promotion from 1804 onwards of the most hot-headed commanders to the rank of marshal was just about tolerable. Rather more questionable

was the creation in 1808 of an "Imperial nobility" which added a host of new aristocrats to the old: four princes, thirty-three dukes, 452 counts, 1,500 barons and 1,474 chevaliers, to be precise. In the same year the inscription "République française" on French coins was replaced by "Empire français". The criminal code of 1809 was without question a step backwards compared to the rightly celebrated *Code civil* of 1804. The emblem of the red bonnet from the time of the sans-culottes disappeared from the façade of the City Hall in Paris before the young empress set foot in the building. In June 1810 the regicide Fouché was dismissed as minister of the interior after Marie Louise had taken over from her beheaded aunt Marie Antoinette the mantle of matriarch of France.

Scenes from the Peninsular War:
  "Just as little."
  "You cannot stand idly by."

Folios 10 and 26 from the series "Los Desastres de la Guerra". Etchings by Francisco de Goya, *c. 1810–1814.*

(Napoleon . . .)
  the antithesis of a gentleman, but he cut a fine figure.
  Sigmund Freud to Stefan Zweig.

[1] WOHLFEIL, R.: *Spanien und die deutsche Erhebung 1808 bis 1814.* Wiesbaden, 1965.
[2] BLAZE, S.: *Mémoires d'un aide-major.* Paris, 1828.

Although sometimes petty, Napoleon's despotic rule was free from malice and megalomania. However, he lacked the real statesman's far-sightedness. The fact that he was successful in most things had a stultifying effect, and even his "grand plan" for the pacification of Europe did not amount to much more than a series of imaginative improvisations. Having shot to the top he could no longer keep control. It was not insatiability which drove him ever onwards; he was constantly forced to act by the force of circumstance.

He could not simply shake off the legacy of the Revolution, which clung to him like some lacerating hairshirt. Wherever his campaigns took him he was obliged to expunge feudalism, to topple monarchs and to flout tradition. He thus continued to find himself the executor and bailiff—as well as the beneficiary—of a great upheaval. He could not free himself from his roots and therefore sought to bury them. His admission to the ranks of the world's most select sovereigns reinforced his contempt and lack of understanding for the interests and feeling of whole nations. New developments which ran counter to his fixed ideas escaped his notice, or else he misconstrued them.

His flashes of insight on St. Helena came too late.

The "Spanish wound" never healed.[1] It was not that every Spaniard bewailed the disappearance of the Bourbons or the autos-da-fé. Anyone who realized what was going on and who yearned to break free from the anachronistic constraints of feudalism could easily warm to the—very moderate—reform programme of the "Josefinos" which at least promised to introduce a trickle of Enlightenment and bourgeois rationality into the country. The court painter Goya was not alone in holding this view. Even survivers from Charles III's era of reform, including a considerable number of administrators, were willing to give it a go. However, this potential liberal faction was split since the new age was ushered in at the point of foreign bayonets. This gave the forces of feudal reaction an excuse to gather round themselves the peasant masses to defend the country against the foreign foe and enabled them to stigmatize the *afrancesados*, the Francophiles, as traitors and to isolate them from the people as if they were lepers.[2]

Hence the Spanish revolt was not a revolution by another name; it was more like a grand-scale Vendée; but nor was that the whole truth. It was led by counter-revolutionaries who saw Napoleon as Voltaire, Rousseau and Robespierre all rolled into one and who regarded his followers as a bunch of diabolical Freemasons and Protestants. The priests hammered this message, both from the pulpit and at the head of armed groups, into the head of every last peasant—for whom the idealized memory of the anti-Moor crusades was still very much alive. They were not just fighting to reinstate their rightful king, they were also determined to resist enslavement by an alien power and incensed by the degrading treatment meted out to their empire, on which hitherto the sun had never set.

Europe learned two important lessons from the Spanish people's revolt. One was military, namely that resistance only held out the prospect of success if it was based not merely on the passive support of the bulk of the population but on their active involvement. Count Palafox, whom European public opinion singled out as the hero of 1809, had shown the way. He was able to hold the besieged city of Saragossa for months because its inhabitants—including the poorest ones—threw themselves with their wives and children into the house-to-house struggle under the sign of the cross.

The partisans' running battle, the *guerilla*, did not win any campaigns, but this was not its objective. Yet it did enable the regular troops, Spanish as well as English, to feel completely at ease on the broad and broken terrain. The whole of Spain was one big support base which supplied their every need and constantly replenished their ranks with volunteers, whereas the French generals, consumed by mutual jealousy, groped their way forward without enthusiasm and in perpetual fear for their supply lines. How could 100,000 or even 200,000 men fight one battle after another and at the same time act as an occupation force holding down 500,000 square kilometres of hostile territory? Furthermore, the enemy learned to make a strategic virtue out of tactical necessity. He rarely engaged in open battle unless he felt at an advantage. Otherwise he withdrew into the woods and compelled the French to undertake exhaustive zigzag marches across the inhospitable terrain. Or else he retreated to virtually impregnable strongholds near the sea whence the ubiquitous British fleet could cover his flanks and rear.

For Spain was now also the site of the Anglo-French war. England had found its most willing and cheapest continental force. In 1809 Wellesley reappeared on the peninsula, this time to stay. A partial victory at Talavera brought him a peerage. Under his new name of Lord Wellington he would be the bane of Napoleon for a long time to come, the first of his opponents to systematically employ the cat-and-mouse tactic and thus to retain an undefeated record right up to the end. When in 1810/1811 forces were freed which tilted the scales in France's favour, the British general withdrew behind the entrenchments which he had previously prepared at Torres Vedras in front of Lisbon. However, there was no power on earth which could shift him from there, and eventually his antagonist ran out of steam exactly as he had done before during the siege of Cádiz. In the meantime the war continued to exact its toll of senseless death and to raise political demands.

Napoleon found his way blocked where he had least expected it, and refused to believe his eyes. But his enemies recognized the fact with glee. Moreover, the powers-that-be had noted that a people could be galvanized by other means than revolutionary agitation and mobilized without any change of leadership as long as nationalism, within a specific political context, concealed the deeper internal class antagonism. There were, however, no guarantees, but a plurality of solutions to choose from.

The choice lay between liberation because of Napoleon, or liberty in spite of him. The question was raised in Spain, but no answer was forthcoming. Spain's American colonies had initially come out in support of Ferdinand and against Joseph, but by 1810/1811 they had begun to break with the mother country, regardless of who was in power. There were uprisings on the Río de la Plata (Argentina), in New Granada (Venezuela) and in New Castile (Mexico). In Caracas Simón Bolívar conceived the idea of independence for half a continent, out of which would one day emerge republican Latin America. Impressed by the radicalization of the colonies, the Spanish Cortes in Cádiz, calling itself the Provisional National Assembly, introduced a liberal constitution in 1812 in the teeth of the preponderance enjoyed by the traditionalist forces. Its repeal in 1814 was one of the first acts of the returning Bourbons. On the other hand it was in the selfsame city of Cádiz that a group of army officers led by Riego sought in 1820 to make up for the lost revolutionary opportunity between 1808 and 1813.

The Spaniards' reaction to French subjugation was unanimously fierce yet superficial in the sense that its aristocratic and clerical leaders found it neither necessary nor desirable to use the chance to sweep away ossified components of the social structure. They thought the existing feudal system, with only a little titivation, would suffice to attain their goal. The reaction of the Germans, whom many believed capable in 1809 of creating a second Spain, was based on different premises. Consequently it expressed itself only in isolated and hopeless patriotic outbursts and was totally uncoordinated. In part, however, it ploughed deeper furrows and thus prepared the ground for the implantation of bourgeois social and state institutions on German soil.

The Rhineland, as an integral part of the Empire, together with the Grand Duchy of Berg, with which it was linked by personal union, participated in the events in France with neither particular enthusiasm nor with any deep-seated reluctance.

Professed Francophobes such as the fiery writer Görres were the exception. In reply to Napoleon's question of how many millionaires there were in Cologne, one of the bankers peevishly answered that there had been five when Cologne became French and that the number had not changed since. Maybe his reply was less atypical than intended, reflecting a widespread attitude: a mixture of anticipation and caution, the readiness to offer loyal obedience but to withdraw it as soon as the situation changed. Few lamented the end of the Holy Roman Empire with its mosaic of statelets. The conservative version of the bourgeois revolution necessarily asserted itself, in accordance with internal French conditions, through administrative channels without any serious problems—and without raising the national question. So enduring was its achievement that Rhenish liberalism, with its broad economic base, continued to maintain its intellectual ascendancy well into the century even under Prussian hegemony.

The knave of hearts. Such topical playing cards were produced by a factory in Hamburg. The heads of the various knaves depict German and French generals. This knave of hearts is thought to represent Schill. Woodcut by Friedrich Wilhelm Gubitz after Philipp Otto Runge, 1809/10.

[1] HEITZER, H.: *Insurrectionen zwischen Weser und Elbe. Volksbewegungen gegen die französische Fremdherrschaft im Königreich Westfalen (1806–1813)*. Berlin, 1959;
BERDING, H.: *Napoleonische Herrschafts- und Gesellschaftspolitik im Königreich Westfalen 1807–1813*. Göttingen, 1973.

[2] FEHRENBACH, E.: *Traditionale Gesellschaft und revolutionäres Recht. Die Einführung des Code Napoléon in den Rheinbundstaaten*. Göttingen, 1974.

[3] BOCK, H.: *Schill. Rebellenzug 1809*. 3rd edition. Berlin, 1981.

The princes of the Rhine Confederation likewise reserved their options in case the European balance of power should alter. Napoleon was realistic enough to take this into account. However, as long as his luck held he had no cause to complain about lack of loyalty from these flexible rulers. As a small but useful third force in Germany they had received sizeable chunks of land from First Consul Bonaparte in the *Reichsdeputationshauptschluss* of 1803. As Emperor Napoleon he continued to grant them his favour. Promotion, dynastic intermarriage and bigger landholdings were all to be had as long as they paid up on the dot: with soldiers and hard cash. They put up with upstarts such as the emperor's youngest brother Jérôme, who was made King of Westphalia, and looked the other way whenever one of their number—such as the Duke of Oldenburg in 1810—fell victim to a reallocation of property.[1]

It was not just in political affairs, which they left well alone, that they kowtowed to Paris. In domestic matters, too, there was a tendency to conform, partly as a result of French "recommendations" and partly of their own wish to modernize. In the economic, administrative and judicial fields standards were adopted which Napoleon wished to see introduced throughout the whole of his Grand Empire: a gradual dismantling of feudalism accompanied by a boost for respectable bourgeois and efficient farmers.[2]

Any intervention on the part of the populace was still most unwelcome. Whenever voices or hands were raised in a bid to initiate some kind of action, they incurred the disapproval of the frightened authorities. None was prepared to commit political suicide. In fact, the princes of the Rhine Confederation—at one with their French overlord—joined in the suppression of their own subjects who proved "unreasonable".

Nevertheless, things did begin to happen, and Spain added fuel to the fire. In the dire straits in which he found himself in 1809 the Archduke Charles was prepared to exploit the situation. However, the idea of a national revolt under the Austrian double eagle in a country which was a variegated mosaic of nations was a contradiction in terms. Meanwhile, in northern Germany courageous but isolated risings by small groups—such as those of Major Schill, the Duke of Brunswick-Oels, Katte and Dörnberg—fizzled out, for although many admired them privately, they were left to their own devices.[3]

There was one notable exception: the serious revolt of the Tyroleans led by the innkeeper Andreas Hofer who fought off three Franco-Bavarian offensives before, abandoned by the Viennese court, he was vanquished. These ultra-conservative alpine farmers, who refused to be dragooned into becoming Bavarians, just as they had in 1702 under Sterzinger, now insisted on their nationality, their traditional religious beliefs (unencumbered by Enlightenment ideas) and the freedom of their mountain pastures. This was the only freedom they were interested in. Andreas Hofer, who was shot in Mantua as a rebel in 1810, died in front of his platoon declaring his unswerving loyalty to king and country. He died a hero, but not—as some youthful admirers supposed—as a German hero.

The German dimension was vividly demonstrated by Friedrich Staps, a student of Protestant theology who tried to kill Napoleon in Vienna in October 1809. The intended victim was inclined to put on a display of generosity redolent of the tyrant Dionysus who, in Schiller's ballad "Die Bürgschaft", ends up embracing his would-be assassin. He interrogated his assailant personally so as to elicit from him an expression of contrition for his misdeed. Instead he had to listen to the fearless young man telling him that, if pardoned, he would endeavour once more to rid Germany of the tyrant. Thereupon the student calmly pronounced his own death sentence.

His act was exceptional, but his motive was not. Hegel was wrong when he wrote in 1808—from a southern German perspective—that the Germans remained just as blind as they had been twenty years before. Jena and Tilsit had occurred since then. Rarely was a state so rudely awakened from retrospective nostalgia and arrogant self-assurance to be plunged into the abyss as was Prussia in the era after Frederick the Great.

The fact that Prussia managed to survive at all it owed to the Russian tsar.

Nevertheless there is some justification for saying that the vanquished profited from their defeat. This did not mean that every Junker examined his conscience and came to terms with the past. But so much lay in ruins and could never again be rebuilt in their dismembered country that anyone who gave serious thought to the task of reconstruction began to think in terms of open spaces and open doors in the French manner.

The Prussian advocates of reform did not need telling twice, and a hesitant and timid king did nothing to stop them. His main concern was to quickly recreate a strong army, and he saw no other way to attain this goal. For their part the renovators would not be satisfied with anything less than a revolution from above, although they could not prevent cold water from being poured on their plans. They came from all parts of the country: Baron Stein from Nassau and the peasant's son Scharnhorst from Hanover, Neidhardt von Gneisenau from Lower Franconia and Blücher from Mecklenburg. The task they had undertaken was by no means easy. Supported by the civil service and burghers, they were looked at askance and even angrily resented as would-be revolutionaries and democrats by the archreactionaries at home and as Francophobes by Napoleon. The latter even forced Frederick William III to dismiss Stein from office after earlier having recommended him for his competence and knowledge. This time he was not far off the mark: the reformers were indeed all set to turn his own weapons, both political and military, against him.

Their measures were radical: the abolition of serfdom, the right of redemption, local self-government, municipal reform, freedom of trade and the introduction of universal conscription altered the state, the army and society as a whole. At one fell swoop they overhauled most of the legislation of the Rhine Confederation. However, they left the absolute monarchy and the nobility's class rule well alone. It was to be a renovation of public life for, but not by means of, the popular masses, whose heartfelt gratitude was taken for granted at the outset.

This was the drawback of the "Prussian road" aimed at liberation from foreign domination and re-admission to the ranks of the independent powers. Following this "revolution without a revolution" both progressive and reactionary Prussians cohabited under the same Hohenzollern roof, their fusion seemingly epitomized by Chancellor Hardenberg. Doubtlessly some would have liked to go further and to overstep the boundaries of Prussia to achieve a national German state in keeping with the time, for which the Romantics were already calling. But that presupposed the

defeat of Napoleon, and this took precedence over everything else. This was also accepted by intellectual champions of the bourgeois reform movement: the Lusatian Johann Gottlieb Fichte in his 14 "Addresses to the German Nation" which he held in Berlin in 1807/1808, Ernst Moritz Arndt from the Swedish island of Rügen, Friedrich Jahn, the initiator of organized physical training, from the Thuringian town of Lanz, Wilhelm von Humboldt, co-founder of the Berlin University, plus the apostles of Kant in Königsberg grouped around Heinrich Schön, who translated their master's categorical imperative from the philosophical to the political plane.

Napoleon himself had played a major role in upsetting the continental applecart, getting people on the move and driving them forward. He could exert pressure to make them dance to his tune but thereby engendered resistance. This did not everywhere and immediately become as noticeable and visible as in Spain, but thereafter it tended to coalesce year by year around certain nodal points. The Emperor of the French paid no heed to such minor disturbances. He still perceived them as unpleasant but harmless side effects of the suffering he had to occasion in order to get his message across. In 1812 he was still sufficiently feared to compel Prussia and Austria to ally with France as he decided to resort once more to the sword to resolve the "Russian problem". "Oderint, dum metuant," as the Roman Emperor Domitian said: "Let them hate me, as long as they fear me!" But what if his last "lightning campaign" in the pacification of Europe—which is how he saw the operation—should get bogged down in the endless expanse of the Russian plain?

Even Frenchmen were now asking themselves this question.

Notes made by Freiherr vom Stein on the October Edict of 8 October 1807. It proclaimed the freedom to acquire landed property, freedom of trade and industry and abolished the personal servitude of the peasants. In spite of all its shortcomings it represented an important part of the Prussian reforms. Staatsarchiv Merseburg.

[1] TARLÉ, E.V.: *1812. Russland und das Schicksal Europas.* Berlin, 1951.
[2] TOLSTOI, L.: *War and Peace* (1863–1869).

From Moscow to Waterloo

French morale fell, and not just among the perpetual moaners who were opposed to the entire line of French policy: the Republicans, who could not forgive Napoleon's attack on democracy, and the diehard royalists, for whom this usurper of the throne and confiscator of their privileges remained the devil incarnate. However, neither group got up to much more than a few conspiratorial antics or posed any real threat as long as Imperial France was basking in success. Anyone who stepped out of line, like the Republican General Malet in 1808, was stuck behind bars as a "lunatic".

Yet Spain destroyed the optimistic attitude which the public—even without prompting—believed was justified after Tilsit and Erfurt. It now seemed that the war would drag on indefinitely. On top of this came a series of military mishaps which could be neither concealed nor explained away: Bailén, Aspern and Torres Vedras. Increasing conflict with the pope, who had been ejected from Rome, alienated the pious. There were also the privations of the "continental system" and finally, in 1811, an economic crisis which in one way or another affected virtually everyone. No one benefited from the fact that, following the latest annexations, France now stretched as far as Lübeck and Cattaro, or that it now had an empress of impeccable pedigree from Vienna, or that a member of the Bonaparte clan now ruled the roost in Cassel while another, who proved recalcitrant, got into hot water in his Dutch fief, so that Holland had to be annexed by France.

The misgivings of the big bourgeoisie were even greater. They were far too commercially-minded to pave the way to imperial recklessness with letters of credit of unlimited validity. They were prepared to be bullied by the tough soldier for as long as he conquered new markets, and the arms boom was also good for business for a while. But in the long run the negative consequences of the war predominated. Woe betide the mighty emperor if he could not halt the slump and in the end were even to be defeated!

Thus the prevailing mood was one of uncertainty. Yet, as Napoleon himself had said, a government such as his must either amaze and dazzle, or go under; it could not stand still. It had at all costs to do something about the general malaise, news of which had by now also reached foreign ears by dozens of channels; it had to act.

It was not an easy decision for Napoleon to break with Russia and to dictate the terms of a general peace not in alliance with the tsar but in opposition to him. Yet he never seriously considered backtracking, apart from on minor points. To have yielded to the first attempt at blackmail for the sake of peace would merely have invited other attempts. Although he considered a three-year campaign conceivable he was confident that, in sheer logistical terms, no one would be able to stand up to the 600,000 men he could muster.

After long reflection he acted, as usual, with speed. On February 8, 1812 he issued instructions for mobilization, on the 24th he imposed a military alliance on Prussia and on March 13 compelled Austria to join. He had nothing to conceal. All through the spring his motley array of divisions—the majority of which were non-French auxiliaries—rolled eastwards. At dawn on June 23 he crossed the Niemen with his main army.[1]

Russian compliance with the "continental system", to which it had originally assented, had become increasingly lackadaisical. Its liaison with France had initially proved advantageous, but by 1811 brought only trouble and cooled accordingly. Alexander was not looking for the fight to which the "English party" at his court encouraged him, but nor did he seek to avoid it. To begin with, Russia was at a great military disadvantage. On the other hand it had considerable reserves which could be deployed more and more as the enemy penetrated deeper into the vast country. This gave rise to the tactic of harrying the French while yielding ground—a strategy of steady withdrawal to save the troops for the intended counterattack.

Russia's social élite supported the war effort.[2] The few who advocated a deal with France were eliminated. Their most influential spokesman, Speranski, was banished. The mass of the peasants did not revolt. In no way did they welcome Napoleon as their liberator from the inexorable burden of serfdom, a role which he in any case did not emphasize in Russia. They regarded him as nothing more than a brazenly plundering foreign invader and atheist whom they obviously must either expel or exterminate. Their armed resistance harassed and dented the entire French line of advance and provided invaluable assistance to their own troops. In this respect the Russians were justified in speaking of a "patriotic war".

Internationally the tsar obtained as many safeguards as possible. He received an assurance from both Vienna and Berlin that Austria and Prussia would largely restrict themselves to making angry noises, just as Russia had done in the year 1809.

He was less successful in trying to drum up support among the Polish nobility. However, in May 1812 he managed to bring the five-year war against Turkey to a timely close and so release his southern army which had been tied down on the Lower Danube. England contributed both weapons and a major offensive while Sweden, on which the tsar had only recently waged war, did a spectacular somersault in return for the prospect of Danish-held Norway as compensation for the loss of Finland. By a strange quirk of fate the newly proclaimed crown prince, Jean Bernadotte of Gascony—hitherto a black sheep among the French marshals and an inlaw of Napoleon's to boot—appeared on the scene as Sweden's staunch champion.

The wastes of Russia were the last hope of both European feudal reaction and the patriotic opposition. Representatives of both camps sought refuge at St. Petersburg: Vom Stein and Madame de Staël, Clausewitz and Arndt, Joseph de Maistre and Pozzo di Borgo, a Corsican archenemy of the Bonaparte clan. In America Moreau waited for his hour to come.

Right from the start Napoleon felt uneasy. He thought of calling an early halt and setting up camp for the winter but then disastrously decided to press on after all. At Smolensk, the first time that he encountered the enemy in large number, he had less than 200,000 men. When he was at last able to fight a full-scale battle, at Borodino on the Moskva on September 7—which left the ultimate outcome of the campaign wide open—he had 140,000 men left and on entering Moscow only some 90,000. Here, after Alexander turned down his offer to negotiate, he had as good as lost the war. What could he achieve, ensconced in the Kremlin 1,600 miles from Paris and without any discernible strategic objective? As the winter approached he was caught in a trap of his own making, and no miracle or enemy blunder came to his rescue.

After kicking his heels for a month in the smouldering capital in the vain hope that Alexander would sue for peace, he was forced to sound the retreat on October 19.[1] However, Prince Kutusov, as he wheeled round from Borodino and gathered reinforcements along the way, cut off his southern line of retreat and seized the initiative.

With hordes of Cossack light cavalry and peasant partisans harrying the unprotected deep flank, the withdrawal soon turned into a catastrophic rout. Finding its supply depots largely destroyed or ransacked and plagued by blinding snow storms, the Grand Army, which consisted mostly of southern Europeans, disintegrated into a disorderly and bedraggled shambles. Spanish, Swiss and German troops deserted en masse. Others, cut off or exhausted, surrendered. Thanks largely to the vigour of Marshal Ney, Napoleon did manage to break through the ring of enemy troops and recross the Beresina, but at the cost of abandoning his baggage train and rearguard. Having got his men into this mess in the first place, Napoleon now got them out again. But few units were left intact as they reached Lithuania, with the emperor walking amidst the Guard for the last part of the way. On December 5 he left the now apathetic rump of his army in Smorgony and sped away in a covered sleigh towards Dresden and thence by coach back to Paris.[2] On the 16th, two days before his arrival at the Tuileries, the *Moniteur*, in its 29th bulletin, tersely announced the destruction of the Grand Army. Throughout Europe, which had had no news for weeks and so was on tenterhooks, the announcement came as a bombshell.

Just how unstable the situation had been for some time, even in Paris, was shown by General Malet's attempted coup on October 22/23. Armed only with a clumsily forged army despatch to the effect that the emperor had been killed in Russia, he set up a provisional government in Moreau's name. It occurred to literally nobody that Napoleon already had a constitutional successor, namely the infant "King of Rome". Malet's bluff was called after just a few hours when Hulin, a veteran of the storming of the Bastille, smelled a rat. But how could a man who was supposedly not quite sane manage, without let or hindrance, to "abolish" the Empire, tyrannize the chief of police and peremptorily arrest the interior minister without being challenged once? And why did

Fouché have the ringleaders shot with such suspicious haste instead of laying bare the whole plot?

France obeyed the emperor after his return, but with a bad grace. Following the carnage in Russia he was left with no choice but to muster 300,000 men from the National Guard—mostly older men and fathers of families—and raw recruits. Time was against him; Kutusov was not for long checked by the French line of fortifications along the Vistula and Oder rivers. The Convention of Tauroggen, signed on December 31, 1812 between the Prussian general Von Yorck and the Russian general Count Diebitsch, paved the way for a national uprising which soon encompassed the whole of East Prussia. Freiherr vom Stein reappeared in Königsberg and issued a call to the whole of Germany. King Frederick William III, who at first wanted to courtmartial Von Yorck for insubordination, escaped from Berlin to Silesia where he succumbed to pressure from the patriots to break with France. On March 17, 1813 he deigned to issue an appeal "To my People", but only after they had already risen. Now allied with the Russians, the reformed Prussian army moved into battle. A number of voluntary corps were formed, and the poet Theodor Körner became their eloquent spokesman.

In May Napoleon reconquered Saxony—and its king—in the battle of Lützen-Grossgörschen. After another victory at Bautzen he drove the enemy back beyond Breslau. Metternich then negotiated an armistice, but this merely facilitated Austria's preparations for entering the war. A political solution to the conflict was put forward which would have required Napoleon to withdraw behind France's "natural frontiers" along the Rhine, the Alps and the Pyrenees. But this was unacceptable to him as the whole world would have seen it as a defeat. Besides, his opponents, now in the unaccustomed position of having the advantage, also wanted a fight to the finish. Following a heavy defeat at Vitoria on June 26 the French lost Spain, and on August 12 Napoleon's father-in-law joined the Coalition. After his marshals, given insufficient forces, had been beaten on the wings, Napoleon, despite a remarkable victory over the Austrians at Dresden, was now threatened with encirclement by three concentric enemy formations adavancing on Leipzig. He lost the ensuing Battle of the Nations,

Take the skulls of a hundred thousand nobles
killed by him
And with these fill to the brim
The base of the monument.
As the centrepiece and crowning element
Place the biggest tiger on all fours
Mauling yet another victim with its claws.
Let all around a ghostly wall of bones be set;
Then from countless widows squeeze
the blood and sweat:
This will serve for ten thousand dismal
lights as tallow—
Thus posterity will see him whom
none shall hallow.

Death's head monument to Napoleon. Lithograph; pen-and-ink plus watercolours.

Page 62:
Truth hounded by evil spirits. Allegory on the situation in Spain following the Peninsular War. Penand-ink drawing by Francisco de Goya. Metropolitan Museum, New York.

[1] ROSTOPCHIN(E), F.V.: *La vérité sur l'incendie de Moscou.* Paris, 1823.
[2] SÉGUR, P. DE: *Geschichte Napoleons und der Grossen Armee im Jahr 1812.* Stuttgart, 1835; GOURGAUD, G.: *Napoléon et la Grande Armée en Russie.* Paris, 1825.

which was fought between October 16 and 19 against a united force of Russians, Prussians, Austrians and Bernadotte's Swedes, and evacuated Germany. The princes of the Rhine Confederation abandoned him with the same alacrity with which they had flocked to his side in happier days.

It was a case of every man for himself, including in Naples. There the emperor's ambitions sister Caroline, desperate to retain the Neapolitan crown, prompted her husband Murat to go it alone and make overtures to England, which would not particularly care which minor potentate sat at the foot of the Vesuvius as long as he kept his distance from France—and the other continental powers. And suddenly Napoleon had no allies or vassals left in all Europe. The only means of payment he now had were promissory notes. Forced loans and requisitions were now levied on French burghers and peasants. As Wellington's troops from Spain advanced on Lyons from Toulouse while the Austrians arrived from Italy, the Russians, Prussians and Austrians under Blücher and Schwarzenberg pressed along the Marne and the Seine towards Paris.

With his back to the wall, the emperor had to call up veterans and seventeen year-old lads to replenish his ranks. Even so, the French were outnumbered by two or even three to one. His only chance was to try and drive a wedge between the allied armies. In the spring campaign of 1814 (which strictly speaking was a winter campaign) he gave a last demonstration of his military genius which Clausewitz, the military theorist on the opposing side, rates highly. He managed to defeat the two hostile armies several more times, but he was unable to deliver the *coup de grâce* since, as a result of exhausting countermarches, he had no reserves left. He succumbed to Blücher at Laon and to Schwarzenberg at Arcis-sur-Aube. Thereupon the two generals, no longer afraid of the emperor, bypassed him and, in true Napoleonic style, headed straight for the capital. The move owed less to Gneisenau's offensive strategy than to their inside knowledge of the mood of rampant defeatism there.

Napoleon clung to the hope that he could destroy the invaders' bases and so cut them off. He could still draw on the troops who manned the fortifications in eastern France. There were risings of peasants who were prepared, with him, to defend

"The Liberators of Europe". Allegorical triumphal procession of the three allied monarchs to the Temple of Concord. Engraving by Daniel Berger after Friedrich Georg Weitsch, 1815.

the home of the Revolution. The sans-culottes of Paris were pressing to be mobilized but Napoleon refused. He insisted on fighting "according to the rules", and at congresses in Frankfurt and Châtillon got his diplomats to put out peace feelers, but in vain. He gave in to their demands one by one, but these past masters of the war of attrition were simply leading him a merry dance. Time was now on their side. On March 12 Bordeaux cheered the arrival, to the accompaniment of English soldiers, of the Duke of Angoulême, a Bourbon prince, while the Vendée took up arms in support of their old king. The pope, who had been hastily released and despatched from Fontainebleau back to Rome with Napoleon's blessings, sided as expected with the allies.

Finally the city of Paris gave the order of the boot to His Imperial Highness. Inside the capital his marshals fought half-heartedly with an eye to the future. With Fouché's assistance prominent personages set their minds to formulating the most acceptable terms of capitulation: an end to the war through the elimination of its "cause", i.e. Napoleon. Carefully prepared subversion gained the upper hand. The leaders of the National Guard and the city council had already been won

CONGRÈS DE VIENNE.

over, while the vacillating military governor Marmont was swayed by the banking fraternity into which he had married. Greeted by clenched fists in the working class districts, the "friendly enemy"entered the city on March 31 and was showered with flowers by the upper crust, among whom the ladies boisterously mounted the cruppers of Cossack steeds. The tumultuously acclaimed monarchs, who were present in person, then declared that they would no longer negotiate with Napoleon, while Talleyrand limped off to persuade the Imperial Senate to depose him. As the ill tidings came in thick and fast,

Napoleon hastened from Saint-Dizier by forced march to Fontainebleau and was about to launch the counterattack when news of the wholesale defection reached him. He tried to intercede to at least ensure that his son by Marie Louise would retain the succession, but time had run out. On the advice of his marshals he abdicated unconditionally and, after the poison he had taken failed to take effect, submitted himself to the will of the victors. By way of consolation they let him keep the title of emperor and granted him a life annuity of two million livres as well as sovereignty over the island of Elba near his native Corsica.

The Vienna Congress of 1815. Jean-Baptiste Isabey exhibited a group portrait of the assembled diplomats in the Paris Salon in 1817. The statesmen are grouped around Metternich (seventh from the left). Talleyrand is seated at the table on the right, Hardenberg in the left foreground. At the left-hand margin of the picture a door has just been opened to admit Wellington, the victor of Waterloo. The scene is framed by the portraits of the eight signatory monarchs, the national emblems of the states and the coats of arms of their plenipotentiaries. Engraving by Jean Godefroy after Jean-Baptiste Isabey, 1819.

Last drawing by Marshal Ney. It was done in the Luxembourg Prison twelve days prior to the execution of the marshal, who was condemned to death after the "Hundred Days" for high treason. Musée du Louvre, Cabinet des Dessins, Paris.

Return of a royalist ("I am being reactivated"). Lithograph by Nicolas-Toussaint Charlet.

I have no wish to be the King of the Jacquerie!
Napoleon to Benjamin Constant, June 21, 1815.

[1] KRÖGER, A.: *Napoleon kam bis Waterloo. Die Hundert Tage im Spiegel der zeitgenössischen Presse.* Munich, 1968.
[2] SIEBURG, F.: *Napoleon. Die hundert Tage.* Stuttgart, 1956.
[3] ZWEIG, S.: *Sternstunden der Menschheit. Waterloo.* Leipzig, 1948.
[4] MARGERIT, R.: *Waterloo, le 18 juin 1815.* Paris, 1964;
LACHOUQUE, H.: *Waterloo.* Paris, 1972.

As Louis XVIII, after twenty-three years of exile, landed in Calais on April 23, Napoleon headed south under escort and protectively dressed in an Austrian uniform and subjected to physical threats from royalists. While war-weary parvenus of the Imperial era clustered around the restored Bourbon throne and relaxed after their feats of heroism in sumptuous surroundings, Napoleon entered his capital Portoferraio on May 4. It seemed that the curtain would fall on the tempestuous drama that was his life under virtually the same patch of blue sky which had witnessed its opening scene. But the appearance was deceptive. It was not this island which was to be his last resting place.

His verdict on the Bourbons, that they had "forgotten nothing and learned nothing", was inaccurate. When Louis XVIII took his leave of his fastidious English hosts he was looking for peace and quiet rather than revenge. No fool, he realized that the far-reaching social and economic changes wrought by the Revolution and many of the tried-and-tested institutions of the Empire were irreversible, that the army marched with pride behind the Imperial eagles stained with their blood, and that the victors were motivated by base selfishness.

Therefore his substitute for a constitution, the Charter, sought to extend a conciliatory hand to those amenable to compromise among the big bourgeoisie, the new nobility and to the ideologues who had been severely maltreated by his predecessor. The peasants were relieved that the restoration cost them nothing and that peace finally had returned.

However, a king who was the puppet of the victors was an insult to a nation which for twenty years had led the world. Although they were pleased enough to see the back of the emperor, they were less than enthusiastic about the imported symbol of defeat. The peace terms were favourable: a return to the "borders of 1792" (actually of January 1, 1793) and no reparations. Yet no one knew whether or how long this spirit of generosity, this willingness to forgive and forget France's many sins, would last. In the wake of a continuous purge the leading positions in the state were increasingly taken over by aristocrats. In the royalist strongholds of the west and south the "white terror" once again gave vent to its spleen at grassroots level.

Only now did it dawn on many that the Revolution was irretrievably lost, and this revived memories of Napoleon—of the 1789 vintage, if not that of 1793. The great divide now ran between the fleur-de-lys and the tricolour.

Meanwhile the allied rulers were taking their time at the Vienna Congress. There was little talk any more of the nations which had fought the war of liberation. They were now more of an embarrassment. The victors gladly accepted the principle of monarchical legitimacy which Talleyrand skilfully proposed in order to rid Bourbon France of the stigma of defeat and to represent its interests as an equal arbiter among the other powers. It was, however, easier to condemn Enlightenment ideas, revolt and usurpation than to agree on the fate of Poland, Saxony or Naples. In 1815 England and Austria initialled a secret pact with France against Russia and its Prussian ally. In view of these circumstances Napoleon weighed the idea of living out his remaining years as the wretched ruler of a small island against the prospects of a return to Paris. He was sent neither the promised annuity nor his wife and child. There were calls to shunt the deposed emperor further afield, to Madeira or the Azores. From Paris came both warning cries and assurances of help. After brief consideration Napoleon outwitted the British patrol ships for the last time and landed with his small guard of honour at the fishing port of Golfe Juan on March 1, 1815.

Whereas his marshals, almost to a man, chickened out, the rank-and-file flocked to his side with cries of "Vive l' Empereur!" Without firing a shot, just as he had predicted, he approached Paris. The press changed its tune daily: "The Corsican werewolf has landed . . . The usurper faces annihilation at Lyons . . . Bonaparte in Fontainebleau . . . The capital awaits His Majesty the Emperor. . . ."[1] During the night of March 20 Louis fled to Ghent. The next day Napoleon returned to the Tuileries where he took his accustomed hot bath.

Never before had he appealed so strongly to the revolutionary heritage, and never had he met with such a response among ordinary folk in both town and countryside. He was now a popular hero, the defender of the nation. Would this signal a new, democratic empire under the now permanent red, white and blue emblem, one which solemnly renounced aggression?

For this he would have had to accept the willing support of the masses and set up a revolutionary dictatorship in the name of the common good, which is what they expected from him.[2] But the leopard was unable to change his spots. He threatened to hang the Bourbon supporters from the lamp posts, but his vituperative bark had no bite. He drew aggrieved Republicans to his side but attempted at the same time to win over their "Notables"; and with his April constitution (the *acte additionnel*) he sought to please both the likes of Fouché and Carnot as well as Benjamin Constant. The bulk of the burghers, especially the wealthy few, were by now heartily sick of him and did not fall for his blandishments. They regarded him as a nuisance. Hence the elections met with apathy and gerrymandering, while Lafayette and Lanjuinais, the Grand Old Man of the Gironde, tried to put a spanner in the works as they both distrusted Napoleon's show of liberalism. He later admitted that as soon as victory was assured he would have dissolved the parliamentary chambers.

He also misjudged the international situation. His spectre cast a shadow over the assembled élite as they danced away in the Viennese ballrooms, and fear made them sink their differences. The four great powers formed a quadruple alliance against the outlaw on the spot. His reconquest of power was due entirely to the personal allegiance of the veterans who hastened to the colours in the tumult caused by the renewed invasion of their country. They gave the "Hundred Days" an aura of military melodrama.[3]

The emperor's only hope was to deal with the allies one by one before they could coordinate their movements. He therefore recrossed the Belgian border and, at Ligny on June 16, duly defeated Blücher whom, however, he was unable either to intimidate or to put out of action. As he faced Wellington's ferocious line two days later at the Mont Saint-Jean near Waterloo the Prussians made a timely reappearance and savaged his right flank. The Imperial Guard was decimated, and the defeat sealed his fate.[4] It was to be his final defeat.

The emperor's act of desperation had rebounded on him. He did not die on the battlefield as he had wished. Instead he resigned himself to a second abdication. Thousands of ordinary people surrounded the Elysée Palace and tried in vain to

make him change his mind. He refused. In Malmaison, the house where the late Josephine had lived, he sat among the tea-roses which she had cultivated and reminisced. Then his intended embarkation for America from the port of Rochefort misfired and, like Themistocles, he bade his enemy for asylum. However, the English government failed to appreciate the joke, de-

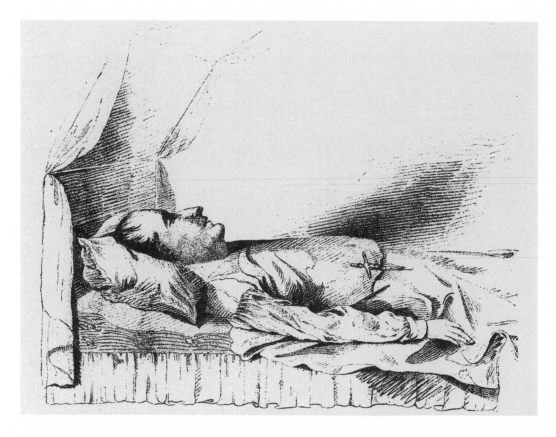

clared him a prisoner of war and shipped him off to St. Helena.

In the second Treaty of Paris—as a punishment for its fickleness—France was fleeced more thoroughly. It had to cede border areas, dig deep into its pocket and put up with foreign occupation forces for an indefinite period. The allied powers signed a mutual life insurance policy: in place of the holy alliance of nations, for which the Jacobins and sans-culottes had striven, came the Holy Alliance of kings. The dream of the freedom fighters faded. Once again it had proved disastrous to trust the word of princes. Promises were unscrupulously broken as soon as the rulers deemed it possible to sever the national bond between leaders and led. Feudal class barriers were re-established. The German Confederation turned out to have been much ado about nothing, while Metternich allowed Italy to survive only as a geographical concept. It was left up to the Spanish patriots to decide whether they would allow themselves to be slaughtered in a colonial war or not. Sooner or later the heroes of the hour would either be thrust into the background and forgotten or else would themselves become the victims of persecution. The only way to deal with democrats was to send in the troops. A new historical era began in which revolutions would launch attacks on newly erected Bastilles using other means and under other banners.

"General Bonaparte", as his jailors pointedly referred to him, was not to be involved in any of this. He was doomed to spend his last few years in inactivity on an island in the South Atlantic, isolated from the outside world and condemned to a life of passive contemplation, his health failing and surrounded by a devoted coterie. It was here that he died in his prime, aged fifty one, on May 5, 1821, probably of a chronic stomach disorder.[1]

[1] *Geschichte der Gefangenschaft Napoleons auf St. Helena von dem General Montholon.* Leipzig, 1846;
BERTRAND, H.: *Cahiers de Sainte-Hélène,* 3 Vols. Paris, 1949–1959.

Cover of the Constitution of the Grand Duchy of Warsaw of July 22, 1807. After the Peace of Tilsit Napoleon formed the Grand Duchy of Warsaw from annexed Prussian territory as a client state in order to strengthen his position in the East. In July 1807 he personally signed the constitutional charter in Dresden. The ornate cover of blue velvet with rich gilding is adorned by the emperor's monogram, the crowned eagle and the Imperial seal. Staatsarchiv Dresden.

Napoleon in his coronation regalia. In 1810 Gérard's teacher Jacques-Louis David, enraptured by Napoleon's appearance, exclaimed: "In the past altars would have been erected in honour of such a man!" Even without altars a conspicuous personality cult was built up around the emperor, whose portraits were distributed throughout the whole of Europe. (Between 1810 and 1812 alone the marble workshops at Carrara are said to have produced some 1,500 replicas of the Napoleon bust by Chaudet.) This version of his portrait in his coronation robes, which Gérard had to paint several times, was given to the King of Saxony in 1810 as a present. Staatliche Kunstsammlungen Dresden, Gemäldegalerie Neue Meister.

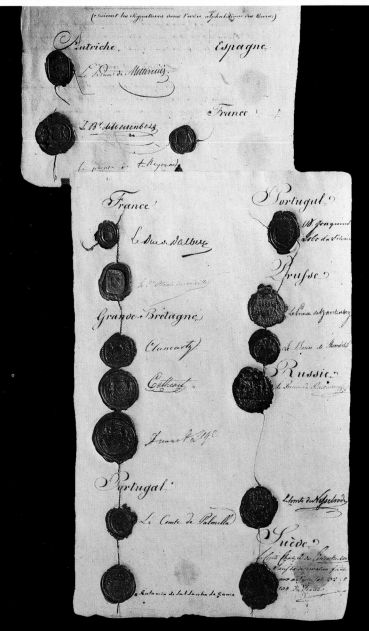

Official document of the Congress of Vienna of
June 9, 1815. Prussian copy bearing the seals
of the signatory states. It sealed the defeat of the
Napoleonic army and created the basis for the
restoration policy of the victorious states.
Staatsarchiv Merseburg.

Left:
The Battle of the Nations at Leipzig: the Allies
storming the city. Coloured aquatint by
J. L. Rugendas after a drawing from nature
by J. Wagner, *c.* 1820. Museum für Geschichte
der Stadt Leipzig.

Russian cavalry at the time of the wars of liberation. Illustration from the "Mohtssche Chronik" of the town of Mühlhausen. Stadtarchiv Mühlhausen.

Order book of an unknown German textile dealer (1787–1803). This double-page entry from May 1801 demonstrates the disruption in trade with England.
For as long as England remained at war with France the consignments of cloth from Manchester were to be transported either by neutral ships or by convoy. Museum für Geschichte der Stadt Leipzig.

Page 76:
Napoleon at Fontainebleau on March 31, 1814 after receiving news of the entry of the Allies into Paris. Painting by Paul Delaroche, 1845. Museum der bildenden Künste, Leipzig.

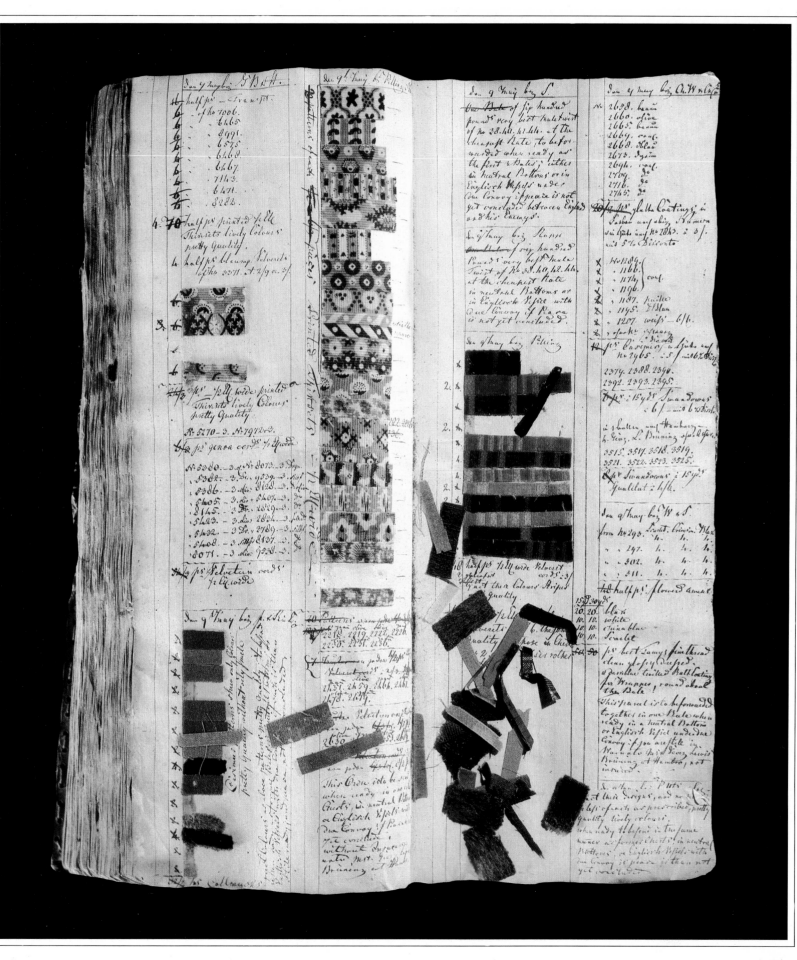

THE EMPIRE
IN BLUE - WHITE - RED

The Village

The Revolution turned the French peasants into free men on free land. However, this freedom did not simply fall into their laps. They had to fight for it against their old masters using flails and pitchforks, grimly defend it against both internal and external attack and themselves implement the destruction of feudalism in their locality. They could not conquer state power—this task fell to their urban counterparts—but nor were they interested in this anyway. They were content to determine events at parish level.

The Revolution altered property relations in their favour.[1] Although the redistribution of land following the confiscation of the estates of the Church and of the emigrés primarily benefited well-to-do bourgeois purchasers, the peasantry did not miss out entirely. Between a third and a half of the auctioned land went to them. This satisfied the most immediate land hunger. And if those sons of peasants whose military service had taken them to foreign parts cared to compare their own lot with the miserable and often servile existence of the peasants, let alone the serfs, there, they would immediately have noticed the huge difference between the French Republic and the Old Régime which continued to prevail in some countries.[2]

They had not needed Napoleon's help for this—and nevertheless folk legend, instead of eulogizing the Convention's sterling efforts to reparcel agricultural land, concentrated on the persona of the "people's emperor", the *roi du peuple*, whose exploits were admiringly related to little children by their grandfathers.

What the vicissitudes of the Revolution were unable to give the countryman was the guarantee of irrevocability: well ordered markets at which he could buy and sell to his heart's content, a sound currency which he could once again confidently put aside for a rainy day, and a truce with the Church which he inevitably needed from time to time. Nor could the peasants be certain that the requisitions would cease or that the state would round up the wandering gangs of brigands; nor, above all, that the returning emigrés would have no claim to their former property which had since been acquired by peasants; nor that tax rates would not rise sky high again as they had under the Bourbons; nor that common land would be made available for parcelling.[3]

The emperor did have a "peasant policy". He was well aware of their economic importance for all his schemes, whether planned or improvised. When he said that his peasants came first, this was neither sentimental drooling nor an idle boast. It was rather a pragmatic precaution aimed at safely channelling the pressure exerted by this mighty mass. The peasantry accounted for almost four fifths of the population. They fed the towns and furnished most of the conscripts. In return they required careful handling—in a word, good government.

This was granted them, inasmuch as higher state interests permitted, and most peasants, however many general and particular bones they had to pick with the townfolk, recognized this. As a soldier Napoleon had impressed them and as emperor—apart from in the Vendée which refused any reconciliation with the "usurper"—he was decidedly popular. They lost no sleep over the loss of the National Assemblies, in which they had not been represented anyway. At long last the country again had a strong ruler, someone with whom they could identify and who was obviously coping successfully with his onerous burden. At the same time the taxes which he levied from them remained within tolerable and acceptable limits. It was a system of taxation which they could comprehend, even though no one parted with his money willingly. The Imperial constitution expressly safeguarded the acquisition of nationalized land. As from 1813 onwards common land was also put up for grabs. The state ensured that the laws were obeyed, and in court the peasant usually got a fair hearing. He and his wife could attend church without any constraints.

Emancipation of the peasantry was not restricted to France. It spread, albeit in an increasingly attenuated form, in the wake of the French armies as they moved across Europe: to Germany, Italy, Austria, Poland and Spain. It was not just a case of Napoleon issuing directives to compliant satellites but also, for example in Prussia, resulted from the efforts of reformers to revive the state after its collapse. Outside France, however, the emancipatory legislation—decreed from above rather than conquered from below—was largely limited to releasing the peasant from the shackles of personal servitude and corvée.

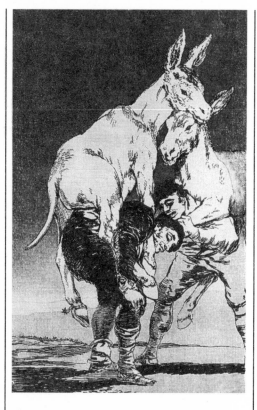

The peasant as loadbearer ("It is all too much for you"). Folio 42 from the series "Los Caprichos". Aquatint by Francisco de Goya, 1797–1799.

Page 78:
Peasant family ("True happiness"). In paintings and drawings in the second half of the 18th century peasants were continually depicted with a mixture of coarse realism and idyllic sentimentalism. Engraving by Simonet after Moreau le Jeune.

[1] BOURDE, A.J.: *Agronomie et agronomes en France au XVIIIᵉ siècle*, 3 Vols. Paris, 1967.
[2] *Histoire de la France rurale, III: Apogée et crise de la civilisation paysanne.* Edited by E. Juillard. Paris, 1977.
[3] BOIS, P.: *Paysans de l'Ouest. Des structures économiques et sociales aux options politiques, depuis l'époque révolutionnaire, dans la Sarthe.* Paris, 1961.

On one score Napoleon came a cropper, namely as a would-be peacemaker. In 1802 and again in 1807 he looked all set to tame the god of war. But nothing came of it, and ever increasing numbers of young men from the villages were sacrificed to Mars. The unceasing and continuously rising toll of lives, to which there was no end in sight, began to provoke resentment and to damage the emperor's popularity. There is much evidence to show that the premature conscriptions of 1809 for the first time caused unrest even among the hitherto reliable peasantry. Had they not already sacrificed enough men? The word spread, perhaps deliberately put about, that Napoleon was a cannibal and an ogre. It was left to the next generation to retrospectively clear his name and to reassess his rule as constituting the "good old days" of the French peasantry.

The Empire was of much too short a duration to produce drastic changes in agriculture.[1] It continued some things and initiated others. The Revolution at least led to the slackening of the inflexible medieval method of farming, which was ultimately dropped altogether. Fallow land was now cultivated and the area of arable land was somewhat enlarged, while there was a corresponding increase in grazing land and in the raising of cattle and horses. But—unlike today—the main form of farming remained the rather less demanding raising of sheep. The officially recommended practice of growing potatoes on poor soil made some headway. The state began the reafforestation of the sandy area of Aquitaine known as "les Landes", now the largest continuous expanse of forest in France. The cultivation of sugar beet in the northern provinces, expressly encouraged to offset the blockade, was still in an experimental stage. Agricultural technology, which lagged way behind developments in England and the Netherlands, remained at a comparatively low level.

Nevertheless, the transition from the old two and three-field system to that of crop rotation was accelerated. The numbers of wild boar and wolves, which had become a scourge, were emphatically reduced by the peasants, who were now permitted to hunt. Neighbourly assistance was still very much in vogue. Small peasants who did not have their own agricultural equipment took turns to harness their horse or mule to a communal plough.

The bourgeois state and social system furthered the process of differentiation within the peasantry, which disintegrated completely as a social class.[2] The law no longer placed any restrictions on inheritance and hence on the fragmentation of land ownership. Under Napoleon's *Code civil* the buying and selling of land was put on a par with the free circulation of commodities and was subject only to the market law of supply and demand, with the latter still tending to be greater than the former. The desire to own a little plot of land was the dream of all Frenchmen in both urban and rural areas. Consequently there was never enough available for everyone at prices they could afford.

Following the elimination of the top layer of property owners, distinctions between the various individual strata of the rural population became more pronounced.

Big landowners and large-scale tenant farmers possessed extensive landholdings plus working capital. They undertook land improvement schemes and employed sizeable numbers of paid labourers. They could afford to adapt to market fluctuations, i.e. to sell when the price was high and to store their stocks when it was low until the rate of profit looked set to climb again, which normally occurred between harvests. Although they were not infrequently personally involved in supervising the work in the fields—so as to set an example and spur the labourers on to greater efforts—they were marked off from the peasantry, from which they seldom stemmed anyway, by the fact that they were agricultural entrepreneurs. Some counted among the notabilities of Imperial France who amassed real fortunes. Most of their male descendants enjoyed a secure middle-class life in the towns as officials or in one of the professions.

Rich peasants, and sometimes powerful middling peasants, were either respected or reviled as "kingpins" who set the tone locally. They were undoubtedly among the main beneficiaries of the revolutionary agrarian reforms since it was above all they who, by means of redemption and additional purchases, were able to supplement their existing holdings. It was they who were chiefly responsible for supplying the local markets and it was from among their ranks that the emperor personally appointed the parish mayor. This post was often a thankless task, for the *maire* found himself between the Devil and the deep blue sea—between government instructions from above and the rather different expectations of his parish council.

The much more numerous small peasants were worse off. They were primarily engaged in subsistence farming, and during the winter months often took a second job as workers at a nearby forge or mine. Their problem was twofold. Both the Revolution and the emperor left the old system of semi-leasehold or *métayage* intact. A peasant whose own parcel of land (if he had one) was insufficient for the upkeep of his family and who thus leased an additional plot had to pay in kind half of everything he produced on it to the owner. In a good year the other half sufficed to keep his head above water, but if the harvest was poor he got into debt with the usurers who plied their evil trade in both town and countryside. Since he had only a little surplus produce—a few sacks of grain, a sheep, a basket of eggs, a chicken, a pat of butter and some seasonal vegetables—which he could bring to market, he was constantly short of money, even when he made a satisfactory sale. And the overall increase in prices worked to the detriment of anyone who had to pay his rent in cash because during a long-term economic boom leasehold rates rose twice as much on average as the price of grain, even though the latter also tended to go up—by some twenty per cent as compared to an increase of thirty-five per cent in leasehold rents.

The free play of market forces rendered the small peasant's life neither easy nor more agreeable. However, it did give a different importance, a distinctly new meaning, to his work: he now slaved away not for his master but for himself and his family, which at least made the effort worthwhile. In 1811 Lady Morgan, a member of the breed of English travelling ladies who were to be found everywhere, wrote a rather effusive but basically accurate appraisal in her book *La France*: "One can observe the way in which such an independent farmer, being the owner of an acre or so of land, plods across his little field with an ass pulling some kind of contraption that resembles a harrow. What counts is that he owns it himself;

he is independent. The little field he is ploughing belongs to him. It is he who sows the seed and he will it be who reaps the reward. His children will garner the fruit of the tree which his hand has planted. The small plot of land upholds his and his family's independence. Each clod of earth is utilized and will yield three times as much as that which was previously got out by less well motivated hands. His modest savings no longer go to satisfy some rapacious collector of tithe or taxes, nor to pay for the sun that shines upon him, nor yet for the air which he breathes."

This did not apply to the agricultural labourer. He could not vote and had no say in the running of his village. With few exceptions he remained the same village pauper that he always had been, whether as a farmhand, itinerant seasonal worker or as a day labourer whose wife and children— e.g. by minding sheep or poultry from the age of five upwards—earned a bit extra whenever the opportunity presented itself. His working day stayed excessively long and onerous, his humble abode defied description and was anything but a "home sweet home". However, he did manage to boost his earning capacity, though not because someone suddenly took pity on the plight of the rural proletariat. The rise in wage rates was due to the situation on the labour market. There was an increasing shortage of labour. Apart from the crisis years of 1810/1811, the amount of jobs available considerably exceeded the number of those seeking work. This was a consequence not just of the general economic revival and the migration of workers to the towns but above all of conscription, which year after year deprived rural France of its strongest labourers. Consequently the daily pay of a trained reaper—about three francs, depending on the region—even drew level with that of a bricklayer in a small town, who was reckoned to earn a good wage. This helped to keep the rural exodus—except in the case of female domestics—in bounds. At the same time it ensured political quiescence among the most wretched countrydwellers in Imperial France.[3]

The reports of the prefects, whose task it was to keep a record of everything that occurred and to inform their superiors promptly, confirmed the fact that the peasants adhered to the customs and habits of their forefathers.[4] A village was a community based on a strictly hierarchical structure

Setting off for market. Colour print by Duthé after Blaisot.

[1] SONNINI, C.: *Manuel des propriétaires ruraux et de tous les habitants de la campagne.* Paris, 1808.

[2] GRATTON, P.: *Les luttes de classes dans les campagnes.* Paris, 1971.

[3] SOBOUL, A.: *Problèmes paysans de la Révolution 1789–1848.* Paris, 1976.

[4] RESTIF DE LA BRETONNE, N.E.: *Le paysan perverti* (1776); *La vie de mon père* (1778).

which was never free from quarrelling but, for all that, few villagers ever left it. It was largely shielded from external influences. It was wary and even suspicious of "newcomers". Nor did the peasants go in for any fads or fashions. What was good enough yesterday would still do the trick today. The conventions which were rooted in the natural rhythm of the seasons regulated their habits, work, clothing and what little leisure time they had. They spoke in a local idiom which was often incomprehensible to the outsider—the *patois*—and their mentality and temperament varied depending on whether they came from Brittany, Gascony, Normandy or Provence. One in every two or three male peasants could just about write and would sometimes read the popular country almanac or even, exceptionally, might buy an "edifying" book.

Lack of cleanliness and hygiene, a diet low on proteins and vitamins plus drunkenness resulted in a high incidence of disease. Villages were often stricken by scabies, scrofula, rickets and puerperal fever. The herbwoman or village quack—who were fairly adept at dealing with minor ailments—were helpless in the face of the epidemics which periodically raged among both animals and humans; and doctors rarely strayed into the countryside. The assistance of certain saints was summoned for some complaints, in return for a sacrificial offering or a pilgrimage to a popular site of veneration. Recourse was often had to the ineradicable power of superstition, whether behind a religious façade or not, which went back to a much older peasant culture of Celtic origin. It was part of the peasant's philosophy and continued to weigh heavily on his everyday life.

Just about all the prefects depicted the peasants as simple and coarse yet more natural than their urban counterparts and thus unspoilt. No doubt their reports were coloured by the sentimentalism of pastoral poetry and the rustic idealism of the Enlightenment. They ascribed to country folk obstinacy coupled with a certain pride, native cunning and a sense of reality. The peasants took life as it came, and celebrated in convivial but rarely extravagant style with communal singing, customary dances, the occasional brawl and a dreadful hangover the next morning.

However, it would be untrue to say that the peasants lived in splendid isolation in their villages,

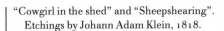

"Cowgirl in the shed" and "Sheepshearing". Etchings by Johann Adam Klein, 1818.

[1] FRANÇOIS HUË: *Le Journal d'un paysan, 1799–1823*. Edited by E. V. Veuclin. Paris, 1866.

J. A. Klein fec. Wien 1818.

away from the major postal and military routes, blind to events happening outside their own neck of the woods, seemingly impervious to and untouched by the march of history.[1] This was not the case, and certainly not after the Revolution. The danger of famine roused them in 1789 and the invitation to list their grievances in the *cahiers* gave them fresh hope. The "great fear" galvanized them and the storming of the châteaux drew them into the fray. The flight and execution of the king, the civil war and the de-Christianization campaign forced them to take sides. There was no letup in the torrent of leaflets, and even the almanac

was politicized. The agrarian laws affected the peasants personally, and they had to keep a close eye on the legal penpushers in case they tried to pull a fast one.

Contacts between town and country grew more intense. There was an increase in traffic and the traffic network, in particular as a result of the "continental system". Newspapers reached the villages as well, of course, as the official bulletins announcing Napoleon's victories. From the pulpit the post-Concordat priests dutifully enunciated the emperor's beneficent deeds and exhortations. But above all it was the veterans of the

Grand Army who brought home with them news of the outside world to their native villages where they enthralled rural youths during the long winter evenings with—more or less truthful—tales of their incredible and magnificent feats. They also introduced new eating habits, in particular a predilection for more meat to which they had grown accustomed in the army and which the peasants were now better able to afford than before. For them, at least, the years of extreme hunger were now a thing of the past.

It may also be true that in addition the Imperial grenadiers brought back horrendous new curses

Stable boy feeding nag. Lithograph by Théodore Géricault, 1822.

La recherche de paternité est interdite.
   Code Napoléon

and syphilis, although they were certainly not the only conveyors of these evils.[1] But they were innocent of the charge of unveiling the mysteries of birth control, the *secrets funestes*, against which the agitated priests railed with all the eloquence at their command in the confessional. From the turn of the century onwards this sterile practice, for which little imagination was required, spread from the towns to the countryside, insofar as this was still necessary. The armed forces did not need to take such precautions as the *Code Napoléon* expressly prohibited paternity suits.

The Château

France is studded with châteaux. They range from Gothic structures with precarious turrets, ornate Renaissance palaces, exquisite Baroque edifices to country mansions, designed either in a lighthearted Rococo style or according to a strict neo-classical harmony. Enveloped by the leafy shade of immaculately tended gardens, perched majestically on a hill or nestling behind a placid lake that reflects their imposing contours, they are priceless artistic and historical gems.

In the 18th century they symbolized something more: the hegemony of the rural aristocracy. The manorial lord was both the local judge and sherriff and the owner of most of the land in the neighbourhood. He was a feudal lord who, although on his own he had little influence on the dense structure of the royal administrative apparatus above him, was within his locality the untrammelled seignorial master of his "vassals". Unless he was some paltry country squire he would delegate the running of his estate to a supervisor whilst he himself hung around the court at Versailles in the hope of receiving further preferment. In between times he busied himself with his pleasures, social engagements or some occupation befitting his status.[2]

The Revolution did away with all this. The aristocracy lost their monopoly of high state and church offices, their pensions, sinecures and military commissions, jurisdictional rights and feudal dues, their share of the common land and finally even their aristocratic titles. Quite a few châteaux went up in flames in 1789 or subsequently, together with their archives and man-

orial records, as the peasants' patience at last snapped. The word "aristocrat" came to have an equally pejorative meaning as "speculator".

A sizeable minority of aristocrats fled abroad, and from 1792 onwards their estates, unless they had been legally transferred in good time to some relative or front man in France, were confiscated by the state. Like the church lands earlier, they were auctioned off as national property, sometimes after being broken up. Thermidor did not alter the situation in any way, and the Directory remained equally implacable vis-à-vis the emigrés: it already had enough trouble on its plate.

It was the Consulate which brought about a change. Bonaparte's policy of reconciliation, which matched the mood of the Republic's weary statesmen, gave the go-ahead for the return of the emigrés which had hitherto been a capital offence. Those who took advantage of the amnesty, from which only the gravest cases of treason were excepted, were entitled to reclaim their former property if it had not yet been bought by anyone. This time most, if not all, overcame their reservations about the Bonapartist régime and accepted the pardon which was proffered to them on a silver platter.

They did not need to be asked twice to relieve themselves of the burden of exile. Back among familiar surroundings, the French aristocracy were able to review the previous decade with the benefit of hindsight.

For the bulk of the survivors things had not gone as badly as had at first seemed likely.[3] Of course, some things were irretrievably lost; thus for the time being they had to wave goodbye to their accustomed extravagant style of living. Yet they managed to salvage rather more than is commonly presumed.

After so many years of neglect the ancestral home, if at all habitable, was often in a poor state of repair and partly denuded, with the gardens overgrown. They bewailed their fate loud and long. The land too, seen primarily as real estate and hence improperly or insufficiently tended, had likewise suffered. Here and there the returning emigrants, usually with good reason, encountered barely concealed mistrust. Since the law was to some extent elastic and rather vague, and sometimes self-contradictory, people bombarded the authorities with petitions or went to court to determine who exactly owned what. One of the

[1] Flandrin, J.L.: *Les amours paysans.* Paris, 1975.
[2] *Der Adel vor der Revolution.* Edited by R. Vierhaus. Göttingen, 1971.
[3] *Denkwürdigkeiten, Rückerinnerungen und Anekdoten aus dem Leben des Grafen von Ségur,* 2 Vols. Stuttgart, 1825–1826.

biggest bones of contention was the ownership of woodland.

It is safe to say, however, that the old nobility, regardless of whether they had stayed in the country or made a judicious return, had no real grounds for complaint about unfair treatment under the Empire[1] once they saw that the hopes which they had nurtured in exile were mere wishful thinking. Rarely has the losing side got off so lightly. Indeed, after reappearing on the scene they were inundated with compliments by the authorities.

At court the Republic's prodigal sons were well received and met with a tolerant and understanding attitude. This did not prevent blue-blooded die-hards from disapprovingly decrying the upstart and his hangers-on at the Tuileries when they were alone. But, with the exception of a few foolish hotheads, they would have nothing more to do with any conspiracies. The Duke of Enghien's execution in 1804 was a painfully vivid memory to them long afterwards, and the "Chevaliers de la foi" (Chevaliers of the Faith), a secret organization led by Grand Master Mathieu de Montmorency (1767–1826) only began to attract support after the Empire had already begun to disintegrate. Until then the royalists kept their

beliefs to themselves, for it was difficult to anticipate which way things would develop. It seemed more propitious to take advantage of the emperor's offer of compromise—or his need for prestigious figureheads of impeccable pedigree. There was also a certain "division of labour" involved. Thus Armand de Caulaincourt functioned as Napoleon's consummate chaperon without ever breaking with his cousin Blacas, who was a close confidant of "Louis XVIII" and in charge of the latter's secret diplomacy.

Younger aristocrats wished to make a career in the army or civil service without bothering too much about the long-term future. No obstacles were placed in their way. On the contrary, the percentage of aristocratic students at military academies shot right up. On the other hand, Napoleon sought to keep questionable individuals well away from the levers of power whenever he could and for as long as he was able. In 1811, for instance, three quarters of his generals were of bourgeois origin. He knew very well that noblemen whom he could still trust when the chips were down were few and far between. Nor did the external glamour of the "good old days" reappear completely, although the aristocracy, forcibly

banished from Paris by law in 1794, gradually began to move back into their townhouses. They now lived less in the Marais area in the city centre, where the imposing palaces of a byegone era— the "hotels" of the Guise and Sully, Colbert and Soubise families—were already falling into decay and had in any case changed hands. They preferred Saint-Germain on the left bank of the Seine, formerly a leafy suburb in the southwest of the capital which looked out onto open countryside. From here the aristocracy set the tone for the *crème de la crème*. Sumptuous banquets or expensive dinners, at which both tables and footmen seemed likely to collapse under the sheer weight, were rare since either the money, credit or the requisite festive spirit was lacking. Of necessity the feudal nobility left this to the *nouveaux riches* or to the eminent "turncoats". Yet this did not mean that they were reduced to the role of passive spectators. They began their ideological counter-offensive in the great salons which were frequented by simply "tout Paris".

These had little in common with the high-class dens of iniquity of the post-Thermidor and Directory periods in which the spirit of hedonism once again reared its frenzied head and became an end in itself. Some of the faces from the past, albeit with a few more wrinkles, now reappeared, but most of them had been swept away by the cold wind of Brumaire. Other venues of social intercourse exerted a magnetic pull on the visitors, while the direct exhibition of female charms gave way to more refined customs which harked back to the traditions of the *ancien régime*.

As before, the salon was a centre of information, a barometer of public opinion and a place for making contacts: of a political, financial, literary or a more salacious kind.[2] There the old aristocracy rubbed shoulders with the new men who, due to the unfathomable vagaries of fate, now had the whiphand. They judged the time not yet ripe to openly challenge them or to try and win them over. They listened to and sounded one another out, struck up useful acquaintances, leaked and spread rumours—sometimes also to foreign ears. Frequenters of salons informed themselves or others about the latest developments in public as in more private affairs. At the same time one was expected to be able to converse with eloquence, to engage in scintillating or at least witty repartee, to divine unspoken thoughts and to display elegance with a nonchalant air.

It was incumbent upon the hostess, to whom the visitors paid their respects, to handle each gathering on her "jour fixe" with a delicate touch and to make it an enjoyable occasion while carefully guiding the course of the conversation. She was expected to draw out bashful patrons and to restrain the more extrovert guests. No salon hostess was more adept at playing with fire without (almost) ever burning her fingers than Madame Récamier, who was idolized by her clientèle.

Julie Bernard was born in Lyons in 1777 of patrician stock and married a much older Parisian banker who was among those who financed the First Consul's celebration victory. He was a Brumairian financial magnate who did not hesitate to put his wife on display and in the process to live beyond his means. Their two palatial residences in the Rue du Montblanc had previously been the domicile of Necker and his daughter, Germaine de Staël. The neighbourhood veritably bristled with aristocratic millionaires: Marmont's father-in-law Perrégaux had settled there in the Hôtel de l'Empire. Ouvrard and Laffitte also moved in. None of them was of ancient lineage, they were all wealthy men of the new era who,

however, deemed it meet to befriend the traditional conservative aristocracy and to open for the latter a few doors which it would have been better to keep closed.

Ouvrard used an "insider" for this purpose: Madame de Montesson. He bought her mansion but kept her on as a grey-haired figurehead. The morganatic widow of the Duke of Orléans knew as a matter of course just about everyone who had survived from the *ancien régime* as well as Bonaparte, whom she had presented with a mathematics prize when he was a fourteen year-old cadet at a military school. He was happy to see her gracefully draw together the social élite from the past and the present and fuse them into a new synthesis which was thoroughly in keeping with his own wish.

What Julie Récamier lacked in aristocratic ancestry she made up for with a charm with which she even captivated fellow members of the fair sex— a rare accomplishment indeed. Her portrait by Gérard, which was reproduced in encyclopaedias around the world, shows a delicate face which smiles in an inviting yet non-committal manner at the beholder, an alluringly aloof lady. She successfully employed her capacity to enchant and bewitch others, e.g. General Moreau and General Bernadotte, Talleyrand and David, Benjamin Constant and her bosom friend Chateaubriand,[3] until she was expelled from Paris in 1812 by Napoleon who at last, and not without good grounds, came to suspect that her salon was a focus of royalist opposition. In 1814, however, she was able to resume her winning ways, this time enthralling Tsar Alexander and an enraptured widower, Frederick William III of Prussia.

Living in town was one thing, earning one's keep there was quite another, assuming one did not want to sully one's hands with honest toil. This option, unlike in the past, was now open to everyone, but it was not everyone's cup of tea. Not every nobleman descended from a long and illustrious lineage was ready or willing to take up a bourgeois profession or to lend a helping hand to the little Corsican lieutenant. Hence many withdrew instead to their country estate.

Here relations had changed a great deal during the previous decade, though not as radically as had at first seemed likely when the Revolution mobilized the peasants. The latter did not rest

Ass tracing his pedigree ("He has located his grandfather"). Folio 39 from the series "Los Caprichos". Aquatint by Francisco de Goya, 1797 to 1799.

Page 86:
View of the Hôtel de Soubise in Paris. During the revolutionary period the palace was taken over by the state and in 1808 it became the site of the state archives. Engraving by Jean-Baptiste Rigaud after Jacques Rigaud, c. 1750–1760.

[1] Marquise de La Tour du Pin: *Journal d'une femme de cinquante ans (1778–1815)*. Paris, 1914.

[2] Sophie Gay (née Nichault de Lavalette): *Salons célèbres*. Paris, 1837.

[3] Chateaubriand, F. R. de: *Über Bonaparte und die Bourbonen*. Hamburg, 1814.

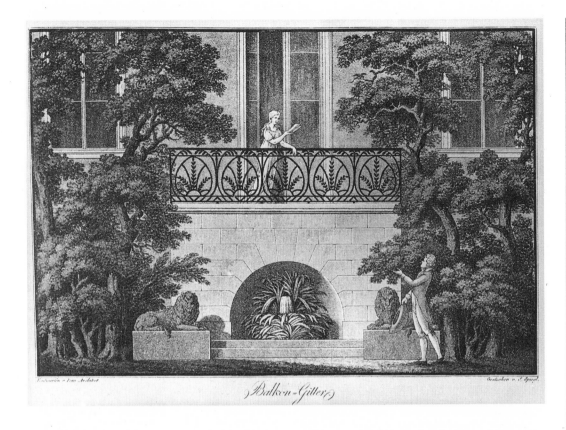

Balcony of a country house. Engraving by Joseph Spiegl after Georg Pein. From: *Ideen zur äussern und innern Verzierung der Gebäude*, Vol. 1. Vienna, 1809.

Departure of the hunter. Aquatint by Jean-Pierre Jazet after Carle Vernet.

until they had freed their land from the last vestige of seignorial privilege. Quite often they forced their terrified lord to utter the imprecise but pregnant declaration that he belonged to the Third Estate. In fact, in the end he could count himself very lucky not to be labelled a "suspect" and so suffer a much worse fate. On the other hand there was no real assault, either by the peasants or by the revolutionary theorists who played a part in the politics of the Revolution, on the big landed estates as such.

This was not the aim behind the nationalization of the church lands or the expropriation of the political emigrés. The "agrarian law" remained a tame paper tiger. The Ventôse decrees of 1794 did prompt Saint-Just to air his utopian idea of a republic of independent producers and of an egalitarian and overwhelmingly petty-bourgeois France, but it quickly vanished without a trace after Thermidor.

The average farmer who—whether big or small—clung tenaciously to his personal property, had no objection to the manorial lord similarly enjoying the fruits of ownership as long as he did not meddle in affairs which did not concern him. The manorial system was finished, but the big landed estates remained, and the Empire did everything in its power to nurture and strengthen them. If a returning emigré reclaimed that part of his land to which he was entitled under the Consulate, he likewise became—in this respect—an agrarian capitalist, i.e. an agricultural entrepreneur within the framework of a modern market economy,[1] just like his counterpart who had remained in France. So did the new nobility who had acquired property either as the result of an Imperial gift or through purchase, so too did the rentier. The latter still preferred to invest a considerable portion of his surplus capital in real estate (often, but not always, within the town), as this retained its value. And so too—in exceptional cases—did the *coq de village* who, whether as a wealthy farmer, cattle dealer, innkeeper or usurer who had managed, from an economic viewpoint but not in his individual lifestyle, to join the ranks of the landowning class.

Thus the old-established rural aristocracy had to get used to this new environment and to unwelcome plebeian neighbours. This by no means meant that the two strata merged into one. Napo-

[1] CAMPARDON, E.: *Liste des membres de la noblesse impériale dressée d'après les registres de lettres patentes conservés aux Archives Nationales.* Paris, 1889.

leon's attempts to play the go-between were even less successful than his efforts on the "marriage marts" which he himself set up in Paris and which were established in the départements by the prefects at his behest to find suitable "heiresses" and wed them to deserving candidates. The aim was the breeding of an élite caste through the amalgamation of the old and new nobility, firmly underpinned by money and land.

Much of the rural nobility led a secluded and modest life far from the pitfalls of shady power politics. Those who could afford it whiled away the time in cavalier fashion with inspections or walks, by riding, driving, hunting and reading or in light conversation with a few friends as of yore. The nobleman was an ardent churchgoer and now devoted more time than before to the education of his children. His lady wife maintained the

rural custom of charitable works, which gained her the affection of the poor. Sometimes this aroused the ire of their less genteel bourgeois neighbour who found it more difficult to assume the role of a fatherly protector of the innocent poor and who could by no means always count on the parish priest as his ally. Many, however, considered ways to boost their income and concluded that they could best do this by managing their

Road sweeper. Etching by Jean Duplessi-Bertaux from the series "The Beggars".

[1] COMTE MOLÉ: *Sa vie et ses mémoires.* Paris, 1922; ROCHECHOUART, L. V. L. DE: *Souvenirs.* Paris, 1889.

[2] CHAPTAL: *De l'industrie française.* Paris, 1889.

[3] LELEUX, F.: *Liévin-Bauwens, industriel gantois.* Paris, 1969.

estates themselves. It was undoubtedly the physiocrats who initiated this economic awareness, but in the 18th century few individuals found agricultural production an activity which both fulfilled them and filled their coffers. In general the local lord preferred to lease his fields to peasants who possessed insufficient land of their own. Some estates, usually extremely fertile ones, he rented out en bloc to a large-scale tenant farmer who in turn either employed labourers to cultivate the land for him or else sublet it in individual lots to smaller tenants. The lord would then retain only his gardens, grounds and stables around the mansion, a chicken-run, a hunting preserve and possibly also a vineyard so that he could make his own wine.

Under the Empire there was a significant increase in the number of manorial lords who used the chance to establish themselves as working landowners, i.e. to develop from rentiers into producers. This tendency took firm root in the course of the century. Undoubtedly the continuing seller's market which resulted from the years of war and the naval blockade played a big part in this, and some very eminent and illustrious individuals led the way. General Lafayette, who defected to the Austrians in 1792 only to be rewarded with a lengthy spell of imprisonment, marked his (temporary) withdrawal into private life by devoting himself to the systematic breeding of sheep so as to cater for the promising wool market. The emperor, who was a keen mathematician, saw to it that the science of statistics now came into its own. These records reveal that, whereas the nobility fared pretty well, the process of revolutionary and democratic agrarian reform remained unfinished. It was the job of the prefects to draw up lists of all the biggest tax payers in their département which then served as a basis for the appointment of "notables of the Empire". Of course, statistics only tell part of the story. It was far easier to avoid paying tax on mobile capital than on immobile landed property, which could be precisely measured and assessed. But concerning the latter, at least, the figures do provide a fairly accurate picture. They demonstrate that although, as compared with the *ancien régime*, the landowning bourgeoisie had made considerable headway, the old feudal aristocracy continued to account for a majority of the big landowners in most départements. In almost every case it was to this class that the wealthiest individuals and therefore top tax payers belonged.

This explains why, despite forfeiting its old corporate privileges and public functions, it continued to exert a strong moral influence in the countryside well beyond the duration of the Empire. Certainly it had to adjust economically to the bourgeois system and its legal stipulations.[1] However, combining the virtues of upholders of tradition with those of major agricultural entrepreneurs, the rural nobility retained their characteristic lifestyle in the aftermath of the twist which their millennial history had taken.

The Workshop

Even during the Revolution Finance Minister Cambon admitted before the Convention: "The English do everything with machines while the French still do almost everything by hand."

The era of large-scale manufacturing, which was starting to alter the face of the earth, did indeed begin in the British Isles at the end of the 18th century. The transition was very painful and led many artisans, who feared the worst from the imminent changes, to resist them. However, nothing and no one could now halt the triumphal forward march of the more productive technology and with it the birth in the cities of a mass industrial proletariat.

Together with the "rest of the world", France slowly began to follow the trail blazed by England. The revolutionary bourgeoisie had improved their chances and had helped to maximize the mobility of entrepreneurial initiative. But the path to the widespread establishment on the continent of fully equipped factories was to be a long one, full of setbacks and often trod only hesitantly. Under the Empire the craft workshop and the manufactory were still the paramount forms of industrial production.[2]

The handicrafts weathered the storm of 1791—when guild restrictions were lifted—with mixed feelings, depending on the particular trade. Marat's fear that, on the one hand, the economically strong forces would crush their weaker counterparts and, on the other, that the abolition of examinations for journeymen and master craftsmen would lead to slapdash work so that it would soon become impossible to buy a decent hat, proved to be exaggerated. Although such things did occur, the enforced competition between the various master craftsmen for the favour of the discerning customers ensured that the supplier of cheap and shoddy goods did not gain the upper hand. The upright tradesman who did a skilful and solid job of work and who showed himself to be reliable was not going to be displaced overnight. By refusing to grant licences the local authorities could combat the danger of individual branches of industry becoming saturated. Thus in prosperous years business was middling to good for most of them. A steady flow of orders enabled many to do very nicely. Many a successful master craftsman was able to enjoy a comfortable middle-class existence: goldsmiths, who under the guild system had already been among the top earners; bricklayers, who became building contractors and landlords; much sought-after cabinet makers from the faubourg Saint-Antoine, who became furniture manufacturers; and weavers, who were able to expand their domestic workshops. Some even opted for early retirement, transferred their business to their son or son-in-law and lived off their accrued income for their remaining years.

In France, as elsewhere, the days of handicraft production were numbered. Though enjoying both demand and respect, this mode of production was merely marking time, whereas established or new manufacturers were extending their industrial empires all over the country, partly through the system of cottage industry but also via the establishment of large centralized workshops in former châteaux, disused monasteries or (more rarely) in new buildings. Such entrepreneurs as De Wendel, Köchlin and Liévin-Bauwens[3] expanded and improved their stock of machines. Douglas installed wool-carding machines while Philippe de Girard introduced his new linen-spinning machine. Completing the picture, scientists and inventors such as Chaptal, Berthollet and Leblanc themselves tried their hand at production. The Empire banked on the inventiveness of such pioneers and granted many privileges to tireless originators of the calibre of Guillaume Ternaux (1762–1833) who opened up new avenues in the cloth industry. On his travels Napoleon made a special point of visiting and admiring their factories. He awarded prizes for in-

ventions and bestowed a decoration on Joseph Marie Jacquard (1752–1834), a silk weaver and mechanic from Lyons, for his design of a power loom in 1805 which could reproduce large-format patterns. Recurrent industrial exhibitions, held on the Champs de Mars or in the courtyard of the Louvre, encouraged the interchange of ideas and the spirit of rivalry. In 1806 more than 1,400 exhibitors took part from all over France. Benevolence of a more subdued kind—owing to its dependence on imported raw materials—was shown to the cotton industry. Yet it was precisely this branch of industry which achieved the most meteoric development, as exemplified by François Richard (1765–1839), a peasant's son who was a symbolic figure of the industrial boom. Having accrued the necessary starting capital by speculating in nationalized land he linked up with a businessman, Jean Daniel Lenoir-Dufresne, to trade in fabrics. By introducing a fixed price system they achieved high profits which enabled them to begin manufacturing the merchandise themselves. Outdoing their English rivals, they combined wool with cotton to produce the greatly prized material known as bombasine. They established workshops for spinning and weaving, at first in the Hôtel Thorigny and in the former monastery of Bon-Secours in Paris, but soon they expanded across Picardy and Normandy with their new premises. When Lenoir died in 1806 Richard added his partner's name to his own since the firm was already well established under the dual title of Richard-Lenoir. A few years later the "French cotton king" was employing a workforce of more than 12,000. Nonetheless it would be presumptuous to speak of the triumph of the manufacturing bourgeoisie at this stage. Just as they had been under the *ancien régime*, the lines of demarcation between industrialists, big businessmen and bankers remained fluid. Though the proportion of capital invested in industrial production rose, it came nowhere near to ousting merchant capital from its leading position. For this the young, venturesome big businessmen still had a far too insecure base. Like so many gamblers these adventurous pioneers of the new epoch often speculated at random, overestimated their reserves with carefree abandon and disdained to put aside any considerable funds for a rainy day. In wild pursuit of the great coup they immediately invested all the

gains which they had quickly managed to accumulate via the liberal use of their elbows in their own enterprises which had in the meantime grown into chains of factories, and in buying up rival undertakings. Not infrequently such breakneck expansion at any price—in true Napoleonic style—led to ruination, and they lost everything that they had staked. Concurrently with the collapse of the Empire in 1814, such captains of industry as Liévin-Bauwens and Richard-Lenoir also went bankrupt.

It was not always management teething troubles or unsound business practices which were to blame. The most highly modernized industry which had achieved the greatest degree of mechanization—the cotton-spinning industry—was one of the victims of Napoleon's economic blockade: the dearth of sufficient imports of raw materials came perilously close to choking the industry to death.

The fact that, on the whole, the rate of change in large-scale industry was fairly gradual also precluded any abrupt upheaval in the pattern of working life.

The working people in urban areas did not as yet constitute a clearly delineated, more or less homogeneous social class with a common character. In particular they still lacked a cohesive sense of class consciousness and an awareness of the social status of labour. An attitude of uncertainty still prevailed which was reflected in the confused contemporary self-portrayals. Most workers classified themselves as part of a generic trade group. Thus the description "weavers" covered both factory employees and homeworkers, journeymen as well as masters. *Ouvrier*, i.e. worker, was a term also used by small-scale employers to describe themselves while, significantly, the expression *indigent* (needy) could be equally applied to either a worker or a poor man. Babeuf's *prolétaire*, a scholarly loanword taken from Roman history and as such a favourite epithet of men of letters (and not only those of a left-wing persuasion) was synonymous with and symbolic of the anonymous mass of the people, the have-nots, all those who had a "deficiency of property", one of the twenty-four million whom the "tribune of the people" counterposed to the "golden million" who constituted the bourgeoisie.

In relation to the actual working folk, the *hommes du labour*[1] this estimate is very wide of the mark. They numbered around two million, give or take a few, although in big centres of industry such as Paris they might account for half of all those employed. The Imperial police kept a permanent eye on them for, owing to their constant fluctuation, it was very difficult to keep tabs on them all. They were regarded as a troublesome element, easily upset if they thought they had been wronged. At the workplace manifestations of a strong corporate identity were widespread and easily led to instances of "riotous assembly".

What made these workers tick?

They were not interested in politics, nor did they identify with any particular political grouping. Their concern was the struggle for better pay and working conditions in this "open" society in which the workers, from both a moral and a legal point of view, were rated as mere "underlings".

Thanks to the Revolution the working day now lasted on average only ten hours or little longer: from 5 a.m. to 7 p.m. in the summer and from 6 a.m. to 6 p.m. in winter, including breaks. This was some two hours less than under the *ancien régime*. On the other hand the number of religious holidays had been substantially reduced, nor was the principle of keeping Sunday a rest day always adhered to. However, by way of compensation they often observed the old custom of skipping work on Mondays. Whereas in handicraft enterprises the working rhythm was hallowed by traditional guild convention and hence was often rather leisurely, a carefully conceived system of deductions from wages and bonus payments prevailed in the factories which fostered higher production. There was virtually no health and safety protection; in the absence of such safety precautions the number of accidents at work rose and was particularly prevalent in the building trade.

Whenever workers submitted demands to their employers these were usually formulated in such a way as to suggest that they were seeking redress for the infringement of traditional rights, or else for what they considered the unfair dismissal of a workmate. Their efforts were not always unsuc-

Large-scale spooling device above the silk-threading machines (left) and sketch of a silk-threading machine (right). Engravings by an unknown artist.

From: *Encyclopédie ou Dictionnaire universel raisonné, mis en ordre par M. de Felice*, Vol. IX. Yverdon, 1779.

The whole world agrees that the previous exhibitions were much less well attended, which testifies to the advances made by our industry.
Champagny to Napoleon, October 4, 1806.

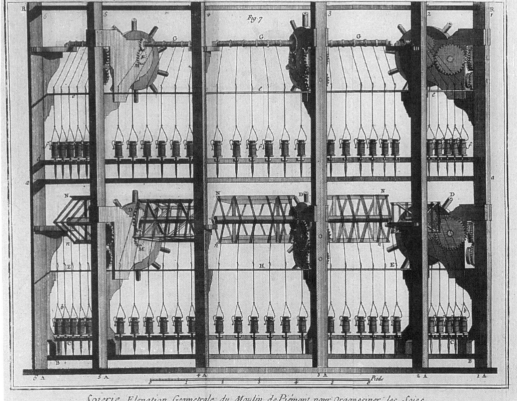

Soierie, Elevation Geometrale du Moulin de Piémont pour Organsiner les Soies

[1] VAUTHIER, G.: *Les ouvriers de Paris sous l'Empire*. Paris, 1913.

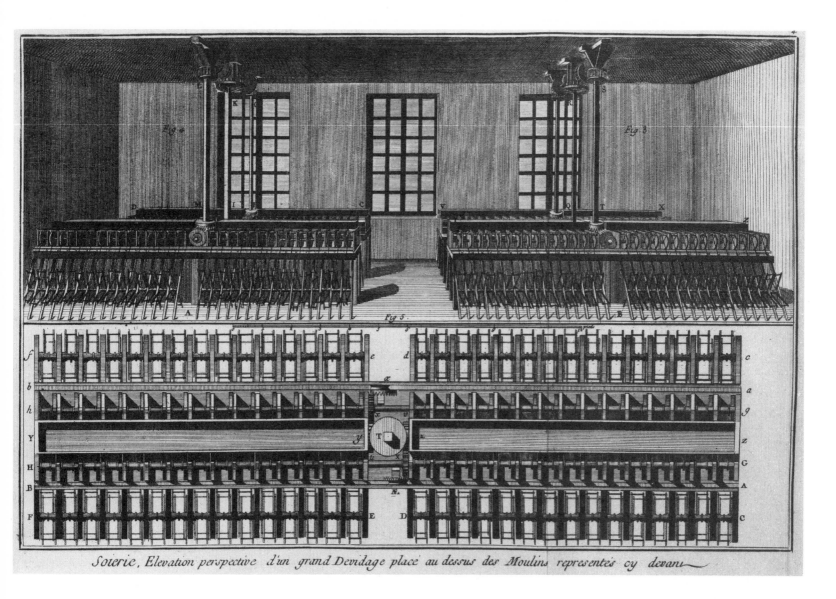

Soierie, Elevation perspective d'un grand Devidage placé au dessus des Moulins representés cy devant

cessful. They demanded that the low price of bread, established during the Revolution, be maintained, and in the capital at least this aim was attained. When a new regulation was introduced which deprived Parisian building workers of their midday lunch break, they replied in October 1806 with a sensational week-long stoppage and managed to achieve their main demand.

In fact strikes were more common than is commonly supposed. They were reported, at various times, from all over the country: from Sedan and Lille in the north to Bordeaux and Lyons in the south. There were strikes in mines and factories, on building sites and in textile plants, at abattoirs and in munitions workshops, but always involving relatively small groups of people, numbering at most a few hundred. They never covered any extensive area, were limited to individual actions or to a particular branch of industry or to a single workforce. Nor did they last long. Both sides were keen to come to a quick decision.

In principle the government favoured the employers, but they also expected them to contribute—e.g. by eliminating the most glaring abuses—to restoring industrial calm as quickly as possible. On the other hand it tended to punish stoppages in pursuit of higher wages, and more especially physical attacks on strikebreakers, with the arrest of the spokesmen or by labour conscription, whereupon the expression of discontent soon ceased. Another tried-and-tested method of cooling down tempers was the threat of banishment from Paris. The workers were reluctant to attempt a head-on collision with the state. Nobody was willing without good reason to give up the high wages paid in Paris or any of the other attractions of life in the capital.

It was therefore easy for the authorities to rid themselves of any troublemakers. They were well enough aware that the law, which ultimately they made themselves, was on their side and that they could resort to it whenever they liked. No right of appeal existed for the victims. The ban on strikes and combinations enshrined in the notorious

Le Chapelier law of 1791 remained in full force. The Imperial authorities needed only to apply it. What is more, the introduction of a labour pass-book, *livret d'ouvrier*, which had to be shown and deposited at the place of work, enabled the employer to keep a very strict check on his employees, especially in the factories.

Yet however innocuous the workers in Imperial France might appear as a whole, they nevertheless tried to get round regulations, which they were either unable or unwilling to attack or infringe directly, in other ways. Convinced that the only way they could achieve anything was through the extension of solidarity and support to one another, they formed, along with a few small employers, charitable organizations or mutual aid associations, known as *mutuelles*, in order to assist each other. This was done, for example, by the glovemakers in Grenoble in 1803 and the shoemakers (among others) of Paris in 1804. They were followed in 1806 by the tanners and

lapidaries and in 1808 by the locksmiths and weavers. Between 1805 and 1813 there were ten printworkers' associations in Paris alone and four silkweavers' organizations in Lyons.[1] In the whole of France there were about a hundred of these mutual clubs, including in Bordeaux and Roubaix. This was by no means a large number, and they never encompassed more than a single craft. It was no more than a tentative start but, as a portent of future developments, several included in their rules the motto: "Beset on all sides, the workers support one another."

Far more numerous than the new mutual clubs were the journeymen's organizations or fraternal societies, which often dated back to the Middle Ages. In theory they were secret fraternities, but everyone (including the authorities) knew about them. They were tightly organized and had their own rituals, recognition symbols and a hierarchy of elected officials, plus hostels and support funds for travelling journeymen and for sick and infirm

members. Not even the Revolution managed to destroy them completely.

They laid great stress on respectability and acknowledged the prevailing order even though the latter often irritably picked on them as illicit or at least not expressly authorized bodies. In cases of both minor and major labour conflict it was often they who, as adversaries of the masters, took charge of the dispute. Their efforts were geared towards freely negotiated contracts and mutually agreed compromises. However, these objectives were by no means always attained in a spirit of peaceful and amicable reasonableness on both sides. At times, such as in Nantes in 1804 and 1806, members of kindred trades engaged in "bloody" battles with one another, e.g. blacksmiths and whitesmiths, or carpenters and roofers. Much energy was dissipated, to the satisfaction of both the masters and the police, on fratricidal strife between rival leaderships, each of which challenged the other's supremacy. Hence the associations never emerged as united and powerful bodies.

In their whole structure the journeymen's associations harked back to the old craft guilds, of which they were antiquated oppositional forms. Although under the Empire the handicraft journeymen probably remained the most numerous and self-assured section of the working population, they were no longer unarguably the leading and trendsetting group. The living and working conditions of the miners, homeworkers, factory and farm workers or day and casual labourers differed markedly from their own.[2]

Although all these groups already existed under the *ancien régime*, they fitted in more easily with a free market economy, despite the fact that they existed only on its margins. It was the "patron" who profited most from the readily available and portable commodity which they had to offer, namely their labour power. Above all it was the factory owners who recognized how much profit could be extracted from the employment of women and children, since they cost only a half or even a third of the price of employing adult males. Whereas a craft apprentice had not started working for his master until the age of fourteen—or twelve at the very earliest—in the wool and cotton industry children began at the age of seven. Nor was this an extreme or exceptional case. At their large factory at Amilly near Montargis the Périer Brothers set on nearly six hundred boys and girls

Gericault del · Chez Gihaut b⁺⁴ des Italiens N⁰ 5 · Lith. de Villain

aged between eleven and thirteen. In some areas, indeed, the demand for such juvenile labour exceeded the supply, and the industrialists were continually besieging the government to allocate more minors to them from the orphanages and poorhouses. Few moral scruples were shown by the manufacturers who, following the Battle of Austerlitz in 1805, applied to have the children of French soldiers who had died in the fighting entrusted to their "care".

What such welfare amounted to in practice can be seen even in the official reports of the prefects: fed on a poor, unbalanced and meagre diet, taxed beyond the limits of their frail bodies and with insufficient leisure time in which to recuperate, very few of these mites grew up to become serviceable recruits. Their height was less than average, and well below that required in the Guards, their constitution was weak and they were prone to consumption. Since sufficient recruits could still be obtained from other sources, no social welfare legislation was introduced to ameliorate their condition. Only in the mining industry was one small advance registered—and even there not until 1813—when the minimum working age was raised to ten.

In most branches of industry the real take-home pay of the workers was a little higher than outside France, albeit substantially lower than in that great magnet of migrants, America. On the whole it showed a rising tendency, and for highly skilled workers might approximate to that of office workers, minor officials or army lieutenants.[3] This is confirmed by the impressions of all foreign observers who travelled through France.

Although the pay of most unskilled and semi-skilled workers was appreciably lower than that of the top earners, even they were not quite on starvation wages. The working man could now feed his family in a more varied fashion than before, and clothe them better. The purchase of bread no longer accounted for half his income. Social advancement was still difficult and extremely rare, but not automatically ruled out. Educational facilities for children of the working class remained deplorable, and they lived in unbelievably appalling conditions which resulted in frequent illness and premature death: dirty, devoid of any hygiene or sanitation, as often as not dank, dark, mildew-ridden hovels in basements or at-

tics into which far too many people were crammed into a tiny space since the rent was so expensive. However, the picture was similar or even worse throughout Europe and would remain so for a long time to come.

Consequently the dire fate of the propertyless labourer was bewailed by many an upstanding philanthropist from the "educated classes". But Robert Owen (1771–1858), a Welsh nonconformist who from 1799 onwards was a successful manager and co-owner of a cotton mill in New Lanark in Scotland, construed philanthropy as the task of gradually improving the lot of mankind, and decided to start with his own two thousand employees. He reduced the number of hours they had to work and inaugurated a sickness and pension scheme for his work force. He provided his workers with, for that time, a very decent standard of housing. He radically cut the working time of the five hundred children from the orphanages and poorhouses in his employ and provided them with a "polytechnical" education in infant, day and evening classes.

Since he still managed to show a profit (which he fixed by statute at five per cent in 1813), his paternalistic philosophy aroused considerable interest well beyond the borders of the British Isles. New Lanark became a centre of pilgrimage for the advocates of reform, and Owen himself energetically publicized his experiment. He exhorted manufacturers to follow suit, since he had established that his approach was beneficial both to himself and others, not least from a pecuniary point of view. An indefatigable letter-writer who corresponded with people all over the world, he witnessed the "great attention given to the dead machinery, and the neglected disregard of the living machinery",[4] and proposed that his fellow employers would do better to devote more time and capital to the latter.

The rejection which his moderate calls for a humane working world met with from the hard-boiled industrialists—especially as he coupled them with a negation of religion—drove Owen further. By 1820 he was no longer merely demanding reforms but also a transformation of the existing social system, which he endeavoured to implement in 1825 in his communistic model community of New Harmony in America: a social utopia by means of which the peaceable Welshman sought to give a wide berth to the class

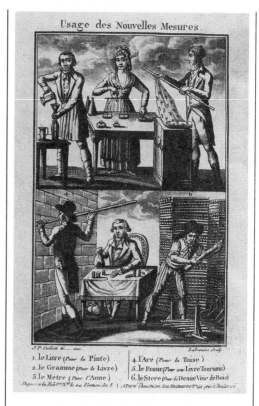

Application of new weights and measures. Engraving by Labrousse after J. P. Delion, 1800.

Page 94:
Blacksmiths. Lithograph by Théodore Géricault, 1823.

Among building workers the disputes arise quickest and are hardest to settle. The reason for this is that often a large number of workers are concentrated on the same site. Some hooligan then puts forward an irresponsible proposal and immediately they all lend their backing as if it were a matter of honour.
Report by Chief of Police Pasquier, 1807.

[1] CHAUVET, P.: *Les ouvriers du livre en France de 1789 à la constitution de la Fédération du livre.* Paris, 1956.
[2] CHEVALIER, L.: *Classes dangereuses et classes laborieuses à Paris, pendant la première moitié du XIXᵉ siècle.* Paris, 1958.
[3] KUCZYNSKI, J.: *Darstellung der Lage der Arbeiter in Frankreich von 1789 bis 1848.* Berlin, 1967.
[4] OWEN, R.: *A New View of Society* (1813).

struggle and revolution. At the same time, as one of the founding fathers of the cooperative movement, he later urged the young working class to take a direct hand in the grand reshaping of society.

Napoleon took great care not to get even remotely involved in such ventures. To his mind it was a big enough achievement to keep the workers supplied with bread and in good spirits. He believed that in the whole of French history they had never had it so good as under the Imperial eagle. True enough, during the first few months of Robespierre's rule they had been able to say whatever they liked, but the cupboard had been bare. Now some branches of the economy were characterized by an almost explosive growth, and Napoleon, as a general and the patriarch of the nation, was directly associated with this: first of all with his cannon foundries and ordnance factories; then through the re-routing of maritime traffic, which created work for coachbuilders, wheelwrights and carters; via the award of contracts for the making of uniforms; and finally on account of his spate of civil engineering and road-building projects. As a result of the craze for silk during the Empire and its propagation throughout Europe—and also thanks to the emperor's personal good offices—the silk weavers of Lyons witnessed a spectacular upturn in trade which had been at such a low ebb during the Revolution and the revolutionary wars. Meanwhile, the fashion and luxury goods industries benefited from the fact that Paris had regained its leading role in matters of taste. Conquests expanded the market, which in turn increased production. To a small degree this was reflected in the wage packet.

However, this relatively rosy picture would be incomplete without a mention of those who lost out during this period: the shipbuilding workers, seamen and those who processed goods from overseas. In these trades traditional jobs were lost due to the effects of enemy action, as it were. Even so, those affected found alternative employment and adapted to the changing times—apart, that is, from those whose corpses littered the battlefields.

It would be inappropriate to make rash generalizations. The workers of Imperial France cannot be lumped together; their personal views and feelings were equally as varied as their economic and social position. Neither the figure of the proud father taking his family out for a Sunday picnic in the country nor that of the unemployed man sinking to the level of a beggar typified the mass of the workers.

The workers had no cause to behave in a particularly pro-Napoleonic manner, but nor can it be said that they went to the opposite extreme. Some of them, having personally experienced the Revolution, may in their heart of hearts have cherished the word "republic" like some magic formula and thought more highly of General Bonaparte than of the Emperor Napoleon. Yet on the other hand it was precisely such men from the revolutionary stronghold of Saint-Antoine, workers as well as petty-bourgeois, who swore never to abandon their leader after his defeat at Waterloo in 1815 but rather to continue the struggle against the Bourbon restoration and the conspiracy of European princes. They offered their reluctant leader their strong arms for this purpose. In this they were partly—but not wholly—the victims of self-delusion.

The Bourgeois

A bourgeois society within a bourgeois state was the goal of the men of the Third Estate as they set about fundamentally transforming France during the Revolution. Outfitted with the knowledge of the Enlightenment, nothing and no one could shake their confidence in their own supreme capabilities or their belief that there was no viable historical alternative to them. On the other hand the political representatives of the bourgeoisie at no time showed themselves willing to expand their understanding of liberty and equality to encompass the mass democratization of society. And they cold-bloodedly dropped those Jacobins who, at a time of intense national crisis, were prepared to countenance such notions of public welfare just as soon as the Republic had weathered the worst of the storms.

Under the Thermidorians the Revolution seemed to them to have run its course. They regarded the terms *citoyen* and *bourgeois* as virtually interchangeable. The advent of the Directory put the propertied bourgeoisie firmly in control, but stability and prosperity still proved elusive. These were achieved under the Consulate and con-

solidated under the Empire. To this extent the Brumairians kept their promise. The price which they demanded and exacted in return was high. The bourgeoisie had to relinquish all hopes of directly controlling the political decision-making process and of exercising power, they had to accept the role of impotent bystanders while the generals chased one another half way round the world, and they had to kowtow to a self-willed and hence often insufferable new supremo who on principle regarded all businessmen as rogues. As long as business prospered they were prepared to put up with being muzzled. Boundless vistas opened up for those who neither passed up the chance nor overplayed their hand.

Yet what exactly was the identity and nature of the bourgeois under the Imperial tricolour? Was he still *le bourgeois gentilhomme*, as portrayed by Molière, or like the hero of contemporary moral comedies penned by such writers as Picard and Collin d'Harleville?

Right at the top of the ladder stood the big businessman who had already inherited and multiplied capital before the Revolution, either as a trader or a banker, a shareholder or a manufacturer, and often combining several of these roles.[1] If he had liquid assets which he was prepared to invest elsewhere, he was referred to as *financier* or *capitaliste*. Subsequently quite a number of owners watched their banks or businesses swept away by the revolutionary tide. Firms in the previously thriving ports of Marseilles, Bordeaux, Nantes, Rouen and Le Havre, which were cut off by the naval blockade, were particularly hard hit. Others clawed their way back up the slippery slope using fair means or foul, and paid the wealth tax without batting an eyelid. Possessing the ability to both act and react quickly, they worked as army contractors on the basis of industrial production or else tried to save their skins as importers and thereby usually managed to survive—often quite nicely.

Under the Directory they soon fell on their feet again and rapidly amassed and surpassed the first million mark—always the hardest hurdle. Claude Périer from Dauphiné was arguably the most important of them. In 1788 he hosted and financed the legendary meeting of the Estates at his château in Vizille near Grenoble, and in 1795 managed to buy up a majority shareholding in the large coal-mining complex at Anzin with a sackful of assignats. Before he died in 1801 he drew up on behalf of the Brumairians the statutes of the newly-founded Bank of France, the leading national credit institution, and accordingly became its first *régent*.[2] He was the founding father of a long-lived dynasty of financial magnates. The family fortune was divided up during the Empire among his eight sons and two sons-in-law. These included some of Napoleon's leading officials—plus Casimir Périer, a future prime minister under the "bourgeois monarch", Louis Philippe. Yet fate was by no means equally as kind to the whole of the old-style bourgeoisie. Considerable numbers of maladroit and conservative rentiers who had failed to invest in material assets, such as the expropriated estates, emerged from the Revolution with incomes dented by inflation and lowered living standards. Quite apart from their other losses, the state's insolvency—though kept within the bounds of moderation—ultimately cheated them out of two thirds of their savings and income. This came to light as early as 1798 during the attempt to restore financial stability (the so-called "liquidation Ramel"), i.e. at a time when Bonaparte had not yet appeared on the scene as he was still playing around in the Egyptian sand. Thus neither the bankers nor their precursors could blame him for it. In spite of this cautionary experience not a few ventured to transfer their trust to the emperor and to buy his bonds, whereupon they once again, though not until 1814, fell from the frying pan into the fire.

More conspicuous, more disreputable and hence more frequently the subject of gossip were the *nouveaux riches*, the ones who cashed in on the boom generated during the revolutionary and war years. Often they had little capital to start with; rarely did they rise from rags to riches through simply backing a hunch at the right moment. Some of them feathered their nests with relative ease by buying and re-selling nationalized property, through currency speculation or by means of pawnbroking. Those who did not set their sights so high invested to their profit in a house, a shop, a tavern or a vineyard, stashed their money safely away or else lent it out at a good rate of interest. They followed the example of the old-established owners of real estate, the *propriétaires*, or simply the *bourgeois*, who lived off their rents, and led a middling sort of existence without upsetting anyone or arousing ill-will.

Jacques Laffitte. Portrait of him in his later years. Steel engraving by Ferdinand Bahmann after Julien.

What do they owe me? They were poor when I arrived and poor when I left them. But their instincts tell them what is necessary, and they reflect the feelings of the whole country.
Napoleon, June 21, 1815.

[1] BERGERON, L.: *Banquiers, négociants et manufacturiers à Paris*. Lille, 1975.
[2] SZRAMKIEWICZ, R.: *Les Régents et les Censeurs de la Banque de France*. Paris, 1974.
[3] *Mémoires de Gabriel-Jules Ouvrard sur sa vie et ses diverses opérations financières*, 3 Vols. Paris, 1826–1827;
WOLFF, O.: *Die Geschäfte des Herrn Ouvrard*. Frankfurt/Main, 1933.

Others gambled everything they had, and for quite a few of these big speculators and profiteers it was sooner or later a question of easy come, easy go. Not everyone was as fortunate as Balzac's *Père Goriot* who by means of his hoarded wealth was able to launch his ungrateful daughter into high society. Even that speculator par excellence, Gabriel Ouvrard (1770–1846) alternated constantly between sensational success and abject failure.[3] He started off as a small-time associate of a businessman in Nantes, speculated in paper, went on to found a finance company, became a contractor to the navy and in 1797 a state banker. After being arrested for fraud he quickly returned to the outside world—and to high living—and made himself indispensable to First Consul Bonaparte. He managed to procure urgently-needed grain from foreign ports and financed comprehensive transactions between the Spanish and French governments. While Napoleon was being crowned Ouvrard, for a time the consort of Madame Tallien whom he kept at Château Raincy, rose to become possibly the richest man in France and the father-in-law of Count Rochechouart of Châtillon-sur-Seine. Even the "continental system" failed to sever the links with the Barings, a family of merchant bankers in London. However, when the emperor asked for an explanation and failed to get one, he fell from favour and spent the period from 1810 to 1813 in prison. Nevertheless, during the "Hundred Days" in 1815 the two men teamed up again before Ouvrard, like others of his ilk, turned to the Bourbons, only to fall foul of their legal niceties too. There is no denying Ouvrard's powerful imagination, sharp intellect and courage, so it is hardly surprising that he became a celebrated figure in French light fiction.

Another man who led a charmed life, though he was much less in the public limelight, was Jean Conrad Hottinguer from Zurich who, like other scions of the Swiss middle classes, settled in Paris prior to the Revolution and soon established his own small banking business. Under the Republic business was bad and on top of this he was suspected of being a royalist. In 1793, therefore, he moved to London where he wed an American woman loaded with money. In her native country he met a fellow cautious fence-sitter—Talleyrand. From then on he had a smooth ride. In 1798 he opened his bank in Paris. Branches in

The Stock Exchange in Paris, constructed from 1808 onwards according to plans by Brongniart. Engraving by Barrière the Elder.

The Corn Exchange in Paris, constructed between 1762 and 1765. Engraving by François-Louis Couché. Both from: Binet (Editor), *Soixante vues des plus beaux palais, monuments et églises de Paris*. Paris, no date (*c.* 1818).

Morning affairs or The door of a rich man. Coloured engraving by Philibert-Louis Debucourt, *c.* 1803.

[1] LHOMER, J.: *Le banquier Perrégaux et sa fille la duchesse de Raguse.* Paris, 1926.

Le Havre and Marseilles soon followed, and the honours piled up. Under the Empire he became, by now a multimillionaire, president of the key Parisian chamber of commerce and as such one of the chief arbiters of French economic affairs, a baron and much else besides. Like Périer he founded a "dynasty" which today still gets into the news occasionally.

However, the most audacious financial whizzkid was said to be Jacques Laffitte (1767–1844), a gifted carpenter's son from Bayonne whom the renowned old banker Perrégaux made his partner in 1800.[1] Under the Empire this moneymaking genius took over the reins of the Banque de France in 1809 and of the capital's commercial court in 1813. Laffitte kept his nose clean and performed a special service: after Waterloo he administered Napoleon's personal fortune which its owner involuntarily left behind in France. Under the restored Bourbon monarchy Laffitte went on to become one of the leading lights of the liberal opposition and one of the men who hoisted Louis Philippe to power.

Much less frequent habitués of the salons were the very busy and at times frantically energetic captains of industry. Traditionally the *manufacturier* was regarded as lacking social prestige. In the jaundiced view of the die-hards who moulded popular opinion, they still exuded an odour of sweat born of manual toil. Certainly, they included men who had begun very modestly as artisans, such as the engraver Christian Philipp Oberkampf who moved to Paris from Germany. This commendable pioneer of the manufacture of high-grade cotton fabrics and public benefactor, who drained and settled the marshy valley of Jouy-en-Josas at his own cost, was ennobled in 1787 despite the fact that he was far from seeking such an accolade. Steadfast as he was, he flatly rejected the gracious offer of a seat in the Senate. When Napoleon paid a visit to his premises he had to resort to a ruse in order to foist the Grand Cross of the Legion of Honour upon the admirably public-spirited but obstinate old man (he was born in 1738): he took the medal from his own chest and bestowed it on Oberkampf, who thus could scarcely refuse.

The dramatic episode was immortalized in the form of a picture and then assiduously hawked around for propaganda purposes.

The French speak of a *bourgeoisie à talents* in contradistinction to the *bourgeoisie d'affaires* within which, under the Empire, merchant capital clearly predominated. The educated bourgeoisie was in turn subdivided into two categories of equal importance: the civil service and the self-employed.

There was no shortage of candidates for the top official posts, and anyone who managed to get himself appointed made sure he did not forfeit the goodwill of his immediate superiors or of the supreme state authorities. This determined the conduct of these officials. The assurance of a job for life, a steady rise up the promotion ladder, a fixed and promptly paid salary and entitlement to a pension exerted a powerful attraction on middle-class young men since no other profession could offer them as much. Working conditions in the office were pleasant in comparison to other jobs and the starting salary, while not exorbitant, was nevertheless more ample than in just about any other country. There was also the additional thrill of being able to exercise a modicum of power, however slight, over subordinate employees.

In Paris alone there were said to be anything up to 25,000 officials, more than one tenth of all those employed. Clearly, not every public employee could be categorized as a member of the bourgeoisie. Indeed, the bulk of the lower grades were pushed to make ends meet, for although they earned on average two or three times as much as a worker, the cost of keeping up socially necessary appearances largely cancelled out this advantage and compelled the minor official to be thrifty and economic in his habits. If he had a lot of children he needed to be doubly parsimonious. He moved almost exclusively in petty-bourgeois circles which were supplemented by fellow public servants and new arrivals from the countryside. Under certain circumstances it was even possible to advance as far as the intermediate grades, and this became for many a diligent clerk the be-all and end-all of his life. It was these middle ranks and the higher echelons which harboured "bourgeois officialdom".

On the other hand the apex of the administrative apparatus, from the heads of chancellery and heads of department upwards, formed part of the leading stratum on which the state depended and which Napoleon consciously cultivated as a government prop. The sub-prefects, comparable to district governors or administrators, and the presidents of the courts were very important personages, not to mention the prefects themselves, who earned twice as much as a senator and four times as much as a bishop. Only the generals were on a par with them. It was a social grouping that set great store by appearances. The precondition was a sound (preferably legal) educational background, if not a university education. The senior official, over whose selection and initiation Napoleon presided with great circumspection, was expected to come from a "good family" which could be either bourgeois or noble as long as it had provided him with an appropriately thorough education. Such high officials also tended to mix primarily with their own sort, both inside and outside office hours, strove after a certain exclusiveness

and hence were seen as part of "high society". A multiplicity of contacts and family ties, of which they made free use, linked them to the world of business and to the officers' corps. Usually they had property of their own, whether in the town or in the countryside. Those who were not ardent churchgoers might join a Freemasons' Lodge of the Grand Orient of France. When the emperor introduced a nobility of merit in 1808 some of them—in accordance with the official pecking order—were elevated for their services to the rank of chevalier, baron or even count. They served the Empire with just as much competence and zeal as they did (following a number of personnel changes, particularly at the top) the Bourbons in 1814, Napoleon again in 1815 and, after Waterloo, Louis XVIII once more, and always with a

demonstrative display of equanimity. It was more difficult to find a common denominator for the professions which were subject to the laws of free competition as well as its distortions.

The Revolution opened the floodgates to the large number of lawyers. Forensically practised eloquence and an intimate familiarity with the law enabled them to dominate the proceedings wherever the unlettered populace gathered, from electoral meetings right up to the three National Assemblies on which they imposed their own mode of speech and thought. The Empire had no use for such institutions, but this did not mean that those versed in the ways of the law found themselves unemployed. They were free to choose between a highly respected judicial profession or administrative career and a job as an advocate or

The family of the French consul Stamaty in Civitavecchia. Pencil drawing by Jean-Auguste-Dominique Ingres, 1818. Musée du Louvre, Cabinet des Dessins, Paris.

We must be governed by the best men; these are the most well educated and those who are most interested in upholding the laws. However, such men are to be found—with very few exceptions—only amongst those who possess property and are thus tied to the country in which it is situated, to the laws which protect it and to the peace which guarantees it; men who have this property and the prosperity which it provides to thank for the education which enables them to discuss with perspicacity and precision the advantages and disadvantages of laws that determine the fate of their country.

Boissy d'Anglas, 1795.

[1] JENNER, E.: *Inquiry into the Cause and Effects of the Variolae Vaccinae* (1798).

a notary, the growing importance of which was one of the salient features of this period in which all significant legal transactions had to pass through the hands of a professional jurist. There was work enough for the pettyfogger and the much sought-after top-flight defence lawyer, while the notary became a veritable bourgeois prototype. On the whole the picture was less rosy for professional men in other fields who had set up on their own account: the many private tutors, publicists and playwrights, painters and sculptors, actors and musicians who had no steady job. Those who had no paternal or maternal inheritance to fall back upon, however slender this might be, lived from hand to mouth and anticipated with dread an impecunious old age. Few were able, like David or Talma, to achieve prominence and hence a secure living.

In stark contrast the position of the medical fraternity, for whom life had previously not exactly been a bed of roses, improved significantly. The reputation of their profession, and in particular that of the hitherto lowly-rated surgeon, the *chirurgien*, received a boost. In the provinces this helped many a medical man to end up as mayor. Advances in medical science such as smallpox vaccination, which was first employed in 1798 in England by Edward Jenner (1749 to 1823)[1] and to which Napoleon subjected his own son, began to find widespread practical application. The discoveries of great exponents of medicine like Xavier Bichat, Broussais, Corvisart, Cabanis and Larrey (who taught at Berlin's Charité Hospital and was acquainted with Hufeland, the celebrated German physician) helped to train a new generation of doctors. Though not immune to professional elitism and snobbery, they kept their demands within relatively reasonable bounds, so that the English traveller Pinkerton was probably right to conclude that the low charges of French doctors did much to further public health and, in contrast to England, largely obviated the need to turn to ignorant quacks.

The same author went on to describe just how widespread quackery still was, not just in the back of beyond but in the "enlightened" capital as well. He related that a carpenter whom he knew had been regularly treated by a bailiff for paralysis with human fat. Pinkerton swore that, however far-fetched this might appear to nineteenth-century minds, it was nevertheless true.

Even Napoleon was unable to put a stop to the profitable and hence roaring trade in panaceas, elixirs and magic potions—to say nothing of exorcisms and other hocus-pocus—in his realm. The government did issue several stringent ordinances aimed at medical quacks which managed to reduce their numbers in Paris by about half and which drew a sharp distinction between the permissible and the impermissible, between the lawbreakers on the one hand and the licensed practitioner, a useful and respected member of society, on the other.

It would therefore be futile to attempt to identify *the* typical representative of the bourgeoisie under the Empire. This is a retrospective abstraction from a variegated spectrum of individuals. The social class to which the bourgeois belonged was blurred at the lower end where it merged with the petty-bourgeois mass. Its apex was not clearly defined; whether it would be able to maintain itself in future by its own efforts depended on the outcome of the Napoleonic episode. One thing, however, was already clearly established: the existence of an urban upper crust full of confidence in their own growing strength. Their domination of the market and its laws was uncontested. They were the leading economic and intellectual force in the land and were determined not to let themselves be displaced by anyone else. Even in physical terms they kept their distance from the masses. Thus the German travel writer Carl Friedrich Cramer noted that "by far the majority of houses in the more salubrious streets of Paris are buildings with a gateway and drive. In this respect they differ from the others which merely have an entrance with a dark staircase and lead in the main to the dwellings of common folk, small craftsmen and even whores. . . . All these houses with a garden and drive have their male or female janitors—a custom which distinguishes them from other large cities such as Amsterdam, Hamburg, Berlin etc."

A greatly enhanced income or savings accumulated over the years also led to changes inside the house or abode. It became possible to alter or extend, enlarge or improve the interior. For its upkeep at least two or three badly paid servants were employed, sometimes Parisians and sometimes countryfolk. The first task was to set up and equip a library, Monsieur's study, a boudoir for Madame and a reception salon in the prevailing Empire

style resplendent with mahogany artifacts, gold-framed mirrors and textured wallpaper. Here the choice was not always judicious, and in the quest for modernity bric-a-brac was installed to excess. "Thanks to the intrepid rediscoverers of antique furnishings, the woman who washes the silk stockings and the millionnaire Kräutermann, supplier of horses to the French cavalry, both now possess candelabra in caryatid form, flowerpots with hawk-necks, chests of drawers with griffin's feet and settees adorned with arabesques. So we blush with shame at the sight of a stool, the simple heirloom from our grandparents. We find our own children less attractive than the beetles which decorate some Egyptian secretaire stuffed full of promissory notes." It is only fair to say that Mer-

cier, the author of these remarks, had a strong aversion to the Empire style and therefore laid his sarcasm on a bit thick: "Must we not fear, in consequence of these newfangled developments, that one day our women folk might give birth to little Egyptian deities?"

Once commercial and professional success brought material security, it was accompanied by recognition in the social milieu in which one moved. The time had now come to indulge in well-mannered social intercourse, to maintain a carriage and to drive out to the public park outside the city gates, to entertain charming guests (or sometimes, if etiquette so demanded, less charming visitors) and in the process to bring the mealtimes into line with the eccentric dining

habits of the aristocracy, as a result of which breakfast *(déjeuner)* practically became the midday lunch, the latter *(diner)* became an evening meal and the evening soup *(souper)* was transformed into a late-night beanfeast after one returned from the theatre. A contemporary observer wrote: "The height of happiness is to be a bourgeois in Paris with an income of 10,000 livres."

This relatively young bourgeoisie were well aware of their prominent position and indispensable role in society and made the most of their chance. Ultimately they too worshipped Mammon as the true measure of all things, just like those above and below them in the social hierarchy. Their bourgeois style of living—*vivre*

Strollers in a public park. Lithograph by Jean-François Bosio, c. 1800/1805.

The joys of motherhood. Coloured engraving by an unknown artist. Nuremberg, c. 1810.

Some ten years ago the form of the furniture in our rooms underwent a profound transformation. Tormented by their artistic imagination and full of revulsion at the monotonous styles displayed by works of the present time, artisans examined anew the art of the classical period. They took a look at the Etruscan medallions of remote antiquity as well as those of the Persians, Egyptians, Greeks and Romans. As a result they have designed our vases, chairs and beds in antique style, x-shaped tables, lyreshaped clocks, ridiculously similar Isis/Osiris/Anubis heads, winged animals, sphinxes that guard our fireplaces etc.
Louis Sébastien Mercier

Monsieur Guillotin, who is held by most to be the inventor of the decapitation mechanism which bears his name . . ., was wont to visit an elderly gentleman who had lost the use of his limbs twice a week and in return contented himself with three livres for each visit.
John Pinkerton: "L'état de la médecine".

[1] MORAZÉ, C.: *La France bourgeoise*. Paris, 1946.

bourgeoisement—now meant an easy-paced life. The yearning for security was regarded as more important than a quick rise to riches, the propensity to unhesitatingly grab as much as possible which characterized the wheeler-dealer.[1] They now ventured to set their sights somewhat higher, but in conformity with the restraints of their middle-class mentality—a step-by-step approach. Those who impetuously infringed the sacrosanct conventions were shunned with horror. They respected the social and political realities of Napoleonic tutelage without necessarily enthusing over them. They did not turn down the benefits which this brought but were careful not to compromise themselves; and there was always the expedient of passive resistance.

All in all the bourgeoisie, in spite of the vestiges of feudal constriction and medieval narrowmindedness that they still retained, were the main pillar on which the new system—whether in military guise or not—rested. They determined its more down-to-earth character, the functional style that

subsequently emerged. They were indeed epoch-makers. They topped up the emperor's personally appointed élite of unobjectionable dignitaries and ennobled helpmates as and when required. More importantly, they were destined sooner or later, in pursuit of profit, to leap over their own shadow and take direct control of the ship of state.

The Salvation of Souls

Karl Marx was the first to opine that "everyone should be able to attend to his religious as well as his bodily needs without the police poking their noses in". At the beginning of the 19th century the powers-that-be put more faith in the tried-and-tested principle laid down by the Peace of Augsburg in 1555 of *cuius regio, eius religio*, i.e. the right of the temporal ruler to determine religious affairs in his domains. The very thought of a possible separation of Church and State, which had fought arm in arm for a thousand years, was

Mutterfreuden.

anathema to most. Even the experiments of the revolutionaries, all of whom were children of the Enlightenment, had been pretty hapless.

Bonaparte's soldierly mentality baulked at leaving such an important section of the ideological front unsupervised. The "red priests" of the Revolution haunted him like so many ghosts. "If the priests are left to themselves they run the risk of turning into democrats." The emperor shared this precautionary paternalism with other crowned heads, both allied and hostile. Yet under his patronage the churches did not fare at all badly.

The Protestant minority in the country took good care not to queer his pitch, as this might have spoiled the happy harmony. Indeed, what did they really have to complain about? The Revolution had freed both the Reformed and the Lutheran Church from the slights which, even after the Edict of Tolerance of 1787, they still suffered. Of a strongly middle-class composition, though some hailed from a peasant background, they supported with all their might the creation of a bourgeois state structure with liberal tendencies and a social formation which promised them the position of respect to which their diligence in the economic sphere entitled them. Mirabeau sarcastically noted that they "do pretty nicely in this world even though, as everyone knows, they are condemned to eternal damnation in the next". Whereas they had nothing to gain from a Bourbon restoration, both Consulate and Empire continued the process of integration to the satisfaction of all concerned. They were able to build churches and hold services without objection. They were subjected to hardly any attacks or abuse from the Catholics. Protestants were appointed to high state offices, and business flourished. As a result of annexations (first to the left and then, after 1810, to the right of the Rhine, including Geneva and western Switzerland) their numbers—they were reckoned to constitute a modest one twentieth of the population—rose appreciably. This also gave rise to friction. A not inconsiderable section of the newly annexed, mainly Dutch and German pastors found it difficult to abandon their ancestral traditions.

In particular little enthusiasm was shown for the formation, although basically sensible and not in conflict with the official catechism, of a countrywide church organization with a separate head

for each of the two Protestant denominations. Yet how could Napoleon be expected to restrain his propensity towards centralization, uniformity and tutelage? Moreover, his interference encroached neither on the dogma, spiritual welfare nor the internal constitution of the religious communities. They were equally at liberty to determine their own liturgy. If criticisms were voiced to the effect that the strength of Huguenot convictions had paled by comparison with the period of persecution, this was surely not a reflection of any continuing harassment but rather of the cessation of the external pressure, of the chance to relax and enjoy the more pleasant aspects of life. It was no longer persecuted martyrs living clandestinely who now constituted the pillars of their communities but successful bankers, manufacturers and businessmen—*la banque protestante.*

Of far greater import in Church-State relations than this handful of heretics or even the unproblematical Greek Orthodox believers in the Illyrian provinces was the See of Rome.

The surging tide of the Revolution had seriously undermined its foundations. The Catholic clergy had lost its status as the First Estate of the realm as well as—and this hurt much more—its earthly property to the tune of some two thousand million francs. It had been incorporated into the state and made to tow the line, its authority had been reduced and restricted to internal church affairs. The papal anathematization of the "civil constitution" had led to schism and the removal of those non-juring priests who remained firmly loyal to Rome.[1] Later the de-Christianization campaign even struck at the compliant constitutional priests. In order to fill the vacuum considerable efforts were made to construct substitute cults: the veneration of revolutionary martyrs, of Reason and of the Supreme Being. Under the Thermidorians a "theophilanthropy" had emerged while the Directorate had ordained a "cult of the décadi".

With bewilderment, amazement and finally disgust believers and non-believers alike had followed the rapidly fluctuating and clumsy inventions of the would-be founders of new faiths. In view of such ideological incertitude it was hardly surprising that the established Church gained much ground at the base. Even people who criticized it on other counts still found it preferable to complete chaos.

The Madeleine Church in Paris. Construction, which was begun in 1764, was resumed in 1806 and continued until 1842. Napoleon wanted to make the church, which is most impressively located, a temple of fame. Engraving by an unknown artist, c. 1818. From: Binet (Editor), *Soixante vues des plus beaux palais, monuments et églises de Paris.* Paris, no date (c. 1818).

Page 104:
Interior of the Dominican church in Lyons which was used by the army as coach house. Lithograph by Jean-Baptiste Arnould after François Bellay of Lyons. The painting on which it was based was exhibited in 1817.

[1] LATREILLE, A.: *L'Eglise catholique et la Révolution française.* 2nd edition. Paris, 1970.

However, it was only with the advent of the Consulate that the Catholic Church was able to unfurl its old pomp anew—with the backing of the authorities. Pilgrimages, processions and church festivals all reappeared. The saints returned to their old niches. Freshly cast bells rang out in place of those which had been melted down during the Revolution, and organs played again. Unlimited quantities of devotional objects were offered for sale. The construction of new church buildings began or was resumed. Priests who had gone underground, fled or who had been deported soon returned in droves, and seminaries trained a new generation of priests who were drawn mostly from bourgeois or peasant stock. Theology was once more taught in untrammelled fashion.

In material terms the clergy were well provided for by a substantial budget.[1] They were treated with all due honour and enjoyed respect. Whenever this appeared rather cool the temporal arm intervened. No one tried to prevent the Church any longer from gathering scattered or anxious believers around its pulpits or from doing its level best to heal the wounds inflicted by radical Enlightenment and de-Christianization. With its Sundays and traditional holidays the church calendar displaced the cult of the décadi. In the mornings—preferably before breakfasting—people went to Mass, had their marriage consecrated by the Church following the civil ceremony, gave their children a Christian baptism after entering the birth in the official register, unburdened themselves occasionally of their sins in the confessional and as a rule received the last rites.

No restrictions were placed on prayer. So was this the same old *ecclesia gallicana* as before? No, the Church of the concordat, while not a new Church, was a different one.

Bonaparte never doubted that the restoration of domestic peace, as the Brumairians had envisaged it in the hope of broadening their base, must include an end to religious strife. Although this was petering out anyhow it was not so easy to find someone willing to take the bull by the horns. The old but still smouldering rancour between the enemies of the Church, those loyal to the Republic and the Ultramontanes could only be buried by means of a dialogue at the highest level, a *do ut des* with the Holy See.

Long, tough and discreet negotiations were necessary with Secretary of State Ercole Consalvi (1757–1824) and due allowances made for various sensibilities before Pope Pius VII, who was elected in 1800, was ready to compromise since the reconquest of his secular power in the restored Papal States depended on the goodwill of France. And so the schism was mended.[2] Yet even after agreement had been reached in July 1801 a whole year elapsed before the First Consul was able to promulgate the concordat on August 15, 1802—his birthday.

All the bishops, both non-juring and constitutional, had to resign. The new bishops, who in many cases were the same ones as before, were appointed by the First Consul and canonically instituted by the pope. The episcopacy became a mishmash drawn from various parties, while hard bargaining preceded the investiture of some candidates. With admirable frankness Bonaparte informed the State Council of what he expected from them. What he desired was a clergy who would rest content with that which their office and their duty dictated. He offered consolidation based on conformism within a bourgeois Republic built on the selfsame principle. In 1803 the First Consul unilaterally supplemented the concordat with a set of "Organic Articles". These both facilitated and strictly regulated the career development of the state-financed church official from his theological study to the way in which he administered his episcopate. The Church in Imperial France included a prayer for Napoleon in its catechism. The architects of the concordat Church were extremely interesting people.

The papal legate, Cardinal Caprara (formerly Count Montecuccoli, 1733–1810) proved to be an adroit diplomat of the old Roman school. He had a thorough knowledge of French conditions and manipulated an extensive network of contacts. He was not lacking in the Italianate cunning with which Napoleon indirectly reproached Pius VII. He believed there was no such thing as a hopeless situation—a solution could always be found. He knew just how to deal with Napoleon and impressed him to such an extent that, when he died, the emperor insisted that he be interred in Sainte-Geneviève, as the "Panthéon" was now known. For the duration of the Empire Caprara thus shared his lasting resting place with Voltaire and Rousseau.

Pope Paul VII. Coloured engraving by Pierre Michel Alix after Joseph Wicar.

Children's love of God. "In the tempests of time religion is the only anchor for weak mortals. Blessed are those families which sow the seeds early in the hearts of their children!" Coloured engraving by Friedrich Fleischmann after Jean-Baptiste (?) Mallet, *c.* 1810.

. . . in particular to show the love, respect, obedience and loyalty which we owe to Napoleon I, our Emperor, to perform military service and to pay the contributions required for the preservation and defence of the realm and of his throne; and also to pray fervently for his salvation and for the spiritual and temporal welfare of the state. . . . To honour and serve the Emperor is to honour and serve God Himself.
Catéchisme impérial

[1] LANGLOIS, C.: *Religion et politique dans la France napoléonienne.* Paris, 1974.
[2] CONSALVI, E.: *Memorie.* Rome, 1950.

Henri Grégoire (1750–1831) represented the opposing faction. A militant "friend of the Negroes" in the Constituent Assembly, Bishop of Blois under the Republic as well as an upstanding member of the Convention, saviour and guardian of works of art and a high-ranking scholar, he had gathered around him during the Consulate all the remnants of the national Church of the revolutionary era and had even set up an ecclesiastical council. He made sure his fellow believers were not outmanoeuvred by the "Romans" and were accepted into the ranks of the reunified Church on an equal footing—no doubt with the approval of Bonaparte, who never liked to be confronted with closed ranks. The real key figure was Monseigneur Emery (1732–1811), undoubtedly the most illustrious theologian in France. Since 1782 he had been Superior of the Society of the Sulpicians (la Société des prêtres de Saint-Sulpice), who tried hard to raise the level of teaching in the seminaries and whose members ran many of the religious institutions. Even during the Revolution he was at pains, wherever feasible, to separate

basic secular and ecclesiastical concerns in a spirit of conciliation. Standing to some extent between the two camps, his undisputed integrity allowed the almost seventy-year-old Vicar-General of Paris to persuade even those with doubts and scruples to accept his formula for compromise. Unyielding on questions of principle and never a yes-man, he later clashed repeatedly with Napoleon and wondered anxiously whether, on being given an inch, the emperor had taken a mile.

As it happened, the emperor landed his biggest fish long after the concordat was signed: Jean Siffrein Maury (1746–1817), a cobbler's son from Venaissin. His riveting southern eloquence helped him to gain admission to the Academy in 1784 and to the States General in 1789 after which he quickly became the star orator of the right-wing opposition in the Constituent Assembly. In 1792 he emigrated to Italy where he was rewarded with a cardinal's post in 1794. "Louis XVIII" appointed him ambassador of the French court to the Vatican—a distinction, however, at which he turned up his nose, returning instead to

France in 1806. His motive is still the subject of scholarly debate. Did this incorrigibly plebeian cleric find a hair in the feudal soup? Whatever the reason, the fact that in 1809 Napoleon, despite the disapproval of Pius VII who refused to give his consent, could find no more effective candidate for the post of Archbishop of Paris than the twenty-four carat preacher with a worldwide reputation needs no elucidation.

The attacks of the revolutionaries on "fanaticism, hypocrisy and superstition" had put the wrangling clergy to a severe test and left a deep and lasting impression on them. Once they had been placed under the spotlight of public criticism the prelates could no longer return to the pleasurably dissolute way of life of the *ancien régime*. Their rich estates were not restored to them, and after all that had happened they did not judge it advisable to lodge a political protest. The field of education had become a purely secular affair and the registry office likewise remained outside their jurisdiction. On the other hand their involvement in the sphere of medical and social welfare was readily welcomed.

Not everyone shared the view of Bishop Le Coz of Besançon who effusively lauded Napoleon as "the most perfect hero yet wrought by the hand of the Creator". They were grateful to him for closing the abyss, both inside and outside the Church. In this respect he was not far off the mark when he spoke of "his" bishops in the same breath as "his" generals or "his" prefects. They even maintained their national ecclesiastical self-discipline and offered to mediate when Napoleon annexed Rome in 1809 and banished the protesting pope—the same pontiff who had earlier so obligingly presided at his coronation—from the Holy City. On the other hand the rupture, which also wrecked an attempted renewal of the concordat in 1813, was very much welcomed by sworn opponents of the tricolour Empire such as the conspiratorial "Chevaliers of the Faith".

Once again they were able, with a semblance of legitimacy, to call for a stop to be put to the "anti-Christ" who had done such violence to the head of the Church, an appeal which did not everywhere fall on deaf ears: less so in Poland and Alsace than in Spain and in the Belgian départements, the Illyrian provinces and in the traditionally troublesome Vendée.

Die kindliche Liebe zu Gott.

In den Stürmen der Zeit, ist Religion der einzige Anker für den schwachen Sterblichen. Wohl den guten Familien, die solchen Saamen schon früh in die Herzen ihrer Kinder streuen!

"Peculiar piety". Folio 66 from the series "Los Desastres de la Guerra". Aquatint by Francisco de Goya, c. 1820–1823.

"What a lovely golden beak!" Folio 53 from the series "Los Caprichos". Etching by Francisco de Goya, 1797–1799.

Religion associates the idea of equality with heaven and thus prevents the rich from being slaughtered by the poor.
Bonaparte

[1] SCHLEIERMACHER, F. E. D.: *Reden über die Religion an die Gebildeten unter ihren Verächtern* (1799): *Monologe* (1800).
[2] NOVALIS (GEORG FRIEDRICH VON HARDENBERG): *Die Christenheit oder Europa* (1799).

Like Robespierre before him Napoleon managed to avoid being drawn into what would have been a thoroughly unwelcome theological tug-of-war. Attempts to pacify the fractious parties failed in this area too, and as soon as the hitherto victorious march of the Imperial banner began to falter the problems re-surfaced once again. For regardless of the intentions—sometimes praiseworthy, at other times less so—of those in charge, European Christendom, having been thoroughly shaken up by events, had long since girded itself up for action. Old factional quarrels died down while new ones flared up. Jansenism was a spent force, and the only place where it just managed to survive was on native Dutch soil. The "natural" religion of the *philosophes*, spiced with a dash of materialism, which for some had ended its useful life with the "terror" and for others with the Ninth of Thermidor—or with Babeuf—was superseded by a counter-current: a return to medieval harmony, a concept which had previously been derided as Gothic barbarism but which now became transfigured through idealization. The shattered hopes that had been vested in Reason now yielded to faith in the Revelation. The German theologian Schleiermacher (1768–1834) called it an "archetypal consciousness of dependency".[1]

The "blue flower" of Romanticism blossomed first on Protestant German soil as an aesthetic protest against the chill wind which reached disappointed idealists from the jaded Directoire in France.[2] Politically and ideologically it was at this stage still an open movement. Thus in 1802 Chateaubriand dedicated his *génie du christianisme* to First Consul Bonaparte personally. Meanwhile, quite often accompanied by conversions to Catholicism (e.g. Novalis, Schlegel, Gentz), socially conservative forces came increasingly to the fore. They condemned the Empire as "the afterbirth of the Revolution" and thus found themselves on the same side as the royalist opposition. Consequently aristocratic mannerisms as well as the Bourbons, transfigured by means of a "golden legend", enjoyed a boost in popularity. An incipient "legitimist" clerical tendency, given an ultramontane nuance by De Maistre, emerged and found expression in 1815; the mortal remains of Voltaire and Rousseau, which had rested in the Panthéon since the Revolution, were desecrated by grave robbers loyal to Church and king.

It is hard to say whether the French again became more pious during the Empire or whether it was just that a sizeable group of sanctimonious souls dedicated themselves to uncompromising reaction. What is certain is that Catholicism, whenever it expressed itself politically, increasingly turned its back on the Napoleonic interlude, which it had initially welcomed with relief, and readily added a religious dimension to nostalgic yearnings for the "good old days". Napoleon had an interest in the Catholic Church as an important and morally uplifting factor of stability within his monarchy, and hence also in the love of religious tradition as an element of calmness and conservatism. His own attachment to it was loose, conventional and of a naive nature. Doctrinal disputes bored him to tears and during Mass, attendance of which had once again become seemly at court, he would occasionally doze off. However, he did not share the ostentatious indifference to religion sometimes shown by his old comrades-in-arms. Once he provocatively asked one of "his" great scholars as he gazed up at the starry sky who else but God could have possibly created it all. On the other hand he took the celebrated reply calmly: "I do not need this hypothesis!" Napoleon himself did need it in order to keep the population obedient. The nature of the creed was of secondary importance. In Egypt he had unhesitatingly paraded himself as a Moslem and boldly invoked the prophets of Allah.

Consequently Imperial France was no less unprejudiced in matters of faith than Prussia which, during the lifetime of the philosopher-king, was greatly envied on this account. There too it was possible for each to "achieve bliss in his own way", or else to pay no heed to the matter as a freethinker as long as one stuck to the rules of the game and avoided causing public offence. Snippets of Voltairean thought could be found in some very high places, for some youthful ideas took permanent root. The narrow-minded saw this as going too far. The conventicles of their so-called "Little Church" never reconciled themselves to the régime of the concordat. The legal equality extended to the Protestant, Greek-Orthodox and Jewish communities seemed to them a betrayal of the "Sole Redeemer", the evil consequences of the doings of godless iconoclasts. In one respect it even appeared as if the diabolical seeds sown by the latter had produced new fruit, for Freemason-

ry which, though a constant thorn in the flesh of Roman orthodoxy, had largely disintegrated in the course of the Revolution, celebrated its resurrection with support from the highest quarters.[1] The moral authority of the Grand Orient of France once more spread over half of Europe. It did not bother these steadfast zealots (in Italy they were actually known as *zelanti*) that their convivial gatherings of well-heeled and dependable dignitaries had little or nothing in common any more with the former network of refractory bourgeois intellectuals under the *ancien régime* from whose midst the first swallows of the Revolution had emerged.

The Great Sanhedrin

French Jewry constituted a small percentage of the population. At the end of the 18th century they probably totalled about 40,000 or, at the most, 50,000, i.e. two Jews to every thousand Christians. In two areas they were concentrated in larger numbers: in Alsace-Lorraine and, to a lesser extent, in the Southwest around Bordeaux and Bayonne. In addition there were small local concentrations, e.g. in the papal city of Avignon, in Carpentras, the ports of Marseilles and in Paris where, however, their numbers did not exceed a thousand.

Colloquially referred to as "Portuguese" or "Spanioles" since most of them had originally been driven from the Iberian peninsula, the Sephardim of southern France had long since settled in their new home and even under the old monarchy had to some extent become integrated into their social environment. They had become indispensable in trade around the Mediterranean, particularly with the North African Barbary states where they could make use of their local coreligionists. Some had become members of guilds and enjoyed the right to vote, normally used French rather than the traditional "Ladino", a language which was spoken from Morocco to Salonika, and took part in public life.

By contrast the Germanic Ashkenazim in the East, who had more recently been incorporated into the French nation through conquest and territorial gains between 1552 and 1766, were regarded as aliens and as protegés of the king. They were subjected to a whole series of special regula-

tions. On the one hand they enjoyed certain privileges, for instance with regard to the autonomy of their communities and money-lending. Yet on the other hand they were burdened with very strict and often degrading stipulations such as residence restrictions, bans on buying land and exclusion from certain trades and professions. They were forced to live in Jewish ghettoes which they were forbidden to leave at night. They differed from Christian citizens in their religion and Yiddish language, their customs and education system, in their special dietary rules and prescribed clothing. Between the Ashkenazim and the Sephardim, who encountered one another virtually nowhere else except in the capital, there were only loose contacts. They differed not only in their circumstances and habits but also in their religious rites.

Agents who, as in Poland, looked after the business of their noble masters, or the (occasionally ennobled) "court Jews" like Ephraim in Berlin, Dobruska in Moravia or Rothschild in Frankfurt, were unknown in France, although it was said that the advice of the experienced army contractor Cerf Berr from Nancy was eagerly sought at Versailles. The conditions of the Jewish communities in European countries varied widely to begin with, but they all had one thing in common: everywhere they were regarded and treated as second-class subjects unless they had been converted to the prevailing religion, particularly as their concentration on the field of trade, especially money-lending and second-hand dealing, was looked down upon. The centuries-old tradition of mistrust, disdain and harassment, which could escalate into pogroms, was something which they encountered daily.

It was only with great difficulty and thanks to urgent intercessions from outside that the highly respected Jewish community of Prague was able to fend off the Empress Maria Theresa's decision to expel them from the Golden City which had been a spiritual centre of Jewry since the Middle Ages. Enlightened cosmopolitans vigorously waged war on all this bigoted prejudice and achieved a measure of success. They placed the demand for the emancipation of the Jews on the agenda, and their sustained outcry ensured that it stayed there. In the person of the Berlin philosopher and Humanist Moses Mendelssohn, a little man with a big heart who was also the model for Lessing's

An elderly Jew. Lithograph by a French artist who signed himself with the monogram L. Ch., c. 1800.

It is now the intention of His Highness to convoke the Great Sanhedrin. This council, which disappeared with the fall of the Temple, shall rise again and bring light in all countries to the people who formally adhered to it.

Actually tolerance should be a temporary phenomenon only: it must give way to true acceptance. Mere toleration is offensive.
Goethe

[1] NABONNE, B.: *Joseph Bonaparte, le roi philosophe.* Paris, 1949.

Nathan, they found an advocate of supreme dignity whose influence stretched way beyond the borders of Prussia.

No society based on a corporate social structure was capable of assimilating the Jews. They remained outsiders. At most some improvements were possible, an easing of tension, the gradual lightening of their burden. Yet these limited measures of toleration such as were practised by Dutch merchants and which Joseph II, following Frederick's example, proclaimed in his realm in 1781, were the most they could hope for. As is always the case with toleration, it proved to be little more than a refined form of discrimination. The odd colonial administration turned a blind eye since they were, after all, free-born white men, but it was not until 1790 that George Washington, President of the United States, was able to assure the Jewish Congregation of Newport, Rhode Island: "It is now no more that toleration is spoken of, as if it was by the indulgence of one class of people, that another enjoyed the exercise of their inherent natural rights." In this he was at one with Goethe.

The whole issue was finally raised and the ball set rolling by the French Revolution and its proclamation of the rights of man and the citizen. It was no longer a question of the right to exist on the margins of society as part of a submissive subculture but rather the granting of full citizenship in accordance with the principles of liberty, equality and fraternity. Was it possible, or indeed permissible, for particular groups of people, on whatever grounds, to be excluded?

It is well known just how much and how long the National Assemblies twisted and turned before the Jacobin-led Convention—and only then under the impact of a successful uprising of black slaves on Haiti—finally agreed in 1794 to abolish slavery in its colonies. This was a hurdle which the United States, in spite of all Thomas Jefferson's fine-sounding pronouncements, had not yet managed to surmount. Though France was better placed in this respect, the proponents of an unconditional and unrestricted integration of the Jews into the French nation, such as Mirabeau and Grégoire, had to combat fierce opposition within the Constituent Assembly before they succeeded in pushing through the emancipatory decrees in instalments—at first for the Sephardim and somewhat later for the Ashkenazim as well.

The final piece of legislation was not passed until November 1791 and was confirmed by the Directorial constitution in the year 1795.

Henceforth the Jew was a *citoyen* like anyone else and had the same rights and duties. Thus on paper at least he had achieved notional equality with all his fellow citizens, and, unless he purchased exemption, was now liable to serve in the army—for Jews a novel experience but one to which many had long aspired. In actual fact this emancipation, in which ideological, legal and economic premises and considerations were variously interlinked, left a lot open. A well-meaning stroke of the pen could not obliterate the onus of centuries.

The champions of emancipation, inside France and abroad, expected that the Israelites of both persuasions would now completely merge in with their host nation, that they would become assimilated. The Jews themselves, however, did not exactly leap for joy at this prospect. The process of adjustment, which cut deep into family life, forcibly brought about many changes in ancient traditions and reduced the hitherto uncontested authority of the rabbis as spiritual and temporal leaders, threatened to undermine the security of their familiar environment and to sunder old community ties before durable new ones could be established. The transformation proved to be neither easy nor unproblematic and in no way realizable in the short or medium term. In addition their fellow citizens, if not openly anti-Semitic, nevertheless remained markedly cool towards the idea of the Jews' full integration. The satisfaction at taking an historic step towards freedom, towards the reconciliation of the Old and New Testaments—to which many Israelites gave eloquent expression—was marred for a large number of them (particularly Orthodox Jews) by the fact that they might lose their Jewish identity in the course of this ardent embrace, an identity which they wished to retain even after they had become part of the "Grande Nation".

One of those Frenchmen for whom this process of adaptation was progressing too slowly was the perpetually impatient emperor. He had no grounds for complaint about his Jewish subjects. News of altercations which reached him from Alsace were merely local conflicts and were in any case often provoked by gentiles. Insofar as they commented at all on political events the vast majority of Jews welcomed the Consulate and the establishment of the Empire as conducive to business and trade. Their leaders always took the utmost care to avoid doing anything that might excite Napoleon's notoriously short temper. Their basic tenet was never to forfeit his benevolence by contradicting or criticizing his measures, even when this would have been warranted.

The enlightened emperor had come to share the revolutionaries' rigid conception of the "one and indivisible" nation. This left little room for the proper recognition of the special character of minorities, whether ethnic or religious. Corsicans, Bretons, Basques, Catalans, Flemings, Alsatians and Rhinelanders—as well as Protestants and Jews—should count themselves lucky to be allowed to be one hundred per cent Frenchmen, or to become such as quickly as possible. The aim was a single and unitary legal and educational system, literature and art, military service, career structure, public spirit and sense of loyalty for everyone.

The sorry experiences of the revolutionary period had shown that it was impossible to mould a variety of historically entrenched creeds into a single state religion. Napoleon preferred to accept the various religious communities as separate "units" which, when it came to the crunch, could be played off against one another and to keep them strongly under his control. He further sought to structure their relations in accordance with state imperatives so that he could exert the desired influence on their internal processes and organs of decision-making. Since each Jewish synagogical community formed an autonomous entity and was not subject to any central "church organization", such an institution had to be invented.

Therefore the emperor convoked an assembly of prominent French Jews in Paris in July 1806. The 112 delegates who, though selected by the prefects, nevertheless constituted a fairly representative cross-section, were presented with twelve questions which in essence boiled down to just one: "Do Jews, born in France and treated as French citizens, regard the country as their homeland? Do they feel duty-bound to defend it and to observe its laws?" To Napoleon's gratifica-

Jewess. Engraving from the *Taschenbuch für die Kinder Israels.* Berlin, 1804.

Page 112:
Napoleon restoring the Jewish cult (May 30, 1806). Engraving by an unknown artist, 1806.

People who have chosen a new homeland, have lived there for several centuries and, even in the face of laws that limit their civic existence, have shown such affection for this country that they preferred to forego the enjoyment of normal rights than to leave it cannot but regard themselves as true Frenchmen. Hence the obligation to defend France is for them both a precious duty and an honour.
Vote of the Assembly of Notables.

tion the answers were in the affirmative. The signatories included some illustrious names: among the laymen the staunch Bonapartist Berr Isaak Berr, who chaired the proceedings, and his son Michel, a lawyer from Nancy; the millionnaire Abraham Furtado from Bordeaux; the Chevalier of the Legion of Honour, Moyse May; plus rabbis of renown such as the Talmud scholar David Sinzheim from Strasbourg and Abraham di Cologna from Mantua.

Since the pronouncements and conclusions of this *ad hoc* body did not have any binding religious or juridical force in regard to the whole of Jewry, the emperor went a step further and resolved to submit the preliminary decisions of the assembly of notables to ratification by a "world congress"—the Great Sanhedrin.

Napoleon had a predilection for impressive historical extravaganzas, which he considered the most effective kind of propaganda. He went so far as to concern himself personally with the design of an appropriate Oriental costume in which the honoured delegates had to present themselves to the ever curious Parisians, who gaped to their hearts' content at the colourful procession. At the same time, however, Napoleon was making a political move. In resurrecting the Supreme Council which, until the Roman destruction of Jerusalem in the year 70 had carried out the functions of a spiritual court of justice, he combined the cultivation of tradition with a claim to moral patronage over Jews throughout the world.

In the event the deliberations of the Great Sanhedrin, which opened on February 9, 1807 under the chairmanship of David Sinzheim, did not go quite so smoothly.

Muted fears were expressed that the august body was expected to abandon, or at least revise, the faith of their forefathers. Some of the participants, including several of the prominent Jews who had attended the assembly of notables the previous year, doubted whether, in spite of the readiness to parley, the Mosaic and Talmudic demands could be reconciled with those of an emperor bent on assimilation. Napoleon impressed his own demands on his minister Champagny on November 29, 1806 from Posen, where he was in the middle of a military campaign.

Naturally Rabbi Sinzheim knew nothing of Napoleon's ambition to act as a cleanser of the catechism as he made his prognosis: "The whole affair is a wonderful thing, but only time will tell whether it has gone well." Still, after precisely one month the assembly dispersed with a tangible achievement to its credit. It agreed on a whole series of resolutions which it proclaimed to the whole world:

Prohibition of polygamy; the validity of marriages to be contingent on obtaining the prior consent of the civil authorities; a civil wedding to precede the religious ceremony; validity of mixed marriages even in the absence of a religious wedding ceremony; a religious obligation to love and defend one's homeland and to fraternally assist both Jewish and non-Jewish fellow citizens; the freedom to perform any job, profession or trade coupled with the recommendation to turn to farming, handicrafts and the arts as practised by their forefathers in Israel; the prohibition of usury.

Clearly this was a motley array of proposals arrived at on the basis of compromise, and not every stipulation was likely to hold good for all time.

The Great Sanhedrin, which in exact accordance with the Synhedrion of antiquity was composed of seventy-one men (forty-six rabbis and twenty-five laymen), had unquestionably set itself an ambitious aim: "To issue decrees which, in keeping with the principles of our sacred laws, shall serve *all* Israelites as an example and a guide. . . . We regard anyone who transgresses against or neglects our declarations and decrees as a manifest and evil sinner against the will of God."

Unfortunately the universality of the Sanhedrin suffered from the fact that its synod members came almost exclusively from France, Italy and Germany. Communities in other countries mostly did not dare—or desire—to send representatives. A compounding factor was that the council's new catalogue of duties was quite obviously geared towards modern bourgeois conditions. This explains the vigorous support expressed by the worldy-wise "Portuguese" Furtado, the Sanhedrin's principal speaker. But to broad sections of the far more numerous and coherent Jewry of eastern Europe it did not mean a thing. It did not even offer them the semblance of a substitute for the "Council of the Four Countries", the umbrella organization for orthodox Ashkenazim in the East which the Polish government dissolved in 1764. Nor did it even begin to respond to the challenge of the mystically spiritual

several of the liberties that had previously been granted.

In contrast to their "Portuguese" counterparts, the "Germanic" Jews, even after 1791, required a permit to indulge in trade. Freedom of movement to or from France was again hedged in with restrictions and the appointment of surrogates to perform military service was forbidden. Furthermore, the new centralized consistorial constitution made the rabbis responsible for carrying out policing duties within their own communities. A revision was to be made after ten years to see whether the Jews had become sufficiently assimilated to merit equal status with other citizens in every respect.

Lax implementation of the decree (especially outside Alsace) weakened its effectiveness and in the end led to it being more or less shelved. However, the spirit of the decree revealed that Napoleon, like many German princes, wished to proceed in accordance with the didactic principle of the piecemeal allocation of rights, since ultimately he understood assimilation to mean coalescence. Unfortunately for him the intended objects of his pedagogical efforts seldom complied with his wish despite the fact that—like the enlightened and liberal individuals of his day—he did not make admission to the ranks of the national bourgeois establishment dependent upon being baptized, though this was welcomed as evidence of the willingness to become rapidly assimilated.

Thus Napoleon's efforts aimed at promoting Jewish advance and those tending to hamper it (both of which were motivated by shrewd political calculations) largely cancelled one another out.[1] He has unjustifiably earned many plaudits (and possibly a few brickbats) in this respect. The chances of social advancement that not a few observers—including later ones—ascribed to the Empire can, on a somewhat closer inspection, be seen to be due more to the dynamism of the Revolution.[2]

Yet the Empire indisputably had one accomplishment to its credit: Napoleon's armies, even if this was not the reason for their mobilization, carried France's achievements all over Europe and wrenched open the gates of the ghettoes wherever they went. By force of arms they cleared the way for the Jews to make their splendid contribution towards world culture in the 19th and 20th centuries.

religiosity, redolent in its intensity of late Baroque Protestant Pietism, of Chassidism. This movement was founded in Poland by Israel ben Eliezer (1700–1760), the *Baal-schem tob* (Master of the Holy Name), and its gospel was propagated by emissaries known as the *zaddikim* (the Pious). French Jewry achieved one irreversible gain from the whole business: they were brought together within a cohesive religious organization. It must, however, be added that they were still far from being out of the wood. Napoleon largely ignored the assurances given to the Sanhedrin whenever he was concerned to regulate the status of citizens of the Hebraic faith of his own accord and to firmly encapsulate their religious community within clearly defined ordinances just as he had earlier done with the Christian churches. Bitter disappointment was caused in particular by the so-called "infamous decree" of March 1808 which summarily revoked or massively curtailed

Jew trading in hides. Engraving from the *Taschenbuch für die Kinder Israels*. Berlin, 1804.

Page 114:
The Feast of Tabernacles. Engraving by Georg Paul Nusbiegel. From: J.C.G. Bodenschatz, *Kirchliche Verfassung der heutigen Juden*, Vol. IV, 2. Erlangen, 1748.

It is necessary to expunge from the Mosaic laws all that is intolerant. Part of them should be declared civil and political laws, and the only religious laws that should remain intact are those which accord with the morality and the duties of French citizens.

[1] Pietri, F.: *Napoléon et les Israëlites.* Paris, 1965.
[2] *Les Juifs et la Révolution française.* Edited by B. Blumenkranz/A. Soboul. Toulouse, 1976.
[3] Rivarol, A.: *Discours sur l'universalité de la langue française.* Prize essay for the Berlin Academy, 1784.
[4] Staël, G. de: *Jahre im Exil. Auf der Flucht vor Napoleon.* Stuttgart, 1975.
[5] Biran, M.F.P.G. Maine de: *Tagebuch.* Hamburg, 1977.

Of Thinkers and Poets

For two hundred years France was the centre of artistic excellence, and the only point at issue was whether the laurels should go to the 17th or to the 18th century. Borne by a cultured language which was the medium of communication used by refined and educated people throughout Europe and beyond, its literature, from poems to the most learned treatises, penetrated into the most remote areas. In the liberal arts people submitted to the judgement of Paris. Many conceded, either grudgingly or willingly, that the city was the sole arbiter in matters of good taste and "reason".[3]

Meanwhile the flames of the Revolution had consumed the promises of the Enlightenment. The moment it put them into practice it had annulled them. This left a stale aftertaste. Something else took the place of its fractured ideals, and this arose not in Paris but at the periphery of the Empire. In this way a remarkable contradiction came about which only slowly dawned on French minds. Renewed pilgrimages to the Imperial capital and the apparent confirmation that these gave to the idea that Paris was still—or once more—the hub of the continent and of European civilization in general concealed the bitter truth that the "world spirit" had drifted off elsewhere and did not revolve around the mighty Napoleon as it had around King Louis XIV at Versailles or later around those twin stars, Voltaire and Rousseau. When a certain reputedly excentric woman bluntly said as much, the emperor was quite indignant. He ordered that Germaine de Staël's book *De l'Allemagne*, which appeared in 1810, should be immediately suppressed. But "a bonfire is no answer", as Camille Desmoulins once told Robespierre in similar circumstances, and in 1813 a second edition emerged in the quieter waters of London whence it circulated around the globe.

As the daughter of Necker Madame de Staël was a well-known figure. In her mother's salon she had already made the acquaintance of half the devotees of Enlightenment ideas in Paris, and during the Revolution she maintained her own scintillating salon in the up-market Rue du Bac as the intimate meeting place of the Feuillants. Following the storming of the Bastille she emigrated and after Thermidor she returned. To begin with she courted the favour of the child prodigy Napoleon but her attentions were not reciprocated, and increasing mutual antipathy finally developed into open hostility. She wrote about him in the most vitriolic terms and he responded with autocratic ire. The onlookers followed this unequal contest with relish and bated breath. The fall from favour and banishment failed to break the spirit of this very rich and soon celebrated lady at her château in Coppet, on the shore of Lake Geneva, even though she was loath to leave her beloved Paris.[4] Constantly harried by the custodians of law and order, she nevertheless indulged in numerous amorous affairs and travelled extensively, including to St. Petersburg. She continued to enthral her readers with two remarkable novels, *Delphine* (1803) and *Corinne* (1807).

Without doubt this emancipated lady, whom Napoleon contemptuously termed an "amazon", owed her public popularity to her talent, the freshness and subjective honesty of her writing, her commitment to her subject matter and her courage in tackling unconventional questions. She was also aided by the fact that at the turn of the century there was hardly any other star in the French literary firmament brilliant enough to outshine her. There were men who were well past their prime such as Bernardin de Saint-Pierre (1737–1814), Restif de la Bretonne and Marie Joseph Chénier; the rehashed neo-classical offerings of bandwagon poets like Legouvé or Delille; playwrights who managed to fill the theatres and whose frivolous fare was gratefully lapped up by the majority of theatregoers who sought amusement or sentimentality but whose names and plays have long since been forgotten: the stereotyped melodramas of men such as Pixerécourt in which God can always be relied upon to help Virtue triumph over Vice; a historical kind of drama which indulged in hero worship and which was thus perfectly in keeping with official wishes: e.g. *Peter the Great* by Carrion-Nisas, *Trajan* by Esménard or Lemercier's *Columbus*. Cultivated and prudent conformists like Louis de Fontanes (1757–1821) enveloped themselves in a mantle of Aesopian academicism which enabled them to survive both the Revolution and the Empire intact and even with honour before they were at last able under the Restoration to give vent to their true feelings.[5] One newcomer did appear

briand, however, he opposed the despotic exercise of power under the Empire and not its social nature as such. In 1815 he even formulated its last constitution. Backed by his lady friend he became one of the theoretical founders of a vitalic big bourgeois liberalism as a social doctrine.[1] However, this gifted writer's preoccupation with politics likewise curtailed his literary output.

Madame de Staël rightly concluded that French literature, cowed by the figure of Napoleon, was producing little or nothing. Thus she wrathfully drew French attention to the very different situation in the Germany of Goethe. In contrast to her model Tacitus, the Roman historian who never actually visited the Germania which he described so impressively, Madame de Staël was able to observe the country at first hand. She acquired her information direct from the horse's mouth, particularly in Weimar: from Schiller, the dramatist of the *Sturm und Drang* whose play *Die Räuber* (The Robbers) earned him honorary citizenship of the French Republic; from the old charmer Wieland; and indeed from the Olympian Goethe himself. And as a supplement to the literary achievements of the German classics she also managed to capture the first expansive gestures of German Romanticism, which she perceived as the initial stirrings of a literary rejuvenation. Out of the two strands she wove a picture which was both a little too flattering and one-sided. For her the Germans, though not quite up to scratch politically or—following the débacle of Jena—militarily, were nevertheless not the drunken brawlers of popular legend but rather the "Nation of Thinkers and Poets".

Celebrated quotations such as the one above have their own intrinsic and extrinsic history. Those who first utter them cannot be held responsible for their later misuse. Madame de Staël's observations were certainly not objective, but nor were they intended to be. Nevertheless, if one thinks about it properly she was not all that wide of the mark.

In the 18th century Germany, or rather the various Germanies (the plural term *les Allemagnes* was current at the time), was acknowledged as the leading force in the field of the educational sciences despite the fact that they reached their true zenith only later at the hands of the Swiss Jacobin Pestalozzi. Like the Italians before them, the Germans were now universally recognized as the

whose return from emigration aroused wild expectations: the Breton nobleman Chateaubriand. At first he identified himself with the great saviour of the Eighteenth of Brumaire, but he was quick to reject the advances of the "Emperor" Napoleon. The author of *René* (1805) and *Martyrs* (1809) was quickly lured away from Parnassus and developed into one of the standard-bearers of Bourbon legitimacy in the blue-blooded faubourg Saint-Germain.

The prevailing atmosphere on the Seine permitted only maudlin or tongue-in-cheek poetry to flourish.

Madame de Staël's Swiss compatriot and protegé, Benjamin Constant, was likewise soon deeply engrossed in politics. Unlike Chateau-

Madame de Staël. Chalk drawing by Jean-Baptiste Isabey.

The poet Chateaubriand. Lithograph by Hyacinthe Aubry-Lecomte after Anne-Louis Girodet-Trioson.

Your banishment is a natural consequence of the path which you have consistently followed for some years. It seemed to me that the air in this country does not suit you at all, nor are we as yet compelled to seek models to emulate among the nations which you admire. Your latest work is not French. It was I who stopped its being printed.
Minister of Police Savary, "Duke of Rovigo", October 3, 1810.

[1] Bastid, P.: *Benjamin Constant et sa doctrine.* Paris, 1967.

foremost music-makers: Handel in London, the Bach family scattered around Germany, Gluck in Paris and the immortal trio who gathered in Vienna—Haydn from Burgenland, Mozart from Salzburg and Beethoven, who hailed from Bonn. By contrast the written word took longer to transcend the language barrier and to attract to it the attention necessary to be categorized as "world literature" (even though the term was coined by no less a person than Goethe himself). At most such best-sellers as *The Sorrows of Werther* were translated.

Nor did many people read German outside northern and eastern Europe, whence young men preferred to study at Göttingen, Leipzig, Halle, Jena, Tübingen or Vienna rather than in Paris.

The uniqueness of the German literary landscape at the start of the century had a twofold cause.

The first was the breathtaking clash of two views of the world and the artistic genres based on them which found a home there and produced some superlative achievements. They pervaded one another and put out offshoots which occasionally—less so in the case of Hölderlin than in that of Kleist—rendered their categorization difficult. Napoleon came to terms with German classicism. He was impressed and even inspired by Goethe's personality, and the feeling was mutual. The creator of *Dr. Faustus* could not see why people took it amiss that he wore an Imperial French decoration, simply because the man who had awarded it lost the Battle of Leipzig. At the turn of the century the Romantics were represented in Jena and Berlin by the Schlegel brothers and their wives and by Tieck and Wackenroder. They viewed both sides critically until the collapse of Prussia and the Spanish rising forced them to unequivocally take sides. The Heidelberg brigade of Görres, Arnim and Brentano, plus the Arndts, Kleist and Körner began drumming up support for a war of liberation.[1] Despair caused by the humiliation of foreign domination overpowered them and also led them astray. Their yearning for peace of mind and incipient national chauvinism were grist to the mill of the rehabilitated forces of conservatism. In company with the latter they no longer opposed Napoleon as a renegade and the gravedigger of freedom but as the heir to and executor of the social upheaval guilty of the wanton destruction of the fruits of organic growth.

It was not a "court on high" but the advancing counter-revolution which asked "the reason why". And so too did their ever more amenable allies, the German Romantics, whose questioning spirit seemed to match the mood of the times. They found numerous kindred souls in other lands, particularly across the Channel among the English and Scottish left who had been similarly shaken by the outcome of the Revolution. In the foreword to their *Lyrical Ballads* of 1800 William Wordsworth and Samuel Coleridge[2] manifestly abandoned the great hopes they had placed in France. Henceforth they were to devote themselves, along with Shelley and Keats in the Romantic literary circle in the Lake district, to the *Weltschmerz* of the agonized individual in bourgeois society for which Byron, that latter-day

The appearance of the earth-spirit. Pencil drawing by Johann Wolfgang Goethe, probably produced in preparation for a performance of Part One of *Faust* in 1812. Nationale Forschungs- und Gedenkstätten der klassischen deutschen Literatur, Weimar.

Gothic church behind a grove of oaks with graves. Lithograph by Karl Friedrich Schinkel, c. 1810.

Slay and kill! No court on high
Will e'er ask the reason why.
Heinrich von Kleist: *Die Hermannsschlacht*, 1808.

Friend, we thought we had sown but a seed
to feed the wretched close at hand; in fact we
have planted a tree, the branches of which
will stretch out across the whole globe and
provide shade for every nation on earth with-
out exception.
Pestalozzi to Stapfer, March 24, 1808.

[1] DROZ, J.: *Le romantisme politique en Allemagne.* Paris, 1966.
[2] COLERIDGE, S.T.: *France. An Ode* (1798).
[3] TRACY, L.C. DESTUTT DE: *Eléments d'idéologie.* Paris, 1801–1815.
[4] KITCHIN, J.: *Un Journal philosophique: La Décade (1794–1807).* Paris, 1965.

Euphorion, found the deepest and most genuine expression.

In the second place it was not just the voices of the aesthetes which rang out at this time in Germany. The poets were joined by the thinkers, if this term can serve to denote the philosophy of classical German idealism.

The *philosophes* of the French Enlightenment had been keen writers who were fond of reflection. In Germany they were academics, professional purveyors of wisdom in the lecture hall. They were often difficult to understand, dry and somewhat pedantic but they thought systematically. Christian Wolff was no greater than Voltaire, nor Kant more important than Rousseau. However, as university lecturers they were specialists in their field. They took longer to acquaint the public with their works, to exercise influence on popular opinion and to dispel petty-minded prejudices. Their weapon of criticism was not yet sufficiently well honed to be able to mobilize the Marxian "criticism by weapons", i.e. an outright assault on the conditions within the state which their theory likewise rejected. Besides, for whom could they have forged the weapons in a country in which no social force was yet available to lead a revolution against privilege and despotism, against prejudice and superstition?

Indirectly these German schools of philosophy—or perhaps we should call them schoolroom philosophies—nevertheless rose to become a moral force. There were the Kantians of the "Tugendbund" (League of Virtue) during the Prussian era of reform; Fichte, who went a step further than Kant and penned the *Reden an die deutsche Nation* ("Addresses to the German Nation") in 1807/08 and in 1810 became the first rector of the University of Berlin; Jean Paul, the most widely read of the writers, with his *Kriegserklärung gegen den Krieg* ("Declaration of War on War" in *Deutsche Dämmerungen*, 1809); Schelling, despite his heavy involvement in Romantic natural philosophy, and Hegel, who thought long and hard before he finally wrote off Napoleon. Then there was Herder, who left a lasting testimony in his *Stimmen der Völker* ("Voices of the Nations"), a work of cosmopolitan tolerance which helped to make the world of the Slavs known in the West, and the Protestant theologian Schleiermacher. Truly the world had never before seen such a wealth of concurrent intellectual and spiritual impulses, which had germinated in the forcing house of the Revolution and which were due to fertilize the study of the humanities during the century, from philology to history. What equivalent could Imperial France offer? One proposal came from the *idéologues*, who attempted to bridge the gap between Enlightenment and Positivism.

It was Count Destutt de Tracy (1754–1836) who popularized the newly coined term "ideology" denoting a philosophical teaching which sought to discover a system of rules for morality, law and statesmanship by means of an allround analysis of mankind.[3] This took up Condillac's sensationism which related all thinking to sensorial perceptions, but abandoned some of the latter's metaphysical concepts in place of which the physician Cabanis (1757–1808) posited physiological explanations. It bore the rudiments of behaviourism which combined the methods of the natural sciences and the humanities. The object of these investigations was the psychic structure of the individual, the contents of his ideas and notions with the aim of deducing practical norms.

These "Idéologues" represented a school of thought that developed from a circle of scholars who in the early years of the Revolution met in the salon of Madame Helvétius, the wealthy widow of the feared atheist, in the salubrious Paris suburb of Auteuil. For this reason they were sometimes referred to as the "Society of Auteuil". Condorcet was a member as was the old Volney. After Thermidor Sieyès, Daunou and Laplace put in a reappearance. By a quirk of fate so too did Garat who as a minister had managed to walk a tightrope between the Gironde and the Mountain with what was for a philosopher a surprising amount of dexterity. The returned emigré Destutt de Tracy, supported by Cabanis, determined the profile of the journal *Décade philosophique*,[4] which earned a name for itself and new members for the group, including the highly promising young physicist François Arago. In 1807, however, it was forced to cease publication under pressure from the authorities.

The fact that Napoleon considered the Idéologues only a load of metaphysical windbags, found them insufferable and constantly crossed swords with them was understandable. Their

clever speeches irritated the pragmatic emperor, and he was further riled by his failure to split their ranks. The only one of their leaders whom he was able to win over was De Gérando.[1] Yet all this does not account for the vehemence of his intervention.

The debate raged less around theoretical points as the Empire aspired to make do without any rigid state dogma. Loyalty to the régime was completely compatible with ideological pluralism. Napoleon's unhappiness with the line taken by the Idéologues was roused by their presumption in seeking to teach him how to conduct the art of politics. He suspected that ulterior motives lay behind these excessively astute and far from unworldly self-appointed preceptors and their numerous admirers. As it turned out—too late for Napoleon—the reality was even worse than he had suspected. Despite his advocacy of reforms Destutt de Tracy had always remained at heart a royalist and indulged in his "extrascientific" mischief with deliberation and success. In April 1814 he had the pleasure of moving the emperor's deposition, to which the Senate agreed. This proves that neither side had been engaged in tilting at windmills.

While the Idéologues' battle with Napoleon's autocratic régime was causing such a stir, two other seminal lines of thought, though ultimately more successful, remained unnoticed by the public and police alike under the Empire: the "utopias" of the high-born aristocrat Claude Henri de Saint-Simon (1760–1825) and Charles Fourier (1772 to 1837), the ruined son of a businessman.

At this stage they bore no trade or water mark: the catchword "socialism" had not yet been invented. This may partly be explained by the fact that the two writers only gradually groped their way towards their goal and were themselves still in the process of formulating their ideas. Both were dissatisfied with the Revolution, the class character of which they recognized, and sought to go beyond the bourgeois order and petty-bourgeois egalitarianism it had set in train to a more perfect societal form.

Saint-Simon had been pondering over the problem since 1803,[2] but it was only under the Restoration that he emerged with a carefully elaborated scheme. His aim was to distribute the overall social product according to individual ability and performance, to iron out social contradic-

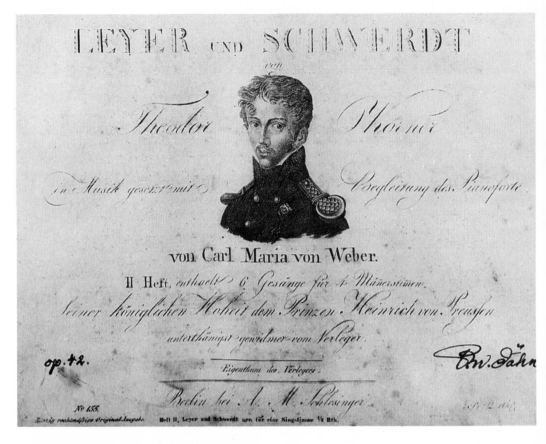

tions among the producers (whom he counterposed to the idlers), to direct and plan production by means of an élite of industrialists and scientists, to replace the exploitation of man by the exploitation of the earth and to transform the state from a medium of domination into a mechanism of provision.

The dialectician Fourier placed the defective functioning of capitalism, with all its contradictions and unacceptable hardships, at the centre of his critique and outlined a course of social development analogous to the Newtonian law of gravity which in the end would lead to "societary harmony".

As exemplary, autonomous models of the latter he proposed to set up social and economic communes known as *phalanstères* (phalanxes). In his main early work, *Théorie des quatre mouvements et des déstinées générales* (1808), he placed at the forefront a moral and educational revolution which he hoped would give rise to the new personality whose task—which would devolve equally on men and women—would be to bring about the "natural and just" society.

Both Saint-Simon and Fourier ruled out any mass action in the implementation of their ideals.[3] They relied on the logic of their arguments, on the process of persuasion and—with astonishing naivity—on the support of sensible, wealthy or influential patrons.

Consequently their perfectionism in no way alarmed the hard-bitten rulers. From time immemorial starry-eyed idealists to whom no one listened had been seen as harmless dreamers and allowed a free rein as long as they behaved peaceably and eschewed violence (and preferably counselled against its use as well). Thus there was no cause to try to stop them from attempting to construct a never-never land of human happiness. In 1803 Fourier even sent his grand scheme for achieving this to the appropriate authority, the minister of justice.

Actually Napoleon agreed with him that much more ought to be done in his domains for the organization of education and science. It was in their disparate views as to how this was to be attained that they differed.

Palais des Beaux-Arts in Paris. In 1801 the Collège Mazarin, which was built to Louis le Vau's design between 1663 and 1672, became the seat of the Academy of Art and in 1805 of the Institut de France. Engraving by François-Louis Couché, 1818. From: Binet (Editor), *Soixante vues des plus beaux palais, monuments et églises de Paris.* Paris, no date (*c.* 1818).

Page 120:
Title page of Theodor Körner's "Leyer und Schwerdt", set to music by Carl Maria von Weber. No. II, 1814.

[1] DE GÉRANDO, J.M.: *Histoire comparée des systèmes de philosophie.* Paris, 1804.
[2] (ANON.): *Lettres d'un habitant de Genève à ses contemporains* (1803).
[3] SAINT-SIMON, C.H. DE: *Du système industriel.* Paris, 1820–1822.
[4] AULARD, A.: *Napoléon Ier et le monopole universitaire.* Paris, 1911.

Napoleon never claimed that organization and the careful selection of cadres determined everything in the field of science and learning, but he did believe that nothing would work properly in their absence. And what he meant by organization was, as ever, centralization, effectiveness and parade-ground neatness. It was based on an outlook that undeniably had a definite social function.

The Empire put its trust in the carefully supervised cultivation of an élite with the aim of fusing property and education. By contrast little was done to educate the masses. By and large they were left to their own devices, to local initiative or to individual zeal. Whereas men such as Chaptal, Champagny and La Rochefoucauld-Liancourt at least deserve credit for the establishment of trade schools, Napoleon is said to have angrily protested: "Am I now to concern myself with the education of dolts?" His interest was directed at the higher educational institutions of which the standard was set by the state-run *lycée.* This replaced the "central school" of the Republican era, which was accused of being too liberal and mod-ernistic, and once again concentrated on providing a classical general education (not unlike the British grammar school). Though, in theory at least, freed from all aristocratic, ecclesiastical, regional and private influences, in actual fact it remained the preserve of children from the upper classes for whom it had indeed been specially tailored. Exclusive, standardized and bureaucratic, it strictly regulated everything from the curriculum and timetable to the school uniform and systematically prepared its pupils for higher education.

Students were in no way reminiscent of itinerant scholars or of citizens as free academics. They too moved within a closed system which was given its unalterable base by the university law of May 10, 1806 and subsequent decrees. It proved so stable that it was not shaken until the student riots of 1968.

Reflecting later on St. Helena Napoleon was still proud of his handiwork. The "Imperial University of France"[4] was a unified body based in Paris with sixteen branches in the provinces of which only a few, such as Montpellier and Strasbourg, enjoyed a reputation in their own right. Thus the pre-eminent position which Richelieu had granted to the Sorbonne in Paris not only remained intact, it was actually strengthened. The traditional number of faculties was increased. Theology, law and medicine retained their old framework while the natural sciences and the humanities were separated.

There could be no question of any academy autonomy or self-administration. The "University of France" was a well-drilled unit just like any other in the militarized state. Its statutes and disciplinary regulations dealt with teachers and taught with equal severity. The rules prescribed precisely what they had to say and to wear: for members of the teaching staff a black cloak with a blue silk palm attached to the left breast. During lectures they wore a black gown with a shoulder piece of etamine, the colour of which indicated the faculty and its trimmings the degree of seniority.

Yet the strict guardians of morality made little headway against the centuries-old tradition of riotous behaviour on the part of the young undergraduates in the old Quartier Latin on the left bank of the Seine in the vicinity of the Sorbonne. This generation of students, whose well-cushioned background gave them little cause for complaint, were not especially truculent, though whether the obligation imposed by the Imperial catechism in its seventh paragraph was a true reflection of the feelings of these future servants of the state is a question best left unanswered.

On the whole, however, the educational system worked well. It began to train a caste of highly qualified middle and top-ranking officials of all kinds whose loyalty—for the time being—was beyond question plus an up-and-coming generation of young men versed in the legal, medical and other professions which were so indispensable to a bourgeois society.

Pure research was not expected from the university sector, which was geared totally towards teaching, especially as effective and promising alternative institutions already existed for this purpose. These catered especially for the "exact" sciences on which research work was concentrated and to which the future belonged.

The composer Spontini. Lithograph by Jean Guérin after Jean-Baptiste Aubry-Lecomte, 1823.

The composer Boïeldieu. Chalk drawing by Jean-Baptiste Isabey, 1815.

Botany lesson in a park. Etching by Jean-Jacques de Boissieu, 1804.

The Owls of Minerva

The upswing which the "exact" sciences experienced at the end of the 18th century and which continued into the 19th century cannot be really credited to the various state leaders. A few ventures were promoted if they held out the prospect of raising their country's economic or military potential, and Leibniz's motto of "theoria cum praxi" found receptive ears among the founders of the academies in Berlin and St. Petersburg. But the incomparably greater position achieved by the natural sciences under the auspices of the Enlightenment did not result from the whims of princely patronage.

The Industrial Revolution emerged first in England and led to a thorough-going transformation of the existing mode of production, which had been exclusively based on handicraft techniques. It would have been impossible without the requisite scientific spadework, and in turn this gave a boost to research which thereby became more directly geared than ever before towards social problems.

By tackling the needs of material production it attained a new social quality. Branches of knowledge which had hitherto struggled to survive and which had depended on speculation for their funding now became autonomous disciplines in their own right. And although they rarely intervened in the political power struggles of the time their influence on basic processes ensured that they made a crucial contribution towards laying the foundations of a rational bourgeois society notable for its high rate of labour productivity.

Owing to the social and constitutional framework created by its successful revolution back in the 17th century, England's lead was both unmistakeable and unassailable. Its primitive accumulation of capital enabled the country to develop a factory system based on the combination of two decisive technical innovations: the invention of machine tools and of steam power.

Without the dynamic development of the natural sciences and their application to the manufacturing process this would have been quite impossible. The British inventors and innovators, engineers and designers whose most celebrative creative era now began were well aware of this.

Their pride in the power of knowledge showed in their words when they spoke before learned gatherings—such as the Lunar Society in Birmingham or the Literary and Philosophical Society in Manchester—where they met up with the theorists and jointly hailed the spirit of progress which, unburdened by considerations of church dogma or the straitjacket of moral precepts, began to unlock the secrets of both nature and society.

Intellectually the French—as also the German and Italian—pioneering scholars were in no way inferior to their English counterparts. However, the backwardness of their social environment forced them to direct most of their attention to other areas. They had first to concentrate on breaking free of the old régime in which hundreds of hindrances prevented them from freely using the fruits of their research to further the national economic effort. The *lumières* and the public authorities confronted and observed one another with well-founded mutual suspicion.

The French Revolution gave the scientists a more hopeful outlook, even though their reactions to it varied. Some thought its amelioration went too fast, others too far. Some saw it as too turbulent, others as too brutal. Still others, such as the astronomer Bailly or the philosopher Condorcet, had benevolently marched in the front (or, like the chemist Lavoisier, at least in the secondary) ranks of the Revolution, only to get fatefully entangled in its unforeseeable twists and turns. Highly desirable material and financial comforts went for a burton as the Jacobins ruthlessly purged and eventually closed down the academies and universities, in which obdurate obscurantists had held out to the last.

Yet it was these selfsame reviled Jacobins who appealed to the men of science to put their knowledge to use in defence of the Republic. This call to go beyond mere fine-sounding words and to perform tangible deeds for their country, aimed at mobilizing their full potential in similar vein to the military *levée en masse* of August 1793, was an unprecedented act unparallelled in history of which only a revolutionary society was capable. The call was heard and heeded.

Prominent mathematicians who included Lagrange, Laplace and Romme, the chemist Berthollet, the mathematician and brilliant military organizer Carnot, the physicist Coulomb and many

The first time a balloon was filled with hydrogen by Alexandre César Charles and the Roberts brothers, 1783. Engraving by Louis Sellier.

Accordingly we could regard the present state of the universe as the effect of its past state and as the cause of the state which will follow. A level of knowledge which would be cognizant of all the forces which set Nature in motion as well as of the various positions of all its components at any given moment—assuming it were sufficiently comprehensive to be able to analyze this data—would summarize the movements of the largest bodies as well as the lightest atom in a single formula. Nothing would be beyond its ken; the future would be just as knowable as the present. The human spirit, in the degree of perfection that it has achieved in astronomy, offers a faint inkling of such a capacity of knowledge.
Laplace: "Essai philosophique des probabilités", 1814.

[1] MONGE, G.: *Géometrie descriptive* (1799); with CASSINI and BERTHOLON: *Dictionnaire de physique* (1793–1822).
[2] CHANTELOUP, J. A. C. CHAPTAL DE: *Mes souvenirs sur Napoléon.* Paris, 1893.
[3] FOURIER, J.-B.: *Théorie analytique de la chaleur* (1812).

others offered their services to the Republic. Gaspard Monge,[1] the son of an itinerant knife grinder and sometime minister of naval affairs, was the co-author with Vauquelin of a paper on steel production for arms manufacture. He also did useful work as the man in charge of cannon casting and rifle production. The chemists Fourcroy and De Morveau took over the task of organizing the supply of saltpetre, of which there was a dangerous dearth, in cellars and cattle sheds with the help of thousands of volunteers. They taught patriotic Frenchmen how to produce gunpowder that "ignites the flash which kills the tyrants". Chappe's optical telegraph—a signalling relay which reduced the time needed to transmit messages between the northern front and Paris to little more than an hour, passed its first test with flying colours in 1794. Military strategy was even extended to the third dimension when the designer Franz Joseph Lange from Klein-Kembs, known in Lyons as L'Ange, set out to master the ethereal element for the Republic by means of an air fleet. A start was made during the Battle of Fleurus on June 26, 1794 when a fully operational "Montgolfière"—a hot-air balloon—took off in order to observe the enemy's movements from on high.

By suppressing the privileges of the nobility the Revolution democratized access to education. Of course this did not occur on the scale demanded and hoped for by the educational blueprints of such democratically-minded revolutionaries as Michel Lepeletier or Léonard Bourdon. But it at least removed those barriers, consisting of a mixture of narrow-mindedness and aristocratic contempt, which were exemplified by the minister of education under the *ancien régime,* who dismissed the tailor's son who promised to become one of the greatest scientists of his age with the terse observation: "Fourier is not of noble birth and so could not enter the artillery even if he were a second Newton!"

Thus the French Revolution was willing and indeed compelled to found and to bequeath to the Empire educational establishments which were to prove immensely fruitful and enduring. These included:

the *Ecole Normale Supérieure,* largely inspired by Lakanal, which provided training and further qualification for the pick of the teaching profession, especially in the field of natural sciences;

the *Conservatoire National des arts et métiers,* the prototype of a science museum based on the idea of the multifaceted cultural commentator Henri Grégoire. It was a permanent exhibition of machines and inventions with workshops and laboratories on the premises of the former monastery complex of Saint-Martin-des-Champs in the Section Gravilliers (the old stamping ground of the "red priest" Jacques Roux);

the *Ecole Polytechnique* (1794/95)—a new-style technical college recommended by Carnot, Monge and Berthollet which was to meet contemporary needs. It was exclusively devoted to the natural and the engineering sciences—in the broadest sense. It went on to spawn many similar colleges all over the world—minus the figure of the illustrious general who became its "gouverneur" in 1804;

the *Institut National* (later known as the *Institut de France*). Enshrined in Article 298 of the Constitution of the Year III (1795), with its 312 members it became much more than a substitute for the academy. It was the real and effective focus and coordinating centre of research work in all areas and throughout the country and at the same time a means of active control over scientific policy which the bourgeois state was neither willing nor able to do without. It thus came as no surprise that when the globetrotting Alexander von Humboldt, fêted as the "second man to discover America", decided that the only place he could locate his gigantic *Kosmos* was in the metropolis of the Grand Empire with its incomparable aids, institutes and libraries.

General Bonaparte was all the more proud of his election in 1797 to the physical-mathematical section of the most renowned scientific body, since even as a cadet he had shown a great penchant for mathematics. On becoming First Consul he gave his seat to Carnot but continued to closely observe both scientific matters and the scientists themselves within "his" realm, sometimes with satisfaction and sometimes with annoyance. The men who represented French science tended to view themselves at this time as belonging to two worlds. Believing in the indivisibility of progress they ranged themselves alongside their fellow colleagues elsewhere as members of a scholarly brotherhood that encompassed the whole world and which in this sense, with an obligation to serve the entire human race, transcended all na-

Sellier Sculp.

tional boundaries. At the same time they had a patriotic pride in their country in which, for the first time, they had full backing and encouragement. Some social critics, accused by Napoleon of disloyalty to the emperor, were plunged into conflict by this dichotomy. On the other hand the Empire did not molest the natural scientists. On the contrary, even though Napoleon did not take up all their discoveries he was shrewd enough to appreciate the public usefulness of their work,[2] to manifest his benevolence and to proffer them all manner of assistance in the expectation of tangible results. He particularly delighted in bestowing honours on them and saw to it that their living conditions were improved. He was pleased to appoint them senators—a lucrative business. In no other sphere did the emperor, whose habitual interference was greatly feared, try so hard to curb his tongue and desist from carping. He did not bring his authority to bear on these men, who were authorities in their own fields. He sought instead to engage them in dialogue, though often to boost his own ego, and even when, in spite of his crip, he made embarrassing blunders this did not undermine the high opinion which he enjoyed among French scholars. He took to heart the Roman saying "Caesar non supra grammaticos", and fared pretty well as a result.

Mathematicians had always enjoyed the highest esteem and France had a particularly bright panoply of stars in this field: Monge (1746 to 1818), who with his descriptive geometry, today better known as technical drawing, created the "language of engineers" and thus the indispensable tool of designers of everything from buildings to machine parts; Jean-Baptiste Fourier (1768 to 1830, not to be confused with his near contemporary, the utopian socialist Charles Fourier). By means of his analysis he introduced a new definition of the concept of functions—a term of decisive importance for the whole of mathematics. This he did with the still heuristic hypothesis that all functions, including discontinuous and algebraically non-representable ones, can be portrayed by an infinite sum of constant trigonometrical functions.[3]

Not infrequently leading mathematicians extended their investigations to the field of celestial mechanics which made their names known to a wider public who were always interested in stargazing and the like. They did not achieve the popularity of the real stalwarts who personally sat behind their telescopes night after night: Herschel in England, who in 1781 discovered a new planet within the solar system: Uranus; or Piazzi in Palermo, who on New Year's Eve in the year 1800 sighted a stellar body with his telescope which disappeared but then returned a year later at precisely the spot predicted by Carl Friedrich Gauss (1777–1855) of Göttingen: Ceres, the first star to be discovered among the teeming mass of the asteroids.

Using mathematical means Joseph Louis Lagrange (1736–1813) cogently demonstrated that, in contradistinction to Newton's view, the solar system as a whole remained stable despite the perturbations in the orbits of the planets around the central plane. Pierre Simon Laplace (1749 to 1827) complemented the consistent mechanical materialism of the French Enlightenment with his five-volume *Mécanique céleste*.[1] He held that the universe was nothing other than an (albeit immensely huge) collection of material particles—atoms or mass points—and that their motions, in strict accordance with the prevailing mechanical laws, set in train all changes in nature. If an astronomer knew the initial criteria of all particles for a given time, place and velocity, then by solving a set of differential equations he could—at least in theory—precisely calculate the condition of the entire universe in the past, present and future down to the last detail. The fact that the emperor was unable to believe this mathematical genius, who subsequently acquired the nickname "the demon Laplace", did not matter. He might query an opinion but he did not, in this case at least, suppress it.

This proved a boon to the mathematicians' close associates, the physicists. During the Revolution they together successfully championed the momentous introduction of the metric system. This overcame the feudal atomization of weights, measures and standards in a triumphal march from Paris to the four corners of the earth. In 1791 a commission set up by the National Assembly and consisting of Lagrange, Laplace and others laid down the ten millionth part of the earth's quadrant as the standard unit of measurement of length and by determining the oscillation period of a second at a latitude of 45° established its relation to the unit of time. This reflected its debt to the Enlightenment theories of natural right. At the same time the commission also undertook the Herculean task of measuring the earth's arc between Dunkirk and Barcelona, and in 1799 constructed an end measure of platinum as the prototype of the new unit of measurement. At Borda's suggestion it was named a "metre", from the Greek *metron* meaning measure. The commemorative medal struck to mark the occasion bore an inscription which testified to the bourgeoisie's sense of mission: "For all times, for all nations."

Of course, such things needed time, nor was Napoleon in any great hurry. For the time being his infantrymen continued to tramp old-fashioned miles and their rations were not yet allocated in the form of kilos, grammes and litres. It took shopkeepers and thrifty housewives a long time to get used to the new system of weights and measures and to scrimp with every centime instead of each sou, though the latter died hard in popular parlance. Even in the realm of the natural sciences, where it had been conceived, the metric system did not fully establish itself until the Empire had long since been superseded. In fact the physicists were very slow to rid themselves of their traditional notions. Lagrange succeeded in formally perfecting theoretical mechanics, i.e. the mathematical treatment of the mechanics of mass points (of an idealized mechanics).[2] He and his contemporaries, like Newton, still saw mechanics as the basis of all physics in the sense that ultimately every physical phenomenon derived from it. Yet it was left to the following generation at the Ecole Polytechnique, working under the exegencies of the Industrial Revolution, to extend the application of mechanics to the relations of forces (including friction) inherent in machines and, in particular, the steam engine.

In the field of optics it was a similar picture. The Englishman Thomas Young, in a famous experiment in 1807, managed to refute the "corpuscular theory" of light that went back to Newton and to demonstrate its undulatory character. However, he gained little credence, especially as Malus discovered the polarization of light by reflection a year later in Paris, which seemed to be incompatible with the wave theory. It was not until 1817 that Young managed to solve the apparent contradiction by positing transverse rather than longitudinal waves, and the hypothesis of an

Alexander von Humboldt. Engraving by Auguste Boucher-Desnoyers after François Gérard's drawing of 1805.

Lavoisier's burning glass for the production of high temperatures in order to thermally decompose chemical substances. From: *Œuvres de Lavoisier*, Vol. III. Paris, 1865.

Lavoisier's rigorous definition, interpreted in a modern sense:

We use the term elements to express our idea of the ultimate point that analysis can attain by any means to reduce a body to its basic constituents.

One day mathematics will rule the world.
Napoleon

[1] LAPLACE, P.S.: *Mécanique céleste* (1799–1825).
[2] LAGRANGE, J.L.: *Mécanique analytique* (1788);
LAVOISIER, A.L.: *Traité élémentaire de chymie.* (1789);
LAMARCK, J.-B. DE: *Philosophie zoologique* (1809).
[1] (p. 128) HUARD, P.: *Sciences, Médecine, Pharmacie de la Révolution à l'Empire.* Paris, 1970.

A *Grande Lentille à liqueur.*
B *Petite Lentille pour rassembler les raions plus près.*
C *Centre de mouvement horisontal de toute la Machine.*
D *Manivelle servant à imprimer le mouvement horisontal.*
E *Manivelle servant à imprimer le mouvement vertical par le moien des Vis 1 et 2.*
F *Vis de rappel pour éloigner de la grande Loupe la petite Lentille ou la rapprocher.*
G *Porte objet aïant le mouvement de haut en bas et de bas en haut celui d'avancer et reculer parallellement à la plate-forme et de s'incliner au degré du Soleil et de s'avancer parallellement aux raions.*
H *Chariot ou Plate-forme portant toute la Machine et les Opérateurs.*
I *Roues du Chariot tendantes au Centre de mouvement par leurs Axes et roulantes sur des bandes de fer incrustées circulairement sur une plate-forme de pierre.*
K *Escalier pour parvenir sur le Chariot, il est soutenu de deux rouleaux excentriques.*

DESSEIN en Perspective d'une Grande Loupe formée par 2 Glaces de 52 po. de diam. chacune coulées à la Manufacture Royale de St. Gobin, courbées et travaillées sur une portion de Sphère de 16 pieds de diam. par Mr. de Berniere, Controlleur des Ponts et Chaussées, et ensuite opposées l'une à l'autre par la concavité. L'espace lenticulaire qu'elles laissent entr'elles a été rempli d'esprit de vin il a quatre pieds de diam. et plus de 6 pouc. d'epaisseur au centre: Cette Loupe a été construite d'après le désir de L'ACADÉMIE Roiale des Sciences, aux frais et par les soins de Monsieur DE TRUDAINE, Honoraire de cette Académie, sous les yeux de Messieurs de Montigny, Macquer, Brisson, Cadet et Lavoisier, nommés Commissaires par l'Académie. La Monture a été construite d'après les idées de Mr. de Berniere, perfectionnée et exécutée par Mr. Charpentier, Mécanicien au Vieux Louvre.

À Monsieur De Trudaine
Par son très humble et très obéissant Serviteur, Charpentier.

"ethereal" medium lingered on well into the century.

It was above all the "electricians" who, grabbing the limelight around 1770 through Mesmer, became the darlings of the public. Working in Paris between 1785 and 1789, Coulomb had discovered that electrical and magnetic forces, analogous to the law of gravity, were inversely proportional to the square of their distances. Galvani carried out his sensational experiments on frogs' legs in Bologna in 1789 while in Pavia Volta refuted this "animalistic" electricity when, using various metal plates, he achieved the same effect through the medium of static electricity. In 1799 he increased the effect by introducing diluted acid between the metals. The secret of the battery had been discovered, and in London in 1807 Humphrey Davy successfully demonstrated electrolysis with a battery of voltaic piles. While Volta was being led round Paris as Napoleon's personal guest other scholars were busy increasing both the scope and spread of his discovery: Nicholson and Carlisle in England, Berzelius and Hisinger in Sweden, Oerstedt in Denmark.

The breakthroughs in chemistry were even more amazing. Its reputation suffered from its long association with alchemy and attempts to manufacture gold. Indeed, many a charlatan like Cagliostro indulged in all sorts of hocus-pocus with the "philosopher's stone" and "elixirs of life" by which even crowned heads such as the Emperor Leopold II were taken in. Even serious experiments such as the work of Georg Ernst Stahl in Germany and Henry Cavendish (1731–1810) in England, who discovered hydrogen and determined the composition of water, were only in small part based on conclusive scientific theories. Undoubtedly the very fact of gathering practical experience and findings was extremely important for chemistry, since this empirical approach made possible new techniques for the extraction of iron and steel and made auxiliary materials available for the machinery of the expanding textile industry.[1] From 1790 onwards Leblanc in Paris was able to produce unlimited quantities of soda, needed for washing raw cotton fabrics, of a purer quality and more economically than the natural soda imported from Egypt or Spain. This he did by adding sulphuric acid to common salt to produce sodium sulphate which he then converted into soda by heating it in a reverbatory furnace with limestone and coal. For a generation France enjoyed a world monopoly of "Leblanc soda". The rigorous scientific reputation of chemistry was finally put beyond doubt by Lavoisier in France and Dalton in England, who built on the chemistry of gas. In 1789 Lavoisier published a textbook which has been called the birth certificate of the new chemistry. It embodied the distinction which he first demonstrated in a series of experiments between chemical elements on the one hand and compounds on the other. He recognized the key to the latter as oxygen, discovered by Priestley in England in 1774. In compound with metals it produces the alkalis and with non-metals the acids, while the neutralization of acids by alkalis gives rise to the salts.

In 1797, in a dispute with Berthollet, Proust supplemented the theory of elements by the law of constant composition, by which the combination of two elements produces a compound. Confirmation of the law with regard to gases was supplied in 1811 by the Frenchman Gay-Lussac and the Italian Avogadro, while among Dalton's achievements was the definition of the relative atomic weight of hydrogen (H) as "1". Berzelius worked out the relative atomic weights of all the forty elements then known and formulated the symbols by which they are still known: a system of abbreviations of their Latin names. In 1812 he introduced the term "organic chemistry" for that largely uncharted area in which the concept of a "vital force", the *vis vitalis*, was still being used by scientists as a metaphysical prop long after the equivalent hypothetical substance in the inorganic field, "phlogiston", had been expunged from their colleagues' vocabulary.

On the other hand, when the naturalists coined the term biology at the turn of the century they reflected their belief that all living organisms, whether plants, animals or human beings, shared common features, which thus necessitated a unified "science of life" that bridged the boundaries separating the individual disciplines of botany, zoology and (possibly) anthropology. This was a fundamental advance which broke important new ground.

With the aim of uncovering a "plan of creation" the researchers groped their way forward, via many detours and blind alleys, to what they perceived as the fixed natural order of things. They sought to classify all living things, on a sliding scale, from the lowest to the highest species, and to determine the concomitant criteria. Others saw them as variations of a handful of basic types. One of these was Goethe. He used the word "morphology" to denote the science of forms and structures of organisms and initially accepted the hypothesis of a primordial plant which he actually tried to find on a visit to Sicily. Another was the anatomist Georges de Cuvier (1769–1832) who distinguished between four different basic types in the animal kingdom. In 1830 he defended his thesis in a spectacular debate at the academy in Paris with the zoologist Geoffroy Saint-Hilaire, who believed in a single basic structure.

In the end, however, this idea of the fixed natural order of things was itself caught in a crossfire of doubts. The idea of perpetual development which ran like a thread through the Enlightenment and which with the Revolution became social reality, was also confirmed by the natural sciences: astronomy, cosmogony, geology and palaeontology each showed in their own that even the earth and the universe had their own history. In 1755 Kant felt obliged to publish his *Allgemeine Naturgeschichte und Theorie des Himmels* ("General Natural History and Theory of the Heavens") anonymously: "Successive continuation of the Creation in all eternity of time and infinity of space, through the incessant formation of new worlds ... Gradual decay and decline of the world system ... Renewal of decayed Nature."

Thus with his views about the historical nature of the solar system the philosopher from Königsberg, as Frederick Engels was later to say, made the first breech in the wall of metaphysical thinking. When in 1796 Laplace published his

Exposition du système du monde, which described the genesis of our planet in terms quite different from those in the biblical story of the Genesis, its main tenets met with undisguised approval from the erudite world.

That the earth and all its life forms must also have gone through various stages of evolution was forcefully demonstrated by Buffon, Intendant of the Botanical Gardens in Paris and a man of encyclopaedic learning in his 36-volume work *Histoire naturelle générale et particulière* (1749 to 1788), which was completed by someone else in 1804. Based on his study of the earth's crust the mineralogist Abraham Gottlieb Werner (1749 to 1817) developed a comprehensive system of geological history.

Fossils likewise provided evidence for the theory of evolution. Cuvier, who was given top posts and showered with honours by both Napoleon and the Bourbons after him, did much to further palaeontology. He showed how inferences could be drawn from a few old bones about long-extinct animals which no human being had ever seen. However, the conclusion he arrived at was erroneous. The only way he could explain the gaps in the evolutionary development of fossils was by means of periodic cataclysms followed by the appearance of totally or partially new creations. Lamarck (1744–1829) got closer to the truth. His theory rejected the notion of cataclysms in favour of a gradual transition from one geological era to the next through evolutionary adaptation to changing environmental conditions.

Hence the Owls of Minerva did not fly from country to country in accordance with the plans and schemes of the Empire. Its boundaries were not their boundaries, nor its aspirations their aspirations. Its style, its deeds and misdeeds were quite different from their own. Nor did their respective chronologies or breaks in development coincide. Indeed, how could there be any coincidence between the necessarily long-term perspective of the sciences and the inevitably short-term political project of Napoleon Bonaparte?

Nevertheless, both in the home of the Revolution and in those countries which combated it the advances in scientific knowledge and learning, which offered irresistible and irrefutable confirmation of the bourgeoisie's appropriation of the world, became inextricably associated with the Napoleonic era.

Page 129:

JEAN-BAPTISTE REGNAULT: Liberty or Death, 1793.
No less abstract or radical than the revolutionary
calendar or other cultural declarations of the
Jacobin era, this composition illustrates the political situation with the aid of pictorial symbols of
the Enlightenment. The genius of France, the
bearer of light, hovers between two allegorical figures: Liberty triumphant (holding a Freemason's
plumbline as a symbol of equality) and Death.
The picture is a smaller version of a monumental
painting, which subsequently went missing, that
the artist presented to "the Nation". Like David,
his rival as both a painter and a teacher, Regnault
continued to enjoy success under the Empire.
This was reflected by his work "Napoleon's
Triumphal Procession to the Temple of Immortality", which was nine metres long, and by a
number of blithely elegant nude studies.
Oil on canvas, 50 × 49.3 cm. Kunsthalle Hamburg.

ISIDORE-STANISLAS HELMAN after CHARLES MONNET:
The Fountain of Rejuvenation was built on the
ruins of the Bastille for the Festival of Unity and
Rejuvenation in Paris on August 10, 1793. Details
of the great public festivals, the most characteristic
and democratic cultural genre of the revolutionary epoch, have survived only in the form of pictorial and verbal reports. These events mobilized
huge numbers of people and occasioned the construction of immense decorative structures from
wood, plaster and cloth.

They included the Festival of National Federation
on the first anniversary of the Storming of the Bastille, a festival to mark the transference of Voltaire's mortal remains to the Panthéon, funeral
marches for revolutionary heroes, the Festival of
Unity and Rejuvenation in 1793, the Festival of
the Supreme Being (Reason) and many others, including the Festival of General Peace in the Year
X, which raised great but false hopes. In charge of
designing the set and decorations for the rejuvenation festival of August 10, 1793, and for many
others, was Jacques-Louis David. The procession,
which included a hearse containing sceptres and
crowns, was routed through several specially decorated public squares spaced well apart from one
another. On the Place de la Bastille stood a giant
figure representing Nature which spouted water
from its breasts.
Engraving, 1793.

Jean Duplessi-Bertaux and Delaunay the Younger
after Carle Vernet's drawing: The removal of
the equestrian statues of San Marco in Venice. In
December 1797 the famous four antique bronze
horses were taken from the façade of the church of
San Marco and brought to Paris as war trophies,
just like many other Italian works of art—including the lion of St. Mark's, the symbol of Venice.
For a few years they adorned the triumphal arch
on the Place du Carrousel until they had to be
given back in 1815.
Etching from the work: *Campagnes des Français
sous le Consulat et sous l'Empire.* Paris, 1806.

AUGUSTE HIBON after CHRISTOPHE CIVETON: The courtyard of the Museum of Antiquities in the Louvre.

Page 133:
The grand staircase of the museum in the Louvre.
Engravings from the work: Frédéric Comte de
Clarac, *Musée de Sculpture antique et moderne.*
Paris, 1826.

Ever since the Italian campaign the plundering of
art treasures was virtually part of the legitimation
of the returning conqueror. Napoleon took with
him to Egypt a special group of scholars who were
to concern themselves purely with philological
and archaeological tasks. Famous works of art
were brought back to Paris from all occupied
countries—from the Belvedere Apollo and Mem-
ling's Danzig altar to Altdorfer's "Alexander's
Victory" and Veronese's "The Feast in Levi's
House". For a few years until their enforced return the capital of the Empire possessed art collections of incredible dimensions which provided
living artists with all the opportunities for study
that they could possibly want. As the "Musée
Napoléon" the Louvre was opened to the public in
1793 and expanded. Under the control of Vivant
Denon, a scholar who often supervised the assembly of booty on the spot, the collections were
systematically arranged in respect of their evolution.

JEAN-BAPTISTE MAUZAISSE and CAMOIN after RENÉ
BERTHON's painting: Vivant Denon in his study.
The private collection of the chief curator of the
French museums contained samples of numerous
different cultures, including non-European ones.
Within the realm of European painting he was
mostly interested in the "primitive" masters on
the threshold of the Renaissance.
Lithograph.

JEAN-BAPTISTE ISABEY: The artist with his wife in the studio, c. 1800/1805.

The versatile portrait painter, miniaturist, lithographer, and designer of theatrical décor, costumes and merit awards has depicted himself at the beginning of his brilliant career under Napoleon. Right up until the end of the Empire he was constantly in the vicinity of the emperor and an indispensable figure in all the salons. Having previously enjoyed Marie-Antoinette's favour, he continued to hold public office under the various regimes up to 1848, but he reached the pinnacle of his career under Napoleon. Precisely because he did not have a distinctive personal style he was able to execute a wide range of commissioned work with ease. Painting. Present whereabouts unknown.

LOUIS-LÉOPOLD BOILLY: Visitors to the Salon in 1808 before David's coronation picture. Painted between 1808 and 1815.

From the time of Louis XIV it was the custom to display the new works of artists annually in a salon within the Louvre, and these exhibitions soon became a big attraction for the bourgeois public. They provided an opportunity for Diderot, amongst others, to develop a model of art criticism. After the Revolution had allowed all artists, and not just those with academic titles, to submit their work the "Salon", which was now supervised directly by the government, enjoyed a further increase in prestige, the number of visitors rose and the controversies surrounding individual pictures and new trends grew more acute. In the course of the 19th century such throngs of visitors were repeatedly depicted, usually with a satirical slant. Boilly's light-

hearted genre picture pays tribute to the great success of David's solemn history painting: he specifically asked David's permission to portray this situation. Fellow artists feature among the inquisitive and interested crowd: older ones such as Houdon, Hubert Robert, Madame Vigée-Lebrun (the portrait painter of the *ancien régime*) plus younger practitioners like Gérard and Gros.

Oil on canvas, 60 × 81 cm. Present whereabouts unknown.

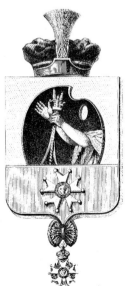

The coat of arms of the artist Jacques-Louis David. In 1808 David was raised to the knighthood as a member of the Legion of Honour. The main field of his coat of arms in the form of a palette shows a characteristic detail from the famous "Oath of the Horatii". David's public career ended in 1815. Just about tolerated before the "Hundred Days", he was regarded as an undesirable figure after Waterloo and emigrated to Brussels. His erstwhile Jacobin sympathies were probably more to blame for this than his Napoleonic past, for many other prominent artists of the Imperial era were readily accepted by the restored Bourbon monarchy, e.g. Isabey, Gérard, Gros, Guérin, Regnault, the sculptor Bosio and others. Compared to the Romanticism of Géricault and Delacroix they became dependable pillars of conservatism.
Engraving.

JACQUES-LOUIS DAVID: The Sabine women intervening in the struggle between the Sabini and the Romans. 1799.

When this picture went on show in Paris in return for an admission charge, the 51-year-old painter stood at the zenith of his spectacular career, which closely mirrored the political ups-and-downs. He was already a successful painter of historical scenes and of portraits and a renowned teacher when, four years before the Bastille fell, he completed his "Oath of the Horatii" in Rome. The work was a monumental tribute to the ideal of Roman civic virtue which was to form the central plank of the revolutionary ethic. The painting made a big impression throughout Europe. The Revolution found in David its artistic impresario, organizer of festivals and state painter. As a member of the Committee of Public Safety, a regicide, the man who had immortalized on canvas the assassinated Marat and a friend of Robespierre, he was arrested in the wake of 9 Thermidor and only escaped the guillotine by disavowing Jacobinism. Yet a year later he was already reclimbing the ladder. As a member of the newly founded Academy of Fine Arts he began a new career under the Directory and the Empire. In 1803 he became Premier Painter to the First Consul. In 1798 he painted one of the first portraits of Napoleon and later painted a huge canvas of the coronation. The fall of Napoleon irrevocably brought about his own downfall. In France he bequeathed to his fellow painters a firmly established theory of art which replaced the old-fashioned academicism but in its turn soon became equally as ossified.

David was unable to maintain the realistic austerity, which is the hallmark of his portraits, in his historical paintings in classical style. Compared to the earlier "Oath of the Horatii" with its rigid and severe compositional framework the Sabine picture, on which he began working in prison, is full of pacification and theatrical opulence. Strict aesthetic rules are already beginning to lead to the emergence of free-standing tableaux. The young woman who has thrust herself into the thick of the fray in order to separate the two combatants was immediately interpreted as a symbol of national reconciliation following Bonaparte's victories. Overnight Bonaparte made him his personal painter and commissioned him to paint the famous picture of him crossing the Alps on horseback.

Oil on canvas, 386 × 520 cm. Musée du Louvre, Paris.

JACQUES-LOUIS DAVID: Leonidas at the Thermopylae.
1800–1814.

This huge picture occupied David intermittently for the whole of his Napoleonic career. The work was begun uncommissioned at a time of victory and great hope in the year of the Battle of Marengo and completed in the year the Empire collapsed. In retrospect this portrayal of the heroic defeat of a Greek army in the Persian War (which Napoleon reputedly advised the artist not to undertake) seems like a dire presentiment—which it was surely not. The artist wanted to depict manly equanimity and martial virtue in the face of a hopeless situation:

"I want to show the king and his men preparing like true Spartans for an encounter which they know they will not survive." The central figure of the Sabine picture, whose outstretched arms drew together all the dramatic movement in the painting, has given way to a melancholy hero who is optically isolated from all the commotion around him and seeks an exclusive dialogue with the viewer. This was a figure which, in various guises, repeatedly reappears around 1800 and thereafter. Despite the classical setting the psychological outlook of the new-style French citizen is clearly apparent.

Oil on canvas, 392 × 533 cm. Musée du Louvre, Paris.

PIERRE-NARCISSE GUÉRIN: The Death of Cato. 1797.
For all neo-classical artists a stay in Rome following
their studies was a crucial phase in their early development. The contest for the Prix de Rome, which included the award of a scholarship for several years,
at the same time sifted out the future masters. Guérin
won the prize, which David was awarded only at the
fourth attempt, for this Cato picture, the first in a series
of historical paintings of antiquity which were often inspired by the classical French theatre. The self-immo-
lation of Cato, a Stoic and Republican, in face of
Caesar's triumphs was, as a prime example of Roman
virtue, a very topical subject. The hero, having plunged
the sword into his stomach, deliberately enlarges the
wound with his hand while staving off the doctor. His
dynamic motion forms a natural focus for the differentiated gesticulations of his horrified friends who,
though full of dramatic intensity, form a well-ordered
sequence in a compressed two-dimensional plane.
The hectic movements of the figures are offset by the
calm solidity of an architectural backdrop adorned
with eagles. In later years Guérin's painting became
more complaisant in common with the general trend
of art in the Napoleonic era.
Oil on canvas, 111 × 144 cm. École des Beaux-Arts,
Paris.

PIERRE-NARCISSE GUÉRIN: Aurora and Cephalus. 1810.
Barely a year after its completion the painting was repeated at the behest of the Russian prince Yussupov,
who bought up a number of paintings in Paris during
Napoleon's time. (Hence the first version hangs in the
Louvre while the second is in the Hermitage in Lenin-
grad.) The felicitous result is characteristic: with its
theatrical play of light the picture represents a late
phase of Napoleonic neo-classicism which combines
romanticizing and decorative elements.
Engraving by François Forster (1821) after the painting, which was exhibited in 1810.

FRANÇOIS GÉRARD: Cupid and Psyche. 1798.
When no heroic subject-matter instilled power and
pathos into their works, the classicist followers of David
abandoned themselves to a gentle sentimentality and
sweet softness which, in view of the turbulent times in
which they lived, were quite astonishing. The hedonistic and sensuous lovers of the Rococo period were
now replaced by ethereal, innocent figures. This was
typified by the predilection for the almost child-like
couple, Cupid and Psyche whose passivity and erotic
coolness are in turn not without ambiguity. The neo-
classical form, emptied of all living substance, gave
rise to a wealth of decorative and luxurious art which
already contained many of the features that were
to characterize "salon painting" up to the end of
the century.
Engraving by Hyacinthe Aubry-Lecomte after the
painting, which was exhibited in 1798.

FRANÇOIS GÉRARD: Belisarius. 1795.
The late Roman general Belisarius was accused of con-
spiring against the Emperor Justinian, convicted and
later rehabilitated. The belief that he ended his days as
a blind beggar, as Gérard depicts him here, is probably
only a legend. But many contemporaries in the revolutionary and Imperial eras could identify with such
vicissitudes. The fact that the lowering, tragic figure is
seen from below heightens the impact which he makes.
We see him striding directly towards the onlooker—
around 1800 such frontal views are more common.
This picture was Gérard's first big success in the field
of historical painting. He also went on to become one
of the most popular portraitists (including at court)
of the Napoleonic period.
Engraving (1806) by Auguste Boucher-Desnoyers
after Gérard's painting.

BÉLISAIRE

142

Page 142:

JACQUES-LOUIS DAVID: Madame de Verninac. 1799.
French neo-classicism expressed itself far more impressively in female than in male portraits. At the turn
of the century many women were painted in this Ju-
noesque form in a thin dress redolent of antiquity, and
not only in France. Serene harmony and the striking
of a happy medium between an imposing and an intimate depiction account for the charm of such pictures.

The bare background devoid of any architectural backdrop accorded not only with aesthetic demands but
also with an ethical ideal of bourgeois simplicity and
stringent truthfulness. This lack of extraneous detail
serves to set off the harmoniously free-flowing lines
and adds gracefulness to the dignified effect. Yet David
rejected the suggestion that he should enter this picture
for the art exhibition of the Year VIII as the display of a
"mere portrait" which seemed to him unworthy of a

painter of historical scenes. – When the lovely wife of
the Prefect of Lyons posed for the picture, her brother
was just one year old: Eugène Delacroix, who even
in David's lifetime overcame the latter's dogmatic
precept.

Oil on canvas, 143 × 110 cm. Musée du Louvre, Paris.

Page 143:

Pierre-Paul Prud'hon: The Empress Josephine in the Park of Malmaison. 1805.

More than a hint of the *ancien régime* accompanied Prud'hon, the left-wing Jacobin who was Josephine's portraitist and Marie Louise's art teacher: a seductively feminine beauty and the charm of a gentle chiaroscuro—inherited from the 18th century—envelop and enliven the obligatory neo-classical elements. David, who misapproved of the underlying conception, at least ceded that "not everyone is capable of erring in the manner of Prud'hon". Devoid of ostentatious or moral severity, the portrait particularly emphasizes the model's sensitive and elegant femininity. The setting draws on a tradition which is especially popular in English painting: daydreaming in a landscaped garden is symbolic of pastoral sentimentality.

Oil on canvas, 244 × 179 cm. Musée du Louvre, Paris.

Anne-Louis Girodet-Trioson: Danae regarding herself in Cupid's mirror. 1798.

From about 1790 onwards Girodet, in comparison with the rationalist neo-classicism of the group of painters around David, began to embody a more emotional stylistic variant with early Romantic features. A capricious imagination and a propensity for theatrical lighting effects are noticeable in this first version of the mythological theme. The second version caused a scandal since Girodet portrayed Danae in the form of a well-known actress and thereby stigmatized her as an avaricious courtesan. The whole episode was characteristic of the atmosphere that prevailed at the time of the Directory.

Oil on canvas, 170 × 88 cm. Museum der bildenden Künste, Leipzig.

ANNE-LOUIS GIRODET-TRIOSON: Atala's burial. 1808. Chateaubriand's story "Atala" tells of two Indians who have had a Christian upbringing and then find themselves in a Romeo/Juliet situation. The book, which appeared in 1801, had already stimulated a number of other artists when Girodet chose the subject of the burial of the beautiful girl who died by her own hand as a subject. The preoccupation with death and burial sites which was typical of the Romantic period right from the start is here coupled with the evocation of a kind of prehistoric age in which Christian and heathen elements converge. Behind the classically drawn but magically illumined figures a truly Romantic landscape opens up: the distant and unknown climes of America. Oil on canvas, 210 × 267 cm. Musée du Louvre, Paris.

ANNE-LOUIS GIRODET-TRIOSON: Insurrection in Cairo. 1810.

This work retrospectively depicts the final throes of the insurrection of October 21/22, 1798 against Napoleon's troops, the destruction of the Arabs in the courtyard of the al-Azhar mosque. By highlighting the splendid group of the Arab with the dying woman and by glorifying the enemy of his own nation and hence the encounter itself, he objectifies the proceedings and raises them to the level of the epic. Just how closely connected this effect is with the disciplined classicist form can be seen from a comparison with Goya's picture of the Madrid uprising.

Oil on canvas, 365 × 500 cm. Musée National de Versailles.

THÉODORE GÉRICAULT: Chasseur officer of the Imperial Guard charging. 1812,

From the start the young pupil of the classicist Guérin sought to emulate the passionate, dynamic power and painterly sensuousness of Rubens. His chasseur officer in the thick of the battle—the sight of a beautiful horse is said to have inspired the picture—is a dramatic amalgum of action, colour and light, although the composition remains carefully circumscribed by the surrounding border. At the exhibition of 1812 this painting won a gold medal. The vista which this opened up, namely the possibility of bursting the bonds of academic classicism from within, was not yet apparent to contemporary observers; it was not until 1819 that Géricault's "Raft of the Medusa"

gave the signal for a new, realistically Romantic style of painting. Another feature of Géricault's as yet unconscious programme was his preference for contemporary subject matter at a time when ancient history was seen as the be-all and end-all of true art—even the ageing Gros was lectured by David to desist from painting battle scenes and to at last choose a theme worthy of himself!

Oil on canvas, 292 × 194 cm. Musée du Louvre, Paris.

ANTOINE GROS: Bonaparte visiting the plague-stricken at Jaffa. 1803/04.

According to a medieval tradition of priest-kings, the French monarchs were credited with the ability to heal the sick by laying their hands on them. Bonaparte, who was still First Consul when he commissioned this picture, seemed to want to recall this special privilege of the sovereign. His visit to the plague-stricken soldiers in 1799 during the Egyptian campaign was meant to boost his troops' morale, and by touching one of the victims he sought to play down the disease. But the solemn gesture which the painter attributed to him just four years later made the general appear as some kind of religious healer in the human hell of this oriental hospital, and this account of an event from the recent past was turned into a myth by the horrific realism, heightened by pathos. The wretched heroes in the foreground anticipate the Romanticism of the "Raft of Medusa" or "Massacre of Chios". Gros, a pupil of David's and Napoleon's busy painter of battles, was a classicist in the way in which he depicted his figures but according to his artistic temperament, which drew him to Rubens, he was a realistic forerunner of Géricault and Delacroix. When the picture was first exhibited, young artists hung laurel wreaths around it.

Oil on canvas, 532 × 720 cm. Musée du Louvre, Paris.

FRANÇOIS GÉRARD: Ossian conjuring up the spirits of the heroes. First version, 1801.

The romantically lugubrious hymns which were ascribed to the legendary Gaelic bard Ossian—and which later turned out to be very free adaptations of folklore themes by the Scot Macpherson—fascinated all Europe from the 1770s onwards. Napoleon was also an avid reader of them. The "Ossian" atmosphere of mist and moonlight, mourning and martial virtue— emotionally lyric rather than Homerically epic—finds fairly frequent expression in French painting around 1800. Gérard executed this composition, which first arose as a commission for Bonaparte's residence at Malmaison, two or even three times. Similar pictures were painted by Girodet, Ingres and others. The whole Ossian ethos was one route from classicism to Romanticism.

Oil on canvas, 180 × 98 cm. Musée National du Château de Malmaison.

Page 151:

Jean-Auguste-Dominique Ingres: Jupiter and Thetis. 1811.

Again and again mythological subjects have a bearing on the present. The inflexible majesty of the king of the gods, whom Thetis is imploring to assist her son Achilles, is reminiscent of the atmosphere of the portrait of the enthroned emperor which Ingres also painted (see illustration on page 42), an imposing embodiment of power which is offset by the female figure. The vehicle of the picture's beauty and expressiveness is a melodious and strictly formal line to which anatomical "correctness" is sacrificed.

The search for a formalistically simplified expression was evident throughout Europe in the decades around the turn of the century. Coming after the Englishmen Blake and Flaxman but before the Lukas brothers of Germany, some rebellious pupils of David, who called themselves the "Primitives" or the "Bearded Ones", strove to achieve a non-sensuous, abstract visual language as exemplified by Greek vase painting. The young Ingres was drawn to them but also found models in the High Renaissance.

Oil on canvas, 321 × 257 cm. Musée Granet, Aix-en-Provence.

PIERRE-PAUL PRUD'HON: Abduction of
Psyche. 1808.
The equal coexistence of widely varying
conceptions of painting during the
Napoleonic period precludes the search
for a uniform Empire style in the field of
the arts. This was only apparent in the
sphere of ornamentation and the applied
arts. With his gentle lyricism Prud'hon
achieved a measure of official recognition
which was hardly less than that enjoyed
by painters of historic themes. When contemporaries compared him with Cor-
reggio or even Boucher they were rightly
counterposing him to David's school.
Oil on canvas, 195 × 157 cm. Musée du
Louvre, Paris.

JEAN-AUGUSTE-DOMINIQUE INGRES: La Bag-
neuse de Valpinçon. 1808.
Ingres was thirty-two years younger than
his teacher David and still a child when
the Revolution began. Aged seventeen he
left southern France in the year the Treaty of Campo Formio was signed for Paris
which he then left nine years later in 1806
for Rome, where he spent the next eight-
een years. Despite a brilliant career,
which began when he won the Academy's
Prix de Rome, and despite a few state
commissions, he remained more on the
periphery. His most important clients
were refined burgesses and aristocrats
among whom his intensely personal style
met with greater understanding than in
the public art exhibitions, where he was
often accused of "bizarreness". The life-
size nude whose fame immortalized the
name of her husband, the collector Valpinçon, comes across as more oriental
than classical—the Egyptian campaign
gave rise to a new exotic vogue—and despite all the stylization the warmth of the
living model is more discernible than
the smoothness of academic precursors.
The unusual motif of the nude seen from
behind here provides an opportunity for
a masterful contrast between the long,
gently curving lines of the body and the
sharply defined linear folds of the curtain
as also between the softly depicted
unbroken surface of the back and the
rich accessories. Fragonard, the last great
painter of the "fêtes galantes", died only
two years before this picture was painted.
But the joyful sensuality of his composi-
tions is already worlds apart from the calm
grandeur of Ingres's nudes.
Oil on canvas, 146 × 97.5 cm. Musée du
Louvre, Paris.

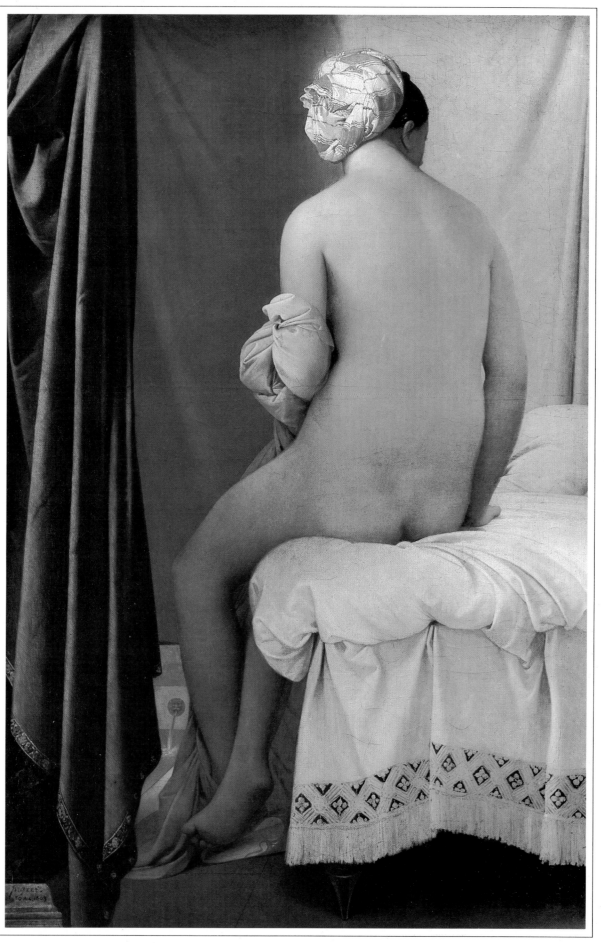

JEAN-AUGUSTE-DOMINIQUE INGRES: The Forestier family.
1806.

The latent source of Ingres's sublime cult of beauty was
a realistic objectivity which is apparent in many of his
portraits. In the same year (1806) in which he painted
the most imperial, abstract and rapt of all portraits of
the emperor he also made a drawing of his bride, Julie
Forestier, a young artist, with her parents. Although by
no means designed to flatter, it does clearly convey
the bourgeois solidity of the official's family. With the
relaxed postures and the satisfied smiles of everyone
grouped around the young lady, who embodies a higher
culture, the result is an unenigmatic depiction of a
milieu without a past history, the cool self-portrayal of
a contented mediocrity.

Pencil. Musée du Louvre, Cabinet des Dessins, Paris.

JEAN-AUGUSTE-DOMINIQUE INGRES: Madame Devauçay.
1807.

This portrait of an Italian lady who was married to a
Frenchman was one of the first of the series of female
portraits which made Ingres famous. No other artist of
the time expressed the characteristic features of each
model so sharply. Each of his figures possesses a certain unmistakable magic, and each is enveloped by a
perfectly harmonious linear rhythm. (In this case the
dynamic outlines of the figure contrast with the rigid
arc of the chair-back.) Ingres was only able to maintain
this balance between reality and ideality for a few
years.

Oil on canvas, 76×59 cm. Musée Condé, Chantilly.

JACQUES-LOUIS DAVID: The three ladies of Ghent
  (Madame Morel de Tangry and her daughters).
  C. 1816–1818.
  Painted soon after David went into exile, this work,
  with its almost frightening realism, anticipates a genre
  which is met with frequently in post-Restoration
  paintings, albeit mostly in a much less incisive form:
  Balzac's world of the provincial bourgeoisie.
  Oil on canvas, 132 × 105 cm. Musée du Louvre, Paris.

LOUIS LÉOPOLD BOILLY: Artist in her studio. C. 1795.
  Boilly belongs to a long line of genre painters who carried on the tradition of the unheroic depiction of everyday bourgeois life, ranging from the frivolous to the
  sentimental, without any fundamental change (except
  in costumes, scenery and compositional formulae)
  from the *ancien régime* to the Restoration. In his later
  years he was also a very successful lithographer. The
  meticulousness of his portrayals sometimes verged on
  caricature, especially in pictures populated with many
  figures. Although such largely sentimental genre
  painting was regarded as something second-rate by the
  official connoisseurs, it was greatly loved by much of
  the bourgeois public, and its popularity was confirmed
  by printed reproductions.
  Oil on canvas, 50 × 60 cm. Staatliches Museum,
  Schwerin.

Martin Drolling: Kitchen scene. 1815.

Minor Netherlandish masters of the 17th century served some of the more modest contemporaries of the classicists as models of bourgeois painting. Like them Drolling portrays this interior with its numerous characteristic details as a large still-life. The incoming light, which underlines the spatial relations of the various objects through sharp contrasts of brightness, plays at least as prominent a role as the figures. The fact that they are both glancing at the onlooker, as if the latter had interrupted their tranquil and timeless work, emphasizes the isolated domesticity of the scene. It hardly seems credible that while this picture was being painted in the quiet of the studio whole nations were locked in mortal combat not far away. This genre continued to exist for several decades side by side with ideal painting.

Oil on canvas, 65 × 80.8 cm. Musée du Louvre, Paris.

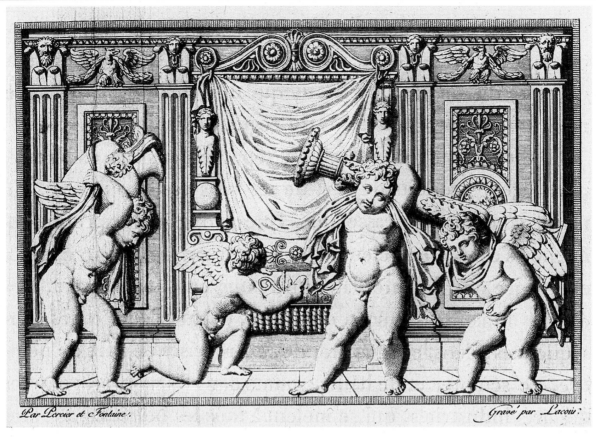

JEAN-BAPTISTE MALLET: Gothic bathroom. 1810.
This extraordinarily versatile painter, who experimented with all the current "lesser" artistic genres of his time, was already fifty when he executed this work. It is an example of the *style troubadour*, an undercurrent in French painting which emerged around 1800 and portrayed an idealized medieval world. In Napoleonic France there was a quite considerable romanticized interest in historic monuments and art of the Gothic period. One expression of this was the Musée des Monuments français which Alexandre Lenoir founded in 1790. Mallet's form of artistic expression, however, was oriented more towards the Netherlandish school of painting of the 17th century. Oil on canvas, 40.5×52.5 cm. Musée de Dieppe.

CHARLES PERCIER and PIERRE FONTAINE: Allegory on the decorative arts. 1812.
Engraving by LACOUR after the drawing of CHARLES PERCIER and PIERRE FONTAINE. Headpiece for the preface of their work: *Recueil de décorations intérieures*. Paris, 1812.

Periods of war do not favour architecture. The Napoleonic administration had to leave most of its ambitious and far-reaching projects for re-designing the capital to future generations. While some bridges and other functional public buildings (indoor markets, abattoirs etc.) were constructed, monumental buildings and radical road construction schemes largely remained at the planning stage. The continuation of the royal Louvre palace undertaken by Percier and Fontaine was more akin to restoration work since the two architects adhered to the old historic style. The Tuileries, Napoleon's official residence, and other older structures were altered or extended.

However, as was to be expected the most characteristic constructions of the Napoleonic era served to immortalize his military campaigns. These include fountains and columns, such as the one on the Place Vendôme for which the relief spiral was cast from the metal of 1,200 captured cannon, and triumphal arches like the small and elegant edifice on the Place du Carrousel near the Louvre or the huge and famous Arc de Triomphe which was completed by Louis-Philippe. For the arrival of Marie Louise in 1810 a provisional structure of wood and painted canvas had to be erected above the newly built foundation walls, and it was only when the emperor's ashes were brought back to Paris that the ceremonial procession was able to pass through the completed arch. Triumphal arches and columns were invented by the Romans, and the choice of such models was preordained: Imperial art looked for inspiration to the Imperial past.

In keeping with the centralism of the Napoleonic state, a handful of artists enjoyed a monopolistic privilege. Thus the most important architectural commissions for the state and for the Imperial family were awarded to the studio of Percier and Fontaine. The cabinet maker Jacob-Desmalter, who carried out many of their furniture designs, attained a comparable pre-eminence in this field and exported his wares to many countries in Europe. For, like the works of its chief exponents, the Empire style could be found wherever the Bonaparte family settled or Napoleon founded a new dynasty, i.e. from Stockholm to Naples. But despite its extensive geographical propagation, this art form remained closely bound up with a particular social stratum which identified very much with the state. In 1871 a fire destroyed those rooms in the Tuileries which had been specifically designed to display Napoleon's supreme prestigious aspirations. On the other hand Malmaison, Josephine's beautiful residence, survived intact.

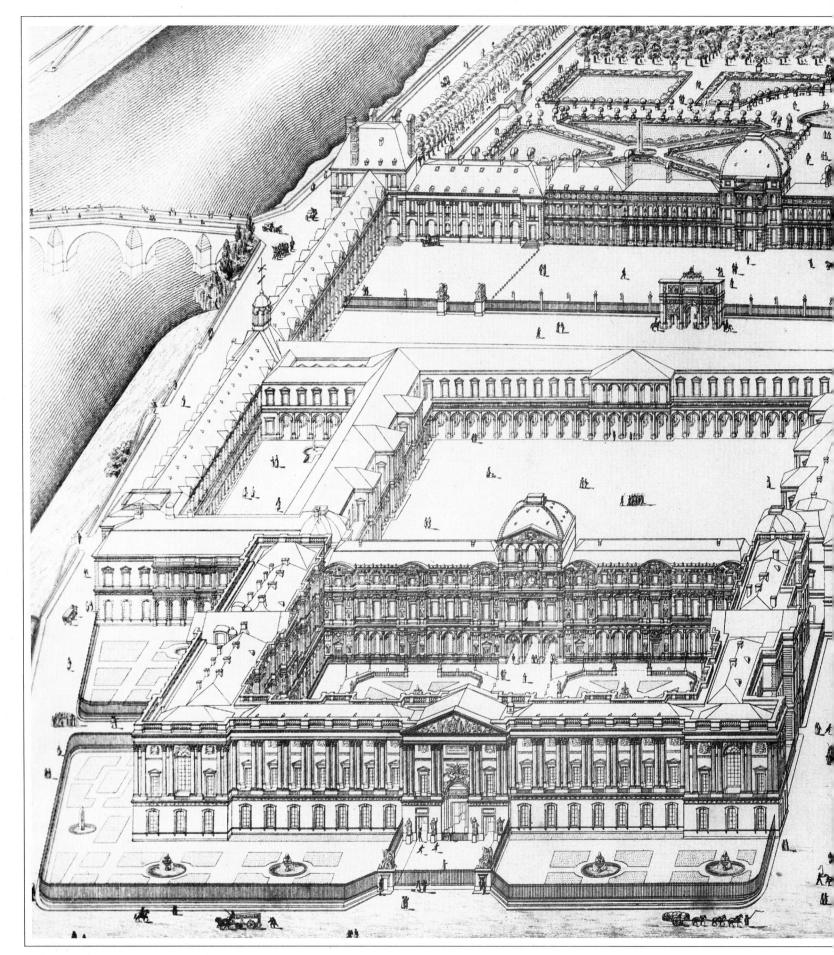

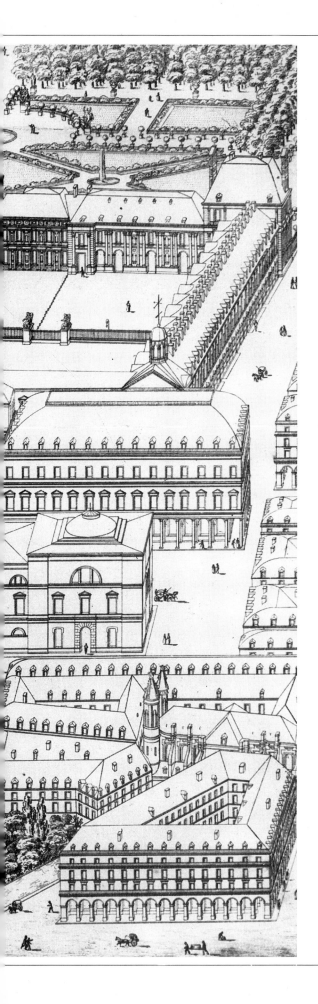

Arc de triomphe de l'Étoile
Côté de Neuilly

AUGUSTE HIBON after MATHIEU PROSPER MOREY:
The Louvre and the Tuileries in accordance with
the design of Percier and Fontaine for joining the
two palaces. View from the east.
The lower half of the sketch shows the inner square
of the Old Louvre dating from the 16th and 17th
centuries with the façade by Claude Perrault.
At the top we can see the Tuileries palace which was
refashioned under Napoleon. In front of it, on the
Place du Carrousel, stands the smaller triumphal
arch, also the work of Percier and Fontaine. On the
left the Pont des Arts, built of iron in 1803, leads to
the Institut on the left bank of the Seine. The con-
necting structure between the multi-winged Louvre
and the Tuileries long remained a mere skeleton.
It was not completed until the reign of Napoleon III.
But not long afterwards, in 1871, the Tuileries
burned down and a few years later was demolished.
Engraving from Frédéric Comte de Clarac's work:
Musée de Sculpture antique et moderne. Paris, 1826.

The Arc de Triomphe on the Place de l'Etoile.
View from the west, *c.* 1825. Lithograph after a drawing by NAUNHEIM.
The colossal triumphal arch situated at the end
of the long axis which leads from the Louvre via the
Tuileries gardens and the Champs-Elysées to the
"star" formed by the Place de l'Etoile (hence the
name) was begun in 1807 according to Jean-François
Chalgrin's designs but was no more than a stump
when the Empire came to an end. The building
proper was not erected until between 1823 and 1836.
Thus the plastic ornamentation does not date from
the Napoleonic era, unlike the architectonic form
in which the massive block has but a single arch
(i. e. no side-arches).

Par Percier et Fontaine.

Lit exécuté à Paris pour M. O......

For twenty years, from 1794 to 1814 Percier and Fontaine collaborated (the latter from 1807 onwards as Napoleon's First Architect). Their work covered a wide range of activities, just as later that of Schinkel did in Prussia: from large-scale projects—which, however, usually only provided them with an opportunity to alter or expand older buildings—and mammoth but ephemeral festival enterprises to interior decoration and designs for furniture and ornate objects of every kind. Whenever they designed a room they concerned themselves with everything down to the last detail.

The specific nature of the Empire style manifested itself unmistakably in the form of interior décor. The social group which had quickly acquired wealth and status furnished their dwellings sumptuously and covered walls and other bare architectural surfaces with a plethora of costly and impressive archaeological decoration. The classicism of the pre-revolutionary period with its modest and rather stiff gracefulness gave way to cooler and more rigorous forms. Striking colours such as red and gold, mahogany and gold (for furniture) or blue and gold came into vogue. Figures, animals and fabulous creatures were now applied in ornamentation much more frequently than the formerly very popular plant and floral motifs, framed by sharp lines in perfect and highly stylized form. Ancient Rome was an important source of political symbols. Thus the eagles, trophies, laurel wreaths and the propensity towards vast dimensions and sumptuousness point back to Imperial Rome. More initimate interiors were decked out in Pompeian fashion. A better knowledge of Greek art, especially vase painting, and the stimulation of interest in ancient Egyptian art following Bonaparte's campaign broadened the classical horizon and the range of stylistic choice.

CHARLES PERCIER and PIERRE FONTAINE: Bedroom of Monsieur O. in Paris, conceived as a temple of Diana. The upper mural zone seemingly provides an open view of the countryside. Between painted pillars appear painted trees, to give the impression that the imaginary temple is set in the middle of a wood. Drapery was a common motif of wall decoration under the Empire.

CHARLES PERCIER and PIERRE FONTAINE: View of the Salle des Maréchaux in the re-designed Tuileries. This hall was decorated with portraits and busts of high-ranking military men. The gallery with its caryatids is an exact copy of Jean Goujon's gallery in the Old Louvre (1550). Engravings by Charles Normand after Charles Percier and Pierre Fontaine, *Recueil de décorations intérieures*. Paris, 1812.

Par Percier et Fontaine.

Vue de la Tribune et d'une partie de la Salle des Maréchaux, au Palais des Tuileries.

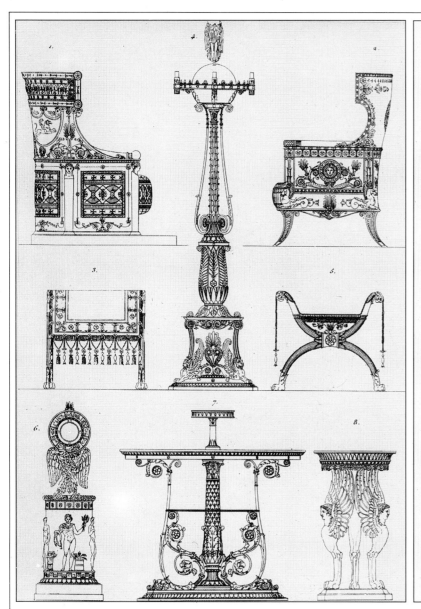

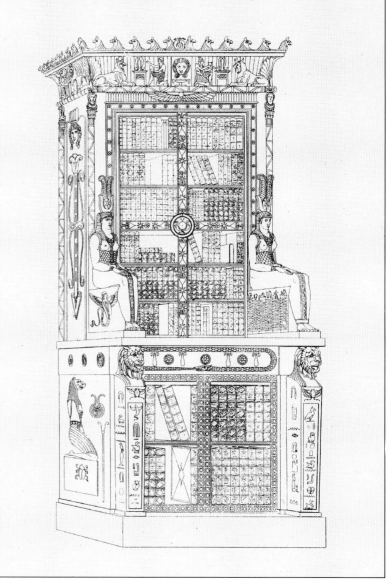

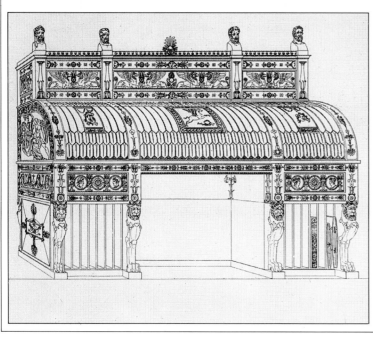

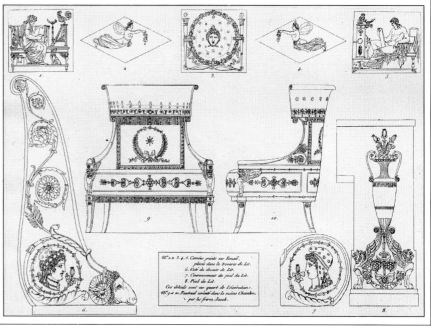

Pl. 59.

Par Percier et Fontaine.

Candélabre portant Girandoles, exécuté à Paris.

Pages 164/165:

CHARLES PERCIER and PIERRE FONTAINE:
  Candelabrum, tea-table, chairs and grandfather clock.
  The designers themselves wrote: "As one can see, we
  have striven to subordinate the embellishment of these
  diverse household furnishings to the requirements of
  utility in every respect."

Bookcase from several different kinds of wood in the form
  of a secretaire; Egyptian style.

Cylindrical secretaire, manufactured by the Jacob factory
  in Paris.

Armchairs and bedroom furnishings for Vivant-Denon.

Large candelabrum of gilt copper.
  Engravings by Charles Normand after Charles Percier
  and Pierre Fontaine, *Recueil de décorations intérieures*.
  Paris, 1812.

Pages 166/167:

Aromatic incense burner, *c.* 1800/1810.
  Bronze, partly gilt. Height 42.5 cm. Staatliche Museen
  Berlin, Kunstgewerbemuseum.

Pitcher, *c.* 1800/1810.
  Bronze, partly gilt. Height 44.4 cm. Staatliche Museen
  Berlin, Kunstgewerbemuseum.

Ringholder, *c.* 1800/1810.
  Bronze, gilt. Height 20 cm. Staatliche Museen Berlin,
  Kunstgewerbemuseum.

Oil lamp, *c.* 1800/1810.
  This ornate vessel differs only in a few minor details
  from the design of Percier and Fontaine.
  Bronze, partly gilt. Height 26 cm, length 23 cm. Staatliche Museen Berlin, Kunstgewerbemuseum.

Two vases from the porcelain factory at Sèvres near Paris
bearing the portraits of the Empresses Josephine and
Marie Louise. Height 55 cm.
Staatliche Museen Berlin, Kunstgewerbemuseum.

Table clock with Amphitrite, *c.* 1800.
Bronze, gilt. Height 55 cm. Staatliche Kunstsammlungen
Dresden, Kunstgewerbemuseum.

ANTOINE-DENIS CHAUDET: Cupid. 1802.
Chaudet owes a large part of his reputation
to the Napoleon busts which, reproduced in
large workshops, were sent in their hundreds
to public buildings in even the most remote
corners of the Empire. His larger-than-life
statue of the emperor which stood on top of
the Vendôme Column was destroyed in 1814.
His work exhibits that juxtaposition of official
stringency and delightfulness that one repeatedly encounters in the art of this period—
as in Imperial Rome, which provided the inspiration for this study of Cupid preoccupied
by his work.
Marble. Height 89.7 cm. Musée du Louvre,
Paris.

JOSEPH CHINARD: Madame de l'Orme de l'Isle. *C.* 1802.
Like many fellow artists Chinard, who spent most of his time in his native Lyons but also lived inbetween times in Rome, was tossed back and forth by the turbulent current of the era. In 1792 he was arrested by the Inquisition in Rome and a year later by the Revolution in Lyons. Later he served as a soldier and then became portraitist to the Bonaparte family. He represented a variant of classicism which still bore traces of 18th-century gracefulness. Like many of his works this bust was made of terracotta, a material which conveys an impression of intimacy and which probably for this reason was frequently used in the second half of the 18th century.
Terracotta. Formerly Collection Reynaud.

171

ANTONIO CANOVA: Tomb of the Arch-
  duchess Maria-Christina of Austria
  in the Augustinerkirche in Vienna.
  1798–1805.
  Stendhal regarded this work as the
  finest example of a tomb anywhere.
  The quiet peace of death—which
  according to the classicist viewpoint
  resembled sleep and which was far
  removed from the dramatic extravagance of Baroque tombs—is symbolized by the withdrawal of the
  allegorical figures into the interior
  of the pyramid. Canova here re-used
  an older design for a tomb for Titian
  which was not executed.
  Engraving by Antoine Réveil (1829)
  after Canova's work in marble.

ANTONIO CANOVA: Hercules and Lychas.
  1795–1815.
  This heroic group of the despairing
  Hercules who dashes Lychas
  (the messenger of death who brought
  him the fatal fiery shirt) against
  a rock turns the violent scene into an
  abstractly stylized ornament. Canova,
  who was born near Venice, soon settled in Rome under papal patronage
  and became famous throughout
  Europe, had no compunction about
  incorporating Baroque motifs into his
  neo-classical forms.
  Engraving by Antoine Réveil (1829)
  after Canova's marble statue.

ANTONIO CANOVA: The three Graces.
  1812–1816.
  The first specimen of the group,
  which was commissioned by Eugène
  Beauharnais, met with great acclaim
  immediately. The motif of the three
  women locked in a mutual embrace,
  which first appeared in antiquity,
  has here been interpreted with particular gracefulness and linear elegance
  which is reminiscent of Ingres.
  Canova's art always retained features
  of courtly decorativeness, which no
  doubt contributed to his popularity
  within the Bonaparte family.
  Marble. Height 182 cm.
  Ny Carlsberg Glyptothek, Copenhagen.

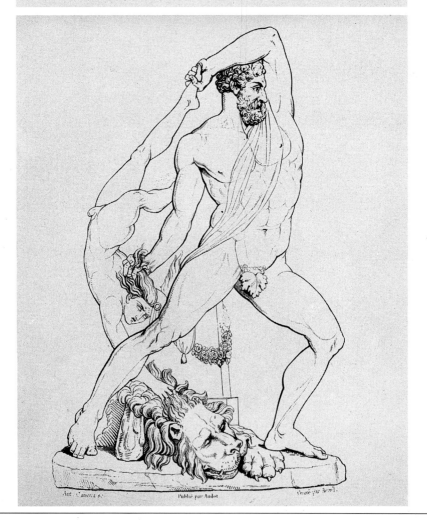

JOHANN GOTTFRIED SCHADOW: Reposing Eros. *C.* 1798.
The Berlin court sculptor Schadow retained all the freshness and grace of early classicism beyond the turn of the century. This youthful figure, whose symbolic slumber suggests a dual function as an angel of love and of death, combines a lively interest in the human body with a knowledge of classical rules.
Marble relief, 55×37 cm. Staatliche Museen Berlin, Nationalgalerie.

BERTEL THORVALDSEN: Ganymede giving water to the eagle of Zeus. This group, which is outlined with ideal clarity, is concentrated into such a small space that, were a backdrop present, it could easily be taken for a relief. The linear principle of classicism has here been realized with supreme casualness. Marble, after a model made in 1817. Height 88 cm. Museum der bildenden Künste, Leipzig.

BERTEL THORVALDSEN: Detail from the frieze "Alexander the Great's entry into Babylon". 1812.
In 1812 the papal Quirinal palace in French-occupied Rome was re-furnished as a summer residence for Napoleon. The theme of this relief in the banqueting hall was intended as a homage to the new landlord. It was not the first time that he had been compared to the conqueror of the ancient world. The frieze, which was 35 metres long and replete with figures, was a sensational and immediate triumph for the sculptor, who adhered on a monumental scale to the strict regularity of classical Greek relief art. For many years Thorvaldsen, a Dane based in Rome, had been regarded as the leading European sculptor and a reformer in his field.   .
Engravings by Samuel Amsler after Friedrich Overbeck's drawings (1815/1816) of Thorvaldsen's relief.

175

Francisco de Goya: Second of May (Rising on the Puerta del Sol in Madrid). 1814.

Goya's paintings attached great importance to the common people, who are absent from most artworks executed at the turn of the century, and in the process distanced themselves increasingly from the idyllic Rococo style in favour of problematic and conflicting elements.

Goya painted two famous pictures to commemorate the Madrid rising, the suppression of which by French troops unleashed the long Peninsular War. The well-known counterpart depicts an execution scene on May 3. The pair were commissioned by King Ferdinand VII after his restoration in 1814. The king was at pains to legitimate his repressive, anti-liberal régime by alluding to his people's struggles and sacrifices. Nor could the court painter, who had compromised himself politically on various counts, avoid misusing his talents in this way. He had himself been obliged to paint over his grandiose "Allegory of the City of Madrid", the initial centrepiece of which had been a portrait of Joseph Bonaparte (whom Napoleon installed as King of Spain)

several times in accordance with the shifting balance of power. However, Goya's picture of the revolt glorifies neither monarch nor rebels. By means of a passionate fervour, which is underscored by the colour, he emphasizes the grimness of the bloody struggle—which he may have witnessed personally—and portrays the act of killing unheroically as an almost technical, dehumanizing process.

Oil on canvas, 266×345 cm. Museo del Prado, Madrid.

Francisco de Goya: Family of Charles IV. 1800.

It was only with the benefit of hindsight that the Spanish court painter was recognized as representing one of the most acute antitheses to Napoleonic neoclassicism, for in his own lifetime he was unknown outside Spain. A contemporary of David's, he grew up in the atmosphere of late Baroque artistic culture and for a time flirted with early neo-classicism. He was already advanced in years and a successful painter of frescoes, genre pictures and portraits when, with the series of etchings known as "Los Caprichos" (1799) and related pictures, he found a means to express social and emotional torments and to fuse them together. His later series of etchings entitled "Los Desastres de la Guerra" were more than a chronicle of the Peninsular War; they were visionary pictures of symbolic significance. A few years before the collapse of the Spanish *ancien régime* he painted a group portrait of the royal family which through its unwavering psychological realism—without irony or caricature—reduced the cliché of the formal portrait to absurdity. It seems as though some bourgeois family has dressed up in royal costumes, an effect which is heightened by the fact that the much criticized Queen Maria Louisa is depicted at the centre. The harsh realism, which defies all norms, and the sensual and impulsive use of colour carry traditions of the Baroque period in transformed guise into the 19th century.

Oil on canvas, 280×336 cm. Museo del Prado, Madrid.

WILLIAM BLAKE: Elohim creating Adam. *C.* 1795.
In English art around 1800 reality and romantic vision stood in particularly close proximity to one another. The most important works of the poet and engraver Blake are books which he wrote and illustrated himself. In enigmatically metaphorical language they present variations on the theme of an expansive, self-made myth: the struggle between a presumptuous, coldly rational, terroristic "Reason" and a humane, libertarian principle which—taking his cue from Milton—he often represented by Satan. In this picture of Adam's creation the awesomely powerful figure of God, which like many of Blake's designs harks back to Michelangelo, appears to be raping Man rather than instilling life into him. Blake's criticism of the fossilized Enlightenment had clearly revolutionary features (and sometimes contained recognizable contemporary references). Colour print finished in pen and watercolour, 42.1×53.6 cm. The Tate Gallery, London.

SIR HENRY RAEBURN: Portrait of Thomas Kennedy of Dunure. *C.* 1812.
In the second half of the 18th century a number of great portraitists left their mark on British painting. Cool elegance, lightness and a certain vague sense of atmosphere were the heritage which they bequeathed to the early 19th century. In a similar manner to his contemporary Thomas Lawrence, the "Scottish Reynolds" immortalized the changed, more sober character of the British aristocracy and bourgeoisie.
Oil on canvas, 127×101.6 cm. National Gallery of Scotland, Edinburgh.

WILLIAM TURNER: Snowstorm. Hannibal crossing the Alps. 1811/1812.

Could Napoleon's contemporaries look at a portrayal of an alpine crossing in ancient times (218 B.C.) without being reminded of Bonaparte's famous march across the mountains into Italy? When Turner exhibited this picture at the London Academy he wrote a commentary for the catalogue in verse-form which spoke of the dangerous consequences of the campaign: but for France or for England? Be that as it may, the event is here neither historicized nor glorified. It has been transformed, even more so than in Turner's Waterloo picture of 1818, into a romantic vision. Above the scenes of carnage and war the all-powerful elements swirl and envelop everything in a thick shroud. The unbridled force of Nature appears as the real subject of the picture. Art around 1800 was full of natural calamities: storms, raging floods and earthquakes, reflecting Romanticism's restlessness and crisis of consciousness. Turner was one of the great Romantic landscape painters. His art first came to fruition during the Napoleonic era and remained fruitful for decades. Celestial phenomena, water, agitated motion and intangible forms were his favourite themes in his pictorial visions. French painting produced nothing comparable. Landscape painting was a fundamental contribution on the part of English art to early European Romanticism.

Oil on canvas, 146×237.5 cm. The Tate Gallery, London.

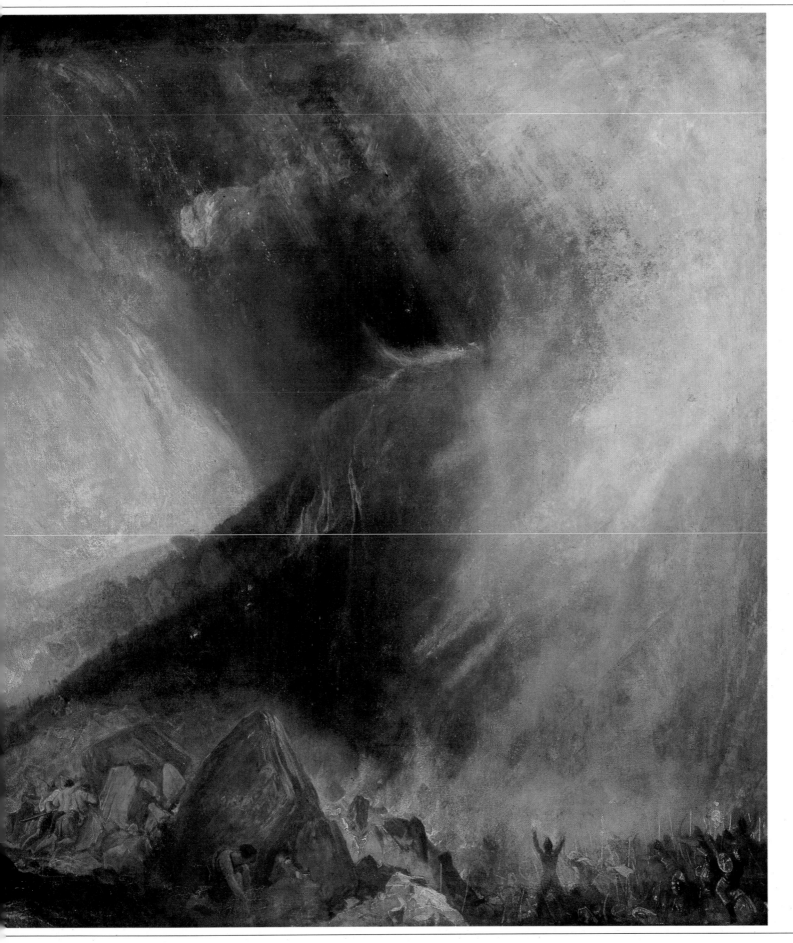

The days when liberal notions and the spirit of rebellion could express themselves in neo-classical form were over and done with once the noble revolutionary ideals had given way to the harsh Napoleonic reality. Rationalist restrictions, propriety and a conformist moral code fitted in only too well with the requirements of an authoritarian state. Thus the reference to a boundless and variegated Nature—largely Romantic in form but feeding on direct, sensuous experience—contained a rejection of a state-ordained mode of thinking. Instead the feelings and perceptions of the individual came to the fore.

Outside France, especially in England and Germany, this occurred most noticeably in landscape painting, a genre which classicist doctrine dismissed as second-rate and unsuited for the representation of grandiose ideas and which possibly for precisely this reason found scope in which to develop. Similarly disregarded by the pre-Romantics at the end of the 18th century, it opened up completely new vistas after 1800.

JOHN CONSTABLE: Boat-building (near Flatford Mill).
Exhibited in 1815.
Constable's verdict on a certain artist whom he admired, namely that he "walked arm in arm with Milton
and Linné", could equally well be applied to himself.
His power to acutely observe Nature's atmospheric
moods and the effects of light, humidity and the wind
in his native county of Suffolk manifested both a poetic
and a scientific awareness. The fresh realism—which
shows up more in small, sketch-type pictures than in
large-scale, more ambitious works—and his free, pas-
tose, painterly method which depended totally on colour also provided an impetus to French Romanticism:
Constable was nearly fifty when his pictures made
a big impression on the young Delacroix in 1824.
Oil on canvas, 50.8×61.6 cm. Victoria and Albert
Museum, London.

CHRISTOFFER WILHELM ECKERSBERG: View through
the arches of the Colosseum. Storm over the city.
Between 1813 and 1816.
Prior to coming to Rome at the age of thirty, the Dane
Eckersberg had studied under his fellow countryman
Abildgaard and then for two years under David in
Paris. However, after arriving in the metropolis of antique art and getting to know Thorvaldsen he adopted a
realistic and objective approach. In this picture the famous amphitheatre of ancient Rome is no longer the
main motif or objective; our interest is drawn through
the arches to the illuminated view in the distance.
Eckersberg was part of the international vanguard
of realistic outdoor painters who turned their backs
on classicism and paved the way for one of the most
important developments of 19th-century painting.
Oil on canvas, 32×49.5 cm. Statens Museum for
Kunst, Copenhagen.

GOTTLIEB SCHICK: Apollo among the shepherds. 1806–1808.

Together with a number of other Stuttgart artists Gottlieb Schick was among the first German pupils in David's studio. After 1806 Prussian painters arrived in France, and for a short time French classicism was the basic model for a group of German artists. During the time he spent studying in Paris (1798–1802), Schick conceived the idea for this principal work, which he executed in Rome without a commission. It is a picture of peace. As a punishment for killing the Cyclops Apollo was forced to tend the flocks of King Admetus. In the process he brought music and poetry to the Arcadian people. The picture exudes the spirit of Schiller, and the artist's identification with him is clear enough. Official French art produced nothing comparable.

Oil on canvas, 178.5×232 cm. Staatsgalerie Stuttgart.

JOSEPH ANTON KOCH: The Schmadribach Falls. 1805–1811.

When the rebellious pupil was expelled from the Karlsschule in Stuttgart in 1791 he cut off his pigtail and sent it back to the school by post to show his contempt. For a while he mixed with the Jacobins in Strasbourg and then went to Rome where he was to spend virtually the rest of his life.

This painter of "historicized" ideal landscapes was the first to explore the possibilities of lonely mountain scapes for Romantic painting. The view upwards from the valley to the snow-capped peaks which feed the waterfall invokes a sublimity which, heightened by many intermediate levels, inspires a feeling of dread. The sight of these falls on the Rhine near Schaffhausen had fired Koch as a young man with revolutionary enthusiasm. A trace of that enthusiasm is still palpable in this later picture with its harshness, sharp contrasts between the rock structures, vegetation, foaming water and ice masses, and with the heroic freedom of the wild.

Oil on canvas, 122×92 cm. Museum der bildenden Künste, Leipzig.

CASPAR DAVID FRIEDRICH: Dolmen in snow. 1807.
For the young Caspar David Friedrich, who was born in Greifswald and then moved to Dresden, the discovery of stone monuments marking prehistoric Germanic burial sites was more than a counterpart to the "Ossianism" of the French painters and a symbol of the venerability of German history at a time when the Holy Roman Empire of the German Nation was collapsing. It also tapped a source of ancient pagan freedom. The mighty oaks likewise convey an impression of great age and lonesome majesty. In other ways, too, Friedrich's work contained repeated allusions to the political situation in Germany before and after the war of liberation. But this was not the only reason for his appeal as an artist: as pure landscapes of a completely new type his pictures were to exert a lasting attraction.
Oil on canvas, 61.5×80 cm. Staatliche Kunstsammlungen Dresden, Gemäldegalerie Neue Meister.

CASPAR DAVID FRIEDRICH: Crucifix in mountain scenery. 1808.
For the North German Romanticist Friedrich landscape was the perfect vehicle for expressing human emotions. There is not a single history painting by him. When he painted his "Crucifix in mountain scenery", encouraged by a private commission, it was actually intended as an altarpiece for the chapel of the Bohemian castle at Teschen, but even this he managed to turn into a landscape, substituting for a portrayal of Christ on the cross a picture of a crucifix on a lonely mountain peak. The subjective intuition of the divine presence within Nature became the subject of a grandiose allegory which defied total interpretation. The consciousness of the irrational— that "mysticism" which so angered contemporary critics but which was closely bound up with the exploration of the effects of light and atmosphere—was also a form of liberation from dogma and hence one of the consequences of the political and intellectual upheavals of this period.
Oil on canvas, 115×110.5 cm. Staatliche Kunstsammlungen Dresden, Gemäldegalerie Neue Meister.

PHILIPP OTTO RUNGE: The artist's parents. 1806.
This portrait of the shipowner and his family from Wolgast reveals the harsh verism in Runge's art which keeps Romantic exuberance in check. The two central figures exude an air of upright middle-class respectability. Both the children and the plants are intended to add a certain symbolic connotation.
Oil on canvas, 196×151 cm. Kunsthalle Hamburg.

PHILIPP OTTO RUNGE: The Morning. First version, 1808.
Runge, who died young, was a loner who was not subsequently emulated by other artists. Living in Hamburg, far removed from the centres of German art, he daydreamed about peasant cottages. He bequeathed to the world the utopian concept of a universal and symbolic landscape art. Many years he spent planning a series of pictures on the theme of the "Four Periods" (of the day, the year, life and the world), the first designs for which took shape in the form of engravings. But he was only able to execute "The Morning" as a painting. It is a complex structure of symbolic references (thus the central figure combines features of Aurora, Venus and the Virgin Mary) in which the objects express certain ideas but in which the direct sensory impression remains paramount: the appearance of light which manifests itself in the colours. Ultimately Runge planned to complete the four pictures in the series—but on a much bigger scale—and then display them in a building of their own. They were to form part of an "abstract, artistic and musical epic phantasmagoria, complete with choirs", which would bring together all the arts: a Romantic substitute for religion in decline.
Oil on canvas, 109×85.5 cm. Kunsthalle Hamburg.

189

HEINRICH OLIVIER: The Holy Alliance. 1815.
Heinrich Olivier from Dessau spent two years in Paris where, together with his brother Ferdinand, he set about painting a large equestrian portrait of Napoleon on behalf of his sovereign. Here he was prompted to head off in a direction that eventually led to this neo-Gothic allegory of the Restoration, for Napoleonic Paris for a brief period was a centre of Catholic Romanticism as proselytized by a group of ex-patriot Germans grouped around Joseph Pilat, a colleague of Metternich's, who were influenced by Friedrich Schlegel. The Musée Napoléon offered favourable opportunities for studying Late Gothic painting. Heinrich Olivier, who volunteered for military service in 1813, was living in Vienna at the time of the Congress. The three monarchs, who appear as a trio of knights in armour, are depicted swearing a solemn oath. This motif has been taken over from pro-revolutionary pictures but given a diametrically opposed meaning. The painting is an impressively single-minded and literal interpretation of the "Holy Alliance"; the archaic Gothic style and the historical accessories express the picture's pro-Restoration project almost too perfectly.
Body colours, 44×35 cm. Staatliche Galerie Dessau.

Franz Pforr: Sulamith and Mary. 1811.

Despite the diversity of the reactions within German art to the shock and helplessness occasioned by the revolutionary wars, the motif of renewal, purification and the return to original and basic values was always to the fore. It was also a fundamental tenet of a group of students at the Vienna Academy who joined forces to form the "Lukasbund". In 1809 they established themselves in the secularized monastery of San Isidoro in Rome where they set about reforming German painting to bring it into line with the tradition of Dürer and of Raphael. One of the "friendship pictures" painted within this circle was Pforr's diptych, the form of which recalls a Late Gothic portable altar. It is dedicated to his friend and fellow painter Friedrich Overbeck. The two female ideals of both painters represent two different but complementary conceptions of life and art. The concomitant lengthy legends reflect their need to discover a new ideological basis for their art.

Oil on wood, 34.5×32 cm. Georg Schäfer Collection, Schweinfurt.

Gay Paree

Sovereigns of both sexes were wont to indulge in the noble art of embellishing their capital cities trough the construction of stately building so as to leave their mark on posterity: appropriately imposing edifices in the prevailing style with the concomitant mews, memorials to their ancestors and churches for the veneration of the Supreme Being whose earthly representatives they claimed to be. They also erected functional buildings—hospitals, theatres and bridges—to evince their altruistic generosity. There was even a spirit of rivalry among some of the sovereigns. Talented architects made use of this ready market to translate their visions into petrified monuments.

Less frequently the rulers concerned themselves with municipal planning. This was more likely in countries where the royal seat was of more recent origin such as St. Petersburg or in a brand-new town like Karlsruhe in Baden. Sometimes it happened that, due to a shift in the political balance of forces, some quiet spot suddenly found itself transformed into a major city and hence underwent a continuous increase in population necessitating the planned construction of whole new residential areas, as was the case with Friedrichstadt in Berlin. There was much to be borne in mind: building regulations and the preservation of green spaces, water supplies and sewers, street planning and lighting. The latter became easier after the introduction of gas lamps in England in 1808. Of crucial importance was the raising of sufficient investment capital and the provision of incentives for potential clients among the nobility and bourgeoisie.

Large-scale historical conglomerations such as London or Paris, however, defied all attempts at radical urban planning. It is hardly surprising, therefore, that the skyline of the French metropolis in 1815 was scarcely different from the one which had presented itself to the revolutionaries in 1789.

The population of Paris did grow, however, from less than 600,000 to more than 700,000—a growth which also affected the city centre.[1] Yet Napoleon's dream of a grandiose "capital of all the capitals" consisting of neo-classical palaces and majestic public buildings could not be realized in the absence of the fundamental pre-

The Pont des Invalides in Paris. It was built between 1806 and 1813 and was known as the Pont d'Jéna until 1814. Three other bridges in Paris were completed during Napoleon's reign. Engraving from Binet (Editor), *Soixante vues des plus beaux palais, monuments et églises de Paris*. Paris, no date (c. 1818).

Page 192:
GEORG FRIEDRICH KERSTING: The elegant reader. 1812.
A friend of Caspar David Friedrich, Kersting was born in Mecklenburg but moved to Dresden. He specialized in tranquil and atmospheric interior scenes. These convey not only the upright simplicity of the cultivated bourgeois milieu of this period but also a special, somewhat constrained form of Romantic spiritualization verging on *Biedermeier*. Oil on canvas, 37.5×37.5 cm. Kunstsammlungen Weimar.

The bonbons and sweetmeats of the finest sort, à l'ananas, à la rose, bijou and suchlike, were much better than those in Berlin; and the boxes, tins and jars in which they are customarily presented to the ladies were of great diversity and daintiness. The sweetmeats filled with various kinds of jelly were also highly delectable. The fact that Bonaparte's portrait was reproduced on everything goes without saying. . . .
Reichardt: *Vertraute Briefe aus Paris 1802 bis 1803.*

[1] LABORIE, L. DE LANZAC DE: *Paris sous Napoléon*, 8 Vols. Paris, 1905–1913.

condition: a "Grand Peace" dictated by France. Thus there was never enough money or time nor the requisite inner tranquility and calm to give a free rein to the urban planners and builders. In 1804 Napoleon even toyed with the whimsical idea of transferring his capital to Lyons in order to be closer to his "second realm", i.e. Italy. But this passing fancy of resurrecting the conditions of Roman Gaul, in which Lugdunum for a time was the seat of administration, soon faded.

What the emperor had in mind was evidenced by the buildings he commissioned. They were nearly all situated in the more salubrious western part of Paris which was not yet as built up as the historic jumble which was the city's core. The plebeian suburbs to the east were completely left out of consideration. The Madeleine Church, begun under Louis XV and neglected during the Revolution, was to be transformed by Vignon into a "temple of fame" replete with colonnade, for which its elevated location seemed to predestine it. In 1808 Percier and Fontaine built a triumphal arch for the emperor on the Place du Carrousel, but this was later outshone by a second arc de triomphe built by Chalgrin and decorated by Rude. Situated in an eye-catching position at the hub of the Place d'Etoile and at the end of the regal Champs-Elysées, it became the trademark of Paris. In 1810 Gondoin completed a column with bronze relief plaques on the Place du Vendôme onto which a statue of Napoleon was hoisted, while a lion from San Marco in Venice was peremptorily relocated in front of the Hôtel des Invalides.

After a refreshing stroll through the immaculately-tended Tuileries gardens one could admire the obelisk which General Bonaparte had kindly sent to the people of Paris from Egypt. The arcades of the new Rue de Rivoli invited patrons to browse at their leisure through the luxurious boutiques before refreshing themselves in one of the exquisite cafés or pastry-shops. The bridges over the Seine (including two recently constructed ones) were named after the sites of glorious battles, which occasioned the somewhat fiery Field Marshal Blücher, after his entry into Paris, to attempt to blow up to the Pont d'Jéna, the name of which offended his sensibilities.

Anyone who revisited the city after a long absence to relive the memory of his youthful indiscretions would have noticed many changes on his walk

The Allée des Orangers in the Tuileries gardens.
Engraving by Schwartz after Müller. From:
R.J. Durdent, *Promenades de Paris*. Paris, 1812.

The Rue de Rivoli in Paris. The construction of
this street, the name of which recalls one of
Bonaparte's early victories, was begun in 1805.
In keeping with a tradition of absolutist Paris
the façades have a uniform pattern.
Lithograph, *c.* 1830.

[1] PINKERTON, J.; MERCIER, L. S.; CRAMER, C. F.:
*Ansichten der Hauptstadt des Französischen
Kaiserreiches vom Jahre 1806 an.* First edition
1807; new edition and selection by Klaus Linke.
Leipzig, 1980:

through the city, some for the better and others for the worse.

Numerous wells had been sunk in various parts of the city, thereby alleviating the task of fetching water. From 1805 onwards a canal linked the Ourcq with the Seine in order to provide the northeastern suburbs with sufficient water. Much was done also to reinforce the wharves along the Seine in the city centre.

Those visitors[1] who were able to take a look behind the glamorous façades would have noted, perhaps with amazement, that the emperor's mania for orderliness was often extended to the humble concerns of everyday-life in an effort to quietly erase all traces of the Revolution from the city's panorama. In 1806 the Panthéon was converted back into a church and in 1811 was adorned with an "Apotheosis of St. Geneviève" by the court painter Gros. The lugubrious tower of the Temple, the fortress in which Louis XVI spent his last days, served as a state prison until 1808. Toussaint L'Ouverture, Pichegru, Cadoudal and even Moreau all made its acquaintance before it was later demolished. The Hôtel de Ville was renovated but the dilapidated archbishop's palace—once one of the main bases of the militant sans-culottes—was merely patched up in a makeshift manner. The "Terrasse des Feuillants" and the infamous Jacobin monastery were razed to the ground.

Amid the hurly-burly of the large and naturally vivacious city, the fact that it was also the seat of government tended to be forgotten except during big military parades or the celebration with music and fireworks of a victory or of some promising peace agreement. It was only apparent in a part of the city centre on either side of the Seine where the ministries were crowded together. The court was still a hive of activity in the Tuileries as was the Legislative Assembly in the Palais Bourbon on the banks of the Seine and the Senate. This was situated a little apart in the Palais Luxembourg, which had served as a prison during the Revolution but was adjoined by a very spacious and popular park. The Hôtel de Ville and police

The Palais de l'Elysée in Paris. This splendid palace (today the residence of the French president) was built in 1718 on what was then the outskirts of the capital. It has changed hands many times. Thus from 1803 to 1808 it belonged to Murat and thereafter to the emperor.

The Arc de Triomphe on the Place de l'Etoile.

The design for the King of Rome's palace in Paris. In honour of the heir to the Imperial throne it was planned to construct a huge edifice on the heights of Chaillot to the extreme west of the city in which not only the court but also large cultural institutions were to be accommodated. Like many other Napoleonic construction projects it remained on the drawing board.

Three engravings, 1814 (section from the marginal illustrations to J. Bonnisel's plan of Paris).

Were one to ask in the Maison de la Commune, the former Hôtel de Ville, to see the room where Robespierre was shot and his brother jumped out of the window it would be a futile exercise, for the whole of the interior has been changed since the prefecture of Paris was moved hither recently from the Place Vendôme.
Pinkerton: "Modifications récentes".

The site of the former meeting place of the Jacobins has been turned into a market intended for the Quartier Saint-Honoré.
Pinkerton: "Fragments".

An air of fragrance, mystery and luxury prevails in the stationery shops which have sprung up here since the establishment of the new régime.
Louis Sébastien Mercier

ELISEE NAPOLEON

[1] CABANIS, A.: *La presse française sous le Consulat et l'Empire*. Paris, 1974.

headquarters were nearby. Also in the centre were the Bourse and the Bank of France, the Supreme Court and the Hôtel-Dieu, the largest of the hospitals reformed by Chaptal. Notre-Dame may also be included here since it was in the voluminous cathedral that the "Te Deum" was sung on important state occasions rather than in the (by later standards) incomparably more beautiful but cramped confines of the Sainte-Chapelle. Not surprisingly the area swarmed with men in uniform—soldiers and officials and guardians of law and order—travelling by coach, on horseback or, if need be, by shanks' mare.

Apart from this the streets were dotted with countless shops and stores, small workshops, taverns and coffee houses. The big expensive restaurants attracted customers less through glittering façades than by the rich selection of meals and beverages on offer.

The mostly narrow and crooked streets, whose state of cleanliness did not improve under the Empire, teemed with people from morning till night. Business was once again booming. Military requirements and the embargo—which for a time was very far-reaching—on goods of the hated English rivals, the unbridled consumerism of the *nouveaux riches* and their apers, the extravagance of visitors and the stability of the franc all stimulated trade. After the long lull of the 1790s many construction projects were commissioned, including by the middle classes. The burgesses refurnished their homes and restocked their wardrobes, wanting once more to dress and bedeck themselves in all their finery. As a result of this, crumbs which were not to be sniffed at fell from the Imperial table to be snatched up by master bricklayers and carpenters, joiners and decorators, producers and vendors of textiles, armourers and goldsmiths, seamstresses and milliners, beauticians and many others.

Nevertheless Paris did not develop into an industrial city during the Napoleonic era. Small-scale handicraft production remained preponderant. In the main it accounted for the many luxury and fashion trades in which the capital excelled. A goodly proportion of the city's production was devoted to the tourist industry, as were many of the small guesthouses and inns, the *hôtels garnis*, in which young journeymen who had arrived from elsewhere, some on foot, stayed as long-term tenants, albeit with the barest minimum of furnishings and comfort. The larger hostelries were reserved for the wealthier visitors.

The police kept their beady eye on newcomers to the city. It was virtually impossible for anyone to slip through their net as the landlords could not expect to prosper without the goodwill of the constabulary.

Those staying in the capital for a longer period who wished to avoid the inconveniences of residing at an inn or a hotel could, if they had the wherewithal, rent (usually furnished) accommodation. There were enough empty dwellings even though cheap housing was lacking for the vast majority of the urban populace.

Expanding manufacturers preferred to locate their enterprises in the provinces where industrial conditions tended to be more favourable and wage rates, though sometimes not to be sneezed at, were rather lower than in the capital. Their interests coincided with those of the government which made no bones about the fact that, for a number of reasons, it feared an overconcentration of workers in the capital and so wished to prevent this. Throughout the Imperial era the working classes proved remarkably docile towards the ruling régime from a political point of view. They were at best apathetic, refusing to offer their services as cannon fodder to either the Bourbon or the bourgeois-republican opposition, let alone coming forward with a programme of their own. Nevertheless Napoleon never overcame his allergic antipathy towards these *classes dangereuses*.

The revolutionary mass actions which he had witnessed in 1789 and 1792 remained too deeply ingrained in his memory. What he had been prepared to tolerate as a young lieutenant was anathema to him once he had become emperor. This was reinforced by practical considerations. Maintaining law and order in the highly sensitive nerve centre of Paris demanded more than the issuing of relevant instructions to the police. It was just as important to stuff cheap bread into hungry mouths, to combat unemployment by official means whenever it reared its head, and to check the spread of epidemics which flourished chiefly in the overcrowded basements and attics of the poorest areas—i.e. to reduce, not swell, the number of slums. As a result Paris remained to some extent exempt from the forest of factory chimneys.

The emperor concerned himself personally with the cultural needs of his subjects and in particular with those of the demanding Parisians. In this sphere too he wished to leave as little as possible to the vicissitudes of chance. Even the big biennial art exhibitions were organized by the government, which at that time was a very rare thing. Napoleon was well aware of the importance of the mass media and was probably the first ruler to operate a systematic press policy. The right to information was recognized and even proclaimed a duty. But his subjects were expected to exercise this right in an appropriately meek and mild manner.

In order to protect the population from "confusion", the number of licensed newspapers was reduced in instalments. In Paris only about a third of the three hundred papers which had existed during the heady days of the Revolution survived the Eighteenth of Brumaire. Thereafter they became fewer and fewer until the emperor decided that the magic figure of five would totally suffice to meet the legitimate needs of the capital, with a handful more for the provinces.[1] Since they all carried—or omitted—approximately the same material, there was a certain logic in this, especially as many Parisians, who had previously been avid newspaper readers, reacted to this state of affairs by dispensing altogether with the monotonous reports of the court correspondents. Consequently the circulation trailed well behind that of the aggressively irreverent London papers which, however, they were not allowed to have in their possession.

Journalism became a tough trade, particularly as the few remaining exponents of the profession were now subject to unfair competition, for Napoleon himself became the "First Journalist of the Empire". He took up the pen in order to dictate to the semi-official *Moniteur* his authoritative interpretation of events in certain important instances. Since they often contained pointers concerning his intentions and sometimes even veiled offers, the lead articles were carefully scrutinized in every capital city. By contrast the Parisians, who were powerless to influence the course of events anyway, attached less importance to them. One illustration of this was that, with the exception of functionaries who were always at pains to keep abreast of the vaguest of indications from above, the *Moniteur* sold pathetically badly in the capital.

On the other hand, whenever there was anything to report on the war front the clearly written *Bulletins de la Grande Armée* found their way into even the smallest village. Once again the unmistakable style of Napoleon could often be detected as the author of these seldom honest but very skilfully composed reports, for he was by no means averse to involving himself directly with propaganda work. The prefects and sub-prefects ensured that they were distributed nationwide, the priests read them from the pulpit and the mayors had them proclaimed into the bargain. In Paris they appeared both in the press and as public posters. They were ubiquitous and all-pervasive. As long as things went well on the battlefield they achieved their didactic aim of civic instruction. But when one defeat began to follow another not even the bulletins written in the finest Caesarean style could save the situation.

The Parisians could not live by bread alone, nor could the more sophisticated among them restrict themselves to a diet of newspapers. First of all they needed air, and the government—fortunately—could not ration this. Everyone who found the bustling narrow streets of the capital too stuffy and claustrophobic fled to the open countryside in his spare time, however limited this was for many working people. The wealthy drove out by coach. The average Parisian, if such a creature existed amid the mixture of native Parisians and migrants to the city, either walked or, more rarely, hired a vehicle.

The Sunday outing into the countryside with the whole family was virtually *de rigueur*. One inhaled the fresh country air, frolicked in the fields and stopped off along the way for refreshment. Among the most popular destinations were the charming islet on the Marne near Charenton, the vineyards of Menil-Montant and the nearby heights of Montmartre with its fine view of Paris and the plain of Saint-Denis, an idyllic location which had not yet been colonized by the *bohémiens*. Others preferred Saint-Cloud, where a deserted château was restored to its full former splendour by Napoleon who also opened up its

View of Paris from Montmartre. In the foreground
   are the quarries of Montmartre. Lithograph (incomplete signature: Gib...), 1804.

Place Vendôme in Paris. In the centre of this square,
   which was re-designed in a uniform style from
   1708 onwards, stood an equestrian statue of Louis
   XIV until it was replaced by a statue of Liberty
   during the revolutionary years. In 1806 this was
   superseded by a bronze column some 43 metres
   high bearing reliefs which gave an account of the
   campaigns of 1805. Etching by Jean Duplessi-
   Bertaux after Zix. From the work: *Napoléon à la
   Grande Armée*. Paris, *c*. 1810.

park to the public. Or one could take a stroll through the woods in the valley of Montmorency and pay a visit to Meudon or Sèvres, where the porcelain factory produced thousands of vases, dishes, plates and cups for the Imperial dining table or for presentation as state gifts, although some were also sold at moderate prices as good-quality household tableware intended for every-day use. Within the international league table

Sèvres porcelain ranked just behind the products of Meissen, which became known in English as "Dresden china" and in France as "porcelaine de Saxe".

During the week the Parisians had to make do with an evening walk which for the men often ended up at the local bar. The Parisiennes, espe-cially if they were still unattached, dressed them-selves up in the latest fashion ready to go out.

They wanted not just to look for themselves but to be looked at. There was no shortage of young—and more mature—men in search of an amorous adventure, which might sometimes end in mat-rimony.

The youth of Paris, in the broadest sense, pre-ferred to wander along the ringroads, the boulevards, which bounded the city in the north and east. They were constructed following the de-

Newspaper vendor. Lithograph by Carle Vernet, *c.* 1820.

The printshop of the lithographer F. Delpech in Paris. Lithograph by Carle Vernet, *c.* 1820.

Fluctuat nec mergitur!
Armorial motto of the city of Paris: Her ship battles with the waves yet does not sink!

[1] ARNAULT, A. V.: *Souvenirs d'un sexagénaire.* Paris, 1833.
[2] TULARD, J.: *Nouvelle Histoire de Paris: le Consulat et l'Empire.* Paris, 1970.

molition of the city's fortified ramparts as broad avenues which were for the most part lined with trees that separated the pavement from the road. Virtually all year round they were busy and full of life. Kiosks and street vendors loudly advertised their wares. Public entertainments, which in most districts took place on open squares, could here be found everywhere. Wandering showmen and entertainers, gamblers and fortune-tellers all went through their paces. Dance music was struck up and ballad singers delighted the assembled throng with their witty and often impromptu offerings.

The strollers included a large number of strangers to the city, both from the provinces and abroad, come to pay homage to the capital. The construction of paved roads, which Napoleon promoted out of military, economic, postal and other considerations, made travelling easier. Fourteen of these first-class Imperial highways (following a decree of 1811) radiated out from Paris, including the main arterial roads to Amsterdam, Hamburg, Mainz, Rome, Milan and Bayonne. On their arrival in Paris the unsprung coaches spewed out their load of mail, freight and thoroughly shaken passengers.

Among the delights to be found in the capital were now attractive public baths. Some, especially the "Turkish" variety, had long existed in various parts of the city, but they could no longer satisfy the demands of the hordes of would-be bathers. Thus new baths were set up of which the main ones were mounted on large, low, covered vehicles moored on the Seine. An enterprising company, correctly predicting the long-term Parisian bathing boom (which was partly caused by Rousseau's "Back to Nature" call) had established a monopoly. John Pinkerton, a British visitor, described the "Bains Vigier", the bathers' favourite haunt: "The baths consist of a wooden structure roughly the size of a 140-gun man-of-war and separated into two sections. They contain one hundred and forty bathing cubicles which at certain times of the day, particularly from 5 to 9 a.m., are so well occupied that one must sometimes wait hours before finding a chance to make use of one's ticket. Since the male and female attendants are paid by the bathers it is reckoned that the owners earn no less than fifty thousand francs (ten thousand pounds) in profits per annum." He did not forget to mention that "the two sexes are kept separate and propriety is fully observed. One enters a long corridor which gives onto the disrobing cabins that, at the side nearest the ladies' cubicles, have only a small square window, which affords but a niggardly prospect. This gives little vantage either to the eye or to curiosity as the beauties tend not to walk up and down along the said corridor."

Opinions varied, even among doctors themselves, as to the usefulness of bathing—and swimming. Not long before, contact with water was still held to be detrimental to health and so it was recommended to avoid the medium as far as possible. Some conceded that this dread of water could have disastrous consequences on the population's physical and mental well-being; yet at the same time they warned against going to the opposite extreme.

The visit to the baths in the morning was complemented by a visit to the theatre in the evening. For different reasons this was also, and always had been, a little problematic. The theatre and the dramatists had always been dictated to, both before and during the Revolution; the only difference was in the method. The Empire likewise tried to ensure that decorum, as it perceived the term, was maintained.

This entailed the avoidance of all obscenity and delicate contemporary questions, no Jacobinism or Royalism on the stage (which after all was a microcosm of the world!). Glorification was not insisted upon; this was an optional extra for sycophants. No author was now put behind bars for what he wrote, as had happened under previous governments. The acting fraternity gained admittance to the respectable ranks of bourgeois society.

The fly in the Thespian ointment was, as ever, the state's insatiable thirst for discipline: a decree of 1807 laid down that Paris was entitled to precisely eight theatres, no more and no less. The repertory for each of them was exactly determined. There was the Comédie-Française, situated from 1802 onwards in the Palais Royal (in 1812 Napoleon issued a benevolent decree concerning its organization—all the way from the Kremlin!); the Odéon, the Grande and the Comic Opera as well as the lighter range of the variety, gaiety and vaudeville theatres and the Ambigu-Comique. The system also had its advantages. It put a stop to the frequent bankruptcies of fly-by-night theatre

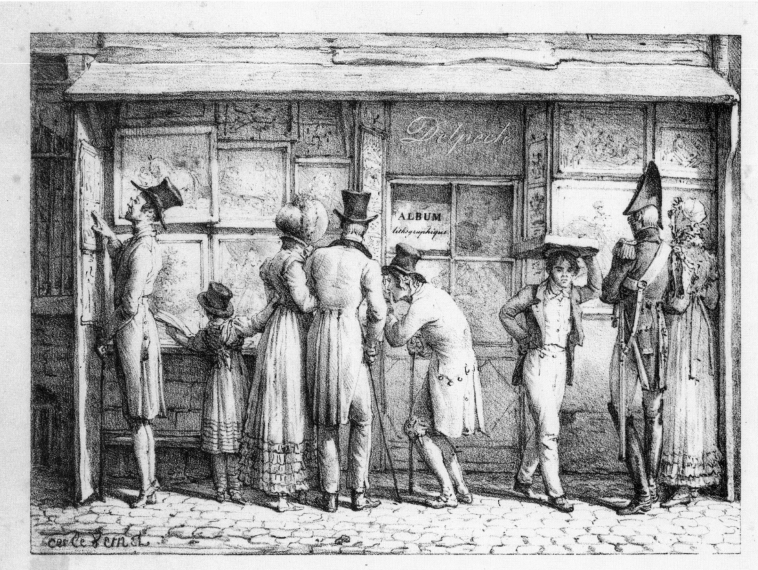

Imprimerie Lithographique de F. Delpech.

operators who used to cheat actors and creditors alike out of their money, and at the same time ensured that they played to a large audience, if not a packed house. Despite the rather meagre literary fare on offer, the spectators were content.[1] They had their favourite actresses to whom—especially at the Comédie-Française—they remained staunchly loyal for years on end.

Some idolized Mademoiselle Georges while others enthused with equal passion over Mademoiselle Duchesnois.

An even bigger attraction for the masses was the music theatre. Here the stage was dominated by such operatic stars as Spontini, Cherubini and Napoleon's favourite Païsiello—an Italian trio of bel canto exponents. They were supplemented by the French singers Méhul and Lesueur, Grétry and Dalayrac, whose tunes were hummed and whistled on every street. The star ballet dancers—Vestris, Gardel and Duport—likewise each had their own firm body of supporters among the public. Vibrant and happy-go-lucky, full of native

wit, an easy harmony of vice and virtue, both lapping up and laughing at its own legend—this was the hospitable face which Paris showed to all visitors. At the same time it was the home of a hundred thousand solid and well-behaved families who went to bed early, listened to what Napoleon had to say and then re-immersed themselves in their own affairs. Yet was it more than the Imperial capital, the administrative headquarters, the main trading centre and a giant vanity fair all rolled into one?[2]

It most certainly was. It had fought out the decisive battles of the Revolution. It was here that the Empire was founded. It was the power house of the forces which would shape France's future for good or evil. From here a dispassionate administrative machine governed the country much more rigorously and uniformly than ever before and reinforced the capital's predominance over the provinces. The Napoleonic régime contributed to this process. On the other hand it was always mindful of the fact that the nation's reserves were scattered throughout the countryside and needed their own foci. One of the purposes of the prefectoral system was to make the départements viable and organic links in the national chain. It ensured that their main centres of population did not atrophy in either material or intellectual terms. Thus Napoleon hit upon the idea of forwarding a portion of the art treasures which he had brought home from his campaigns as "trophies" (i.e. the spoils of war), and which the Parisians had been able to enjoy in the Louvre, to provincial towns. He himself selected suitable paintings which would unobtrusively provide for the people living in small towns and in the countryside a visible record of the emperor's successes. And if propaganda considerations underlay the decision to set up provincial museums, they nevertheless stimulated a sense of appreciation for, and enjoyment of, art among broader sections of the population than had previously been the case in France.

Notwithstanding this, Paris was to remain the intellectual centre of the nation. It did not lose one iota of its magnetic appeal. However, the point was whether it would be able to exert the same attraction outside France, in the same way that the Tuileries was the centre and symbol of the most massive concentration of power in the contemporary world or that the Louvre became the Mecca of the fine arts. The capital's printers were the first to have occasion to doubt this. In 1810 the police reduced the number of permits in this field from almost two hundred to sixty, and these had to swear an oath "never to print anything contrary to their duty to the emperor or to the interests of the state"—a careless attempt to ease the censor's unpleasant task which, however, was hardly conducive to fostering a new generation of philosophers or to making the city the literary centre of the world.

Some inhabitants of the capital confused the reality with the appearances, since the whole world seemed perpetually to be doing obeisance to their Lutetia. The force of its attraction, following all its deeds and misdeeds, did not cease with Napoleon's exit. In fact, its charms even conquered the hearts of the conquerors in 1814. Its very name seemed full of mystic promise: Gay Paree! Young Russian officers carried their impressions back with them and were still inspired by them as they launched their Decembrist revolt of 1825, which was the prelude to a succession of revolutions in their vast and distant land which would one day shake the world.

Fashion Fads

Rarely has the world of fashion undergone such a period of turbulent upheaval, such a rapid succession of changes in taste, as in the final decade of the 18th century. The leading forces of the Revolution were intent on making a demonstrative break with past sartorial habits but without reverting to the feudal tradition of socially differentiated dress standards.

The debate began in the spring of 1789 over the seemingly trivial question of what costume should be worn by the delegates to the States-General. The plain black outfit which the members of the Third Estate were made to wear in order to sharply distinguish them from the ostentatiously clad representatives of the privileged orders and to remind them of their inferior status, soon became a mark of honour for the bourgeois revolutionaries. Heated debates in the National Assembly and the press over the pros and cons of a standard national costume showed just how seriously sartorial questions were treated in the era of Liberty and Equality. Indeed, feelings ran so high at this time that in extreme cases some French patriots regarded the donning of culottes, the knee-length breeches of the *ancien régime*, as a sufficient reason to denounce the wearer to the revolutionary tribunal. One must appreciate how intensely feudal dress constraints were hated in order to be able to understand the egalitarian fanaticism which motivated the great David and other like-minded artists to design a Frankish national costume and to organize exhibitions of revolutionary fashion at national festivals at which

actors took the role of models. Yet the futility of these and other such efforts aimed at dictating fashion trends was shown by the vehemence with which the women market traders of Paris defended themselves in a pitched battle in 1793 against their intolerant and trouser-clad sisters from the "Society of Revolutionary Republican Women" who tried to force them to wear the red bonnet.

Following the abolition of royalty and royal etiquette and the concomitant Republican ban on producing luxury fashion accessories Paris, where the first fashion magazine had appeared in 1785,[1] seemed set to forfeit its international reputation as a trend-setter in this respect. The English court, which had hitherto made no great splash on the fashion scene, now crept stealthily into the lead. The entire European aristocracy transferred its attention from Paris to St. James Palace. At the same time this reinforced the preference shown by supporters of bourgeois reform for the freer French manner of dressing. The abolition of dress regulations became a standard demand in the programmes of liberal forces in Europe in their struggle against the trappings of feudal privilege.

Hair set in curls and French robes were proudly displayed by the bourgeoisie while the courts at St. Petersburg, Vienna, Berlin, Dresden, Munich and elsewhere revived ancient and long-forgotten edicts in an attempt to at least titivate the old façade. On the other hand the *Allgemeine deutsche Real-Enzyklopädie für die gebildeten Stände* ("General German Encyclopedia for the Educated Classes") could still report in the year 1822: "The whole world knows that in all parts of the globe people obey the dictates of the London tailors with the same alacrity with which they heed the prescriptions of the Paris milliners. Together they would seem to dominate the entire earth which they have divided up, so to speak, into two halves."

This is a most apt description of the international division of labour between the two front-runners which gradually asserted itself. The twin centres of haute couture reflected, each in its own way, the triumph of a new social order which also included grotesque aberrations. Bourgeois fashion was to indulge in some wildly extravagant experiments before the pattern of violent fluctuation subsided into a more normal rhythm.

La famille anglaise à Paris.

English family in Paris. Engraving after Carle Vernet.
From: *London und Paris*, 5th annual volume (1805).

Even in the closing stages of the Revolution fanatics and fellow travellers alike often enthused over such revolutionary symbols as the giant red, white and blue cockade, the short tunic and drainpipe trousers of the sans-culottes, the clogs and the Phrygian liberty bonnet more for reasons of snobbery, exhibitionism or dissimulation than from real sympathy or a genuine urge to parade their revolutionary convictions. Much to the annoyance of the pedantic Robespierre, who continued to dress in a punctiliously conventional manner, Léonard Bourdon took a fancy to keeping his hat on inside the Convention as a sign of great brashness. But it was not until the Thermidorian reaction set in that the *merveilleuses* (marvellous) and the *incroyables* (incredible) specimens of the "gilded youth" marked the culmination point of the fashion revolution set in train in the days of the "terror" by a conscious revolt. They buttoned up their jackets lopsidedly, dressed in a deliberately slovenly way, wore boots that were too big and swathed themselves in voluminous neckerchiefs—all in the name of restored freedom. A cudgel, which sometimes belaboured the backs of Jacobins and sans-culottes, replaced the ornamental rapier of the idle rich.

Now that the bourgeoisie at last held the reins of power the adoption of exquisite materials and designs sharply distinguished them from the "grey masses" in the same way that the dazzling court had previously marked itself off from the "canaille". Even upstarts in Paris saw London court society as the paragon of elegance. Indeed, the British had long since freed themselves from over-refined modish habits and had moved towards a more functional style of clothing. Already marked by bourgeois business acumen and under Puritan and Quaker influence, they preferred reserve and sobriety which was reflected in subdued tones, high quality cloth and bespoke tailoring. The "robe à l'anglaise" democratized fashion without incurring the accusation of vulgar levelling. The nobility's old privileges evaporated, but only to be replaced by a hierarchy of money in which senseless extravagance and ostentation flew in the face of sound business practices.

Nudity is the national costume of mankind.
Jean Paul

[1] KLEINERT, A.: *Die ersten Modejournale in Frankreich*. Berlin (West), 1980.

Chevelure à la François 1.ᵉʳ. Chapeau en Barque. Charivari de Breloques.

A gentleman by no means dressed as well as he could afford: being more than he appeared increased his credit-worthiness.

The standard revolutionary uniform finally disappeared as a manifestation of egalitarianism in France after Brumaire when the Consuls and other high-ranking state officials, along with the many elected—or rather appointed—members of the representative bodies, adorned themselves with ceremonial vestments copied from ancient Rome: a fad for fancy dress which culminated in the extravaganza of the Imperial coronation in 1804. Napoleon's garments were exquisitely tailored by Leroy and Josephine's by Madame Raimbaud. The choicest materials and embroideries, by which the *nouveaux riches* could show off, were first paraded by the highest civic officials of Imperial France in a kind of social fashion show instituted by the triumphant victors, who were still very affected in their handling of their new-found power. The costumes of the Roman Republic, which the Convention inaugurated and the Directory imaginatively took further, evolved in the course of the changing scenario into those of the Augustan principate,

enriched by the golden bees which a somewhat ill advised Napoleon borrowed from the quaint symbolism of the Merovingians.

The wives of the Notables, who in 1808 became the Empire's new nobility, improved on the change of political scenery in their own way. The richest among them employed their own personal dressmakers after Josephine had led the way with Mademoiselle Minetti. The Greek chemise, with its extremely high waistline and revived train, became such a flimsy garment that it was only suited to be worn inside the salon or when posing in front of the easel. Skimpy dresses, worn without the conventional but hampering underwear, became so transparent that they were popularly referred to as "nude fashions".

"Silk was invented so that women could walk around naked with their clothes on," as an old Arab proverb has it.

Ladies of genteel refinement—not to mention the less respectable members of the fair sex—often declined to wear even petticoats, let alone outer clothing. In cold weather this was almost an affront to Nature and as such was completely at odds with the fashion habits of the more ordinary middle-class women. Never at a loss for a *bon mot*, people began referring not to well-dressed but to "well-undressed" women. A charming party game soon came into vogue: weighing the apparel of women of the world. Their entire outfit, inclusive of shoes and jewelry, was not supposed to weigh more than half a pound. The record was said to be held by the delightful wife of Hamelin, a Swiss army contractor, who strolled through the Tuileries gardens arrayed in nothing but a gossamer veil until the importunate gawking of passers-by compelled her to retire. Naturally the ballerinas were unbeatable in this field since they enjoyed the unfair advantage of being able to perform, as Mademoiselle Saulnier did when she played Venus in the *Judgement of Paris*, in the altogether.

Around 1800 the cashmere shawl, worn instead of a coat, arrived from London and conquered the hearts of the continental ladies. They did not so much wear it as drape themselves with it, covering their hair with it "à l'Iphigénie".[1] Madame Gardel instructed women in how to wear it properly, and the best place to buy one was Corbin's in the Rue de Richelieu. Napoleon's threat to punish any contravention of the ban on English

Chapeau en Bateau. Habit Couleur Crotin. Culotte de Peau.

imports went unheeded, not least by Josephine who possessed more than three hundred such items, none of which cost less than 15,000 francs (as much as a high official earned in a year). Even the fact that he reputedly ripped up one or two of her early purchases in a fit of pique failed to deter her. Not until 1812 did some slight relief come to the aid of the French balance of payments when the square "Turkish shawl" from Vienna won the favour of fashion-conscious females and thus conquered the market.

Another accessory of the *ancien régime*, which had long been frowned upon, regained popularity. The old pouch filled with liquid fragrances fell into disuse, but the new perfumes, which were concocted according to secret recipes that smacked of alchemy, were put instead into little flasks of glass or metal encased in an embroidered bag or metal basket.

Essences of musk, ambergris, myrrh, roses, irises and violets were most popular as were cloves, cinnamon, lemon, rosemary, marjoram and aniseed. The Parisian manufacturers' monopoly of these so highly desirable odoriferous substances remained unbroken.

Precious stones glittered everywhere, inlaid in combs, brooches, clasps, diadems and other items of jewelry. Imitation or even genuine jewelry, procured as booty by the menfolk, was often worn in superabundant profusion: bracelets and bangles around wrists and ankles, rings on the fingers and toes, chains looped six or seven times around the neck, earrings and pendeloques. For his coronation as King of Italy in Milan in 1805 Napoleon himself made do with the historic "iron crown" of the Lombards whilst for his wife he had eighty-two antique gems plus 2,275 pearls made up by the jeweller Nitot into a diadem, a comb, a necklace, earrings and two bracelets. Apparently it was all so heavy that it could not possibly be worn. Puffs and muffs, frills and lace, including the incomparable products of Alençon, Chantilly and of course the extra-fine variety from Brussels (from which the canopy of Madame Récamier's bed was made), heralded the end of the last restrictions which had been imposed by the Spartan idea of virtue held by the boorish Jacobins. The Roman sandal was replaced by the heeless slip-

Coeffeur.

Clapeau à la Robinson. Cheveux à l'Enfant Pantalon de Tricot Bottes à la russianle.

on shoe. The levelling of dance habits—instead of minuets for some and folk dances for the rest everyone now took up the waltz—necessitated a light but tightly fitting shoe. The cross-ply shoe worn by female dancers at that time has survived to the present day.

A change occurred among the male of the species. In 1803 a German writer[2] in Paris could still scoff: "The place is swarming with Englishmen trying to look like Parisian fops. There is nary a more uproarious spectacle than to see some enervated Briton dressed up in French style by his tailor. He prances and stomps in his unaccustomed get-up like an unbroken horse harnessed to a sleigh." But soon the sons of Albion turned the tables, and one in particular rose with the greatest of ease to become the unchallenged arbiter of elegance: the dandy George Bryan Brummell (1778–1840), known as Beau Brummell. He was a friend of the Prince of Wales and party to all the latter's pranks. Later the two fell out, and later still Beau Brummell, having fled from his creditors to Calais in 1816, ended up in a poorhouse in Normandy where he eked out the remaining years of

Three illustrations from the series "Incroyables". Coloured engravings by Georges-Jacques Gatine after drawings by Carle Vernet, 1810.

Bottom:
Ladies' hairdresser. Coloured engraving by Joly. From: *Arts, Métiers et Cris de Paris.*

Just as there is a music mania and a dance mania, so there is also a mania for watches. They are worn in rings, and such miniature gems even show the correct time. Not content with this, high society ladies even wear them around their necks as jewellery.
Louis Sébastien Mercier

[1] KRÜNITZ, D.J.G.: *Ökonomisch-technologische Enzyklopädie*, Vol. 92, Letter M. Berlin, 1803, p. 518 ("Drei Berlinerinnen").
[2] KRÜNITZ, p. 514.

A Paris chez Martinet, Libraire, rue du Coq, N.º15. *Le Goût du Jour. N.º 44.*
Les Mélomanes ambulans.

his life. However, in Imperial France he was celebrated by French followers of fashion as their idol. In "dandy clubs" they vied with one another over the niceties of sporting a necktie and other intricacies of stylish dressing.

This did not represent a return to the gaudy garb of the old French aristocracy. They dressed more modestly, less flashily. Yet they did go in for a certain amount of excentricity, and no dandy worth his salt wore the same clothes for more than three weeks. In France as elsewhere top quality material and perfect fitting became the hallmark of

"democratic" bourgeois fashion. Everyone could dress as he pleased, regardless of the effect. One recognized one's peers by their dress—by the "price-tag" or the tailor they used. The best supplier of coats was Catin, of trousers Acerby and of opulent waistcoats Thomassin, who still made certain concessions to the "good old days". The clothes were of silk and velvet and exquisitely embroidered. Napoleon himself—to the chagrin of those with spindly legs—gave the signal for the reintroduction of the aristocratic knee breeches with accompanying long white stockings since he

deemed them necessary at any self-respecting court. In the long run, however, he was swimming against the tide.

It was said of Beau Brummell that in order to get a pair of gloves that fitted perfectly he had the hand, the fingers and the thumbs made by three different firms. The number of pairs people got through was enormous: gentlemen changed their gloves up to five times a day. Small wonder, then, that the emperor, who was keen to protect his delicate hands and so preferred gloves of the softest leather or cloth, consumed nearly three hundred

LA VACCINE EN VOYAGE.

À Paris chez Depeuille Rue des Mathurins Sorbonne aux deux Pilastres d'Or.

Travelling representatives of the newly introduced process of vaccination. Coloured engraving by Depeuille, 1800.

Page 206:
Travelling music lovers. Coloured engraving by Pierre Martinet.

La cravate, c'est l'homme.
Balzac

pairs in 1806. He could always turn his gloves, like his victories, to account: when he removed his glove during a battle it was the signal to attack. The soul of a man was embodied in his cravat. It was the linchpin of the male wardrobe. The wide range of different ways in which one could tie it reflected a man's disposition or character. Monsieur Demarelli was acknowledged as the connoisseur in this field. This item of attire had to be of a dazzling whiteness and was likewise changed several times per day. From this developed a welcome craze for washing and cleanliness.

When a gentleman went out he no longer carried a gnarled stick—this was retained only by Freemasons as a secret mark of identification when they raised or lowered the thick end in a particular fashion. The normal walking stick was thinner and more elegant and was often adorned with tortoiseshell. Napoleon even possessed one which had a musical box built into it. For visits to the salon this was replaced by a slender cane which could be dexterously twirled or stroked.
Snuffboxes were often made of gold. Those which Napoleon gave away as tokens of his favour were

often richly beset with brilliants. The only jewelry permissible for men, apart from the finger ring, was the tie-pin and possibly a hat clasp and a pocket watch. Lucky was the man who owned or acquired a genuine "Breguet". The fame of this precision instrument maker, after whose death pre-eminence in the construction of timepieces irrevocably passed to the assiduous Swiss in the Jura Mountains, was sullied by impostors. Even during the lifetime of Abraham Louis Breguet (1747–1823) the number of imitations passed off in his name considerably exceeded Breguet's own handmade masterpieces of technical design, consummate craftsmanship and simple overall harmony of appearance. The latter played their part in the introduction of rubies and, from 1800 onwards, of the second hand.

The petty-bourgeoisie aped the fashions of their bourgeois counterparts, though naturally they had to cut their coat according to their cloth. Quite often they wore cast-offs from the rich which tailors accepted as part payment. Standard dress consisted of underclothes, long pantaloons with braces, a coloured waistcoat (sometimes called a *gilet*), a short English jacket in a variety of forms and colours but preferably brown, green and blue (*bleu foncé*) and then a redingote (a long, double-breasted frock coat) plus a "carrick", a cape worn in case of bad weather which went on to become the standard insignia—almost a uniform—of coachmen for many years to come. On their heads men wore either a two or a three-cornered cocked hat and, to an increasing extent, the "stovepipe" or topper. The shako was adopted by many women. The men liked to wear a kind of pumps known as *escarpins* or else, modelling themselves on the dashing soldiers, the ever more popular boots, with or without tops. On the other hand it was not the done thing for civilians to sport the drooping moustache worn by Napoleon's *grognards*. Instead they grew long and full sidewhiskers (*favoris*) and shaved off the rest.

The bulk of the population were hardly affected by all this. They wore their working clothes just as they had always done. For them the Empire was in truth merely a passing episode. Clothes were handed down from one generation to the next. In the countryside especially a strict distinction was drawn between everyday clothes and those reserved for special occasions. This "Sunday best"

Silver-gilt mirror frame for the Empress Marie Louise, designed by Adrien-Louis-Marie Cavelier and Pierre-Paul Prud'hon. Engraving by Jean-Antoine Pierron.

[1] BOEHN, M. VON: *Menschen und Moden im neunzehnten Jahrhundert. 1790–1817.* Munich, 1908.

varied according to the money available but without breaking the tradition of regional costumes which had developed in the 18th century. It was the farmer's showpiece at festivals and celebrations or when he went to church, and later it was handed on to his heir. At work cheap linen or woollen clothes were worn until they literally fell to pieces. The job of making and altering them was normally done by someone within the family. Design and colouring remained virtually unchanged for many decades. On the other hand the exigencies of the Napoleonic Wars left their mark on the field of fashion.[1] The army was offered an ever wider range of uniforms and the emperor likewise required his officials to wear a uniform in keeping with their status and position. A new convention established itself: a black umbrella for men. It broke the monopoly previously enjoyed by the ladies who protected themselves from rain and shine alike by means of their delightful little parasols. Fur gained ground as a material for gloves, muffs and trimmings. The first real fur coat, however, did not appear until 1808. It reached Paris from Russia and soon caught on. There was a general ban on the import of goods made in, or shipped from, England. As an economic weapon against the enemy, which was not open to frontal attack, Napoleon decreed the exclusive use of French-made materials right across his extensive European sphere of influence. The working classes now often wore old military uniforms since these were made of rather more hard-wearing fabrics. In the course of the wars a wave of Francophobia developed in Germany among fervent patriots, especially young students, which led to a revival of traditional German fashion, with a high-collared black dress-coat and an open-neck shirt. After Napoleon's defeat the focus of political struggle shifted from the battlefield to the princely ballrooms of Vienna. For a short while the Austrian capital, as it hosted the Vienna Congress, made a name for itself not just in the fields of music and dancing but also in fashion, becoming the world's third most important centre of modish dress. However hard some conservative die-hards strove to revive the paraphernalia of feudalism, their efforts were doomed to failure. In its essential features bourgeois fashion continued to set the pace in Vienna, where it saw out the Empire style and ushered in the *Biedermeier* style.

Madame Récamier. Painting by FRANÇOIS GÉRARD. 1802. Before Gérard his teacher David had begun a portrait of Julie Récamier, who had a great many admirers. But he abandoned it after the model had turned to the younger artist. David's conception had been a bleak and idealized neo-classical image with almost utopian features. Gérard has restricted the classical tradition to little more than the clothing. His wistful and casual figure with an architectural and rural backdrop, which he seems to have borrowed from portraits of English aristocrats, conveys the fresh and striking picture of a real woman. Musée du Petit-Palais, Paris.

Page 210:
Parisian fashions. Coloured engravings from the series: "Costumes parisiens de la fin du XVIIIᵉ siècle et du commencement du XIXᵉᵐᵉ siècle".

Pages 211–213:
Twelve illustrations from the *Journal des Luxus und der Moden*, published in Weimar by F.J.Bertuch and G.M.Kraus. These coloured engravings date from the annual volumes of 1796 to 1815.

Costume négligé d'un jeune homme.

Collet haut. Pantalon large.

Turban de Drap d'Or. Aigrette d'Oiseau de Paradis.

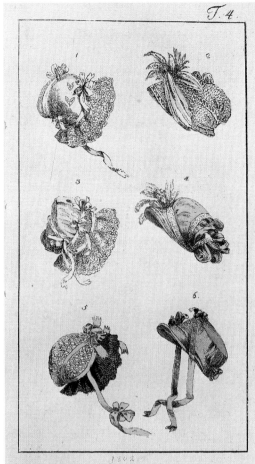

Le Diable,

ein neues Modespiel in Paris.

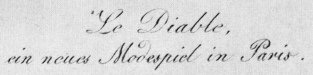

T. 29

T. 13

T. 29

T. 8

T. 13

T. 11

1796

1797

1801

1802

1804

LES MÉRVEILLEUSES.

Les Merveilleuses. Coloured engravings by Louis
Darcis after Carle Vernet, 1797. Carle Vernet is
regarded as the "inventor" of the caricatures of
the "Incroyables" and the "Merveilleuses".

Page 216:
Représentant du Peuple Français. Costume des
Deux Conseils. Coloured engraving by an un-
known artist.

REPRESENTANT DU PEUPLE FRANÇAIS.

Costume des Deux Conseils

A Paris chez Bonneville, Rue Jacques N° 195.

Pleasures of the Palate

In olden days it was probably the Chinese who came closest to raising cookery to the level of an art. However, in the Western world next to nothing was known of the one hundred or so courses of a gala banquet which eunuchs in the Middle Kingdom prepared for the divine Son of Heaven according to recipes which they guarded as state secrets. More was known about the strongly spiced and extra-sweet delicacies of the Orient. Dishes which the Italians copied from Byzantine and Arab sources made them the acknowledged leaders in this field in Renaissance Europe. A Florentine princess from the House of Medici who married a future king of France in 1533 and brought with her in her baggage train a host of first-rate cooks—as a sort of human dowry—stimulated an appetite for more exotic culinary delights in her new homeland.

During the period when Rabelais sired his *Gargantua and Pantagruel* and Luther aired his coarse "Table Talk", meals were still characterized by the glutton's unbridled desire to stuff himself full: "Why do ye not belch and fart—was the food not to your liking?" asked Luther. But by the end of the 17th century men like Pierre de la Varenne or Pierre de Lune had surpassed their Italian masters. Their cookery books became standard works and were repeatedly reprinted well into the 18th century.

Henceforth the privileged strata of "La douce France" cultivated the pleasures of the table, and the literary sources of the "great" 18th century are full of reports about this delectable aspect of life. Following the example set by Duke Philipp of Orléans, high-ranking personages embraced the habit of "composing" new dishes in their own private kitchens which they often named after themselves so as to be remembered by posterity. The Marquis de Béchamel achieved this, for instance, with his famous sauce. So too did the Marshal du Plessis-Praslin for his chocolates (*pralines*), though it was actually his cook who invented them in 1772. The tradition continued after the Bourbon restoration with such amateur cooks as Louis XVIII (1814/15–1824) and his steward, the Duc d'Escars (more correctly des Cars). Not even the urgent entreaties of ministers seeking an audience could distract them from their dabblings.

Even when the duke paid for it with his life after consuming an indigestible gravy the king, who survived the experience, was unperturbed. He is reported as having blithely expressed his sorrow with the words: "Poor old d'Escars. It's just as well that my stomach is stronger than his!"

However, the common man—the *roturier*—in 18th century France was also able to partake of the blessings of the new cuisine. François Massialot had already paved the way with his *Cuisinier royal et bourgeois* in 1691, and Menon carried the process much further with his cookbook for housewives entitled *La cuisinière bourgeoise* (1746) which became a lasting success.

The changes which the Revolution then brought about also affected French cuisine.

Uncertainty and a declining currency brought stagnation to the food and drink industry, and many a Parisian at the beginning of the 1790s, such as the women fish sellers quoted by Johann Friedrich Reichardt in his *Vertraute Briefe* ("Intimate Letters from France", 1793), longed for a return of the old government since under it "things were better and there was more money about". The titbits which the gourmet found indispensable could be had for neither love nor money, and so Balthasar Grimod de la Reynière (1758–1837) complained in retrospect: "It is a most lamentable fact that during this whole terrible period not a single decent turbot was to be had." One's heart bleeds for the poor man!

However, after things had sorted themselves out, the producers and purveyors of foodstuffs once more applied themselves to their business, so that the provinces again began to supply their specialities, from the truffles of Périgord to the goose's liver (which Jean Joseph Klose, the Marshal Contades's cook in Strasbourg, turned into the "divine" *paté de foie gras*) to the capital where, in spite of everything, there were still enough wealthy customers to ensure a roaring trade.

For a time a more serious obstacle to epicurean living was presented by the fact that the Revolution had wreaked particular havoc among those circles of people who had excelled at cultivating the finer pleasures of the palate. Those members of the feudal élite who survived all the trials and tribulations either stayed abroad or preferred to live inconspicuously. Anyone who still possessed great wealth or property took good care not provocatively to advertise the fact in the new egalitarian Republic. For the time being there were to be no more sumptuous repasts in the residences of numerous nobles and a few newly enriched bourgeois which had provided an opportunity to show off the expertise of their personal cooks and to try to outdo one another. There were to be no more banquets to which the hosts invited whole crowds of gourmets for their physical and intellectual delectation which artists, scholars and writers (not forgetting those merry old souls at every dining table, the worldly abbés) supplied the icing on the cake, so to speak.

Under the Thermidorians, and even more so under the Directory, a new generation of refined socialites emerged, and it soon became clear that they were just as partial to leading a life of luxury as their predecessors.

They were certainly a mixed bunch and remained so under both Consulate and Empire. There was Napoleon's officer corps, for example, in which well-bred former courtiers rubbed shoulders with rough peasants. There were old blue-blooded aristocrats who had survived unscathed and now started making money out of stocks and shares, alongside their peers of all ranks who had been newly ennobled by the emperor. Then came surefooted social climbers of the most diverse sort, solid bankers and *nouveaux riches* who had made a quick pile through army contracts. Consequently their eating habits were extremely varied. However, the expense to which they went after all the lean years of virtue was directly proportional in each case to the social prestige that they had acquired or regained. They all wanted to prove something, both to themselves but more especially to other people.

As a result dining tables were sumptuously adorned with silverware, crystal glass and floral decoration. For, as Reichardt noted,[1] "Parisians now prefer a large and splendid meal not just to a good poem but to many other things besides". The new French opulence reminded him of the "inexhaustible wealth of the Greeks and Romans from the period which the French seem to have elevated to their supreme ideal in every respect". His comment that after the Eighteenth of Brumaire "people drank at every opportunity in far greater quantity and quality than before" may have been merely his own subjective impression. No increase in alcoholism was recorded during this era of the bourgeois *parvenus*.

Leading politicians likewise distinguished themselves as generous hosts. For them this was also an exercise in "political gastronomy", to use Brillat-Savarin's phrase. Although not a new practice, it was raised to a higher level in France around 1800. In various forms it has remained a dependable means of oiling the diplomatic wheels to the present day. Lebrun supplied plentiful, if somewhat unimaginative, fare, and this was usually parallelled by the after-dinner discussions. Talleyrand is credited with being the first man to sprinkle Parmesan cheese onto his soup and to wash it down with a glass of dry Madeira. Cambacérès, initially Second Consul and subsequently Napoleon's arch chancellor, entertained fifty guests to an exquisite meal at his home every Saturday, and each Tuesday he gave an intimate dinner party. His dining table enjoyed the reputation of being the most distinguished in Paris, if not in the whole of France.

This new generation of epicures eagerly accepted advice designed to stimulate their taste buds even further. Grimod recognized this fact and capitalized on it. After the Revolution he had pre-cious little left apart from his propensity for gourmet living for which he had been notorious even before 1789. Now he sought to pass on his expertise by writing "gastrosophic" articles for a receptive public. Between 1803 and 1812 appeared eight volumes of his famous *Almanach des gourmands*, and in 1806/07 the *Journal des gourmands et des belles, ou l'épicuricien français*, which was followed by other publications. He took his work so seriously that he even checked out the claims of businessmen and accordingly praised or criticized them by name in his magazine. This made him into something of an arbiter of the delicatessen trade in Paris. Later he even founded a "jury of tasters" over which he presided himself.

Others also dabbled in this field with success. In 1801 Joseph Berchoux published his poem "La gastronomie", which brought the hitherto unknown rhymester fleeting fame, and in 1807 an Imperial cookbook was bestowed on the nation in the form of Alexandre Viard's *Cuisinier impérial*. The high favour which was enjoyed by such "products of pleasant Parisian literature devoted to the main object of hedonistic living in the capi-tal" was once again registered by Reichardt, who as a German had a particularly keen eye for the striking features of everyday life in Paris.

The Revolution also influenced gastronomy in the capital in a quite different and lasting manner: it promoted a swift and huge increase in the number of restaurants.

As early as 1770 public dining places had already existed in France which, compared to the usual public house or inn or to the few hostelries with a communal dining room and a set menu—the *table d'hôte*—represented an advance in the field of catering. After 1789, however, there was a dramatic rise in their number and quality within Paris. In the wake of the social upheaval many aristocratic, clerical or even big bourgeois households had broken up following the flight or ruin of the lords and ladies, so that their cooks, who were often masters of their trade, had lost their livelihood. They were forced to seek alternative employment, which at that time was no easy matter. There was an abundance of unemployed domestics. A few of the more enterprising among them then tried to earn a living by setting up on their own account. They opened up (at first small) taverns in which they offered nourishing, "restorative" soups. Later they acquired a licence to extend their menu. These public eating establishments were soon being dubbed restaurants, a word derived from the Italian *ristorante*.

People went there not just to eat and drink but also to talk politics. In competition with the traditional coffee houses they became meeting places for people of varying political persuasions. Thus the Jacobins assembled "chez Barrère", which caused one French emigrant to whisper the slightly exaggerated comment to Count Trauttmansdorf in Vienna that it was impossible to understand the Revolution unless one had dined at Barrère's.

There were other reasons why these restaurants came in very handy for post-revolutionary France. For one thing it was possible to order a three-course meal to be delivered to one's own house, and even a supper could be supplied in this way. On the top of this there were many people who no longer indulged in social entertaining commensurate with their position or who for the time being had to cut down on their spending and so preferred to eat out. In this new society men, including officers who were often bachelors, likewise made use of the convenient opportunity to enjoy a decent meal in accordance with their ability to pay. And of course there were also visitors from the provinces or abroad who needed to satiate their hunger or slake their thirst during their stay in the capital. "I confess," wrote Reichardt, "that for those who can afford it this mode of living seems to be the most pleasant as far as Paris is concerned. One receives what one pays for, is completely independent and can dine just as one pleases. Were one a gourmand one would be equally well and delightfully catered for as at a grand banquet where the sheer boredom often takes one's appetite away." He added quite correctly that the expense incurred was not much greater than that attendant upon a private invitation.

In Paris there were hundreds of restaurants for a wide palette of social groups, including those of modest means who now nevertheless were intent on eating better and more plentifully: "hairdressers, servants and farmhands". Naturally the mass of the poor people could not afford to eat

there. Eight to ten main courses of meat or fish prepared simply but well were advertised on a handwritten menu with the prices next to them. The cost of a meal—inclusive of wine—was two to three livres, the equivalent of half a day's pay. Other restaurants sprang up which offered a particular speciality, from the beer cellar frequented by military men to places which provided seafish, shrimps and mussels. Others specialized in oysters, which *bons vivants* had devoured with particular voracity under the *ancien régime*. Under the Consulate Grimod was even able to say with impunity he knew from experience that the relish of eating oysters only began to pall after the fifth or sixth dozen.

Naturally the leading Parisian restaurateurs provided a far more copious selection of food than did small innkeepers. Among the most famous were Beauvilliers, who took up the métier as early as 1782, the Véry brothers and the Frères Provençaux, who introduced a Mediterranean flavour. Other renowned establishments were those of Méot, Robert, Rose, Legacque, Henneveu and Baleine.

Stopping by a country inn ("The good evening"). Coloured etching. Nuremberg, *c.* 1815.

Bottom:
A bourgeois dining room. Coloured etching by Louis Philibert Debucourt after a painting by Martin Drolling, 1821.

Page 218:
Kitchen scene. Painting by Martin Drolling. Privately owned.

Those who want to eat well go to the Second Consul, those who want to eat a lot to the Third Consul and those who want to eat quickly to the First Consul.
Bonaparte

At present two poetical booklets and one of prose are all the rage in Paris among those who enjoy reading and those who enjoy living and which are reprinted after only a few weeks. . . . In truth these currently provide the most interesting reading matter for men of the world in Paris, and even their wives are more disposed to follow the piquant accounts of the so-called base pleasures than is the case in our country.
Reichardt, *Vertraute Briefe aus Paris 1802 bis 1803.*

[1] (p. 217) REICHARDT, J. F.: *Vertraute Briefe aus Paris geschrieben in den Jahren 1802 und 1803.* 2nd edition. Hamburg, 1805.

These caterers of renown not only established a lasting reputation for the French cuisine, they also cultivated the art of serving. Many an impressed guest took Véry's menu and wine and spirits list, which were all marked with the prices, home with them as souvenirs and in this way preserved them for posterity. Reichardt, who remarked that they resembled more a complete kitchen lexicon, was pleasantly surprised to find, when he totted them all up, that out of a total of one hundred and fifty meals which appeared on the menu only seventeen were either not available or were already sold out.

What the regular customer could expect to find in a good Parisian restaurant around 1800—and even more so thereafter—was noted down by Brillat-Savarin, the leading authority in this field: "At least twelve soups, twenty-four hors d'oeuvres, fifteen to twenty meals of beef, thirty of poultry and game, twenty-four of fish, fifteen roasts, twelve patés, fifty entremets, fifty desserts. In addition the would-be gourmet can wash this down with at least thirty kinds of wine of his choice, from Burgundy to Tokay and Cape wine, plus twenty to thirty varieties of fine liqueurs, not to mention coffee and the mixed drinks such as punch, mulled wine, Cardinal and suchlike beverages." The ingredients came from many different countries, and this supported Brillat-Savarin's thesis that "a meal such as one can partake of in Paris is a cosmopolitan entity in which every part of the world is represented by its own products".[1] Even the shortages occasioned subsequently by the "continental system" hardly made themselves felt.

The epicurean Anthelme Brillat-Savarin (1755 to 1826) has found a niche in world literature as an author of books on cuisine. A lawyer who was a member of the Constituent Assembly, he collected the material for his *Physiologie du Goût* over the course of several decades. All the while, day in day out, he would wander through his beloved Paris, inspect and frequent inns and restaurants, himself even experiment at the sideboard, stove and oven, thereby enriching the cookbook by many a page. His pride and joy was a yeast cake in the form of a ring soaked in rum with choice fruits which was served hot.

His opus was still far from being completed and put to paper when the Empire crumbled. He attributed to the Parisian "gourmandise" the fact that France was nevertheless saved from national bankruptcy, since the occupying forces could not resist their temptations and through their gorging contributed more money to the state coffers than the enormous sums which were pumped out of France by the victors as reparations. Thus he wrote in humorous vein: "When the Britons, Germans, Teutons, the Cimbrians and the Scythians invaded France they brought with them insatiable appetites and stomachs of unusual dimensions. They did not rest content for long with the simple fare which their reluctant hosts placed before them; they craved more refined treats. Soon the capital was one enormous dining room. These intruders ate at the inns and restaurants, in the bars and hostelries, indeed even in the street. They filled their bellies with meat, fish, venison, truffles, patés and especially with fruit. . . . The casual observer did not know what to think of this constant and endless scoffing for its own sake. But every true Frenchman laughed and rubbed his hands with glee. They have swallowed the bait, he said to himself, and at the end of the evening they will pay more talers back than the francs which they received this morning from the national exchequer."

The caterers of Paris seized their chance. In particular Beauvilliers and Véry were much sought after by the gentlemen of the Holy Alliance for the duration of the occupation. We know what sort of tasty morsels they were offered from an account by the poet August von Kotzebue, who detailed Véry's menu with the same reverence as his compatriot Reichardt a few years earlier.

European rulers concentrated their efforts on luring away French chefs. They had their eye especially on Marie Antoine Carême, who was employed by Talleyrand for twelve years but also arranged banquets for Cambacérès[2] and Prince de Condé.

With the help of this chef extraordinaire Talleyrand was able to reap political dividends at the Vienna Congress in 1814/15 by which time Napoleon had been forgotten. As far as the history of French gastronomy is concerned, it must be admitted that Napoleon did not achieve any glory. On that stage he at most played the part of an extra. Throughout his life the little Corsican stuck to solid bourgeois food, and in his later years his painful stomach disorder precluded any overindulgence.

A Parisian café. Lithograph by François Bellay after Louis-Léopold Boilly.

Véry's menu:
- *8 assorted potages*
- *14 hors d'œuvres*
- *11 assorted meals of bœuf*
- *10 of mouton*
- *16 assorted dishes of veau de Pontoise*
- *27 assorted entrées de volaille*
- *6 patisseries*
- *16 kinds of poisson*
- *13 assorted roasts*
- *29 entremets*
- *26 desserts of fresh or cooked fruit, cheese and the like*
- *55 sorts of fine wines from France and from abroad*
- *25 sorts of domestic and imported fine liqueurs*

Reichardt, *Vertraute Briefe aus Paris 1802 bis 1803.*

[1] BRILLAT-SAVARIN, A.: *Physiologie du goût.* Paris, 1825. New edition in German edited by M. Lemmer: *Physiologie des Geschmacks.* Leipzig, 1983.
[2] PAPILLARD, F.: *Cambacérès.* Paris, 1961.

People soon realized that the new ruler was neither a glutton like Louis XVI, a gourmand, nor a gourmet, a connoisseur of good food. Rather he deserves the epithet of a Spartan eater. Brillat-Savarin categorized him as one of those people who "like to do two things at the same time and eat purely out of necessity". He regarded lengthy dining as a waste of time which he thought he could ill afford. He never ate for longer than a quarter of an hour, had all the courses served at once and did not eat them in the conventional order. It is also said that he masticated little but literally gulped down his food. What is more, he sometimes disregarded the prescribed etiquette at the royal dining table and assumed the table manners of a serving soldier, dispensing with knife and fork altogether.

The emperor nevertheless had some most capable chefs in his employ and paid them handsomely. For example, his last cook Laguipère, who died during the retreat from Moscow in 1812, had such a good name that Carême dedicated his work *Le cuisinier parisien* to him in 1828. Yet it was clear that talented cooks had too few opportunities to show off their skills at the Tuileries and in Saint-Cloud, and so they did not remain in the emperor's service for long. Lecomte was probably best able to demonstrate his prowess, for his forte was confectionery, and for the Imperial dining table he sculpted historical scenes from marzipan, sponge cake and puff pastry with which he probably pleased his employer more than with any other kind of meal.

Brillat-Savarin severely criticized the conspicuous irregularity with which Napoleon took his meals. No doubt the exigencies of his frequent

A mother à la mode—A mother like all mothers should be. Watercolour engraving by Alexis Chataigner, *c.* 1800.

The 400 kitchens of the individual households with all their superfluous utensils are replaced by one fine and large single kitchen in which men, women and children who have the inclination and skill for cooking will prepare the food for all the members of the commune on a long range of ovens as in royal kitchens. The foodstuffs will be delivered at cost price and will vary in their composition and preparation in accordance with the tastes and means of each individual.

Victor Considérant: "Exposition du système de Fourier", 1845.

Lamartine drooled:
It combined the fire of the south, the serenity of the north and the gracefulness of France. Thus it was a living monument to the beauty of all countries.

[1] DELDERFIELD, R. F.: *Napoleon in Love.* London, 1959;
SAVANT, J.: *Napoleon und das zarte Geschlecht.* Stuttgart, 1960 .
[2] MÉNÉVAL, C. F. DE: *Napoleon und Marie Louise. Geschichtliche Erinnerungen.* Berlin, 1906.
[3] ROSTAND, E. DE: *L'Aiglon* (1900).

military campaigns played their part in this. However, his stewards hit on a ruse to combat this. Bearing in mind that when he felt like eating he required a piping hot meal to be served immediately, they arranged the field kitchen in such a way that he could be served at once at any time and any place with poultry, cutlets and coffee. In 1800, when Napoleon had just become Consul, the system did not yet function perfectly, and following the lengthy Battle of Marengo the ravenous general had to make do with a chicken done in sauce hastily improvised by his adjutant. Napoleon, exhausted after the rigours of the close-run affair, found the chance concoction so delicious that he ordered "chicken Marengo" regularly thereafter and thus guaranteed the dish—right down to the present time—an assured place in every good-quality cookery book.

Somewhat less successful was the proposal which emanated from the lower reaches of Imperial French society: Charles Fourier, the utopian socialist who dreamed of organizing communes of two thousand people living in a single complex of buildings, had to devise a way of feeding them all. He came up with the idea of the first communal canteen. His suggestion fell on deaf ears but nonetheless went on to outlive Napoleon's chicken.

Sex à la bourgeoise

Whenever 18th-century commentators bemoaned the decline in moral standards their main target was sexual dissipation, which was the epitome of moral laxity. The courts were foremost in setting a bad example, in particular the French court which under Louis XV and his (admittedly clever) Madame Pompadour cultivated the system of petticoat government as a sophisticated norm which was eagerly imitated even in the most minor German principality. Confirmed bachelors like Frederick II of Prussia were frowned upon. His chastity gave rise to malicious gossip, and so refined society heaved an audible sigh of relief when his nephew and successor Frederick William II bestowed his favour on a plurality of coquettes. In countries in which women governed, such as Russia, or at least ruled the roost, as in Spain, they turned the tables and, to the amusement of a tolerant public opinion, main-

tained their favourites in the form of men like Potemkin or Godoy.

Persons of rank, both secular and ecclesiastical, went to great lengths to keep pace with these developments. Envied philanderers and amorous ladies kept the scandal sheets well stocked with salacious stories. On the other hand the lower classes were expected to exercise Christian self-restraint, while their free and easy manners and its consequences were bewailed by their social superiors: relationships not blessed by the bonds of holy matrimony and children born "out of wedlock". Many of the latter were fathered by clerics who, despite having taken a vow of celibacy, succumbed to temptation. Out of both economic and social considerations feudal governments, in France as elsewhere, had been interested in maintaining and upholding the family as the basic unit in the ordered social hierarchy.

The Revolution then introduced a "Roman" emphasis on virtue—*la vertu du citoyen*—as a pugnacious middle-class code of honour. Though it did not demand ascetic renunciation it declared war on lascivious living as something unworthy of the new man and the free citizen. The Republican system had a simple and orderly conception of morality. The true patriot, the good sans-culotte, posed as a devoted husband and father. Petty-bourgeois astringency was not consistent with carnal vice. "Depravity is counter-revolutionary!" a totally shocked Robespierre thundered with Jacobin pathos at the happily hedonistic Danton and his fellow rakes. "Anaxagoras" Chaumette, the judge of public morals in the Paris Commune, reserved his most vituperative fulminations for prostitution, gambling and licentiousness, which he equated with aristocratic lackeys and enemies of France.

Subsequently the Directory reimbursed its subjects for all this decreed (or simulated) extramarital absteminousness many times over. The orgy reigned supreme, and the warning cry of Babeuf, the "people's tribune", went unheeded: "Just wait! These shameless hussies, these high-class brazen wenches who now deign to prostitute themselves in your bourgeois arms will put paid to you just as soon as they have managed to restore the old state of affairs!"

Then social mores underwent another change. After severing her liaison with the financial shark Ouvrard, the highly desirable Madame Tallien married her third husband, Count Caraman, who later became Prince de Chimay. Josephine Beauharnais, the tender and generous-hearted widow who as Madame Bonaparte allowed herself a few discreet adventures, went on to become empress and thus to outstrip the celebrated English beauty Lady Hamilton, who in Naples eased the onerous burden of naval hero Lord Nelson as his last love. There could be no denying the fact that this required the application of a new set of standards.

As for Napoleon, even at the peak of his power he displayed a degree of uncertainty in this regard. He was not cut out to be a Romeo and dreamed of conquests of quite a different kind. Getting on reasonably well with his ageing wife, he did allow himself a few amatory escapades[1] with younger women: with Pauline Fourès and Marguerite Joséphine Weimer, whose stage-name was Mademoiselle Georges; with the singers Giuseppina Grassini and Emilia Pellapra, the ladies-in-waiting Duchâtel and Dénuelle, and with the Polish countess Maria Walewska (1789–1817), of whom he was genuinely fond. However, these were all mere passing fancies, and he was careful to keep up appearances. Besides, they served less to satisfy his physical gratification than to confirm his potency, as his marriage had failed to provide the heir to the throne which he so badly needed following his sudden and unorthodox elevation to royal status. And his belated separation from Josephine in 1809 was decidedly dictated by dynastic rather than lecherous considerations, even though the public at large believed the oppo-

site. They contrasted the young general who had wed an older courtesan with the forty-year-old emperor who married a virgin barely half his age: Marie Louise of Austria.[2] This prompted him to refer to the executed Louis Capet as "my poor uncle". It was a most unfortunate turn of phrase, coming as it did from the lips of the heir to the French Revolution. Indeed, many people thought he overplayed the role of a model bourgeois husband who loved nothing more than to while away the time playing with the son he had so longed for, the "King of Rome", his legitimate heir who was destined never to wear a crown.[3]

The cosy family idyll did not endure. The obedient princess from the House of Habsburg and future Duchess of Parma did not shed any tears for her belligerent husband when he finally dis-

appeared from the scene. She consoled herself over her loss in the arms of Count Neipperg, who had been carefully groomed for this eventuality by the Viennese court. In retrospect the tortuous paths of Austrian political expediency seemed to justify the instinctive scepticism of the plebeian Babeuf.

However, the moral code of the Napoleonic Empire was dictated by precisely the same logic of political expediency.[1] The definition of marriage given by that intellectual giant (and life-long bachelor) Immanuel Kant as a contract for mutual sexual usage was in practice regarded as insufficient because it was incomplete. In ruling circles the institution of marriage was seen firstly as a question of politics and only secondarily as a question of economics. Of course not everyone allowed himself—or herself—to be so shamefully horsetraded in this manner. Even Napoleon could not assert his matrimonial intentions for all his marshals, nor even for every one of his brothers.

Self-respect sometimes proved stronger than the will of the brand-new monarch. Yet on the whole it was considerations of social expediency rather than simple attraction which determined the choice of a partner (hopefully for life) and the establishment of a home and a family. The Bonapartes, for example, were required to intermarry with European royalty, the new nobility to make matches with the old-established aristocracy, and mixed marriages were encouraged with the various nations of the Grand Empire so as to cement French hegemony. The emperor particularly recommended German maidens and drew attention to their special merits.

Dancers on the stage ("Operatical Reform, or la Danse à l'Evêque"). Etching by James Gillray, March 14, 1798.

Page 224:
Paris brothel. Engraving by an unknown artist.

Leipzig—le "petit Paris"—also had something of a reputation:

You will scarcely ever come across so many vile creatures and depraved girls of every kind as at the time of the trade fair in Leipzig. Most of them come from our dear Berlin, from Dresden, Frankfurt, Dessau, Halle, Jena: in short, this venomous mob gathers from all over the world. In the evenings the streets are teeming with these strumpets in their corsets and flimsy gowns.

August Maurer: *Leipzig im Taumel*, 1799.

[1] MOLÉ, L. M. DE: *Essais de morale et de politique.* Paris, 1806.

Operatical Reform;—or—la Dance a l'Eveque.—

Tis hard for such new fangled orthodox rules, That our OPERA-Troop, should be blam'd. *'Since like our first parents, they only, poor fools, Danc'd Naked, & were not asham'd!'*—Morning Herald.

Marriage was regulated by the bourgeois *Code Napoléon* which, however admirable an achievement by contemporary standards, was very much made by men for men. Naturally it did not exclude love-matches, which defied the new social system just as they had defied the old one. Yet the law with its regulations concerning the marriage contract, the male head of the family's sole right to exercise legal responsibility and to dispose of the family's wealth, and the incapacitation of women—who were relegated to the sphere of the kitchen and bedroom—set the future course in both town and country. When marrying—or divorcing—it was the Code that determined such matters as dowries, claims to inheritance, relationships and prospects of social advancement. In the long run this had a negative influence on population growth. Much to the chagrin of its rulers, who were helpless in the face of this phenomenon, France led the way in Europe in family planning. Whereas the deliberate decision to have fewer children had hitherto been largely confined to the rich upper classes, it was now accompanied by a trend towards falling birthrates among the wealthy middle classes and farmers who thereby sought to keep the second-generation fragmentation of property within bounds. The ability to finance a decent education with promising career prospects for their children also played a major part in their calculations. No dramatic drop in the birthrate occurred for as long as the decline continued to be roughly offset by the high birthrate among the lower classes. But it did herald an increasingly disturbing trend towards demographic stagnation in France in the further course of the century.

Marriage and the marriage contract as a form of channelling physical desire were one thing. But there were also extramarital—and often more passionate—affairs. In the face of emotional outpourings in which the first stirrings of "romantic" love were manifested, the state, like Cupid, could afford to turn a blind eye. Hölderlin's *Diotima*, Schlegel's *Lucinde*, Karamzin's *Poor Liza*, Chateaubriand's *Atala*, Madame de Staël's *Corinne*, Kleist's *Käthchen* and Goethe's *Gretchen* agitated the feelings and consciences of sentimental souls but did not disturb public order.

Prostitute and procuress ("She is praying for her welfare").

Girl in prison ("Because she was sensitive"). Folios 14 and 31 of the series "Los Caprichos". Etching and aquatint by Francisco de Goya, 1797–1799.

Certain other illnesses, the names of which one is reluctant to utter, are understandably nothing unusual in a country in which people live so intensely, though not profoundly (this passion is, like much else besides, somewhat superficial). It is said that few young people manage to avoid being presented with these unwelcome gifts. In Paris there is no lack of institutions devoted to the most feminine of arts which are most adept at infecting them. The streets, particularly around the Palais Royal, are filled with them; their priestesses, especially in the evenings, roam this focal point of pleasure and amusement in hordes on the look-out for patients for their practice.
John Pinkerton: "L'état de la médecine".

Suspicion was aroused by expressly erotic art, and its most famous victim was the Marquis de Sade (1740–1814). He had already miscalculated once during the Revolution when he had hoped for a favourable reception for his risqué novel *Justine* ("or the Mishaps of Virtue") in 1791. Instead he caused a storm of outrage among the puritanically minded. Following a brief spell as secretary of Robespierre's Piques Section, he barely escaped the revolutionary tribunal and then got into hot water with General Bonaparte when he made so bold as to dedicate the new edition of his book (with candid engravings) to the "spouse of a cocotte" in 1797. Sexual perversions were the last thing that the prudish upholder of law and order wanted. Though no doubt chronically overwrought, De Sade was no more insane than the cantankerous Republican general Malet, who was for a time his fellow inmate. Yet at the behest of his family he was detained in various institutions during three different régimes and ended his eventful life with a final ten-year stint in the lunatic asylum of Charenton. No one lifted a finger or had a good word to say for the man who gave his name to "sadism", the moral leper who threatened to infect others.

The other master of pornography at the turn of the century fared better. Not to speak of that much-travelled Venetian Giovanni Giacomo Casanova (1725–1798), who worked as a librarian for Count Waldstein in a Bohemian castle where he ruefully recalled the abundant sins of his youth and, plagued by gout, imbibed milk and piety. Restif de la Bretonne, erroneously reviled as a vulgar version of Rousseau's reached his peak as a writer with his *Monsieur Nicolas* in 1797 but thereafter continued to be read, usually in secret and with avid intensity, by both sexes. The friend and portrayer of the Parisian tarts, who captured for posterity something of both their compelling charm and the misery behind all the glitter, was unsurpassed in the graceful way in which he blended truth with fiction. However, his astoundingly early sharp social criticism soon faded; the utopian communist allusions in his first works were no longer "opportune" and so were abandoned. This put him above suspicion. When Napoleon ascended the throne the frivolous Restif was seventy and destitute. A year later he was given a job—with the police of all people! But the secret of how he came by it went with him

to the grave in 1806. Perhaps his admirer was one of the two thousand men and women who made up the variegated crowd of literary figures, countesses and ladies of easy virtue who came to pay him their last respects.

The number of mourners was perhaps boosted by the fact that an ancient quarrel had just flared up anew. From time immemorial most rulers and their critics had concurred on the need to tolerate prostitution as a regrettable but unavoidable evil. Regardless of the sixth commandment, it was an essential safety valve. It protected the citizens' property rights in respect of their wives and daughters against undesirable lady-killers by diverting the excess demand for love to the market where it could be had for hard cash. Opinions differed, however, as to the best method.

The prostitutes were in no way a marginal group. In Paris alone their numbers were put at between ten and thirty thousand, depending on the criteria applied, and in London there were at least as many. They included various categories: high-class tarts who maintained salons for their discriminating and free-spending clientèle which were sometimes combined with or camouflaged by a gambling den; women who were kept on a long-term basis by a fixed patron (who in return enjoyed, or at least laid claim to, exclusive rights); girls who were regularly employed by a madame or brothel-keeper; those for whom it was a part-time or spare-time occupation, married and single women who supplemented their meagre wages at night a bit of pin money; and, in addition to the occasional sinners, a host of freelance professionals who solicited for custom in the street and in taverns. They could be found all over the city and in every price range, but their main haunts were the Palais-Royal and the city's theatres. Their pimps ensured that the boundary between the demi-monde and the underworld was a very fluid one, so that it was not only in the field of public health that the authorities had a hard job on their hands.

The streetwalkers of the Imperial era, whose desirability and elegance were praised by many others besides Restif, came from virtually every walk of life: Bohemians, "fallen" middle-class girls who had been disowned, and adventuresses of the most diverse provenance. The bulk of them, dismissed servants, newcomers from the countryside, penniless widows, underpaid workers and unemployed women, were driven onto the street by extreme penury. Some managed to find husbands or to open up a little shop, but for most it was a slippery downward slope. Neither Marengo nor Austerlitz was of any use to them.

The authorities were quite happy for strangers or visitors from the provinces to seek their pleasure in the capital. Nor did they take it amiss if the city's own bachelors and frustrated husbands indulged. Only sodomy and homosexuality were criminalized as sins against Nature. But the main problem was how to stem the widespread propagation of venereal disease which accompanied all this anonymous promiscuity. It was very hard to prevent carriers of the disease from keeping quiet and transmitting it to others. Although regular medical checks were obligatory, few bothered to scrupulously comply, for if an infection were diagnosed their sole source of income would be cut off. The patient was then put into compulsory quarantine in one of the often rightly feared "women's hospices" but were only in very rare cases cured. It was to take a hundred years before a reliable means of combating syphilis was found.

In 1807 Napoleon opted for a legal measure which had already been practised in the Middle Ages (though the numbers involved had been far lower): the establishment of state brothels and the allocation of an identity card to each prostitute or *fille publique*.

The emperor was unable to come up with a similar solution for the army. Once beyond the national boundaries the soldiers were used to taking advantage of the local women. On the other hand the movement of troops across France led to a great number of local problems. Fortunately, with the exception of the guards the troop units never stayed long in the same place, so that official investigations usually came to naught, though there was the odd exemplary punishment here and there. Many officers brought back wives, with or without a marriage certificate, from the occupied countries despite the fact that this was strictly forbidden. Once in France the women were frequently abandoned to their own fate. The moral dissipation which spread throughout the army during the long years of war ended up having a negative effect back home as well, thus jeopardizing morality and righteousness in a country in which they had hitherto prevailed almost unchallenged.

Robbers and Cops

The arm of the law was nowhere long enough to penetrate into the darkest recesses of society. The state's security network was not yet foolproof, so that in every country bands of robbers stalked their prey. As fast as one bunch could be rounded up—and strung—another appeared. Conditions were such that people in dire straits, social flotsam, vagabonds, adventure-seekers and fugitives (whether innocent or guilty) were thrown together. In the dense forests they formed their own communities of predatory outlaws and for a time lived by their own rules in a kind of no man's land.

Pirates demonstrated the highest degree of organization and also enjoyed great prestige, from the old filibusters of the Caribbean to the motley buccaneers of the Far Eastern seas. In the Barbary states of the North African Maghreb and in the Persian Gulf the pirate captain was even considered a member of the ruling class and his profession was viewed as one of the most reputable. But packs of thieving landlubbers also formed something approaching a social institution in China and the Ottoman Empire as well as in many parts of Italy, such as the Papal States and areas further south where the local authorities in some cases persuaded the bandits to turn from stealing to soldiering.[1]

In border areas smuggling was a way of life. As a rule poor peasants living in the vicinity of the smugglers' dens were often left in peace as a guarantee of their tacit neutrality, if not their active goodwill. This was sensible, since only the well-to-do, whether the home-grown variety or passing visitors, were worth fleecing. Many a bold robber captain like Cartouche, Mandrin and Robert, whose daring was renowned, achieved a measure of fame as folk-heroes which long survived their own violent deaths, especially in areas where the tyranny of the lawful rulers was a much greater scourge for the locals. All the same, the noble outlaw and avenger of the poor, as exemplified by Karl Moor, Rinaldo Rinaldini and Dubrowski, belonged more frequently to the realm of fiction than to the more prosaic everyday world.

France was plagued by brigands before, during and after the Napoleonic era. Famine and the

Joseph Fouché. Engraving by Friedrich Wilhelm Bollinger.

The Morgue in Paris. Steel engraving after C. Reiss, c. 1840.

[1] CINGARI, G.: *Giacobini e sanfedisti in Calabria nel 1799.* Messina, Florence, 1957.

[2] RAUCHHAUPT, K.: *Aktenmässige Geschichte über das Leben und Treiben des berüchtigten Räuberhauptmanns Johannes Bückler genannt Schinderhannes und seiner Bande.* Authentic edition based on the original case files. 3rd edition. Kreuznach, 1899;
MINOR, A.: *Räuberbanden im Goldenen Grund: Schinderhannes und andere.* Camberg, 1970.

[3] BARGELLINI, P.: *Fra Diavolo.* Florence, 1932; *La riconquista del Regno di Napoli nel 1799. Lettere del cardinale Ruffo, del rè, della regina e del ministro Acton.* Ed. by B. Croce. Bari, 1943.

[4] JULLIAN, L.: *Projet sommaire d'une loi répressive du brigandage, portant création des commissions spéciales.* Paris, no date (1801).

[5] DAUDET, E.: *La Police et les Chouans sous le Consulat et l'Empire.* Paris, 1893.

collapse of state authority in the countryside in 1789 followed by the civil war which the counter-revolution unleashed in 1793 boosted the numbers of footpads and other unsavoury customers. Things became even worse under the Directory since there was now more loot up for grabs whilst at the same time the people's revolutionary vigilance was on the wane. In annexed or occupied territories banditry was often accompanied by nationalistic phrase-mongering, but this did not alter its basic nature. In Rheno-Hesse Johann Bückler, known as "Schinderhannes" (1777 to 1803)[2], struck terror into every heart before being executed at Mainz. Michele Pezza from Calabria (1771–1806) achieved what was tantamount to world renown under the name "Fra Diavolo"[3] after Cardinal Ruffo, generously turning a blind eye to his criminal sidelines, appointed him colonel of the counter-revolutionary Viva Maria militia in 1799. He successfully routed the godless French in Naples. However, they returned with Napoleon, and "Brother Lucifer"—to the delight of some and dismay of others—got his comeuppance.

The Republic also bequeathed to the Empire a special breed of highwaymen.[4] They were harder to handle than the run-of-the-mill thieves, who were fairly successfully dealt with by an enlarged and well equipped rural gendarmerie based on the old *maréchaussée*. For in Brittany and the Vendée defeated royalist soldiers or failed conspirators, both aristocrats and peasants, reverted to the guerilla tactics of sniping and ambush which they kept up for years. On the other hand many an outright highwayman eagerly donned the political mask and merged in with the anonymous mass of the royalist Chouans. The two groups ensured that using a stagecoach (or many an inn of ill repute—and not only in the more notorious areas) was less of a thrill than a fright. The assailants were familiar with the local terrain, were rarely betrayed by the stolid rural population and were exceedingly mobile. Thus although their ranks were thinned it never proved possible, to the despair of the security forces, to disperse or destroy them completely.[5] Furthermore their leaders, when the going got really rough, could always retreat across the Channel to England.

In the last years of the Empire the security of persons and property, following a temporary improvement, took another turn for the worse. A big new group of people went underground: young men who increasingly sought to evade the incessant stream of call-ups from 1809 onwards by fleeing to the countryside.

After seventeen years of war they no longer believed, as the Roman watchword would have it, that it was a sweet and noble thing to sacrifice themselves on the field of honour to the insatiable god of war.

Those who did not get sufficient assistance from their kith and kin had to help themselves as best they could, even if they had no natural aggressive streak or criminal bent, and especially if they had no inclination to help pave the way for a Bourbon restoration and the return of feudalism. Naturally the gendarmerie tried to recapture these reluctant soldier-boys, for often as much as a third of the troop contingent failed to report for duty, which on a national scale meant the loss of whole divisions. Yet the main thrust of police work was combating the activities of political opponents of the régime.

This was a wide-ranging task which involved surveillance, counter-intelligence and espionage and demanded a highly sophisticated organization. Contemporary observers all concurred that Joseph Fouché (1759 to 1820) had perfected such a system.

This former Oratorian priest, "terrorist" and Thermidorian conspirator was in charge of the police from 1799 to 1802, from 1804 to 1810 and again in 1815, becoming the Duke of Otranto. His secret police cost the taxpayer a pretty penny and was also a great nuisance as it aimed at an (albeit inconspicuous) omnipresence for its organs. Its intention was to learn everything it could about as many people as possible. Such painstaking surveillance of both Frenchmen and foreigners required an army of agents and informers, the widespread interception of mail, bribery, spying as well, of course, as systematic snooping into people's private lives and personal affairs. Recourse was also had to blackmail. The police collected and stored information for future use, so that no one, not even the leading lights of Imperial French society, could be sure that Fouché did not keep a secret file on them which might sooner or later be used to compromise them. Nor did they know what was in it. It is not hard to imagine the unease which this caused. After all, who among

all these *parvenus* and rehabilitated personages had nothing to hide, who in one way or another, did not have a skeleton lurking in the cupboard? Who, after all that had transpired, had not made provisions for the eventuality of another sharp turn in the course of events? Who relished the prospect that the police would or could poke their noses into affairs that did not concern them? For people of a nervous disposition Fouché was a nightmare.

What is more, the minister, though he put his police apparatus at the service of the emperor whom he loyally protected,[1] also had his own "historical" perspective which by no means always coincided with the usurper's express wishes and caprices. He exceeded the bounds of his responsibility and authority as a police official. Whereas Napoleon considered that the main threat emanated from the left, for Fouché it came from the right. His own ultimate intentions remain a mystery, especially as little credence can be given to his *Mémoires*. Did this political realist try to defend the substantive achievements of the bourgeois revolution as far as was practicable under the given circumstances, negotiating the hurdles presented by an ossifying régime through a policy of flexible compromise, and did he hold an invisible protective hand over a few of the old campaigners as a latent democratic reserve? Did the man whose fall from favour in 1810 was so widely acclaimed, having in his hubris given up the Empire for lost, take a running jump at the Bourbon bandwagon with the ulterior motive of rescuing whatever he could from the debris of 1789? Or did he play for such high stakes simply because he was an inveterate gambler and an incorrigible plotter? Or was he merely concerned to save his own precious skin? It would seem that he was far too astute to warrant such a simplistic interpretation.[2]

It was not only Fouché's cunning that Napoleon mistrusted. By 1809 there were concrete grounds for suspicion against him: contact with royalist emigrés in England, unauthorized peace feelers which banking supremo Ouvrard put out at his request, and one or two other things. In his defence Fouché could claim that a ministry such as his needed to have fingers in many pies and must also be in possession of highly explosive material for bargaining purposes. But was he to be believed? Had the secret police chief, in spite of—or

possibly because of—his undoubted professional ability, himself become a security risk for the Empire? His conduct in 1812, 1814 and 1815 spoke against him.

Fouché's rival and successor Savary (1774–1833) did not arouse such fears. From his time as an adjutant in Egypt up to Waterloo and beyond he remained Napoleon's trusty lieutenant. Straight as a dye and a paragon of reliability but with no in-

tellectual pretensions, a general and from 1808 Duke of Rovigo,[3] he always got involved but, with the best will in the world, did not always get it right.

Even in a powerfully expanding country there are never enough resources available to be able to tackle every problem at once. Thus the fight against common-or-garden urban crime had to take a backseat.[4] The introduction of a new Criminal Code did not do the trick. Moreover the *Code pénal* of 1809, which came into force two years later, showed just how far France had moved away under the Empire from the humanitarian educational ideals of the Revolution. It had a lot to say about the prosecution of wrongdoers, in particular those who transgressed against the sanctity of bourgeois property, but nothing about preventive or curative measures aimed at checking and averting criminal acts. Although an increasing number of lamps—by 1814 there were over four thousand—made it a little safer to walk home through the main streets of the capital at night, there were just as many instances of theft, fraud, burglary, assault, rape, manslaughter and murder in Paris as in the two other European cities of comparable size, London and Constantinople. Hence the executioner could not complain about lack of work. Funnily enough his was the only profession in revolutionary France that was still hereditary.

The Sanson family founded their "dynasty" in Paris in 1688 when the sun king awarded them a monopoly.[5] Charles Henri (1740–1793) made history in 1792 when, in order to decapitate a non-political common thief, he renounced the hatchet and carried out the first execution using the guillotine. He was also the man who, albeit reluctantly, beheaded Louis XVI in 1793. His son Henri (1767–1840) showed the same diligence in implementing the sentences of the revolutionary tribunal, and neither Napoleon nor Louis XVIII after him ever felt the urge to hold it against him: a case of continuity amidst discontinuity.

A decree of July 5, 1808 proposed to tackle the problem of beggary before which the three National Assemblies had demonstrated their impotence. In order to eliminate this handmaiden of crime and to keep the supposedly workshy rural and urban vagrants off the streets it ordered the construction of a workhouse in each département which would provide the poor with shelter, a living and (underpaid) work. In areas in which such a *dépôt de mendicité* existed begging was strictly prohibited. In all other areas this ban applied only to those who were healthy and fit for work and to habitual scroungers. Paragraphs 276 to 281 of the *Code pénal* laid down stiff penalties in the case of repeated offences, but this completely failed to have the desired deterrent effect.

Organized crime came through the *ancien régime* and the revolutionary years more or less intact. Such one-off coups as the theft of the crown jewels in 1792 or the mass forging of assignats during the paper money glut did not recur during the Empire. On the other hand the underworld and its widespread network of fences did profit from the expansion of the market across Europe, the increased mobility in the cosmopolitan Imperial capital, from the arms boom and the influx of tribute (of which not a little remained clinging to sticky fingers) and finally from the flowering of luxurious living among the old and new rich, a process which was not just welcomed but positively encouraged by the highest authorities in the land. Finally, the shortages caused by the "continental system" were an invitation to swindling and black marketeering.

Corruption got out of hand, for the big thieves in the administrative apparatus and the major contractors and speculators who were in league with them continued to get away with murder. Tax evasion, when perpetrated by those in high places, was viewed as a mere peccadillo. A forebearing Napoleon himself was content to simply dismiss his private secretary and former fellow pupil Bourrienne after the latter had managed in a short space of time to siphon off a cool million from public funds into his own pocket.

In pursuit of minor villains, however, the Imperial police—or more precisely its prefect, Baron Pasquier, who was answerable for the capital's moral conduct—came up with, or rather was talked into, a novel idea.[6]

When Jean François Eugène Vidocq made his proposal to the police authorities in 1809, the 36-year-old baker's son from Arras in Artois already had a highly turbulent life behind him. Even as a pugnacious youngster, according to his own testimony, he had been admonished by citizen Robespierre to use his excess energies for something better than brawling. He became a soldier, first in France, then with the Austrians and then back in France where, after a few more escapades, he arrived just in time to share in the glory of victory at Valmy and Jemappes. Thereafter, however, he went completely off the rails. He committed theft, fraud and forgery on a grand scale and so languished in the galleys at Nantes for many years. This was not a reformatory in which Beccaria's call for the humanization of the

The Saint-Lazare Prison in Paris. It was set up during the Revolution in a secularized monastery. During the day the inmates were allowed to walk up and down the corridors. Painting by Hubert Robert. This painter of famed "phantastic prospects" replete with classical ruins was entrusted with the task of planning museum affairs in 1792 but then taken into custody in 1793/94 following a denunciation from which he was not released until Thermidor. Musée Carnavalet, Paris.

Dulce et decorum est pro patria mori.

[1] HAUTERIVE, E. DE: *La Police secrète du Premier Empire. Bulletins quotidiens adressés par Fouché à l'Empereur*, 5 Vols. Paris, 1908–1964.
[2] FOUCHÉ, J.: *Mémoires*. Paris, 1824. Critical edition by L. Madelin. Paris, 1945; COLE, H.: *Fouché. The unprincipled Patriot*. London, New York, 1971; ZWEIG, S.: *Joseph Fouché. Bildnis eines politischen Menschen*. Berlin, 1982.
[3] (J. J. SAVARY:) *Memoiren des Herzogs von Rovigo, als Beiträge zur Geschichte des Kaisers Napoleon*. Leipzig, 1828.
[4] DESMARETS, C.: *Mémoires*. Paris, 1833.
[5] SANSON, H.: *Tagebücher der Henker von Paris 1685–1847*. Leipzig, Weimar, 1982.
[6] PASQUIER, E. D.: *Napoleons Glück und Ende. Erinnerungen eines Staatsmannes 1806–1815*. Stuttgart, 1907.

cruel and often sadistic penal system might have struck a chord. With its slave-driving character this institution set out rather to break the spirit of the delinquents, who were seen as inherently criminal, using physical and moral means.

Not even the massively built Vidocq could shoulder such a burden indefinitely. He escaped twice, and so began a long chase with his pursuers until both he and they tired of the cat-and-mouse game. When he offered to put himself at the service of the emperor along with his great wealth of experience, knowledge and useful contacts with the Paris underground, Pasquier decided to give him a chance. After all, Napoleon himself made use of the reformed smuggler Schulmeister from Baden to carry out special assignments with great success.

Vidocq was put in charge of a sizeable special unit composed of fellow ex-convicts. He soon became the talk of the town by means of a series of brilliant, if not always strictly legal, blows against his former professional colleagues, among whom he signed up more expert assistants. The success rate of crime prosecution in the capital showed a welcome improvement, and soon Vidocq made himself so indispensable to his erstwhile enemies that he was able with impunity to outlive the Empire by a dozen years in the same post.[1] Property owners of all colours, whether their allegiance was to the tricolour or to the fleur-de-lys, were all delighted to be able to set a thief to catch a thief.

Yet in addition to his less appealing qualities, Vidocq must also have had some winning ways and possessed an unusual charisma, perhaps because even in seemingly hopeless situations he never gave up. This enabled him to captivate not only the experts and the sensation seekers. He popped up again in the July revolution of 1830 and—at Lamartine's side—in the February revolution of 1848. His rich imagination thought up many more ingenious ideas. Some, such as the paper factory run by former prisoners as a form of rehabilitation, came to nothing. Others went on to make history in their own way, such as the establishment of the first detective agency. (And what would have become of the detective story without the invention of the private eye?) It was no accident that this master of adaptation, like no other shady double-dealer, was reincarnated, in a multiplicity of guises that matched his real life, in the books of illustrious friends which he inspired as a

Membre du Tribunal Civil

figure of world literature: at the hand of Eugène Sue, Balzac, Victor Hugo and Alexandre Dumas. The *Secrets of Paris*, Vautrin, Jean Valjean and *The Count of Monte Cristo* all owe something to him.

Burgeoning Bureaucracy

Bureaucracy was by no means an invention of the French Revolution. The Chinese could look back on an impressive two millennia and the Egyptians on as many as four thousand years of penpushing. In Europe a decline set in following the downfall of the Roman Empire. It was not until much later with the advent of the absolute monarchies, which sought to tame unruly local potentates and to open up further hunting grounds for the treasury, that a stable apparatus of officials was created which transformed the atomized feudal state with its personalized relations into a modern, centralized administration. In the 18th century the system had not yet been perfected, i.e. it did not as yet encroach upon all areas of life. But a start had been made from which later emerged

Messager d'État

what were often enduring dynasties of officialdom of a classical kind, such as those of Prussia, Austria and Russia.

In France the process did not always run smoothly. Both the general and more specific instructions from above often ran counter to currents at the base. Since distortions were already becoming apparent in the social fabric, every purely administrative correction with which the French people were involuntarily presented increased the tension between the contending social forces and brought about that frictional, antagonistic and confused jostling of feudal and bourgeois projects which was one of the main factors responsible for undermining the *ancien régime*. Trivial embellishments at the administrative level did not suffice to stop the rot.

In the final analysis the Revolution did not leave many of the prevailing state mechanisms intact. Instead it created new ones. In particular it devoured many of the purchasable offices, including the highly prized judicial posts. The widespread hatred of "despotism" as exemplified by the government at Versailles—more so by the ministers than the king—found expression in a decentralization of power. The citizens now governed themselves, no longer subjects but *citoyens*, each an integral part of the sovereign body which henceforth was known as "the Nation" or "the French people". The citizen did this via the election of officials at public meetings at which they were called to account. He was no longer answerable to them but they to him. Despite all the teething troubles among both electors and the elected this was already a remarkable achievement of youthful democracy. The paid administrators were joined by part-time assistants, which tended to somewhat blur old lines of demarcation.

The *fonctionnaire* or *officier public* was understandably a highly political animal. Often he owed his post to patriotic activities in the past, and thereafter he concerned himself officially with politics. Hence this reformed apparatus of civil servants was caught up in the debate on the nature of the Republic. They possessed a minute amount of power, which made the contending parties all the more eager to win them over to their side and to keep them there. Under the conditions of war and civil war, however, the revolutionary Jacobin government, which during the

Girondist "federalist revolt" in the summer of 1793 found its staunchest adversaries among the administrators of the départements, did an about-turn. The official—right up to ministerial level—was now once again appointed, instead of being elected by a majority vote, and was subjected to strict supervision and control by politically reliable extraparliamentary bodies such as the Jacobin Club and its affiliated societies.

The Directory in its turn slackened the reins once again. Its administrative principles, like everything else, were based on a policy of balance and compromise. It reinstated the six ministries, which had been dissolved by the revolutionary government and replaced by subcommittees of the Convention, and built up the Republic's superstructure. It showed indecision at the level of the départements but to its credit introduced a useful reform of municipal government which sought to meet the wishes of the local property-owning bourgeoisie without curbing the Parisian mandarins' freedom of decision-making. Otherwise the Brumairians, when Napoleon became First Consul, could choose from a wide range of options.

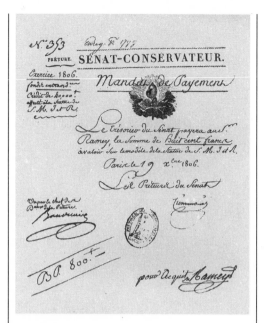

Notification of payment from the Senate to the sculptor Claude Ramey for his statue of Napoleon of 1806.

Official robes of French representatives of the people. Coloured engravings by Labrousse, 1796. The sartorial debate which had raged since the beginning of the Revolution produced designs for new official robes. A supplementary ordinance to the constitution of the Year III, which contained illustrations, laid down the dress regulations of civil servants.

Membre du Tribunal de Cassation.

Membre du Pouvoir Exécutif.

[1] *Mémoires de Vidocq.* Paris, 1828.

A visit by the First Consul to the northern départements. Bonaparte and his staff are welcomed by representatives of the local authorities. Engraving by an unknown artist, 1803.

Public consultation period during the Directory. Engraving by Alexis Chataigner.

The Revolution's clearly delineated administrative structure of départements, cantons and communes functioned well and acquired such vital force that it was adopted worldwide and has survived right down to the present day. Neither the Consulate nor the Empire found any cause to amend it much. Its mode of operation was redefined: instead of a genuine local or regional apparatus of self-administration it became a smoothly running machine controlled by a single hand. In particular the stress was laid on the uniformity and indivisibility of the state authority as personified by the omnipotent Napoleon Bonaparte, who held all the reins of power in his hands.[1]

The administration was rigidly structured from top to bottom. In charge of each département was a prefect to whom the sub-prefects in charge of the cantons were answerable and, below them, the maires of the communes. They were all appointed on the basis of recommended lists, which later were submitted by the locally registered Notables, by the First Consul and after 1804 by His Imperial Highness. They were the local embodiment of state power, not practitioners of local parish-pump politics. The departmental, communal and cantonal councils, whose remit was strictly confined to budgetary matters, were likewise appointed by the government. At all levels public servants were expected to regard themselves as the government's authorized representatives.

The system arose at an early date: on February 17, 1800 with the creation of a new caste, the prefects, two thirds of whom Napoleon selected personally on his brother Lucien's advice. Lucien, without batting an eyelid, described the role assigned to them as that of blind tools of the government. They were the delegated representatives of the First Consul—and from 1804 of the emperor—in the whole of France and beyond. In his speech at the time of their inauguration Napoleon was even more explicit, telling them that he did not want "men of the Revolution".

Indeed, no one who saw them in action would ever have mistaken them for such. In fact these worthy governors tended more to overemphasize their loyal subservience. They endeavoured to make the "prefects' ball", held in honour of the emperor's birthday (which inconveniently fell on

The prefects are the organs of the law and the instruments of its implementation. They have neither the right to express their own wishes nor their own opinions.
Lucien Bonaparte, 1800.

[1] *Le Cabinet des Tuileries sous le Consulat et sous l'Empire. Mémoire pour servir à la vie de Napoléon, par M. de comte de . . .* Paris, 1827.
[2] SAVANT, J.: *Les Préfets de Napoléon.* Paris, 1958.
[3] REVEREND, A. DE: *Armorial du Premier Empire.* Edited by J. Tulard. Paris, 1974.

August 15, i.e. in the "close season"), the primary social event in their département. An ornate uniform, though as a rule of civilian origin, underlined the military nature of their function and of the central authority which they represented.[2]

It would be no exaggeration to say that prefects, who were largely recruited from the big bourgeoisie and the aristocracy, formed a distinct caste. They were among the first to be elevated to the Imperial nobility in 1808. The much sought-after post of prefect tended to become something of an hereditary position.[3]

This was hardly what Napoleon had intended. Still, he could not prevent it and, besides, he himself set the example in this respect. Thus De Jessaint, a fellow pupil of his in Brienne, remained prefect of the Département Seine-et-Marne for a full thirty-four years. It has been calculated that he survived thirty-seven ministers of the interior under the Consulate, the Empire, the first restoration, the "Hundred Days", Louis XVIII, Charles X and Louis Philippe. His son and grandson also became prefect.

Paris was an exception to the rule, and special provisions were made for it. In view of what had happened to the upholders of law and order during the Revolution after the sudden leftward turn of its self-confident commune, the capital was allowed neither a city council nor a municipal leader. Instead there was a mayor for each of the twelve arrondissements into which the restive forty-eight sections had been reorganized back in 1795. For practical purposes the capital as a whole was governed by the prefect of the Département Seine which in addition to Paris itself included two other arrondissements within the city's precincts. He took up residence in the historic city hall on the Place de Grève so as to visibly reinforce his position. Since, however, his responsibilities far exceeded those of a normal prefect, an additional post was created to relieve him of part of his burden: the chief of police, who possessed complete authority in matters of law and order. He thus loomed large in the lives of the people of Paris. Some malicious commentators saw this as the ultimate reinstatement of the old division of powers between the notorious head merchant and the king's lieutenant, and that consequently the Bourbons should be begged for forgiveness!

This whole structure was firmly underpinned by an information system which would bear comparison with the flood of bumf generated by the revolutionary government. An incessant stream of directives, instructions and enquiries flowed down via official channels from the government to the lowest administrative echelons. In the reverse direction short and medium-term situation reports were required. In the case of the prefects these were forthcoming: in all a million and a half of them are said to have been written during the Napoleonic era—and all done without the aid of a typewriter using a simple quill! Researchers, for whom these comprehensive reports are indispensable social documents, have cause to be truly grateful to their authors.

When it came to the practical realities of running the Empire it was a different story. Information flowed more or less efficiently from the minister via the prefect to the sub-prefect, and vice versa, but often it did not get any further. And how many of the stolid mayors in rural France were, with all due respect to the emperor, at all qualified to draft the desired analyses or even capable of writing them down, unless some literate village scribe was at hand? And there was no end to what their superiors wanted to know from them in rapid succession: information about the state of the economy and the harvest, data on demographic trends, indications as to the mood of the population etc. The intermediate-level officials, however, learned to live with the fact of missing links in the chain of information. They covered over these gaps as best they could before passing on the reports and usually kept the shortcomings of their subordinate colleagues to themselves, especially as nobody was able or willing to wade through this whole mountain of paperwork anyway. This was the sad but not unmerited outcome of such an unquenchable thirst for information. Furthermore, these reports were often tailored to suit the emperor's preconceived opinions, as far as these could be ascertained, which in turn merely served to reinforce Napoleon's prejudices. As a result, much of what was happening in the country never came to his notice, so that he was much less well informed than he imagined. Even his frequent tours of inspection did not alter the fact that he knew precious little about the vast number of Frenchmen who blithely ignored him and his glorious deeds.

Since the quality of the government was to a large extent gauged by its civil service, it had to ensure that the officials discharged their duties correctly

and competently, which on the whole it did. It allowed few misdemeanours to go unpunished, for expressions of public discontent cast a poor light on the government itself. To many people keeping one's own house in order was proof of inner strength. Thus whenever comparisons were drawn with other countries, the administrative system of Imperial France, in the opinion of unbiased observers, often showed up exceedingly well, even in the eyes of politically hostile countries. Even its adversaries, such as the Prussian reformers, drew many a useful lesson from France's example.

Nevertheless there were a certain amount of careerists, dullards, thieves and cheats among their number. The temptation was particularly strong in occupied or annexed territories where for a time French administrators, in accordance with the rights of conquest, were able virtually untrammelled to tyranically impose their will on a powerless and hence frightened local population: "Vae victis!" ("Woe betide the conquered!"), as their ancestor Brennus is supposed to have

jeeringly remarked to the defeated Romans. Such conduct was sometimes referred to as "colonial practices". The possibly once-in-a-lifetime chance to make a quick and substantial killing, which was scarcely feasible in the native environment, in places eroded the probity of officialdom—and the higher the post, the greater was the likelihood.

Material security gave more reliable backing to the morale of the public servants than any patriotic sermonizing. The enormous differentials between the income of the highest office holders and that of the lowly clerks remained. However, following a law of 1809 even the latter were assured of receiving their salary punctually and in solid metal currency—and by means of a pension fund after their retirement as well. And it should be borne in mind that the "franc Germinal", coined in 1803 with a silver content of five grammes, maintained its parity right up until the outbreak of the First World War in 1914! The Order of the Legion of Honour (*Légion d'honneur*) proved even more durable. With its

Coat of arms of the Emperor and of a few other top dignitaries. Engraving from: *Neue Wappenkunde des französischen Kaiserreiches*. Rudolstadt, 1812.

Cover of the first edition of the *Code Napoléon* of 1804. Bibliothèque Nationale, Paris.

But the main point was that the people were assured of achieving their aims under him. This is why they flocked to him just as they would to anyone who could instil a similar sense of certainty into them. They are like actors who fall under the spell of a new director whom they believe will give them good roles to play.
Eckermann: *Gespräche mit Goethe*.

Just as this ceremony which was celebrated at the Invalides could be regarded more or less as the first in which the regent of France appeared in his new Imperial dignity, so it made a no less impressive impact through the most grandiose display of external military pomp.
John Pinkerton: "La légion d'honneur".

My real claim to fame lies not in the forty battles I won, for the defeat at Waterloo will erase the memory of them all. The thing which cannot be destroyed and which will live forever is my Code civil.
Napoleon on St. Helena.

institution on May 19, 1802 Bonaparte found an effective incentive to spur on the ambition and zeal of his officials as well as his army officers and scholars. Initially it was a simple certificate of merit for "special services to the motherland", and even in this form the First Consul only managed to get it accepted in October as the Republican "Pour le mérite" award after overcoming unexpectedly stiff resistance from uncompromising opponents of all honours systems in the Chambers and even within his State Council. The Empire, however, demanded more pageantry. In 1804 Napoleon deliberately chose the Hôtel des Invalides (not its chapel) as the venue for the first

solemn award ceremony at which he bestowed the decorations from out of a golden basin at his feet.

Thereafter the Order, whose grand master was (and still is) the prevailing head of state, was awarded in five different categories: chevaliers, officers, commanders, grand officers and grand crosses. It was worn on a red ribbon: in the form of a silver cross for the chevaliers and a gold cross for the other classes. In form and legend they were all similar. They all bore the inscription "Honneur à la Patrie" plus a picture of the Emperor Napoleon with accompanying monogram enclosed in a central oval. The chevaliers wore—and still wear today—a thin red ribbon in the button-hole of their suit, and members of the higher classes a rosette.[1]

The Legion was lavishly endowed. It was allocated the Hôtel de Salm in Paris as its headquarters where it has remained to the present day. In 1807 it received the most prestigious girls' boarding school in France which the emperor built at Château d'Ecouen. At his behest Madame Campan was put in charge of it, an unquestionably outstanding teacher who up to 1792 had been governess to the children of Louis XVI. This was a pointer for holders of decorations and especially for those who aspired to join their ranks.

Whatever might transpire in the political stratosphere far above the heads of ordinary mortals, neither the state machine nor those who operated it ever let themselves be stampeded into making fateful drastic changes. Regardless of what régime was in power—and quite a few changes were rung over the years—the Napoleonic administrative structure, its achievements and personnel were bequeathed with only minor modifications from one government to the next. Testifying to the continuity of an essentially bourgeois state institution, including in its numerical strength, the process recurred with a fair degree of regularity—in 1830, 1848, 1852 and 1870. It demonstrated that the "non-political" public officials, starting with the Bonapartist career civil servants, had acquired the timeserver's ability to quickly adapt themselves to changing circumstances.[2] Indeed, can one really find fault with this mentality in a country in which change at the top seemed to be the only constant factor?

Usually the civic official was concerned not just with administering things but also people as well.

Sooner or later almost everyone strayed across his path. It was his job to represent "higher" state interests vis-à-vis the ordinary citizen, who no longer had a charter of human rights to which he could appeal. As a result the state and state power tended to become conflated in popular consciousness. Only the executive arm was visible as it swung unchecked above the disenfranchised majority, wielding not just executive but also judicial power. Within certain limits, which it set itself, the administration might pay some heed to public welfare since it was easier to govern a prosperous nation, but it had no need to. It was equally capable of governing by other means.

On the other hand the administered masses did have a means of legal redress in the form of the legal code. They seldom had cause to complain about the lack of formal equality before the bourgeois law in all its solemnity. Nothing remained of the confusion of corporate exemptions and special privileges, of canonical and common law, of local and regional variants. Five Imperial civil codes guaranteed that everywhere justice was dispensed and administered equally for everyone. There were codes of civil law, civil procedure, commercial law, criminal law and criminal procedure. For all the justified criticisms which in particular passages in the later, post-Restoration civil codes incurred, it was for that time a unique and immense achievement. The *Code civil* of March 21, 1804, which from 1807 carried Napoleon's name, remained unsurpassed. It went on to play a role—either directly or indirectly—in bourgeois legislation throughout the whole course of the century, from South America to Japan.

Naturally the *Code civil* was not the brilliant brainchild of Napoleon, as the name might imply, but rather the quintessential juridical distillation of the Enlightenment and the bourgeois revolution at which jurists had slaved away for a decade. Way back in 1793 a commission under Cambacérès had placed before the Convention a draft code consisting of 719 paragraphs. It was rejected as being too technical and detailed for the masses to understand.

In 1794 a second version comprising only 297 paragraphs fell by the wayside, and a third containing five hundred paragraphs met a similar fate two years later. A new commission foundered with Jacqueminot's draft in 1799. In 1800, how-

Palais-Bourbon. To the palace, which dates from 1722, a façade was added between 1804 and 1807 based on a design by Poyet. Since 1795 the Palais-Bourbon has been the seat of the French Legislative.

Palais de la Légion d'Honneur. In 1804 the building, which was constructed in 1786, became the home of the Grande Chancellerie of the newly inaugurated Legion of Honour. Engravings by François-Louis Couché, *c.* 1818. From: Binet (Editor), *Soixante vues des plus beaux palais, monuments et églises de Paris.* Paris, no date (*c.* 1818).

The spirit of moderation is the true spirit of the legislator.
Political and social welfare is always located between two extremes.
J. E. M. Portalis

[1] TÉSTU: *Etat de la Légion d'honneur.* Paris, 1814.
[2] BEUGNOT, J. C. COMTE: *Mémoire.* Paris, 1866.
[3] CAMBACÉRÈS, J. J. RÉGIS DE: *Lettres inédites à Napoléon, 1802–1814.* Paris, 1973.
[4] ROISSY, J. G. LOCRÉ DE: *Esprit du Code Napoléon.* Paris, 1805.

ever, after the Consulate had been proclaimed, its successor managed after three years of intense discussions, in which Bonaparte did indeed play an active part, to at last clear the final hurdles with a bloated code of 2,281 articles. Its principal architects were Portalis (1745–1807) and Cambacérès, Tronchet, Maleville and Bigot de Préameneu.[3]

The code consisted of four parts: a general section on law and its application, the law of persons, the law of property and the acquisition of rights, including the law of inheritance and contract law. Yet it formed an organic whole united by a common overall perspective. Its declared aim was to legislate for a new and better society, to provide the first ever purely national, ahistorical and inherently logical statute book which obeyed the dictates of reason only. Anything which contradicted reason could not be regarded as legally valid. Basing itself on sublime common sense, it laid claim to universality, general validity and comprehensiveness.[4]

The *Code civil* presupposed that human understanding possesses the innate capacity to order all legal relations. Logical conclusions will supply the answer to all questions. There is thus no need to resort to other sources. No loophole in the law is incapable of being filled. Thus the law, which is self-sufficient, almost resembles absolute right.

The formal qualities of the code, which has been called one of the most elegant achievements of jurisprudence, were of a very high order. It was clear and lucid and understandable to the layman. It avoided extrajuridical elements and kept the exceptions to the rules to a minimum. Many of its epigrammatic formulations went on to acquire a proverbial status in the French-speaking world.

The *Code civil* synthesized traditional customary law, the *coutumes*, with Roman law, Rousseau (whom Bonaparte greatly admired) and some of the bourgeois revolution's main tenets. Combining cautious liberalism with moderate conservatism, it saw its principal task as maintaining the social status quo of free male property owners and heads of families. Consequently its chief beneficiary was the bourgeoisie, who henceforth would never under any circumstances allow their legal bible, this indispensable instrument of legitimation and legalization of their class rule, to be wrested from them.

The Grand Army

Countless bivouack fires had twinkled during the night. It was still dark as the bugle sounded the reveille and the *corps d'armée*, to the rhythm of beating drums, started to take up their allotted positions along the straggling line of battle. Divisions, brigades and the emperor's own regiments behind their eagle standards formed deepset ranks. Grenadiers, fusiliers and carabiniers dressed in blue and white uniforms arranged themselves into battalions, halted and leaned on their rifles. Companies of *voltigeurs* broke up into loose formations of *tirailleurs*.

Behind them the serried columns of the Imperial Guard, with a strength of six to eight companies, prepared to attack. Squadrons of cuirassiers, dragoons, chasseurs and hussars lined up in neat rows and the horses pranced under the weight of their colourfully bedecked riders. To yelled commands the artillerymen aligned their guns and cannon, their muzzles glinting yellowish brown. Marshals and generals in gold-braided uniforms appeared atop their chargers, followed by their sprightly adjutants. In their midst, seated a little apart on his patient mount, was the stocky figure of Napoleon who, plainly dressed, surveyed his troops with a keen eye. The *grognards* with their drooping walrus moustaches intoned a hearty *Vive l'Empereur!* The call reverberated from man to man, from weapon to weapon until it was lost in the distance. Orders were barked, and soon the artillery thundered forth. Explosions rent earth and sky and plumes of greyish white smoke drifted upwards into the cool morning air. The battle had begun, and was fought amid a deafening din.

These were the terms in which court painter Horace Vernet and others depicted the scene. Napoleon, who amongst other things was a masterful director, did his bit with theatrical gestures to weave a web of myth around his battles which determined destiny and to foster the notion that his Imperial reign was synonymous with France's greatness, honour and glory. He persuaded soldiers and officers alike to blindly trust in their leader and to go through fire and water for him.

The reality was less glamorous and more gory. Napoleon's battles claimed a huge toll of casualties among the combatants of both sides. More than once the outcome was balanced on a knife-edge, and often victory was due less to the great man's strategic genius than to the unpardonable errors of the other side. When these were minimal or Napoleon himself acted rashly he was sometimes forced to suffer defeat. Though rare, this did occur, and then it presented Napoleon with a major headache, for the backbone of the Empire, his ultimate argument both at home and abroad, was the army.

It played a crucial role in the coup of 18 Brumaire but with a multitude of different expectations and aspirations. A majority of the army supported the establishment of a strong government led by one of their own whom they hoped would provide the nation with a surer political lead and themselves with more ample supplies of all that they needed. It saw its key task as safeguarding the hard-won Republic against anarchy and tyranny. Initially only a handful of high-ranking officers had backed the idea of a personal dictatorship in the hope that it would bring them power, money and glory, while others harboured doubts or reservations or else begrudged Napoleon his meteoric rise. If the First Consul in 1800 aimed to disarm this military opposition by dispelling all their misgivings—or even better, through action—he would have to satisfy as many expectations as he could as quickly as possible. Confidence-building measures were required in order to win over the entire army and to convince more than just his old Italian army of his military prowess. Henceforth he was addicted to achieving success.

The Battle of Marengo cleared the air. It was a close-run thing, but the result allowed him to present himself to the army as the unchallenged victor and to make full use of his sole command of the French armed forces. Only then did the Bonapartist military dictatorship begin to alter the apparatus of power and to bend it to its own will.

This process of systematic remoulding was set in train from 1801/02 onwards when there was a temporary lull in the fighting. Some troop contingents returned while others stayed put as occupying forces in Italy, Switzerland, the Netherlands and the annexed German territories. They were accommodated in old military camps. Generals and staff officers of questionable loyalty as well as key units which were regarded as politically unreliable—in particular from Moreau's Rhine

Standard-bearer of the French army. Lithograph by Nicolas-Toussaint Charlet. From the series *Costumes militaires*, c. 1820.

Grand military parade before the emperor in the courtyard of the Tuileries. Engraving by Le Grand after Nodet.

He is a man who is loved by no one but whom everyone prefers [to an alternative—the Author].

Count Ségur on Napoleon.

[1] FUNCKEN, L. and F.: *L'uniforme et les armes des soldats du Premier Empire.* Paris, 1973.
[2] COMMANDANT LEVY: *Routes et voyages de Jacques-Louis Thieur, sergent-major au 16e de ligne (1799–1814).* Dunkirk, no date.

army—were shipped off to St. Domingue in the Antilles in 1802 as an expeditionary corps to restore the colonial yoke of the French plantation holders there. Fever and disease killed off most of them.

The reforging of the army, in which the traditions of the revolutionary wars were still alive, into an institution dedicated to the person of Bonaparte gradually gave the armed forces a new sense of purpose. The presentation of ceremonial sabres, muskets and titles was designed to foster the fighting spirit of each officer, sergeant and private.

As a result of the reorganization the half-brigades were given back their old name of regiments. They kept the numbering system introduced after 1796 but were given new standards: the simple banner with the inscription *République française* was replaced by ornately decorated regimental colours on which the motto *Empereur des Français* was emblazoned as the bestower or donor. In addition he endowed each regiment, in the manner of the old Roman legion, with a troop eagle and standard. The red, white and blue of the tricolour was maintained but the division of the fields was different. Gold embroidered inscriptions, laurel leaves and wreaths and braiding provided a dazzling finish.

After becoming emperor Napoleon also restored the rank of marshal, which was bestowed on a total of twenty-six generals. Courtly titles which had been emptied of their military content, such as *connétable* and *colonel général*, were likewise revived, as were designations dating back to the *ancien régime* such as *carabinier*, *chevaux-léger*, *dragon*, *lancier* and other names of infantry and cavalry units.

New uniforms were designed. They were meant to replace the improvised outfits worn instead of the prescribed ones from 1792 onwards.[1] This motley garb, dictated by force of circumstance, was seen as symbolic of revolutionary simplicity and Republican integrity. But now each regiment was given in addition to its compulsory battle-dress a ceremonial uniform again—or at least a better made pair of clean trousers which the soldiers had to carry with them wherever they went. Each army section and unit was assigned its individual tunics and trousers with their own particular colours and cut. Their lapels, turn-ups, cuffs, shoulder-pieces, piping and other trimmings

aped monarchical pomp and circumstance. The *citoyen* under arms left the stage and was replaced by the Imperial grenadier.[2]

In the following years Napoleon ordered repeated changes in design by means of which he sought not only to make his troops more elegant but also to raise their morale. Many of the alterations were, however, not executed, either because there was a lack of money or materials or because of the renewed outbreak of war. Even the introduction of the new uniforms met with immense difficulties. Only the Imperial Guard, which had developed out of the First Consul's Guard, quickly received the new tunics. The rest of the army had to make do for the time being with the replacement of their hats, which smacked of Republican symbolism, by the shako. For a period many battalions even lacked shoes and overcoats until the spoils of war and the impositions exacted between 1805 and 1807 gave the war ministry in Paris the means to supplement the soldiers' clothing and to secure sufficient material and cloth for the mass production of the Imperial uniforms.

The reorganization of the army was accompanied by increasing misgivings concerning the infliction of punishment. Notions of equality and liberty still obtained. Military service was seen as an ever greater bane from year to year. Nevertheless almost all the soldiers and officers regarded themselves as free-born Frenchmen and doughty defenders of their country. Something of a comradely relationship existed between the officers and the troops, as was only proper among free men. During a campaign they all ate out of the same field kitchen and all slept together around the same camp fire. The feeling that they were citizen-soldiers and not hired mercenaries still eased the task of maintaining discipline. On the other hand physical duress and privations in the field soon led to moral degeneration. Marauding, pillage and rape were then the order of the day. Instances of insubordination towards superiors and even towards the emperor himself, which had previously occurred only in exceptional cases, became more frequent during the Spanish campaign. Astonishingly enough Napoleon managed right up to the end to fire his troops' courage by appealing to their sense of honour and patriotism, whereas there was a fall-off in the quality of their once exemplary marching ability which even the most earnest entreaties could not restore.

It is a myth that the Napoleonic soldier carried a marshal's baton in his kitbag along with his dress uniform. In theory the Republican system of promotion, based on nomination, election and length of service, was retained but in practice many things changed. The battalion or regimental commander sent his recommendations for appointments and promotions to the war minister who then made his decision, largely on the basis of the candidate's length and record of service in the field and the number of vacancies available. Promotions from the rank of colonel upwards were the prerogative of the emperor. In many units the heavy casualty rate increased the pros-

pects of advancing to the rank of battalion or squadron commander. But very few officers got as far as regimental commander by dint of their own efforts, i.e. without patronage. Napoleon preferred to occupy the topmost ranks with the sons of wealthy and noble families whom he took under his wing. They were sent to military colleges after which they could expect to rise relatively rapidly via the post of staff officer to the rank of adjutant. From among the adjutants proper (*aides de camp*) often emerged the *adjudant-majors* who were deployed as chiefs of staff or as adjutant generals. Though it was said that none of these ambitious officers could ever be appointed colonel without

first having distinguished themselves as troop commanders in the field, in effect it sufficed to display a dashing valour and contempt for death in front of the emperor.

Only a minority were the recipients of such favour. Even so, in general there were no restrictions of birth, fortune or education in the selection of officers under the Empire. Even age was not so important. Apart from the graduates of the military academies it was experienced sergeants and volunteers who were appointed to plug the gaps in the officer corps. Non-commissioned officers, however, had little chance of rising beyond the rank of lieutenant. Better prospects existed for

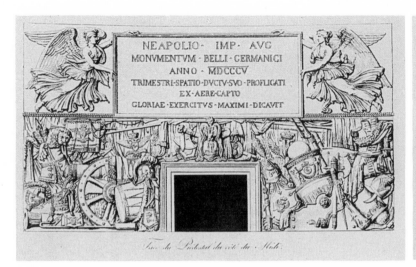

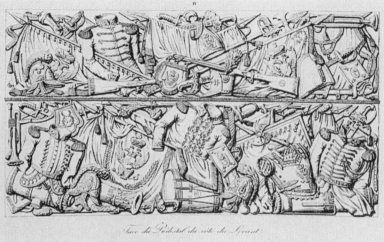

the young cadets who, after brief service as a *cadet-sergeant*, became lieutenants, advanced to captain or company commander whenever a suitable vacancy arose and later made it to battalion or squadron commander. But it was also these young men who as lieutenants provoked many a salacious scandal in public hostelries and places of entertainment, at the card table or through amorous adventures.

When reviewing the troops the emperor liked to award some instant promotions on the spot. This covered decorations, pensions and titles of nobility. Though such occurrences were infrequent, their number was swelled by rumour. Stendhal's Julien in *Le Rouge et le noir,* for example, dreamed of being promoted from lieutenant to colonel by Napoleon as the result of some glorious feat of arms. Such impromptu awards were in fact theatrical gestures designed to nurture the image of Bonaparte as a caring leader within the army. For in reality his adjutants or secretaries had carefully prepared and usually discussed the seemingly off-the-cuff decisions beforehand.

Every day innumerable officers who either had or claimed to have friends in high places fawned upon the war minister in Paris under a variety of pretexts in order to try and further either their own career or that of a close relative or friend. These fops frequented the cafés and theatres and kept prostitutes or honourable married women whose husbands were serving their country in some far-flung corner. Many officers' wives were paid a small proportion of their husband's salary directly by the military authorities. Yet unless they had a fortune of their own or were supported by their parents they often had to earn a living as best they could.

Many officers' wives joined their husbands if they were garrisoned in towns or fortresses. Non-commissioned officers and the rank and file also liked to have their womenfolk with them in the garrison. Hence when a battalion moved out it was often followed by a train of civilian vehicles. Their numbers dwindled only in the vicinity of the front line, and even there some families were still to be found. Napoleon issued decrees which aimed to prohibit wives and children from accompanying the men, but in vain. He liked to marry off his young military protegés to ladies-in-waiting or to the daughters of the old nobility but made it virtually impossible for them to enjoy a common "camp life" by means of frequent transfers and assignments.

The bulk of the army was recruited from the sons of small peasants and craftsmen. The cities provided a much smaller contingent. However, being literate and numerate these had a much greater likelihood of becoming corporals and sergeants. The decrees of 1798 and 1800 made all men aged between twenty and twenty-five eligible for conscription. Furthermore, they could only be demobilized in time of peace and not in war. Conscripts were called up just as soon as the Legislative Assembly, and later the Senate, had decided on the numbers required for a particular year. Each annual contingent provided about 190,000 men of whom some 100,000 were fit for active service. Married men and widowers with children

were immune from conscription but could still join the army or navy as volunteers. The law also exempted priests, doctors, notaries and—for a time—students. However, with the exception of the priests they were all obliged to serve in the National Guard up to the age of forty, and this applied equally to those who were unfit for service. The sons of wealthy parents often enlisted of their own accord with an eye to embarking upon a career as an officer. Others bribed the recruitment commission to obtain a declaration of nonfitness for duty. All those eligible for military service had to draw lots to determine which of them were actually recruited. But in case of need those whose number had not been called had to resubmit themselves up to the age of twenty-five, unless they married in the meantime.

Thus general conscription was an obligation which was limited to the poorer strata of the population. Since the Empire was more or less perpetually at war, even those who had served for a full six years were not released from duty. Moreover, in 1800 Bonaparte did the property-owning bourgeoisie a further favour with the introduction of the *remplacement*, i.e. the right to buy exemption from military service. Although the price rose from year to year, in practice it bought little more than a postponement since it was usual to re-conscript men who had purchased exemption as long as they remained single. The military authorities used the sums thus raised, which were enough to whet the appetite of any poor man, to entice unmarried men whose names had not been drawn out of the hat as well as married men, from

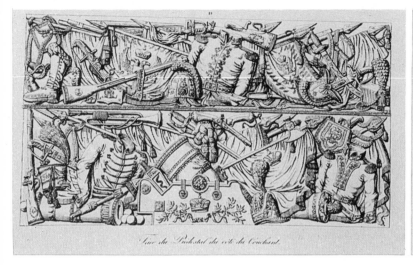
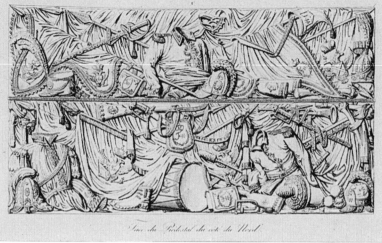

among whom the non-commissioned officers were then recruited.

Conscripts frequently escaped military service by taking to their heels. The number of these draft dodgers (*réfractaires*) grew year by year. To fill the gap Napoleon fell back on even younger men. By the end of his reign it was adolescent boys plus the sick, lame and lazy who were recruited to the army. Men who had been rejected for military service years earlier on the grounds of ill health or disability had to present themselves again, and many of them were now pronounced fit for duty even though this was not the case. Young men often married much older women or widows with children merely to avoid being conscripted. At the end of 1799 France disposed of an army of 470,000 men including the troops stationed in Egypt. By the end of 1801 the number had dropped due to the loss of many older or invalided soldiers, including many who had volunteered in 1792/93, to 415,000, a year later to 400,000 and in 1803 right down to 340,000. Of the seasoned soldiers who had joined up prior to 1801 and who had seen active service about 175,000 remained with the colours. The stricter enforcement of conscription, which netted 30,000 men in 1800 and 120,000 in both 1801 and 1802, enabled the numerical strength of the army to rise fairly rapidly to 493,000 in 1804 and up to 562,000 in 1805. On the other hand every campaign brought heavy losses through disease, injury, desertion and marauding. During military operations it was reckoned that stragglers and those who got left behind accounted for between twenty and twenty-five out of every one hundred troops, of whom only a fraction managed to rejoin their battalion in time. The number of marauders increased from 1807 when it no longer proved possible to provide the fighting troops with food and fodder. The growing size of the armies and the speed of their movements multiplied the difficulties. Attempts to supply themselves through requisitioning did not work whenever the French battalions moved through areas which were poor or which had already been bled dry. The first thing Bonaparte did was to set up baggage trains organized along military lines, which if required could meet the army's needs on enemy territory. Secondly he started preparing storage magazines and supply lines. But since little money was available for this purpose the magazines fell short of what was needed. The means of transportation at his disposal for maintaining the lines of communication remained minimal and had to be supplemented by requisitioned vehicles whose drivers were naturally loth to obey orders and escaped at the earliest opportunity.

The campaigns of 1799 and 1800 showed that the tactical superiority which had been built up in the previous years had been dangerously eroded. The Russian armies now demonstrated an unflagging fighting spirit while the Austrian regiments no longer adhered to the ossified linear formation. The Republican army division of 1792/93, which combined all three branches of service, had ceased to exist. Instead of a fighting formation of 10,000 men who were tactically closely coordinated there were now only divisions consisting of

Reliefs on the plinth of the Vendôme Column. Etchings from the work *Napoléon à la Grande Armée*. Paris (*c*. 1810).

Even Wellington believed that
an officer, indeed an ordinary soldier, could hope to be rewarded for his services with the power over a kingdom.

A bon mot of unknown origin was in circulation:
In the Napoleonic armies there are three categories of heroes: the high-ranking officers, who enjoy both wealth and glory; the other officers and the soldiers, who enjoy glory but not wealth; and the war commissars, who earn wealth but no glory.

"School for mutual instruction" in Metz. Children aged ten and eleven teach army veterans how to read. Lithograph by Jean-Henri Marlet, c. 1810.

The Guard in battle. Lithograph by V. Bassus, 1818.

a few thousand infantrymen with little artillery. For this reason the army commanders had begun to deploy several divisions jointly and to reinforce them with cavalry and artillery. This practice was now given official blessing. Bonaparte amalgamated between three and five infantry divisions, each with its own brigade of cavalry and battery of artillery, to form a *corps d'armée*. It was under the control of a *commandant en chef* who from 1804 onwards usually held the rank of marshal. As a new combat unit, the *corps d'armée* represented a force to be reckoned with. It also facilitated the system of a centralized troop command.

Marengo graphically brought home to Bonaparte the supreme importance of having a strong reserve. In forming his Guard he had two aims in mind. Firstly, serving in the Guard was to remain tied to certain basic principles and act as a spur to personal ambition. Officers and men alike had to prove they had taken part in campaigns and battles before they could be admitted. Secondly he saw the Guards' main role as fulfilling the important tactical task of leading a concentrated assault on the enemy line at the decisive moment. It formed a numerically strong élite unit. Often reinforced by the grenadier battalions of the corps, it remained under the personal command

of the emperor along with the newly formed reserves of artillery and cavalry units. Its officers and men received better pay, smarter uniforms and a higher status vis-à-vis the troops of the line. It grew from a few thousand men to tens of thousands, and when few seasoned troops were left outside the Guard it accepted raw recruits as long as they could read and write. The Imperial Guard, which was commanded by a marshal, comprised all three branches of service. Later it was divided up into the Old Guard, the Young Guard, and, for a time, the Medium Guard. The exaggerated expansion of this special force, which resulted from Napoleon's overreliance on the tactic of driving through the enemy line with massed forces, deprived the line regiments of their most capable soldiers and hence much of their fighting spirit.

However, the principle of élite formations was extended to the troops of the line, and this led to more unjustified differentiations. To the élite belonged the grenadier and voltigeur companies of the infantry battalions (in the light infantry the carabiniers and *voltigeur* companies) as opposed to the fusilier companies, even though it was the latter which bore the brunt of the fighting. The cavalry, too, had regiments which were privileged

Menu based on the rations for non-commissioned officers and the rank-and-file:

Breakfast: white bread, cheese, brandy
Lunch: soup, $^1/_2$ pound of meat, vegetables,
$^1/_2$ litre of wine
Tea: soup, vegetables, $^1/_2$ litre of wine
Officers receive in addition:
rum or coffee and a choice of egg dishes,
poultry or fish.

In every letter that General Marmont writes he brings up the question of provisions for the troops. I repeat that in the mobile and offensive type of warfare waged by the Emperor there are no magazines. It is the task of the generals in charge of the army corps to obtain the necessary supplies from the local territory through which they are passing.
Berthier on Napoleon's behalf to Marmont, October 11, 1805.

compared to other units. This preferential treatment shown to the Guard, the grenadiers and the *voltigeurs* encouraged many officers and soldiers to seek a transfer to such an élite unit in which they hoped for more rapid promotion, higher pay, more decorations, titles of nobility and pensions. Intrigue and nepotism contributed towards stimulating mutual antipathy between the Guard

and the line, between grenadiers and fusiliers. As a result they sometimes failed to actively support one another in the field and even refused their help under one pretext or another.

Following the campaigns of 1800 some generals of the Rhine army began to develop their troops' combat tactics by issuing special instructions. Bonaparte adopted this method and introduced it

wholesale in the camps of Boulogne into every battalion and division as he started amassing an assault force with which to invade Britain. The camps, which had been in existence for many years, and the surrounding training area made it easier to boost the troops' tactical strength. Two thirds of the assembled soldiers were raw recruits without any campaigning experience. By the same token they had not yet acquired their older comrades' aversion to square bashing. Drill exercises were the main element of the training and tested the men to the limits of their physical endurance.[1] However, this allowed them to improve their rate of fire and to speed up the transition from one formation to another. Since the drill book of 1791 had remained in force, it was no problem to reintroduce the firing line and square of the battalion, which had previously been employed with success by individual units, into the combat strategy of the entire infantry. Henceforth the tactic of the infantry consisted in the volleys of the battalion line coupled with the sniping of the *tirailleurs* and the columnal attack. Changing formation and the transition from marching to battle formation were practised ad nauseam. Marching was likewise part of the drill programme.

There were parallel drills for the artillery and the cavalry. After the troop units were reorganized, the divisions were given the many guns and cannon which were captured from the enemy. The artillery sections of the corps, the Guard and the artillery reserve were allocated predominantly French-made equipment. Although the number of cavalry regiments increased, the bulk of the new units could not be made immediately operational owing to a shortage of horses. In 1802 cavalry bands fell into abeyance for a while because of a lack of chargers. It was not until the victories at Ulm, Austerlitz and Jena had provided extensive booty that it became possible to temporarily make good the equestrian shortfall. By 1813, however, it had once again become a major problem.[2]

The troops assembled in the camps on the Channel coast, who accounted for about half of the army, placed an increasing strain on the state's finances. In late August 1805 Napoleon decided to form the well-trained units into an assault force which he designated the *Grande armée* and to deploy them along the upper reaches of the Danube against Vienna.[3] Thereby he shifted the huge cost of their upkeep henceforth onto the conquered or occupied territories. It was his declared intention to make the defeated nations themselves pay for this instrument of subjection. Numbering over 200,000 when war first broke out, the *Grande armée* represented the maximum force which could still be effectively commanded with the means then available. However, in contravention of the golden rule, which was ascribed to Napoleon, that one should never fragment one's forces but always aim for maximum concentration, he had a mere 70,000 men at Austerlitz in early December while the other two thirds of his army were deployed along several other routes or else were still bringing up the rear. It was only the grave blunders committed by the enemy and the excellent training of his own troops that enabled him to win the battle in grand style.

His luck held once more at Jena and Auerstedt in 1806 but he had a hard time of it at Eylau the following year. With the invasion of Spain in 1808 Napoleon's military leadership lost much of its effectiveness. He refused to draw the appropriate lessons, and since his heavy defeat at Aspern in Austria in 1809 was followed only a few weeks later by the great victory at Wagram, he felt justified in sticking to his strategy. The size of the *Grande armée* was further increased until it exceeded the half million mark in 1812.[4] Yet its core units from the Boulogne days now consisted almost entirely of recruits surrounded by a few veterans. Incidentally, these *grognards*, with ever fewer exceptions, were no greybeards but men aged between thirty and thirty-five. They were supplemented by the units of foreign mercenaries and the combined troops of the Italian and German states. The whole thing was held together solely by a "skeleton" which comprised the Imperial Guard and the many thousands of seasoned non-commissioned officers and line officers. They made it possible for France to wage war until 1814 despite the fact that the Imperial army's combat strength had long since been overstretched and exhausted by Napoleon's strategy of immoderation.[5]

The Blockaded Sea

The Empire was not blessed with years of peace. The French people had to learn to live with the legacy of war bequeathed to them by the Revolution and the counter-revolution: twenty years of war, in fact, just as Jacques Roux had predicted in 1793. On land the enemies came and went, but at sea one foe was ever-present—England.

The two countries on either side of the Channel had been traditional enemies for centuries, and their wars had taken many forms. In olden times French knights had stormed into London, and their English counterparts had returned the compliment. The latters' expulsion from France was coupled with the name of a national heroine, the peasant girl Joan of Arc from Lorraine, the "Maid of Orléans". Subsequently, however, England became a naval power and once again began to harry France. In the 18th century it grabbed her biggest colonial possessions and, through its policy of preventing any European power from becoming preponderant by always assisting its weaker rivals, ensured that on the continent, as elsewhere, the Bourbon bubble eventually burst. There was no shortage of continental mercenaries willing to do the job in return for hard cash, called "subsidies".

England was the driving force behind all the wars, from start to finish: against the Convention, the Directory, the Consulate and against Napoleon, whose Imperial dignity it refused to recognize. It regarded a Europe under French supervision, not to mention military domination, as a threat to its vital interests which amounted to economic and political expulsion from the continent, quite apart from the fact that France had gained in strength from its social transformation and was able to compete on equal terms with British merchant and industrial capital. Hence every red-blooded Englishman was basically at one with the government on the need to oppose "Old Boney" from Corsica wherever and however possible. The war against Napoleon was popular and supplied the splendid cartoonists with an inexhaustible theme.

It was not to Napoleon's liking, however, since his traditional tactics were of no avail in a battle between "fish and snake" which rarely permitted a direct encounter. He would have gladly put an

*His appearance fired the men with enthusiasm.
Although Ney's corps consisted largely of
raw conscripts for whom today was probably
the very first time that they had seen action,
hardly any of the wounded young men passed
by without shouting "Vive l'Empereur!".
Even the maimed, who perhaps only had
few hours to live, paid him this tribute.
And if I heard one of these dying fanatics
cheer, I must have heard fifty of them.*
Major Odeleben, 1813.

*War, when not resorted to in self-defence but
waged aggressively on a peaceable
neighbouring nation, is an inhuman and
heinous undertaking, for it not only threatens
the innocent victim of its aggression with
death and devastation, it also inflicts terrible
and undeserved suffering on the nation which
wages it.*
J. G. Herder

[1] BALDET, M.: *La vie quotidienne dans les armées
de Napoléon.* Paris, 1964.

[2] ERCKMANN-CHATRIAN: *Histoire d'un conscrit
de 1813* (1864).

[3] *Armeen und A(r)mouren. Ein Tagebuch aus napo-
leonischer Zeit von Baron Üxküll.* Hamburg,
1965;
BLOND, G.: *La Grande Armée, 1804–1815.*
Paris, 1979.

[4] GOURGAUD, G.: *Napoléon et la Grande Armée
en Russie.* Paris, 1825.

[5] BLAZE, S.: *La vie militaire sous le Ier Empire.
Mémoires d'un aide-major.* Paris, 1828;
*Von Marengo bis Waterloo. Memoiren des Capi-
taine Cognet.* Stuttgart, 1910;
CHOURY, M.: *Les Grognards et Napoléon.*
Paris, 1968.

[6] LADY A. PLUMPTER: *A Narrative of a Three Years'
Residence in France (1802–1805).* London, 1810.

end to it, and in the Peace of Amiens in 1802 the First Consul very nearly succeeded. But the truce did not hold for long. Rather than let France hold sway on the continent England's rulers, as they freely confessed, preferred carnage to a "miserable" ceasefire.

Word of what was happening on the other side of the Channel was spread by amateur and professional observers alike, for even after the resumption of hostilities British globetrotters of either sex continued to travel the length and breadth of Europe.[6] The (largely hypothetical) danger that the Imperial grenadiers might one fine day cross the Channel was extinguished by Nelson's naval victory at Trafalgar in 1805. From now on the British Navy could ply the world's oceans at its own leisure and discretion and run up the Union Jack wherever it was worthwhile to tear down the tricolour or the flag of a French ally: in the Caribbean or on the Cape of Good Hope, in Ceylon and the Mascarene Basin, in Pondichéry and Batavia. On top of this a blockade was imposed on May 16, 1806 on all French coasts, which enabled the English cruisers to search neutral shipping.

On November 21, a furious emperor, who had just entered Berlin, proclaimed the controversial "continental system". He issued some pretty dire threats and a year later made an even more ambitious claim: by countering the English naval blockade with his continental blockade he would "conquer the sea by means of the land". The charge has been levelled against him that in so doing he chose the wrong weapon and turned his back on a golden opportunity which presented itself to him in the form of Robert Fulton.

The American Fulton (1765–1815) was a mediocre artist and a fanatical amateur inventor, one of a numerous breed such as his compatriot Rumsey who set out to apply the steam engine to ship propulsion. This prompted him to start designing vessels. In this connection he visited England and in 1797 France, which he hoped would support him in his ambitious plans.

He made an encouraging start. Despite a few teething troubles his submarine "Nautilus" successfully completed its first trials in 1800 and 1802. The American envoy in Paris, Livingston, who was himself an amateur inventor with an eye for the main chance, collaborated with him, and in 1803 the first paddle-steamer ploughed its way along the Seine. Yet First Consul Bonaparte

showed no interest in either of these maritime innovations, and so in 1806 Fulton returned disconsolately to the States where his "Clermont", popularly nicknamed "Fulton's Folly", made its maiden voyage along the Hudson from New York to Albany on August 17, 1807, thereby inaugurating the age of the steamship. A mere twelve years later the converted sailing ship "Savannah" made its way across the Atlantic.

Napoleon passed up the chance to get in on this historic act. Was his indifference simply due to the limited technical horizons of the Corsican yokel who was thus incapable of grasping the significance of the new inventions, or because as a landlubber he was not overly interested in nautical matters?

Fulton was likewise snubbed by President Jefferson, that most enlightened American, and also, after a slight hesitation, by the English themselves until Trafalgar settled the matter definitively. Nobody denied that his inventions were very promising, but the man himself was not needed. In 1812 the British launched a steamer of their own, the "Comet". And why should any navy give serious attention to an idiosyncratic and costly novelty which was still in its infancy and a long way off becoming a fully operational weapon? It was rather Napoleon's realism or pragmatism which led him in his struggle with the British lion to shy away from banking on the submarine which, in spite of Jules Verne's novel, would need more than a century before it could launch its first lethal torpedo.

The economic warfare which Napoleon—of necessity—waged was a seemingly modern phenomenon. But whether it could be applied, executed and maintained in the teeth of its stronger economic rival and wealthier opponent was a moot question. Was it possible to sever its vital commercial artery and to permanently paralyze its export industry by a simple decree?

Initially things looked hopeful. For simplicity's sake Napoleon sent French troops in to secure the ports of Tuscany and the Papal States and to close them to English ships. Austria and Prussia, having just been defeated, had no option but to toe the line; Spain and Denmark joined in of their own accord, the Netherlands and Portugal under pressure. His brother Joseph in Naples obeyed without demur. The highly important Tsar of Rus-

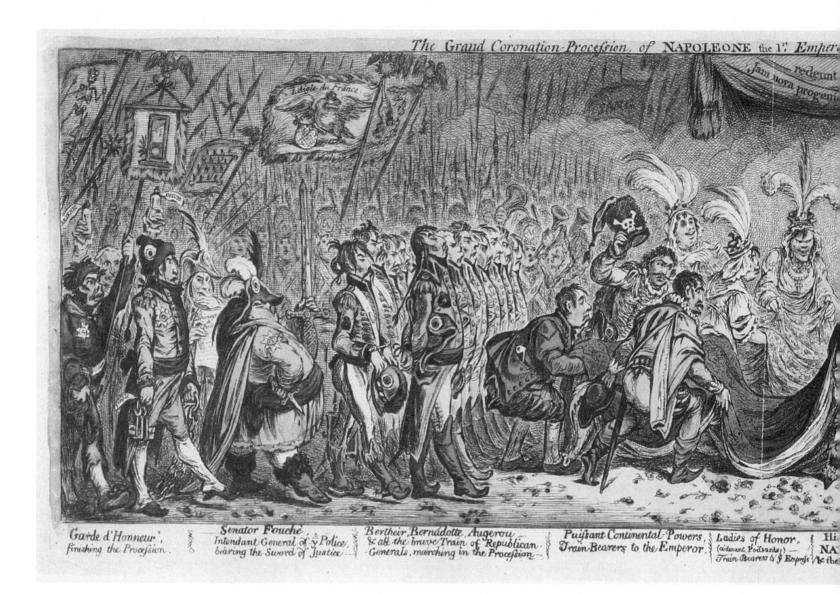

Garde d'Honneur, finishing the Procession.

Senator Fouché Intendant-General of y Police, bearing the Sword of Justice.

Bertheir, Bernadotte, Augerou & all the brave Train of Republican Generals, marching in the Procession.

Puissant Continental-Powers, Train-Bearers to the Emperor.

Ladies of Honor, (aidmant Poissardes) Train-Bearers to y Emprise.

sia assented in accordance with his promises made at Tilsit, though without enthusiasm. At the start of 1808 Sweden, Sicily and—to some extent—Turkey were the only European countries still open to British shipping. As a result symptoms of a crisis began to show in England and Scotland. Exports declined and markets shrank.

Trouble was brewing in the textile industry, and there were outbreaks of labour unrest. The value of the pound wavered since the issue of paper money could no longer be properly covered. In addition British measures to tighten its blockade threatened to lead to a diplomatic break with the United States of America.

However, France was still far from home and dry. A wave of national indignation and a desire to teach perfidious Albion a lesson were no guarantee of being able to cope with the unwelcome but unavoidable side-effects without too much suffering.

At first optimism prevailed. The chambers of commerce, representing the biggest of the businessmen who were directly affected, expressed their agreement. As a result of the naval balance of forces the dockyards, ports and overseas trade, which had previously provided great and rapid riches were already in the doldrums. They were delighted each time a ship managed to penetrate the blockade and put in to port. The

new French counter-measures could not make matters much worse. The same was true of the deep-sea fishermen of Britanny and Normandy who had lost their fishing grounds on the Newfoundland Bank.

The coastal towns did indeed fall on hard times. Their pulse began to beat even more slowly.[1] They could not live from a bit of coastal shipping alone. Wine and brandy exporters were stuck with their normally highly prized wares. Only a few ports in the Channel managed to balance this to some extent through the outfit of privateers and the sale of seized booty. Yet those who possessed capital could invest it elsewhere, and those who lost their livelihood normally found alternative

London. Publish'd Jan.y 1.st 1805. by H. Humphrey 27 S.t James's Street.

| His Holiness Pope PIUS VII conducted by his old Faithful Friend; Cardinal Fesch, offering the Incense | Talleyrand-Perigord Prime Minister & King at Arms bearing the Emperors Genealogy | Madame Talleyrand (ci devant M.rs Halhed the Prophetess) conducting the Heir Apparent in y.e Path of Glory | The Three Imperial Graces. viz T.heir Imp. High.s Princes Borghese, Princess Louis (chi-devant of J. Emperor) & Princess Joseph-Bonaparte | His Imperial Highness Prince Louis Buonaparte Marbœuf High-Constable of the Empire. |

The coronation procession of Napoleon, mercilessly satirized. The coronation procession, which initiates the reign of Satan, is made up of gross figures of vice and stupidity.
Etching by James Gillray, 1804.

Visit to a sick man. The dying English prime minister Fox is haunted by his contemporaries and by personifications of his misdeeds and failures.
Aquatint by James Gillray, 1806.

[1] VION, A.: *La vie calaisienne sous le Consulat et l'Empire*. Paris, 1972.

employment without much difficulty by changing their trade. Government contracts were a help, and the French coast did not become a totally depressed area. Industrialists hoped to gain much from the whole affair. The response among the entrepreneurs testified to this. For them the blockade put up a welcome barrier to rival British goods and acted as a prohibitive protective tariff. Some branches of industry—including major ones such as iron and steel—expectantly predicted that it would greatly boost the demand for their manufactures on the bloated "national" market formed by the Empire plus its satellites. Krupp was not the only man who used this propitious opportunity to found a firm.

Admiral Nelson. A naval battle is depicted beneath the medallion. Engraving by Edward Scriven after Robert Bowyer.

Battle of Trafalgar. Painting by William Mallord Turner. National Maritime Museum, London.

The Emperor made an exaggerated claim:
England, which is being punished by means of the selfsame instrument which it sought to viciously apply itself, must now impotently watch its wares being rejected by the whole of Europe and its ships sailing aimlessly around the world laden with useless riches through oceans which it thought it controlled. The English search in vain between the Öresund and the Dardanelles for a port which will accept them.

[1] HARSANY, F.: *La vie à Strasbourg sous le Consulat et l'Empire.* Paris, 1976.
[2] CROUZET, F.: *L'Empire britannique et le blocus continental (1806–1813).* Paris, 1958.

Nevertheless shortages arose, which were largely self-imposed, in the area of raw materials and colonial goods. New sources of supply and, more especially, new overland transport routes had to be discovered and opened up. This stimulated a resumption of canal building and the expansion and improvement of the Imperial road network. Transit cargo increased by leaps and bounds, and cities like Strasbourg and Lyons became huge emporia.[1] Schemes to divert trading routes which almost defied the imagination were undertaken in order to evade the English blockade. Thus cotton, which had already acquired vital importance, found a completely new path from the Levant via Constantinople and Üsküb, Bosnia and Kostajnica to Napoleon's Illyrian provinces and from there via Milan and the newly opened Mont Cenis Pass to Lyons. In 1811 a new road extension was inaugurated through the Simplon Pass to Switzerland. Overseas goods, which had previously needed only to cross the Straits of Dover, were now re-routed via Salonica, Belgrade and the Danube to Germany whence they reached France. Of course, these were not ideal solutions. The cost of re-directing traffic overland was several times higher and so did just as much to raise the price of the finished product as the losses incurred along the more hazardous maritime routes. The consumer energetically bemoaned the threefold increase in the price of his sugar, coffee, tea, tobacco and other comforts. Since the shortages continued unabated, the mere issuing of instructions could do nothing to counter it.

However, there were some rays of hope. Although in the mechanization of the textile industry France still lagged far behind England at that time, De Girard's and Jacquard's mechanical innovations initiated a higher stage of technical advance. Chaptal succeeded in mass-producing all the acids needed by the arms industry in the requisite quantity and quality. The annual production capacity of rifles, which was spread over a number of old-established and newly created ordnance factories, exceeded two hundred thousand.

Attempts to grow cotton in southern France and Italy failed, but efforts aimed at obtaining sugar from beet instead of the tropical cane met with lasting success in Prussia and France. Franz Karl Achard, a Berlin chemist of Huguenot descent and director of the Physical Section of the Prussian Academy of Sciences, succeeded after lengthy experimentation in putting into practice Marggraf's findings on the sugar content of the humble forage plant. In 1801 he set up the first sugar beet processing factory at Kunern (Konary) in Silesia. It inspired great hopes, and amid the favourable market situation there was no lack of praise and encouragement on either side of the Rhine for this very welcome stopgap. The only snag was that it would take decades and many technical improvements before sugar beet would be able to provide a complete substitute for sugarcane—far too long for a hard-pressed Napoleon and his sweet-toothed Imperial subjects.

In 1809 the battle between the two contenders entered a new phase. England displayed an additional weapon: large-scale smuggling organized along quasi-military lines. For this purpose strong bases and copious supply depots were set up on unassailable islands: on Heligoland in the North Sea, Cephalinia in the Ionian Sea and Lissa in the Adriatic, in addition to those which already existed, such as on Gibraltar and Malta. Here boats took on board their illicit cargoes. The English were aided by the Spanish resistance to Napoleon, which ripped open the western flank of the "continental system", and Russia's growing reluctance to forfeit the increasing benefits of its trade with England simply in order to do France a favour. But as soon as its Baltic ports began to re-admit British ships (which were camouflaged as American vessels), the much sought-after goods started to trickle from the East back into the Grand Empire via routes which could no longer be termed secret.

A fierce struggle for control of the coasts broke out. In 1807 the emperor had justified the occupation of Portugal with the need to plug the Lisbon gap. Several different considerations lay behind the liquidation of the Papal States in 1809: after all, the pope's main activity had hardly consisted in spreading the mantle of Christian charity over contraband articles. However, there can be no doubt that the desire to cut Austria off from the "British" sea and its mercantile siren signals played a big role in the artificial formation in 1809 of the "Illyrian provinces". And in 1810 Napoleon's brother Louis had to pay with his crown when, so as to keep in with his Dutch subjects, he turned a sympathetic blind eye to the ac-

tivities of the customs officials. In a revealing move which highlighted the tyrant's sense of geography, the emperor peremptorily annexed "this accumulation of silt washed up by French rivers". For good measure he also gobbled up the German North Sea ports of Emden, Oldenburg, Bremen and Hamburg. He even stretched a tentacle into the Baltic by grabbing Lübeck in order to be able to manifest his presence in those reaches, too, should the need arise.

Not only all Europe but even the citizens of France themselves were concerned at this land grabbing. Such heterogeneous and far-flung acquisitions could never all be assimilated. But if

the whole business was simply meant to serve to combat the British strategy of smuggling it was quite absurd. The longer and more indented the coastline, the more difficult and indeed impossible did its surveillance become. The customs officers and gendarmes did not suffice, and so whole battalions of infantry had to be drafted in. Their absence elsewhere was sorely felt, and ultimately the "continental system" swallowed up more of the Empire's military resources than a lost battle.

Meanwhile the powerful blows exchanged across the English Channel from one shoreline to the other hit home. Britannia's famed ubiquitous

fleet was put through a stiff test.[2] The economic recovery which followed the slump of 1808 ended fairly abruptly two years later. A poor harvest, the overreliance on credit and a logjam of goods after the markets (largely at knock-down prices which did not even cover the costs) had been flooded and surfeited, combined to make it difficult to get rid of merchandise at all. The French defensive measures did have some success, though. Corsaires in Dunkirk, Calais, Boulogne, Cherbourg and St. Malo, whom Napoleon fitted out with patents which legalized their piracy in international law, inflicted numerous painful blows on the enemy's merchant fleet. It was equally as hard for the larger vessels to pick off the nimble little privateers as it was for the less well-armed merchantmen to shake them off. Keeping both blockading and overseas fleets permanently under sail was a costly business, and the war which the British mercenary army waged doggedly on the Iberian peninsula was even more so. Lest they might forfeit the indigenous population's sympathies or the important support rendered by the guerillas, the British, unlike the French, could not live off requisitions. They had to pay their way with gold which was thus, on top of the subsidies, a constant drain on the nation's resources.

The pound now actually fell, and by 1811 the country was facing an economic crisis. Some exporters went bankrupt, industrial production slumped while a second bad harvest afflicted the land and drove up the price of bread. From Nottingham the machine-breaking Luddites went on the rampage throughout the industrial heartlands of the Midlands, Yorkshire and Lancashire. They were the victims or threatened victims of unemployment who, confusing cause and effect, smashed the inanimate objects of their anger as Satanic destroyers of their traditional handicraft livelihood. In June 1812 ruthless British attacks on American ships and seamen incited a declaration of war from the United States, which for years had sought to manoeuvre between the two adversaries. This closed yet another trade route and market. It seemed as though Napoleon's intuitive tactic of bleeding the eternally evasive enemy to death economically, and thereby to shatter its social fabric and so exhaust both its military resources and its will to wage war, might yet come up trumps.

Yet France was in an even worse position, although the crisis which beset it in 1810/1811 was of a different nature than the one which shook England. To explain it away as the coincidence of several unfortunate circumstances, as Napoleon did, would be to trivialize it. The government's lack of steadfastness in combating the imbalances which emerged during the interaction of economic growth and the effects of war can be dismissed neither as a phenomenon of peripheral importance nor as the inevitable consequence of the blockade. The truth lay somewhere in-between.

The orchestrated system of large-scale smuggling, which with the help of hundreds of thousands of overt and covert participants constructed an extensive network both at home and abroad, managed to establish a parallel market in France and the adjoining countries which was almost totally impervious to government control since the demand always exceeded the supply. This gave rise to wild speculation in colonial goods into which considerable sums of capital were sunk. Unable to beat this conspiracy of self-interest, the emperor hit on the idea of joining it and set himself up as the chief conspirator.

A series of decrees, the most important of which were passed in July and August 1810, laid down a new system of licences. Signed by Napoleon personally, they were—for a fee—issued exclusively to French ships. They empowered these to sail from France to foreign ports (including English ones!) where they could unload their cargoes and restock their holds with all the wares which were in short supply back home. Their allocation on the continent, after being approved by a government commission, was the job of French wholesalers. The prices of colonial goods (the chief of which where cotton, sugar and indigo) were fixed by the government. In practical terms they were based on black market levels but had the advantage of legality and so could dispense with the supplementary risk premium. In other words the emperor beat the illegal underhand dealers at their own game.

The main losers were France's allies, both willing and reluctant. They were categorically forbidden to trade directly with England or with overseas partners. The advantageous position which Napoleon had helped French industry to attain on the continent was now extended to French commerce. The first practical demonstrations of the working of the legislation on the blockade elicited a uniform response from those affected. In November 1810 there was a four-day public bonfire of confiscated English merchandise, from fragrant cloves to the finest cloth. This exemplary act took place in Frankfurt/Main, which was not only the birthplace of Goethe and Rothschild but also the richest trading centre for contraband. The losses were reckoned in millions and did lasting damage to the city's prosperity.

The ruthless enforcement of the licensing system unleashed panic among trading circles all over Europe. This spread from the states of the Rhine Confederation to Italy[1] and from there to France itself, for the hub of all this speculative wheeling and dealing was, naturally enough, Paris which, along with Lyons, was engulfed by the ensuing wave of bankruptcies. In place of the thunderous (or perhaps coldly calculating) applause which had hitherto greeted the emperor's triumphs, a stony silence now prevailed. Even large banking concerns such as Laffitte and Fould were now struggling to survive. Reneging on debt repayments became the order of the day, and in 1811 the entire textile trade—silk, cotton and wool— was hit by a serious sales crisis. Almost half of the handicraft producers had to shut up shop, and factories laid off their workers in droves.[2] Even in Paris, which thanks to the government's measures of support was in a much better position than Rouen, Lyons, Nîmes and many other commercial centres in the country, still had twenty thousand registered unemployed in the spring. In the summer businessmen (perhaps deliberately exaggerating the problem) estimated their turnover at only a tenth of the previous year's figure.

Adding fuel to the fire there were also serious shortfalls in the harvest which, as in England, raised the price of bread. The capital itself remained calm as a result of Napoleon's pragmatic intervention. He had quickly discovered that, although it was unjust to hold down the price of bread in Paris, this was necessary since it was the seat of government and, besides, the soldiers were reluctant to fire on women carrying their children on their backs who clamoured for bread outside the bakers' shops.

When it came to the provinces he did not have the same scruples. At the start of 1812 the combination of unemployment and the disappearance of grain from the market led to looting and the burning down of farms, attacks on mills, bakeries and carts and barges laden with corn. Gangs of vagrants and beggars, whom the authorities thought they had brought under control, stalked the countryside anew. Posters appeared on walls containing blood-curdling messages from the hungry to the sated which made the property-owning bourgeoisie's hair stand on end. In Charleville, Rennes and other towns there were demonstrations and riots in the market place. The police and gendarmerie were no longer able to cope. The régime's authority was in jeopardy. In order to re-establish its credibility a bloody example was made of the town of Caën in Normandy, where the excesses had been no greater than in other places. Soldiers moved in and on March 15, 1812, following the verdict of a court-martial, four men and two women workers were shot by a firing squad.[3]

Eventually the crisis was dealt with, but not before a certain amount of confidence had been lost. Bonfires of confiscated contraband intended as public spectacles were no substitute. The business community bore a lasting grudge for the losses—and the fright of their lives—which they had suffered. It would be fruitless to speculate whether the wounds inflicted would have healed satisfactorily and whether the "continental system", the economic rampart which Napoleon erected but himself repeatedly punctured, might nevertheless have achieved its aim if it had been systematically continued. The emperor decided to crown it all with a grand flourish in the old style. In order to plug the one major breech he returned to conventional military methods and ideas in 1812 with his Russian campaign. His aim was to bring London to its senses via Moscow.

For the sea remained closed to him. This was brought home to Napoleon in 1815 when a British ship, instead of taking him to freedom in America, delivered him into British captivity.

Court Life

Every potentate needs a court, whether he really wants one or not. Shielded from his subjects, he can disport himself there in higher spheres which are inaccessible to the masses. In this way the sovereigns were able to keep their distance from the *canaille* in the capital: in Versailles, which set the example in this respect, in Schönbrunn and Potsdam, in Aranjuez and Belém.

Such courts obey laws of their own and in the course of the centuries develop certain rules which become encrusted with the patina of nobility and are collectively known as etiquette. At intervals they are revamped by means of prescriptive instructions. Whether such a court inspires among the populace at large excessive respect or—in times of social upheaval—excessive repugnance is neither here nor there. It is a self-contained microcosm, an expensive but necessary adjunct of the throne and upholds the viability of the latter through a plethora of ceremonial rules

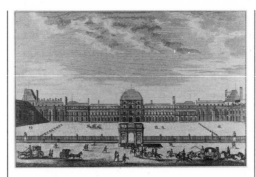

The Tuileries palace as seen from the courtyard side. Steel engraving by François-Louis Couché, 1818. From: Binet (Editor), *Soixante vues des plus beaux palais, monuments et églises de Paris*. Paris, no date (c. 1818).

The Devil noted every misdemeanour perpetrated by him and his siblings . . .
Goethe

Joseph	*(1768–1844)*
Lucien	*(1775–1840)*
Elisa	*(1777–1820)*
Louis	*(1778–1846)*
Pauline	*(1780–1825)*
Caroline	*(1782–1839)*
Jérôme	*(1784–1860)*

[1] Tarlé, E.: *Le Blocus continental et le royaume d'Italie*. Paris, 1928.
[2] Vincent, O.: *Napoléon et l'industrie française. La crise de 1810–1811*. Paris, 1947.
[3] Lavalley, G.: *Napoléon et la disette de 1812*. Caën, 1912.

and regulations. Regardless of the changing occupancy of the throne, it reflects the indispensable continuity of authority in a blaze of pomp and circumstance paid for by the humble tax payer.

How this was done has always depended on the *genius loci*. The pigtailed Manchu rulers inside Peking's "forbidden city" were more formal than the Ottoman caliphs on the Golden Horn, the tsar of all Russians more extravagant than King Stanislaw Poniatowski in the truncated electoral monarchy of Poland. The court was more elaborately ceremonial in Spain (which still hankered after the fading chimera of a Catholic world monarchy) than in Protestant England, which had sent Charles Stuart's royal head rolling. Cheeseparers such as Frederick the Great in Prussia and Joseph in Austria had given way to more free-spending successors who did not allow the war against revolutionary France to spoil their pleasure in sumptuous junketing.

The monarchs addressed one another as brother or cousin and constantly expressed their mutual affection, which was not without a basis in reality. For although they stemmed from different branches of the family tree and were endowed with their own individual grain, they were all chips off the same "divine" block and (at least in Europe) virtually all related to one another by birth or marriage, however tenuously. Even when they pitted their mercenary armies against each other in the search for territorial aggrandizement, the rulers of the western world still regarded themselves as an exclusive club which steadfastly refused admittance to anyone of inferior rank, whatever his pedigree. The members of this big "family" kept company with one another, argued with, married and cheated each other. Napoleon knew if he wished to gain entry into this most select set he had to batter down the door.

He decided to chance his arm, and his martial means of persuasion proved effective. Who could resist such compelling arguments as long as his luck held? Several members of the Bonaparte clan now jumped on the dynastic bandwagon, and one or two married into ancient ruling houses. Napoleon himself led the way as the son-in-law of the last Holy Roman emperor. His own son had no need to be ashamed of his father's pro-Jacobin and revolutionary past since he could look back on his mother's side to an ancient genealogical tree of Imperial pedigree.

The small gallery in the palace of Malmaison. In this chamber, which today serves as a music room, contemporary pictures were displayed—by Granet, Bergeret, Prud'hon, Richard and others. Watercolour by Auguste Garneray, 1812 (completed by his sister in 1832). Palace of Malmaison.

View of Malmaison palace. The château, which was built at the beginning of the 17th century, was purchased by Josephine in 1799 and then extended and furnished by Percier and Fontaine as the private residence of Napoleon and Josephine Bonaparte. After their divorce in 1809 Josephine withdrew to Malmaison. Coloured lithograph by Ermer (?), c. 1800.

Napoleon in his study at the Tuileries. Painting by Jean-Baptiste Isabey.

To reflect this Napoleon required a convincing façade of courtly trappings. As First Consul Bonaparte he had with great farsightedness already taken the first step when—regardless of the Republic—he took up residence in the old Bourbon palace of the Tuileries in Paris.[1] It became his permanent abode which he left only for short-stay visits elsewhere, e.g. to Saint-Cloud. However, as master of the world he could not possibly leave it in the state in which he found it in 1800.

The building itself was not in too bad a shape although, having been built by Catherine de Medici as a Renaissance palace in the 16th century, it had long stood empty prior to 1789 and had badly suffered under the depredations wrought by the storming crowd in 1792. Little was left of the Louis Seize interior after the building, now that its original purpose had become redundant, was turned into offices, and it was no great problem to gradually restore it to splendour and glory.[2] Renowned specialists were entrusted with this task. Bonaparte consulted them frequently, and they did a workmanlike job. Lucrative contracts were awarded to manufacturers of wallpaper, Gobelins, silk and mirrors, to painters and sculptors, cabinetmakers and gilders who were among the best in Europe.

By the time the Empire was proclaimed in 1804 the Tuileries had regained the old sparkle. A rich selection of sculptures and pictures were on display, and anyone who wished to inspect more of the spoils which Bonaparte had looted from Italy could do so in the main gallery of the adjacent Louvre. It was covered in its entire length by paintings representing all the famous schools. Just about everything was put on public display. One exception was Altdorfer's "The Victory of Alexander", taken from Munich, which for some reason Napoleon hung in his bathroom at Saint-Cloud. Self-proclaimed experts found fault with the new interior as it evidenced a certain dryness, ponderousness and jaggedness. This new "Imperial style", which had evolved from the Directoire, was dubbed accordingly "Empire". Sébastien Mercier called it "antiquomania". Perhaps the emperor's new home simply lacked a feminine touch. The coquettish Josephine paid little attention to interior design and whenever she did, her good-natured generosity was all too often exploited by shrewd contractors.[3]

[1] THIBAUDEAU, A.C.: Geheime Denkwürdigkeiten über Napoleon und den Hof der Tuilerien in den Jahren 1799 bis 1804. Stuttgart, 1827.
[2] LACHOUQUE, H.: Bonaparte et la cour consulaire. Paris, 1958.
[3] DUCREST, G.: Mémoires sur l'Impératrice Joséphine. Paris, 1828.
[4] ROEDERER, P.L.: Aus der Umgebung Bonapartes. Tagebuch. Persönliche und politische Notizen eines Vertrauten der Tuilerien. Berlin, 1909.
[5] Mémoires de Madame la Duchesse d'Abrantes, ou Souvenirs historiques sur Napoléon, la Révolution, le Directoire, le Consulat, l'Empire et la Restauration, 18 Vols. Paris, 1831–1835.
[6] SARDOU, V.: Madame Sans-Gêne. Paris, 1893.

Taste was very much a matter of personal discretion even in those days. But it must be said that the tendency to overdo things which all upstarts have in common was kept within bounds and a sense of moderation prevailed. The interior décor betrayed the methodological military mentality of Napoleon who even as emperor could not restrain his natural impulse to poke his nose into every trivial detail that caught his eye. The usurper lacked both the inborn and the acquired nonchalance of the self-assured heir. On the other hand he shared the Englishman's passion for flowers, which had spread to Europe, and had a running order with Madame Bernard: in return for six hundred francs per annum he received a fresh bouquet every day. Out of season many of these floral decorations had to be fetched all the way from the Côte d'Azur.

A dilemma soon became apparent. How could he reconcile the court's function as the external expression of his power and majesty with the Republican heritage? After all, his royal seat was a brand-new creation and so lacked the aura of age-old reverence acquired by older courts with their historic relics and artefacts. His throne had been forged by the Revolution's all-consuming fire and bore its indelible hallmarks. It was of little avail that its occupant avoided any reference to its provenance with the utmost discretion and tact whenever possible. Thus he had the famous manège, the arena within the Tuileries in which the nation's elected representatives had condemned Louis XVI to death, ploughed up. Yet the Convention had met within the palace in the theatre hall from May 1793 onwards, and it was there that the Council of the Ancients had been presented with the *fait accompli* of 18 Brumaire. Could he possibly erase all memories from a room in which, as both First Consul and then emperor, he for years called together his State Council and listened to their views?

Nevertheless Napoleon went to great trouble in an effort to establish by degree a truly "noble" rather than bourgeois court.[4] Why should the system which, despite the occasional hiccup, functioned so well in England not also work in France: a universally recognized, proper court within a bourgeois state? He forgot—or overlooked—the fact that George III (1760–1820) in London, despite his steadily deteriorating state of

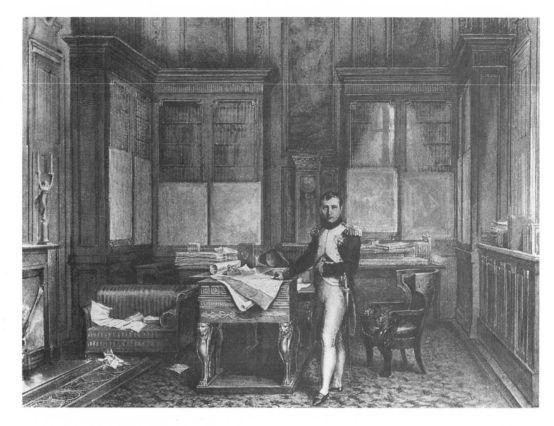

mental health, could more than match his arrogant fellow peers and cousins on the continent with a 700-year-old lineage that stretched back to the Guelphs, whereas the Emperor of the French was seen as an impertinent usurper who had only very recently established himself. His *lèse-majesté* was very far from being forgotten. Bonaparte was man enough to attempt this impossible feat. In doing so he was handicapped by his indecorous entourage.

It was a difficult task to try to accustom the gruff soldiers who had followed him through thick and thin in Italy and Egypt to refined manners in keeping with the magnificent robes which now covered their scarred bodies. He heaped decorations and titles, châteaux and riches on these generals and marshals—the second lieutenants and captains of the Revolution—along with their lady wives (insofar as they restricted themselves to just one), but he was unable to make demure courtiers out of them. Laure Saint-Martin Permon (1784 to 1828) coped well with her elevation to the title "Duchess of Abrantes" and even went on to write her memoirs,[5] while her husband Junot (1771 to 1813), one of Bonaparte's oldest comrades-

in-arms who was known as "Sergeant Storm" (*sergent la tempête*) and became his secretary in Toulon in 1793, ended up completely insane. Monsieur and Madame Lefèbvre failed to learn the usages of social etiquette at the Imperial court. He, the son of a miller, continued to blithely disregard all conventions as "Duke of Danzig" and Commander of the Guard, while his wife, a washerwoman from Alsace called Katharina Hübscher, brought a breath of fresh air into the musty royal corridors with her unabashed plebeian candour which secured her immortality in the world of literature as "Madame Sans-Gêne".[6]

Napoleon was very keen that civilians who had made a name for themselves either during or after the Revolution should also be present at his receptions. But they, forced to rub shoulders with the military men who outnumbered them, often felt equally ill at ease in these unfamiliar surroundings. As for the legitimate aristocracy, apart from a few sticklers for principle, they complied with the obligatory invitations to appear at court for tactical reasons, but did not take the whole charade seriously. Those who did so courted the danger of being tarred as turncoats. One group sulked because they were out of favour with the Republic, and the other because they were out of favour with the monarchy.

Even as First Consul Bonaparte operated with circumspection on this non-reconnoitred terrain and never went for the big kill. He used each opportunity as it arose to gain ground as inconspicuously as possible and then to consolidate his position in peace and quiet. He employed a palace governor—General Duroc—and a commander of the Guard—General Murat—plus several dozen office workers and of course a whole host of servants. Madame de Rémusat, a pert court chronicler who was proud of her family's long membership of the *noblesse de la robe*, had an observant eye, as is reflected by her mémoires: "Each day he introduced a few innovations into his life style which bestowed on his domicile great similarity with a royal palace. He also acquired a taste for a certain prestige as long as it did not adversely affect his personal foibles. He imposed a ceremonial on his entourage. It is his firm conviction that the French allow themselves to be easily seduced by superficial splendour."[1]

In June 1801, for the first time since the Revolution and in the wake of the peace which had been concluded that year, a state reception was held in the Tuileries for the Spanish Bourbon rulers of Tuscany which, ceded by France, now became the "Kingdom of Etruria". The occasion was used to reintroduce embroidered liveries and a refined protocol, which was entrusted to an old hand at the job who performed his role "comme il faut". In spite or maybe because of this, State Councillor Bénézech caused quite a stir. He was an old aristocrat and one-time minister of the interior under Louis XVI who adapted flexibly to the changing times and new masters. By 1802 the "Consul for life" was sporting the once taboo culottes while Josephine surrounded herself with ladies-in-waiting, even though they were not allowed at this stage to describe themselves thus. Extravagance was avoided and refinements such as Talleyrand provided at his garden parties were lacking. Yet as the Imperial coronation approached in 1804 there was a demand for more dignitaries and titles: arch chancellor, grand almoner, connétable, grand admiral. Duroc became Marshal of the Palace, Cambacérès Arch Chancellor, Talleyrand Lord Chamberlain,

Berthier Master of the Hunt and Caulaincourt Chief Equerry[2]—all high-ranking titles for very high-ranking people. After the empress the princes and princesses of the new ruling house were all given their own household along the same lines but of more modest dimensions. In 1808 Napoleon belied the decision of the Constituent Assembly of 1790: the whole courtly menagerie was organically rounded off through the creation of the new Imperial nobility, the "noblesse de l'Empire".

Like all courts, the Tuileries was not devoid of irksome formality and tedium.[3] Efforts were made to entertain the guests through amusing or edifying offerings, but they were not always successful. The people of Paris were choosy and scornfully critical. They were not impressed by a mere crown. Diplomatic receptions were held one after the other, nor was there any shortage of audiences, open-air entertainments in the palace gardens including fireworks, festive banquets and concerts of sacred music. Card games were also played, but not for high stakes and more for fun. Napoleon got a big kick out of cheating. This was rather unfair of him since he knew no one would dare challenge him. His response to this was that it was his partners' own fault if they failed to pay close enough attention. At chess, too, he was a bad loser—like most poor players. One fraudulent opponent once made the grave mistake of forgetting this fact when, in the gardens of Schönbrunn, he pitted a supposed chess automaton against him which promptly beat him. In his fury the emperor smashed the machine—and out popped a hidden dwarf!

In their early years many of the Bonapartes displayed a proclivity towards sentimental literature. Napoleon himself wrote *Clisson et Eugénie*, Lucien *La Tribu indienne*, Joseph (who later turned to science like Louis) a novel, *Moina ou la villageoise du Mont Cenis*. On the other hand none of them could play a musical instrument. Napoleon sang with relish but off-key.[4] Apart from this he was content to listen to the musical delights of the Italian opera and in particular the castrato Girolamo Crescenti. He loved drama, especially tragedy. Ever since he was a child he had nurtured a weakness for ancient Roman subject-matter brimful of heroism.[5] His favourite dramatist was always Corneille. The Comédie-Française, the most famous performers of classi-

cal theatre in the world at the time, made frequent visits to the palace. François Joseph Talma (1763–1826), who during the Revolution had acted as the spokesman of the socially ostracized Thespian fraternity in their struggle for civic equality, enjoyed the emperor's confidence. However, there is no evidence for the assertion that he gave Napoleon private tuition in deportment and dramatic gesticulation nor for the claim that his pupil practised such poses in front of the mirror.

Poor dancer that he was, Napoleon did not enjoy the season of grand balls which were an unavoidable evil, especially as he became more corpulent in later years. He was no great fan of the traditional courtly minuet and offered no objection when Josephine's successor, Marie Louise, replaced it with the Viennese quadrille.

The motley crowd who made up court society did not represent a political force to be taken into consideration in its own right. They were a façade or window-dressing for the self-willed sovereign. The Imperial court had its racy moments, but it was no hotbed of unbridled dissipation. It was more homely than under the Bourbons. The biggest bone of contention was money. Minor upsets were the order of the day rather than real scandals. This did not alter the fact that the Bonaparte and Beauharnais families clashed with one another, that cliques formed and then dissolved again, or that gossip and intrigue flourished.

In his own imperious way Napoleon was a good brother, a decent husband and a dutiful father in accordance with Corsican conventions. In fact he overdid things in this respect. But he also ordered his brothers and sisters about and was then surprised that one or two of them resisted his attempts to do what was best for them. This led to many a stormy scene. His siblings were also Bonapartes, and some had inherited their mother's obstinacy and choleric temperament. Napoleon did not constantly remind them of their origins and of all that he had done for them. But perhaps it was not ingratitude that caused to give vent to their spleen. They simply found it difficult to cope with the meteoric rise which for them had been largely a free ride.[6]

The eldest sister Elisa probably fared best. This strong-willed and capable woman married "beneath her station" but of her own accord when she wed a much older Corsican captain, Felice Baciocchi. She was not of a quarrelsome nature, and from 1805 onwards governed Piombino and Lucca so well that she was also put in charge of Tuscany and made a grand duchess to boot. This meant that for most of the time she stayed at her own court in Florence where Paganini (1782 to 1840)—easily the best violinist in the world at the time—possibly compensated her for the delights of Paris which she had to forego.

Napoleon's favourite sister "Paoletta" was endowed with great beauty but had to pay a high price for it. Her husband, General Leclerc, died of typhoid fever on St. Domingue. The second marriage of the "Duchess of Guastalla" to a prince, Camillo Borghese, turned out to be a mistake, but being a cheerful soul she soon got over it. She was deservedly immortalized in marble by Canova as "Venus Victrix".

Her love affairs were the talk of the town but caused less umbrage than her strained relations with Marie Louise, the new empress. The newly wed Napoleon, caught in the crossfire, came down in favour of his second bride and reluctantly dismissed Pauline Borghese from the court. But she bore her brother no grudge and in 1815, when everything was at stake, was the only one to return to him the jewelry which he had presented to her in happier times.

The youngest sister, Caroline, gave birth to four children by her husband Murat. Her untrammelled ambition, which permeated the very fabric of the Tuileries, incessantly goaded the courageous but simple-minded cavalry commander whom she had wed into reaching ever higher. Even the gift of the Neapolitan crown in 1806 failed to satisfy her since she felt it was simply a move to get rid of her, and she never forgave Napoleon for refusing her the Spanish throne. It was Caroline who established contacts with the Italian opposition, talked Murat into abandoning the sinking ship in 1813 and persuaded him to change sides twice, for which he paid with his life in 1815.

His relationship with his brothers was overshadowed even more strongly by politics. The least problematical was Jérôme, the youngest. He also stepped out of line when in 1803 he married one Miss Patterson in Baltimore, but in 1807 he complied with Napoleon's instruction to leave her in return for the Kingdom of Westphalia and the hand of Princess Catharine of Wurttemberg.

Laetizia Bonaparte, the mother of Napoleon. Lithograph by Bellagny, c. 1835.

[1] RÉMUSAT, C. E. DE: *Napoleon I. und sein Hof. Memoiren 1802–1810*, 3 Vols. Cologne, 1880–1882.
[2] *Unter vier Augen mit Napoleon. Denkwürdigkeiten des Generals Armand de Caulaincourt.* Stuttgart, 1956.
[3] *Cérémonial de l'Empire française.* Paris, 1805.
[4] FLEISCHMANN, T.: *Napoléon et la musique.* Paris, 1965.
[5] HEALEY, F. G.: *The Literary Culture of Napoleon.* Geneva, 1959.
[6] WEINER, M.: *The Parvenu Princesses.* London, 1964.
[7] GARNIER, L.: *Mémoires sur la cour de Louis Bonaparte.* Paris, 1828.
Um Napoleon. Memoiren der Königin Hortense. Munich, no date.

The playboy-king in Cassel possessed more exuberant vivacity than nous but did not interfere in other people's affairs and in times of need did his bit. Though no great soldier, he was at least present at Waterloo.

His differences with his big brother were soft murmurings compared with the scenes staged by the short-tempered Lucien. Though muddled and volatile, he never repudiated his Jacobin sympathies. His poor eyesight precluded a military career, and he remained the family's refractory Republican. He played an extremely active role during 18 Brumaire and at the start of the Consulate but, disinclined to travel the monarchical road, avoided the Tuileries and withdrew to Italy where he shunned all offices and honours. As something of a practical joke he acquired the title of Prince of Canino (which his descendants still bear) not from the hand of the emperor but from the pope as his "feudal lord". He sired a whole crowd of children together with his second wife and rejected the hand of a Spanish infanta. In 1810 he intended to emigrate to America, but fell into the hands of the English and was interned. Thus the two brothers remained at loggerheads until 1815. However, not even Lucien left Napoleon in the lurch during the "Hundred Days".

Louis was quite a different kettle of fish. He was stubborn in a quiet and awkward way. He felt sorry for himself—with some justification—as the victim of the cynical scheming of his tyrannical brother whom, however, he did not dare resist. Initially Napoleon had intended to marry Josephine's daughter Hortense to General Moreau in order to bind his rival to himself. When this plan fell through he presented her to Louis, but the two of them did not hit it off. Neither the governorship of Paris nor the acquisition of the Dutch crown in 1806 made the marital straitjacket any easier to bear.[7] Hortense, who spent a lot of time with her mother and was involved in palace politics, led her own life, so that doubts were expressed as to the paternity of the child who was to feature in history as Napoleon III (1852–1870). But this was not the only reason why he tired of his royal burden. What riled him even more was that the emperor ordered him to rule Holland in the manner of a French tax collector or recruiting sergeant rather than as a responsible and paternal monarch—scruples which

Thank goodness he is always preoccupied with some important venture. Otherwise his ebullience would be quite unbearable.
Josephine on Napoleon.

redounded to his credit. In the year 1810 he hung up his crown and, after the Netherlands had been directly incorporated into France, moved to Austria and then to Italy where he lived anonymously.

Napoleon was very fond of Joseph, the first-born. He felt a sense of guilt ever since he, the younger brother, became head of the clan and tried to make up for it. He showered titles on Joseph: First Prince of the Blood, Grand Elector of the Empire, Master of the Chair of the Grand Orient. It was always he who received the best country going—Naples in 1806, Spain in 1808.

Nevertheless a certain tension remained. Joseph never renounced his right of succession in France. Even as the sovereign of another state he did not regard himself as having been adequately compensated and maintained his claim. Napoleon promised faithfully that it would be honoured but carefully avoided settling the question of the succession definitively. For as long as he had no legitimate son of his own he was inclined to choose one of his nephews. The birth of the "King of Rome" in 1811 clarified the situation.

Overnight it swept away speculations in which half the Tuileries had participated. However, it still left open the question of a regency in the (by no means impossible) case of an ascension of "Napoleon II" to the throne as a minor. In theory if, for example, he himself were killed on the battlefield the Austrian Marie Louise could act as regent, but was this practicable? In 1813 he became even more reluctant to let the ever-loyal Joseph be pushed aside when the latter became a king without a country. As lieutenant general of the Empire he now stood in for Napoleon on the field of battle in the event of the emperor's absence, but without success. In 1814 he was partly to blame for the feeble defence of Paris and in 1815 succeeded where his more illustrious brother failed—he managed to emigrate unhindered to the United States.

By means of her maternal authority Madame Mère, a most formidable old dragon and a prophetess of misfortune, tried with decreasing success to provide some semblance of cohesion to this whole argumentative brood inside and outside the palace. Though under five feet tall she

This was the first service which I was able to perform for Your Majesty.
Fouché to Napoleon.

[1] FAIN, A. J. F.: *Neun Jahre Napoleons Sekretär, 1806–1815. Memoiren.* Berlin, 1926.
[2] WAIRY, L. C.: *Napoleon I. nach den Memoiren seines Kammerdieners Constant.* Leipzig, 1904; MARCHAND, L. J. N.: *Mémoires,* 2 Vols. Paris, 1952–1955.
[3] MASSON, F.: *Napoleon zu Hause. Der Tageslauf in den inneren Gemächern der Tuilerien.* Leipzig, 1895.
[4] VERBRAEKEN, R.: *Jacques-Louis David jugé par ses contemporains et par la postérité.* Paris, 1973.
[5] BAUSSET, L. F.: *Denkwürdigkeiten. Erinnerungen und geheime Geschichten über das Innere des Palastes von Napoleon.* Stuttgart, 1827.

possessed remarkable strength of character, was nobody's fool and a regular old battle-axe into the bargain. She was very sceptical about the viability of her son's Imperial régime and had no time at all for the offspring of "that trollop" who had managed to hook her inexperienced son and ensconce herself in the Tuileries. Although the emperor's children by adoption were well-behaved and exemplary in every way, she thanked her lucky stars when Eugène de Beauharnais was appointed viceroy of Italy and set up his own home with Auguste Amalie Wittelsbach in Milan while Stephanie followed her husband, Hereditary Prince Charles Frederick, to Baden. The officer's daughter Laetizia Ramolino (1750–1836) never accustomed herself to the French way of life, and spent her last few years in Rome where she abandoned herself to an increasingly uncompromising religiosity.

On the other hand the conversion to the Lutheran faith of Jean-Baptiste Jules Bernadotte from Gascony (1763–1844) had precious little to do with religion. The only appearances he put in at the Tuileries were in the line of duty, despite the fact that Joseph's wife and his own spouse were sisters. To make matters worse, his wife, Désirée Clary, had once been as good as engaged to Napoleon. But this did not prevent him from appointing Bernadotte marshal and Prince of Pontecorvo. When in 1810 the Swedish Diet unexpectedly elected him crown prince, Napoleon gave the go-ahead for him to found a dynasty which outlived the reigns of all the Bonapartes. Bernadotte earned this by burning his bridges and joining the final coalition against France. In 1818 he ascended the throne as Charles XIV of Sweden and Norway.

Fouché was long able to fish in troubled waters at the court. He had his informers inside the palace who had their ears to every keyhole. This permitted him to know at an early stage which way the wind was blowing. Sometimes he collaborated with Josephine in order to thwart the schemes of Bonaparte's family, who hated the pair of them. This worked well until they both appeared as hindrances to Napoleon's Austrian marriage in 1810 and had to go. Fouché in no way underestimated the importance of an assured succession for the stability of the régime, and as a realist accepted the personal consequences of this union

philosophically, which was at least another nail in the Bourbon coffin. When an ungrateful Napoleon nevertheless confronted him with the accusation that he had voted for the execution of Louis Capet in 1793, he made a splendid and deeply ironical exit.

If certain initiatives were nevertheless forthcoming from the Tuileries, they did not emanate from the old and new nobility which comprised the court. The palace was also the nerve centre of the entire Empire. This consisted of Napoleon's office and the concomitant chancelleries. Here the fate of millions within France's huge orbit was determined. It was from here that decrees, edicts and ordonnances which altered people's lives were issued. It was likewise here inside his headquarters that the great man himself, pacing up and down in his room or else strolling in the garden between the borders, made his final decisions concerning war and peace.

Napoleon's daily programme was regulated by a strict rhythm which was recorded for posterity by Baron Fain in his *Mémoires*.[1] Some of his personal servants and valets, before whom he could afford to be his real self, also kept diaries or later committed to paper what they—or others—considered worthy of note.[2] They tell us that Napoleon was an intensive sleeper who required only a few hours' rest, a daily change of underwear and a very hot hip bath (later two). The rest of the day was taken up with the art of (sometimes disciplined, sometimes undisciplined) governing—hard labour which was the price he paid for his immoral lunge for power.[3]

He could express himself concisely and succinctly, especially on paper, but could also talk nineteen to the dozen. But it cost him a lot of effort to listen without interruption. He had little time or inclination for diversions. He disliked intensely having to sit for painters and sculptors since he lacked the necessary patience. Portrait painters such as Appiani, Gros, David,[4] Isabey, Vernet, Ingres and Gérard all discovered this to their cost. Perhaps this explains why the Napoleon busts of the old Houdon and the young Canova were not among their better works.

By contrast he performed his courtly duties most conscientiously as a necessary evil and a concession to other people's exploitable and re-usable vanities. On the other hand (notwithstanding Balzac's poetic licence) he could not abide dressing

up, not even for the military parades of which he grew so fond. His slovenliness was deliberate, as when he accepted the surrender of an enemy on the field of battle wearing—in sharp contrast to the immaculately dressed generals around him—a badly fitting and usually stained uniform and mud-caked (but comfortable) boots. Nevertheless he possessed a ceremonial rapier and a hatpin studded with 121 small diamonds and twenty-two solitaires which included the "Sancy", the most exquisite gem from the French crown jewels. This headgear, which it was not really practical to wear in battle, fell into Prussian hands during the debacle at Waterloo in 1815.

At court receptions the names of the dignitaries were always announced together with their full titles, e.g. "Her Majesty, Empress of the French and Queen of Italy", but Napoleon himself was referred to simply as "l'Empereur". The effect was intended. He knew full well that in spite of his lack of height—according to Bausset, prefect of the palace,[5] he was "five foot two and a bit tall"—people bore him respect, whatever his appearance and regardless of whether he behaved phlegmatically or ranted and raved. He had just as little need of extensive commentaries as of the ornate "N" to which he reduced his signature.

The Legend

The Republican Empire did not endure long enough to be able to re-shape the way in which the population lived. The Empire style to which it gave rise prevailed for a mere decade. What survived were less the social (and antisocial) customs associated with it than institutions which owed their efficacy to the greater freedom of manoeuvre which the Revolution provided for the head of state. Its smoothly running public institutions continued to be used for a long time to come, in some cases right down to the present day. However, they were incapable of firing the imagination of millions; they were not the stuff of which legends are made.

France, and with it Europe, experienced some extraordinary and breathtaking moments. Nevertheless the little Corsican who was primarily responsible for them was unable to refashion the French nation in his own image. For his subjects the Imperial era was more of an episode whose

scenes of high political drama, akin to a bull in a china shop, wrought more havoc than anything else. It was a venture that cost more than it earned. The Empire arguably left deeper traces outside France in countries in which, through either the deliberate or unauthorized export of revolution, it introduced the principles of bourgeois emancipation, demolished rotten structures and tore down barriers which not even the victors of Waterloo could resurrect. Napoleon's bellicosity unintentionally helped his adversaries to overcome obstacles, since in order to stand up to the crowned "bastard" of the Revolution they were forced willy-nilly to adopt both his and its achievements, whether with or without ulterior motives. National and social movements arose which, despite their kaleidoscopic diversity, were real enough. They acquired their own momentum and mapped out the future pattern of developments for the rest of the century: in Spain and Germany, in Italy and the Balkans, in Russia and Scandinavia, in the Orient and Spanish America. They acted as catalysts in the re-awakening of national consciousness. Thus the first political poem in Slovenian literature, penned by Valentin Vodnik, begins with the line "Napoleon spake: Illyria, arise!"[1]

This brings us back to the question of the "demiurge": can he be likened to a comet which, both illuminating and scorching everything in its path, soon disappeared from view and in the final analysis did not affect the course of history?

When the restored Bourbon king in Paris learned of his death he called it a news, not an event.

Manzoni's ode *The Fifth of May*, which Goethe translated into German and Berlioz set to music, exercised great restraint in its verdict. Napoleon's name was not mentioned at all, but the poem began with two succinct and pregnant words: "*He was* . . .". The leading Italian Romantic poet suspended judgement on the man himself: "Was he truly great? Let posterity decide."

Posterity has been unable to come to an unanimous decision.[2] No serious commentator could really credit him with the qualities which are commonly associated with greatness: supreme

[1] *Ilirija ozivljena* (V. Vodnik, 1811)
[2] GEYL, P.: *Napoleon for and against.* (Utrecht, 1946) London, 1949;
HAACK, H. E.: *Über den Nachruhm.* Bonn, 1951;
HEGEMANN, W.: *Napoleon oder "Kniefall vor dem Heros".* Hellerau, 1927;
MALRAUX, A.: *Eichen, die man fällt.* Frankfurt/ Main, 1972;
STÄHLING, F.: *Napoleons Glanz und Fall im deutschen Urteil. Wandlungen des deutschen Napoleonbildes.* Brunswick, 1952.
[3] MASSIN, J. and B.: *Ludwig van Beethoven. Materialbiographie. Daten zum Werk und Essay.* Munich, 1970;
ROLLAND, R.: *Beethoven. Von der Eroica zur Appassionata.* Wilhelmshaven, 1970.
[4] GONNARD, P.: *Les origines de la Légende napoléonienne.* Paris, 1906.
[5] *Mémoires pour servir à l'Histoire de France sous Napoléon écrits à Sainte-Hélène par lès généraux qui ont partagé sa captivité* (G. Gourgaud, C. Montholon). Paris, 1822–1827.

intellectual effort, inexhaustible creativity, sublime self-sacrifice or total personal identification with the historic mission of making the world a better place.

In this respect he compares most unfavourably with his contemporary Ludwig van Beethoven[3] (1770–1827). This leaves his deserts as the greatest general of the inchoate industrial era—in some respects the last outstanding instance of his kind—and as a rational ruler and shaper of society with the ability to think incisively and the energy to act decisively. In retrospect we can also identify Bonaparte's ineradicable, inestimable and incalculable contribution towards hoisting the bourgeoisie to its finite period of power on this planet—as one of the handmaidens of history which Hegel characterized as "ruses of reason".

In his overeager assessment of 1814 Chateaubriand found the ousted emperor wanting, referring to his "false greatness" *(un faux grand homme)*. By contrast Junot's widow concluded her reminiscences under the July monarchy of 1835 in the conviction that "even today this incomparable figure still commands great respect".

The legend demanded more, and in his remote seclusion on St. Helena, which prompted public opinion to pity him and to see him as Prometheus chained to a rock amid the savage sea, the prisoner worked away diligently at concocting this.[4] He had acquired some experience in the area of public relations, having acted as his own court chronicler after his first Italian campaign. On St. Helena he replaced his Imperial bulletins by well chosen maxims and aphorisms which were often meant for particular ears.

"I found magnanimity only among the canaille, which I neglected, and real rabble only among the nobility, which I created" is one of the carefully aimed barbs in his *Mémorial*. Here he was addressing those enemies who opposed him not as the destroyer of revolutionary democracy but on the contrary, as the accursed standard-bearer of "plebeian" social change. He conjured up the prospect of a "new era" which he belligerently brandished at all *anciens régimes* in the name of the "indelible and indestructible great ideas of *our* (!) Revolution": "Its noble and grandiose truths must be preserved for all time, however much we may have weighed them down with chandeliers, frippery and other baubles." Hinting

at a polarization of forces in the class conflict, he predicted that the aristocratic restoration would be short-lived. The "two principles" would continue to wage war on one another after his death, and the forces of progress, with which he equated his "system", would prove victorious. Since other survivors from the Year II joined him in exile he, like them licking his wounds and blending fact with fiction, could not bequeath to all Frenchmen

a heritage of liberal opposition in the political testament which was of such crucial importance to him.

The heroic saga which he and his followers on St. Helena evolved and polished circulated around the world.[5] On Corsica itself his name was long overshadowed by that of the abrasive champion of the island's independence, Pasquale Paoli (1725–1807)—but then prophets are rarely

heeded in their native land. Even in France, the "hexagon", his memory did not everywhere inspire the same degree of reverence as among the peasants in the border area of Alsace-Lorraine who often still had his picture hanging in the living room. Bonapartists, whose aim was not only to cherish his image but to couple this with a political vision, comprised a comparatively small minority: demobbed army officers on half-pay; former non-commissioned officers and soldiers who wallowed in the idealized memories of campaigns[1] in the course of which they had trudged through half Europe (cp. Heinrich Heine's[2] "Zwei Grenadiere", which Robert Schumann set to music); public servants who had learned to value a system of administration that functioned like clockwork and by which they had done pretty

nicely; and petty bourgeois souls who had been driven into the arms of the great disciplinarian by national pride or jingoism—if not by a fear of freedom—and who now truculently refused to revise their position. They did not constitute a power in the land but more an element of powerlessness. The prevailing mood was against them, and they lacked both a unifying idea and a common fulcrum.

Some individuals—such as the son of Babeuf, the "enragé" Varlet, the sans-culotte Vingternier or Balzac's banker in *La Maison Nucingen*—may have had a thousand different reasons to mourn the passing of the Imperial era. The decisive factor was not their feelings or admiration for the two-faced warrior but their hatred of the Bourbons who, after at first proceeding cautiously, attacked

Napoleon's coffin on its way to its last resting place in the Eglise des Invalides on December 15, 1840. Steel engraving by Outwaithe.

Napoleon awakes for posterity. Bronze monument by François Rude, 1846, situated in a wood at Fixin near Dijon. A former captain and the sculptor himself were solely responsible for realizing this work, which was publicly unveiled before a great crowd on the eve of the revolution of 1848. The rock of St. Helena, the dead eagle and a chained sword are the allegorical attributes.

[1] BALZAC, H. DE: *Napoleon. Seine Lebensgeschichte, erzählt von einem alten Soldaten.* Munich, 1973.
[2] HOLZHAUSEN, P.: *Heinrich Heine und Napoleon I.* Frankfurt/Main, 1903.

A father getting his son to kneel before a statuette of Napoleon. Woodcut by Auguste Raffet. Closing vignette in: Jacques de Norvins, *Histoire de Napoléon*. Paris, 1839.

Napoleon with two riders. Coloured lithograph by Henri de Toulouse-Lautrec; originally an idea for a poster to mark the appearance of a book about Napoleon by W. Milligan Sloane, 1895.

[1] STENDHAL: *Vie de Napoléon* (1827).
[2] BAINVILLE, J.: *Napoléon*. Paris (1931); Munich, 1950;
DRIAULT, E.: *L'immortelle épopée du drapeau tricolore. Napoléon-le-Grand, 1769 – 1821*, 3 Vols. Le Chesnay, 1930.
[3] GUÉRARD, A. L.: *Napoleon. Wahrheit und Mythos*. Dresden, Berlin, 1928;
JONES, B.: *Napoleon. Man and Myth*. London, 1977;
PRESSER, J.: *Napoleon. Das Leben und die Legende*. Stuttgart, 1977;
TULARD, J.: *Napoleon oder der Mythos des Retters*. (Paris, 1977) Tübingen, 1978.
[4] JAGGI, A.: *Der Befreiungskampf Europas zur Zeit Napoleons I.* Berne, 1944.
[5] Scott, W.: *Die Geschichte Napoleons. Geprüft von Ludwig Bonaparte*. Stuttgart, 1829.

with a vengeance; their hatred of the arrogant aristocratic clique who could not restrain their impulse for revenge which they had nurtured in exile; and their refusal to simply forget everything that had happened since 1789 as if it had been a figment of their imagination.

The multi-volume *Mémorial de Sainte-Hélène*, which Las Cases published between 1822 and 1827 as the allegedly authentic reminiscences of Napoleon himself, provided the semblance of an alternative. Of course, it was presented with stealth and by no means represented an unbiased and original contribution towards a critical historical analysis of the Imperial era. Yet it responded to a need that was greater than anyone could have expected. The astonishingly long-lived impact of the work provided a firm foundation for the Napoleonic legend, the wide-ranging ramifications of which have endured to the present day. Novelists and poets were the first to seize upon it: the inimitable Béranger in his popular chansons and those two sons of generals, Victor Hugo and Alexandre Dumas. Under its influence Musset and Vigny renounced their royalist views. The ghost of the "man who could do everything because he wanted everything" stalked through both Balzac's *Comédie humaine* and Stendhal's[1] *La Chartreuse de Parme*. It crept into the work of Eugène Sue and Thackeray's *Vanity Fair*, inspired Wilhelm Hauff's *Bild des Kaisers* ("The Image of the Emperor") and Grabbe's *Napoleon oder die Hundert Tage* ("Napoleon or the Hundred Days").

Although Carlyle did not like him and ranked him far behind Frederick II, he elevated Napoleon to star status in his *On Heroes, Hero-Worship and the Heroic in History*. This provided a cue for Michelet and Tolstoi, who countered this image with their habitual pungency, but also for countless others to chip in with their contribution.[2] The dead Napoleon, whose mortal remains were brought to Paris in 1840 and placed in the crypt of the chapel at Les Invalides, began to acquire a mythical aura.[3] A nephew whose intelligence (but not his pedigree) was beyond doubt managed to make political capital out of his uncle's image. Simply on the strength of his illustrious surname he was able in 1848 to get nearly three quarters of the voters to elect him president and in 1851 to stage his own "Eighteenth Brumaire of Louis Bonaparte". This "Second Empire" was a pale re-

flection of the first. Out of respect for the "King of Rome", who had died in 1832 without ever having come to power, the new Napoleon styled himself "the Third". His empire crumbled in 1870, but this did not prevent other "tomcats" (to cite a famous simile)[4] from claiming resemblance to the great "lion": as alleged saviours in times of need, envoys of Providence or simply as Cyclopean forgers of the nation's happiness who stood "beyond good and evil" such as Dostoevski's *Raskolnikov* and Nietzsche's *Overman*.

The Napoleon image changed with the passage of time and adjusted to the new realities. Of necessity it lost the graphic immediacy which it had had for Byron and Mickiewicz, for Pushkin, Lermontov and Karl Marx from Trier—who was born three years after Waterloo and three years before Napoleon's death in Longwood—as well as for Walter Scott,[5] who transferred Burke's antipathy towards democrats to the "false" emperor. It was not abandoned by the great writers: Stefan Zweig, Bernard Shaw and Louis Aragon sublimated his image by means of cerebral empathy with the deceased. The attempts by Mussolini and Philipp Bouhler (as authors!) to resurrect him lay on a different plain altogether.

His reputation as a soldier underwent a strange evolution. Initially it was regarded everywhere as unrivalled, but after Königgrätz and Sedan it was forgotten. Ironically it was rediscovered not in France but in the Prusso-German Empire. In 1885/1886 M. Yorck von Wartenburg, a general staff officer, published his work *Napoleon als Feldherr* ("Napoleon—the Strategist") in Berlin which was still being reprinted when its author met his death in distant China in 1900. Napoleon's strategy based on quick and decisive thrusts elicited the undivided attention of the general staff whose head of the military history section, Von Freytag-Loringhoven, had several studies made on the subject and in 1910 himself produced a book on this topic: *Die Heerführung Napoleons in ihrer Bedeutung für unsere Zeit* ("Napoleon's military strategy and its importance for our epoch").

In France, too, the supposed Napoleonic method of waging war came back into vogue around 1890. Unfortunately, neither the Germans nor the French had much to show for their analysis of Napoleon's tactics and strategy. In 1914 both powers saw their strategic doctrines disintegrate.

Nevertheless the unique genius of General Bonaparte (not the achievements of the Emperor Napoleon) continues to pepper the writings of military analysts who refuse to content themselves with examining his campaigns within their concrete context.

The Napoleon that everyone knows from the hackneyed efforts of painters of historical scenes which found their way into school textbooks—of unimpressive build but with the "classical" Roman profile, a tricorn on his head and his fingers lodged between the buttons of his waistcoat—has become a popular figure that tends rather to raise a smile than to strike fear into anyone's heart, in France as elsewhere. This is the result of the handiwork of the lesser Muses for whom Napoleon was always a productive source of subject-matter for engravings, illustrated broadsheets, gifts and for the theatre. Nor have the media of film and television been slow to latch onto the theme. And not all of their efforts can be dismissed as trivial light entertainment: see Wajda's *Mortal Remains* or Bondarchuk's *War and Peace* and *Waterloo* with their striving for veracity. But even these films tell us little about the specific features of the French Republican Empire. It has remained a neglected area.

A deeper impression is conveyed by the diaries, collected letters and memoirs of the actors involved. A veritable mountain of paper has been handed down by a generation of avid writers. However, they must be treated with great caution, for insight is mingled with invention, the bombastic with the sober, significant accounts with trivial tittle-tattle from friend and foe alike, belated vindictiveness with posthumous declarations of love. Both winners and losers have had their say; they reveal or conceal, pardon or accuse, they rejoice or despair—or else maintain a verbose silence: marshals and diplomats, professional politicians and armchair pundits, officials and scholars, poets and actors, more or less respectable citizens, court employees and infantry privates. Some details are observed more sharply by female eyes. Some seek to deflate the legend, others to inflate it. Few of the key figures did not favour posterity with their recollections, few followed the example of that "grey eminence",

Allegory on Napoleon's immortality. Woodcut by Nicolas-Toussaint Charlet. From: Las Cases, *Mémorial de Sainte-Hélène*, Vol. 1. Paris, 1842.

Symbolic gravestone of Napoleon in the ocean. Vignette (woodcut) by Auguste Raffet in: Norvins, *Histoire de Napoléon*. Paris, 1839.

[1] Worth consulting is J. Tulard: *Bibliographie critique des Mémoires sur le Consulat et l'Empire écrits ou traduits en français*. Paris, Geneva, 1971.
[2] Wieland, R.: *Napoleon und ich*. Halle, Leipzig, 1982.

Hugues Bernard Maret (1763–1839) and kept their thoughts to themselves. Maret was one of the founding fathers of the *Moniteur*, a Feuillant and a Brumairian, the Duke of Bassano and the head of Napoleon's chancellery, in which guise he accompanied his master everywhere. From 1811 to 1813 he was foreign minister and as such partly responsible for the breach with Russia. He was very devoted to the emperor but even so has been stigmatized by some as his "evil genius".

Fitting the miriad jigsaw pieces together to form a complete picture is a fascinating but difficult task which requires great patience.[1] Nonetheless blank spaces and missing pieces remain, for those who stood in the background rarely put pen to paper. They appear only in the pages of official records which give some account of the lives they led. Fortunately they were filed away by pedantic bureaucrats and thus preserved for posterity.

The guild of historians—or would-be historians—concern themselves with assessing such records with varying degrees of skill and success. A handful of the decidedly too many tens of thousands who tried their hand at this went on to make a name for themselves, from Adolphe Thiers who, though not for this reason, even headed the French government in 1871, to Emil Ludwig who, as an "amateur" and spoilsport, attracted the ire of the learned professors in 1924. In their favour it must be said, however, that the professional biographers of Napoleon included a goodly number for whom the Corsican general did not obscure their understanding of the epoch but actually clarified it.

Writers will continue to argue for, against and about the emperor and the Empire as well as the virtues and vices of its society on both suitable and unsuitable occasions. Many verdicts will be corrected, many existing prejudices will be got rid of and perhaps, here and there, a new one adopted. For the field is open to anyone.[2]

But no one is likely to dispute the fact that in the final analysis the Grand Empire cannot be accused of mediocrity, unless one judges it by the wise old saying of the Chinese peasants, to wit:
The best kind of government is the one
which is the least noticeable.

APPENDIX

FRANCE

GREAT BRITAIN

NORWAY

SWEDEN

Finland

DENMARK

PRUSSIA

RUSSIA

WARSAW

RHINE CONFEDERATION

AUSTRIA

SWITZERLAND

Illyrian Provinces

ITALY

LUCCA

OTTOMAN EMPIRE

Moldavia

Walachia

Serbia

MONTE-NEGRO

NAPLES

SARDINIA

SICILY

Morocco

Algeria

Tunesia

Tripolis

BARCA

Egypt

PORTUGAL

SPAIN

Atlantic Ocean

North Sea

Baltic Sea

Black Sea

Mediterranean

Bay of Biscay

Balearic Islands

Ionian Islands (Brit.)

Petersburg

Moscow (2nd capital)

Borodino

Smolensk

1812

Stockholm

Copenhagen

Gdańsk

Tilsit
Friedland
Eylau

Kolberg

Berlin

Warsaw

Leipzig
Jena

Amsterdam

Waterloo

London

Amiens

Paris

Lunéville

Basle

Berne

Austerlitz

Aspern
Vienna

Wagram
Pressburg

Leoben

Campo Formio
Arcole

Milan

Mantua

Marengo

Laibach

Jassy

Belgrade

Bucharest

Istanbul

Naples

Palermo

Cagliari

Rome

Corsica

Corfu
(French)

Crete

Vitoria

Sarágossa

Madrid

1810

1812

Torres
Vedras

Lisbon

Cádiz

Trafalgar

Gibraltar (Brit.)

Algier

Tunis

Fes

Malta (Brit.)

Heligoland
(Brit.)

Aboukir

Cairo

Giza

o capital cities

● venues of peace treaties

⚔ sites of battles

⚔ sieges

.... border of Imperial France 1789

Imperial France

French dependencies

states allied with France

0 100 200 300 400 500 600 km

Chronological Table

1762 Rousseau: *The Social Contract*
1763 End of the Seven Years' War
1768 The Genoese Republic cedes Corsica to France
1769 Napoleone Buonaparte born in Ajaccio (August 15)
James Watt: low-pressure steam engine
1772 First Partition of Poland
1774 Discovery of oxygen by Priestley
Goethe: *The Sorrows of Werther*
1776 4.7.: Declaration of Independence by the United States of America
Adam Smith: *The Wealth of Nations*
1781 Kant: *Critique of Pure Reason*
1782 Schiller: *Die Räuber*
1783 End of the American War of Independence
1784 Cort: invention of iron puddling
Beaumarchais/Mozart: *Le Mariage de Figaro*
David: "The Oath of the Horatii"
1785 Cartwright: invention of the power loom
1786 Death of Frederick II of Prussia
1787 Start of the political crisis in France
1788 Beginning of the colonization of Australia by England
1789 Start of the French Revolution
Sieyès: *What is the Third Estate?*
Lavoisier: *Traité de chimie*
Galvani: discovery of current electricity
1790 Death of the Emperor Joseph II
Burke: *Reflections on the Revolution in France*
Radishchev: *Journey from St. Petersburg to Moscow*
1791 Constitution of the French constitutional monarchy
Thomas Paine: *The Rights of Man*
Mozart: *The Magic Flute*
1792 Francis II becomes emperor
Start of the French Revolutionary Wars
Rouget de l'Isle: The Marseillaise
Successful slave revolt on St. Domingue (Haiti)
Convocation of the Convention and proclamation of the French Republic
1793 Execution of Louis XVI
Entry of England into the war and formation of the First Coalition against France
Royalist uprising in the Vendée
Civil war, Jacobin dictatorship and establishment of the revolutionary government in France
De-Christianization campaign
Buonaparte: *Le Souper de Beaucaire*
Condorcet: *Esquisse d'un tableau historique des progrès de l'esprit humain*
David: "Death of Marat"

1794 Abolition of slavery by the Convention
Polish uprising under Kościuszko
Chénier/Méhul: *Chant du départ*
Ninth of Thermidor (July 27): Fall of Robespierre
Chappe: invention of the optical telegraph
Founding of the Ecole Polytechnique in Paris
1795 Conquest of the Netherlands by French troops
Peace made in Basle with Prussia and Spain
Germinal and Prairial risings in Paris
Constitution of the Year III
Suppression of the Vendémiaire insurrection in Paris by General Buonaparte (October 5)
Beginning of the rule of the Directory ("Directoire")
Third Partition of Poland
Kant: *Perpetual Peace*
Introduction of the metric system in France
Restif de la Bretonne: *Monsieur Nicolas* (completed)
1796 Death of the Empress Catherine II of Russia; Tsar Paul I
Babeuf: *Conspiracy of Equals*
Napoleon Bonaparte's Italian campaign
Alliance between France and Bourbon Spain
De Maistre: *Considérations sur la France*
Leblanc: production of soda
1797 Execution of Babeuf and Darthé
Founding of the Cisalpine Republic
Directory's coup of 18 Fructidor (September 4)
Peace of Campo Formio between the French Republic and Austria
Dissolution of the Republic of Venice
Frederick William III King of Prussia (until 1840)
(Marquis de) Sade: *Justine*, 2nd edition
1798 Founding of the Roman and Helvetic "Sister Republics"
Bonaparte's expedition to Egypt
Occupation of Naples by French troops
Formation of the Second Coalition against France
Industrial exhibition at the Champs de Mars in Paris
Jenner: inoculation against smallpox
Coleridge: "France. An Ode"
Schlegel, Tieck: the journal *Athenäum* (until 1800)
Gros: "Bridge of Arcole"
1799 Resistance in South Germany, Switzerland, Italy and the Netherlands to the Second Coalition; Bonaparte's campaign in Syria
4.5. Defeat and death of France's ally, the Sultan Tipu of Mysore in Seringapatam (India)
18.6. Coup of 30 Prairial against the Directory
9.10. Bonaparte's return to France
9./10.11. Coup of 18 Brumaire, dismissal of Directory
14.12. Death of George Washington

15.12. Proclamation of the French Constitution of the Year VIII: Bonaparte becomes First Consul with Cambacérès and Lebrun as his fellow Consuls
Humboldt/Bonpland: Expedition to America (until 1804)
Discovery of the Rosetta Stone
Laplace: *Traité de mécanique céleste*
Monge: *Traité de géométrie descriptive*
Novalis: *Die Christenheit oder Europa*
David: "The Rape of the Sabine Women"
Beethoven: The "Pathétique"
1800
7.2. Plebiscite on the constitution of the Consulate
13.2. Bank of France founded
17.2. Law reorganizing the administrative structure: the prefectorial system
18. to 20.2. Amnesty for the Chouans
19.2. Bonaparte moves into the Tuileries
14.3. Pope Pius VII (Count Chiaramonti) until 1823
18.3. Legal constitution
14.6. Battle of Marengo
3.9. Malta occupied by the English
20.10. Partial amnesty for the emigrés
3.12. Moreau's victory at Hohenlinden
24.12. Attempt on Bonaparte's life ("infernal machine")
Toussaint L'Ouverture made President of Haiti for life
Fulton's submarine "Nautilus"
Volta: "Voltaic pile"
Carlisle/Nicholson: electrolysis of water
Senefelder: invention of lithography
Davy: *Researches Chemical and Philosophical*
Young: Theory of light and colour
Fichte: *Der geschlossene Handelsstaat*
Schleiermacher: *Monologe*
Karamzin: *Poor Liza*
Jean Paul: *Titan* (until 1803)
Goya: "Family of Charles IV"
Paganini: 24 Capricci per violino solo
1801
5.1. Decree of Senate deporting 130 "Jacobins"
9.2. Treaty of Lunéville
4.3. Thomas Jefferson President of the USA (until 1809)
6.3. Resignation of Prime Minister William Pitt, leader of the "War party" in England
9.3. Reopening of the stock markets in France
23./24.3. Assassination of Paul I; Tsar Alexander I (until 1825)
15.7. Concordat signed (but not enforced until 1802)
31.7. Organization of the national gendarmerie in France
Achard: start of industrial sugar-beet production in Silesia
Davy: discovery of the electric arc
Gauss: *Disquisitiones mathematicae*

Destutt de Tracy: *Eléments d'Idéologie* (until 1815)
De Pixérécourt: *Célina*
Pestalozzi: *How Gertrude Teaches her Children*
Schiller: *The Maid of Orléans*
David: "Bonaparte at Mont-Saint-Bernard"
Isabey: Portrait of Bonaparte
Haydn: "The Seasons"
Beethoven: "Moonlight Sonata"

1802

26.1. The Cisalpine Republic becomes the Republic of Italy
25.3. Peace of Amiens signed
26.4. General amnesty for the emigrés
1.5. Law on public education, creation of the Lycée on December 10
19.5. Creation of the order of the Legion of Honour
20.5. Restoration of slavery in the French colonies; arrest of Toussaint L'Ouverture on June 7
2.8. Plebiscite confirms Bonaparte as Consul for life
11.9. Piedmont annexed by France
13.9. Wholesale uprising on St. Domingue
Industrial exhibition in Paris
Grotefend: deciphering of cuneiform script
Gay-Lussac: law of thermal coefficients
Ritter: discovery of ultraviolet rays
Ampère: *Considérations sur la théorie mathématique du jeu*
Chateaubriand: *Le Génie du Christianisme*
Delille: *La pitié*
Foscolo: *Ultime Lettere di Jacopo Ortis*
Kleist: *Der zerbrochene Krug*
Novalis: *Heinrich von Ofterdingen* (published posthumously)
Gérard: "Madame Récamier"

1803

23.1. Reorganization of the Institut national de France
19.2. "Act of Mediation" to re-establish the confederation of the 19 Swiss cantons; end of the united Helvetic Republic
23.2. Reichsdeputationshauptschluss of Regensburg
16.3. Law on the notaries
28.3. Exchange rate of the "franc Germinal" fixed
7.4. Death of Toussaint L'Ouverture as a prisoner in Fort Joux in France
12.4. Law on working in manufactories and workshops
3.5. Louisiana (repossessed by the French in 1797) sold to the USA
12.5. Peace of Amiens broken, Anglo-French war resumed
July French army assembled in Boulogne for invasion of England
20.8. Clandestine return of Cadoudal from England to prepare assassination attempt

1.12. Introduction of employment record books
Fulton's steamboat "Pyroscaphe" on the Seine
Trevithick: first steam locomotive
Berthollet: *Essai de statique chimique*
Cabanis: *Rapports du physique et du moral*
De Staël: *Delphine*
Beethoven: "Eroica"

1804

21.3. *Code civil* finalized (implemented in 1806)
Duc d'Enghien shot in Vincennes
27.3. At Fouché's prompting the Senate agrees to the idea of Napoleon Bonaparte becoming hereditary emperor
March Start of Serbian revolt against Turkish rule under Karageorge (until 1813)
10.5. Pitt back in power in Great Britain
18.5. Constitution of the Year XII; decree of Senate on the Imperial dignity
19.5. Appointment of 18 marshals of Imperial France
28.6. Execution of Cadoudal and some of his fellow conspirators
10.7. Fouché reappointed minister of police following his dismissal in 1802
15.7. Order of the Legion of Honour bestowed for the first time
11.8. Holy Roman Emperor Francis II declares himself Emperor of Austria as Francis I
First flower show in London
Charles Fourier: *Harmonie universelle*
Schiller: *Wilhelm Tell*
De Senancour: *Obermann*
Gros: "The Plague at Jaffa"
Goya: "Maja vestida, Maja desnuda"
6.11. Plebiscite on the constitution of the Year XII
2.12. Coronation of Napoleon I as emperor in Notre Dame cathedral in the presence of Pope Pius VII

1805

9.3. Press office founded in France
17.3. Republic of Italy becomes kingdom under Napoleon
11.4. Third Coalition formed against France
4.6. Ligurian Republic (Genoa) annexed by France
7.6. Eugène de Beauharnais becomes Viceroy of Italy
9.7. Mehemet Ali becomes Pasha of Egypt
17.8. Army camp at Boulogne dissolved
21.10. Nelson's victory and death at the Battle of Trafalgar
2.12. Battle of Austerlitz
26.12. Peace of Pressburg (Bratislava) between France and Austria, end of the Third Coalition
27.12. Flight of the Bourbons from Naples
Jacquard: invention of "Jacquard loom"
Sertürner: isolation of morphine
Gay-Lussac: *Théorie cinétique des gaz*
Fichte: *Die Bestimmung des Menschen*

Jean Paul: *Freiheitsbüchlein*
Scott: *The Lay of the Last Minstrel*
Canova: Pauline Borghese as "Venus Victrix"
Prud'hon: the Empress Josephine as "Venus Victrix"
Turner: "The Shipwreck"
Beethoven: *Fidelio* (first version)

1806

1.1. Gregorian calendar reintroduced in France
23.1. Death of William Pitt the Younger, British prime minister
30.3. Joseph Bonaparte King of Naples
4.4. "Imperial catechism" published
10.5. Imperial University of France founded
5.6. Louis Bonaparte King of Holland
24.6. Gambling casinos banned in France
12.7. Rhine Confederation formed under the protectorate of Napoleon
1.8. Dissolution of the Holy Roman Empire and of the Diet of Regensburg, Francis II lays down his Imperial title (on August 6)
26.8. Execution of the Nuremberg bookseller Palm, author of the pamphlet *Deutschland in seiner Erniedrigung*
14.10. Battle of Jena/Auerstedt
27.10. Napoleon enters the undefended Berlin
21.11. "Berlin Decree" proclaims "continental system" against England
28.11. The French enter Warsaw
10.12. Assembly of the Jewish Notables in Paris
11.12. Saxony joins the Rhine Confederation
30.12. Turkey declares war on Russia
Pont d'Austerlitz inaugurated in Paris, work begun on the construction of the two triumphal arches
Lamarck: *Recherches sur l'organisation des corps vivants*
Hegel: *Phenomenology of Mind*
Brentano/Von Arnim: *Des Knaben Wunderhorn* (until 1808)
Goethe: *Faust*, Part I
Legouvé: *La mort de Henri IV*
David: "The Coronation of Napoleon" (Le Sacre)
Beethoven: The "Appassionata"

1807

1.1. Napoleon meets Maria Walewska
7./8.2. Battle of Eylau
2.3. French decree on the status of the Jews
7.3. Tory cabinet formed in England under Canning and Castlereagh
25.4. Decree on the Parisian theatres
4.5. Franco-Persian treaty against Russia
27.5. Sultan Selim III deposed in Constantinople
31.5. First elevations to the Imperial nobility
14.6. Battle of Friedland
9.7. Treaty of Tilsit, end of the Fourth Coalition
22.7. Grand Duchy of Warsaw founded

9.8. Talleyrand replaced as foreign minister by Champagny

16.8. Jérôme Bonaparte King of Westphalia

17.8. Maiden voyage of Fulton's paddle-steamer "The Steamboat" ("Clermont") along the Hudson from New York to Albany

19.8. The "Tribunate" abolished in France

1.9. Code of commercial law published

5.9. Law on estate registration

9.10. Start of the Prussian era of reform under Freiherr vom Stein: "October Edict" abolishes hereditary serfdom

27.10. Secret Franco-Spanish treaty on the partition of Portugal

23.11./17.12. "Continental system" intensified by "Milan Decrees"

30.11. French troops under Junot occupy Lisbon, the Portuguese court flees to Brazil

Davy: isolation of chemicals by electrolysis

Corvisart: *Traité sur les lésions organiques du cœur*

Fichte: *Reden an die Deutsche Nation* (until 1808)

De Staël: *Corinne*

Ingres: "La Source"

Méhul: *Joseph*

Spontini: *La Vestale*

1808

1.3. Formal decision of the Senate to create an Imperial nobility ("Nobles de l'Empire")

17.3. Decree on tertiary education

19.3. Abdication of Charles IV of Spain

2.5. Insurrection in Madrid, abdication of Ferdinand VII on May 5

May/June Anti-French revolts throughout Spain

24.5. Parma and Tuscany annexed by France

2.6. Joseph Bonaparte King of Spain

9.6. Conspiracy of the Republican general Malet uncovered in Paris

15.7. Murat King of Naples

22.7. Surrender of French army under Dupont at Bailén

28.7. Mahmud II becomes sultan (until 1839)

30.8. Capitulation of Cintra; French expelled from Portugal by English expeditionary corps

27.9. to 14.10. Summit meeting in Erfurt

4.11. to 4.12. Napoleon's Spanish campaign, entry into Madrid

19.11. Municipal reorganization in Prussia

24.11. Freiherr vom Stein dismissed at Napoleon's behest

Fourier: *Théorie des quatre mouvements*

Saint-Simon: *Introduction aux travaux scientifiques du XIXᵉ siècle*

Schlegel: *Von der Sprache und Weisheit der Inder*

Kleist: *Die Hermannsschlacht*

Lesueur: *Le Triomphe de Trajan*

Gérard: "Austerlitz"

Gros: "Battle of Eylau"

Ingres: "Oedipus and the Sphinx"

Beethoven: "Pastoral" Symphony

1809

29.1. Talleyrand, still grand chamberlain, falls out of favour with Napoleon

13.3. Coup d'état in Sweden, Gustavus IV deposed

April Fifth Coalition formed against France

Rising in the Tyrol under Andreas Hofer

17.5. Papal States annexed by France

21./22.5. Battle of Aspern/Essling

31.5. Death of Joseph Haydn in occupied Vienna

10.6. Napoleon excommunicated by Pope Pius VII

5./6.7. Battle of Wagram

6.7. Pope removed from Rome to Savona

8.7. Metternich becomes Austrian foreign minister

28.7. Arthur Wellesley (later Lord Wellington) victorious at Talavera in Spain

17.9. Treaty of Frederikshavn: Finland ceded to Russia by Sweden

12.10. Attempt on the life of Napoleon in Vienna by Friedrich Staps

14.10. Treaty of Schönbrunn (Vienna), creation of the "Illyrian provinces" by Napoleon, end of the Fifth Coalition

15.12. Senate decree on Napoleon's divorce from Josephine

Vauquelin: discovery of nicotine

Gauss: *Theoria maius corporum*

Carnot: *De la défense des places fortes*

Chateaubriand: *Les Martyrs*

Goethe: *Die Wahlverwandtschaften*

Jean Paul: *Krieg dem Kriege!*

Turner: "London seen from Greenwich"

1810

9./12.1. Marriage of Napoleon and Josephine annulled by the Paris church authorities

3.2. Censorship re-introduced in France

20.3. Andreas Hofer shot in Mantua

1./2.4. Civil and church wedding ceremony of Napoleon and Marie Louise of Austria

May/September Start of War of Independence in Spanish America

3.6. Fouché replaced as police minister by Savary

3.7. Louis Bonaparte abdicates as King of Holland

August Onset of economic crisis in England

21.8. Marshal Bernadotte elected Crown Prince of Sweden

14.9. Feudal contributions and services made redeemable in Prussia

11.11. Wellington holds the lines of Torres Vedras in front of Lisbon against the French under Masséna

10.12. Northwestern German and Swiss territories annexed: Senate decree on the 130 French départements (on December 13)

31.12. Russian tariffs imposed on French merchandise

Opening of a university in Berlin, inspired by Wilhelm von Humboldt

Gall: *Anatomie et physiologie du système nerveux* (until 1825)

Hahnemann: *Organon der rationellen Heilkunde* (homeopathy)

Goldsmith: *Histoire secrète du Cabinet de Bonaparte*

Kotzebue: *Die Grille*, a journal published in St. Petersburg

De Staël: *De l'Allemagne* (second edition, London, 1813)

Kleist: *Prinz Friedrich von Homburg*

1811

1.1. The *Code pénal* of 1809 comes into force

20.3. Birth of the "King of Rome"

March French withdrawal from Portugal

March/May Spate of machine-breaking in England by the Luddites (defended by Lord Byron in the House of Lords)

17.6. to 20.10. National Council of French bishops in Paris

27.7. Hidalgo, the priest who led the Mexican revolt against Spanish colonial rule, is shot

28.8. Economic crisis in France: a council of supply summoned in expectation of catastrophic harvest

7.9. Freedom of trade introduced in Prussia

21.11. Suicide of Heinrich von Kleist

5.12. Surrender of Turkish army to General Kutusov in Slobodzié

Krupp works founded in Essen by Friedrich Krupp

Brockhaus: Conversations-Lexikon completed

Goethe: *Dichtung und Wahrheit*

Goya: "Los Desastres de la Guerra"

1812

23.2. Concordat cancelled by Napoleon

24.2. Franco-Prussian treaty of alliance

2.3. Riots in Caën provoked by food shortages

11.3. Emancipation of the Jews in Prussia

14.3. Franco-Austrian treaty of alliance

18.3. Proclamation of a liberal constitution by the Spanish Cortes in Cádiz

9.4. Russo-Swedish pact of Åbo (Turku)

4./8.5. Regulation of corn trade in France

28.5. Russo-Turkish Peace Treaty of Bucharest

18.6. USA declares war on Great Britain

19.6. Captured pope arrives at Fontainebleau

7.9. Battle of Borodino on the Moskva

14.9. to 19.10. Napoleon in Moscow

15.10. From Moscow Napoleon decrees statute on the Comédie-Française

29.10. Execution of General Malet and fellow conspirators following their abortive plot on October 23 in Paris

27. to 29.11. Battle of Beresina

5.12. Napoleon abandons army and returns to Paris

16.12. Publication of 29th bulletin in the *Moniteur* informs Europe of the route of the Grand Army during retreat from Moscow

30.12. Russo-Prussian Convention of Tauroggen
Completion of the Panthéon in Paris
Bell's steamship "Comet" on Clyde in Scotland
Laplace: *Théorie analytique des probabilités*
Cuvier: *Recherches sur les ossements fossiles des quadrupèdes*
d'Ivernois: *Napoléon administrateur et financier* (London)
Arndt: *Kleiner Katechismus*
Byron: *Childe Harold's Pilgrimage*
Jacob and Wilhelm Grimm: Collection of fairy tales
Krylov: *Fables*
Beethoven: 8th Symphony

1813

2.1. Napoleon visits Delessert's sugar refinery in Passy

25.1. New Concordat signed at Fontainebleau but revoked by the pope on March 24

28.2. Russo-Prussian Treaty of Kalisch

17.3. Prussia declares war on France: Start of the Sixth Coalition War

2.5. Battle of Lützen-Grossgörschen; Scharnhorst dies of his wounds on June 28

4.6. to 10.8. Armistice of Pläswitz

21.6. Wellington victorious at Vitoria in Spain

29.7. to 11.8. Failure of the Prague "Peace Congress"

12.8. Austria declares war on France

26./27.8. Battle of Dresden; Moreau, fighting on the side of the Allies, dies of his wounds

8.10. Bavaria abandons Napoleon: Treaty of Ried

16. to 19.10. Napoleon defeated at the Battle of the Nations in Leipzig
Owen: *A New View of Society*
Davy: *On some Chemical Agencies of Electricity*
Körner: *Leyer und Schwerdt* (published posthumously in 1814)
Blake: *The Day of Judgement*
Shelley: *Queen Mab*
Beethoven: "Die Schlacht bei Vitoria"

1814

1.1. Blücher crosses the Rhine at Caub

11.1. Murat comes to terms with the Allies

21.1. Pope released and Papal States restored

27.1. to 4.4. Napoleon's "French campaign"

3.2. to 19.3. Abortive Congress of Châtillon

30.3. Capitulation of Paris; Allies enter capital on March 31

1.4. Provisional Government formed under Talleyrand

6.4. Napoleon abdicates unconditionally

3.5. Louis XVIII arrives in Paris; Napoleon lands on Elba

11.5. Coup d'état in Spain to restore Bourbon absolutism

29.5. Death of Josephine at Malmaison

30.5. First Peace Treaty of Paris

4.6. Louis XVIII proclaims his "Charte"

7.8. Ban on Jesuits lifted

14.8. Norway annexed by Sweden by the Convention of Moss

1.11. Vienna Congress opens

24.12. Peace Treaty of Ghent between Great Britain and the USA
George Stephenson's steam locomotive
Maine de Biran: *Rapports du physique et du moral*
Constant: *De l'esprit de conquête et de l'usurpation*
Saint Simon/Comte: *De la réorganisation de la société européenne*
Görres: *Der Rheinische Merkur*
Leopardi: *All'Italia*
Scott: *Waverley*
Chamisso: *Peter Schlemihl*
Goya: "El Dos de Mayo"

1815

1.3. Napoleon lands in the Golfe Juan

20.3. Napoleon enters Paris

21.3. Provisional government formed, B. Constant asked to draw up new constitution

25.3. In Vienna the Allies agree on the Seventh Coalition War and outlaw Napoleon

22.4. Imperial constitution supplemented by the "Acte additionel"

3.5. Murat, having sided with Napoleon once more, is defeated at Tolentino and flees to France

8.6. German Confederation created at the Vienna Congress

18.6. Battle of Waterloo

21.6. Napoleon ignores pleas from the people to resume the struggle as a revolutionary war; on June 22 he abdicates once again

6.7. Allies re-enter Paris

15.7. In Rochefort Napoleon boards the English ship "Bellerophon"

31.7. "General Bonaparte" declared English prisoner of war

2.8. Marshal Brune murdered

19.9. Fouché dismissed

24.9. Talleyrand dismissed

26.9. "Holy Alliance" of European monarchs formed

13.10. Murat shot in Pizzo

15.10. Napoleon arrives in St. Helena

20.11. Second Peace Treaty of Paris
Say: *Catéchisme d'économie politique*
Ricardo: *Essay on the Influence of a Low Price of Corn in the Profits of Stock*
Béranger: "Chansons"
Tegnér: *The Eagle Awaking*
Gros: Portrait of the Duchess of Angoulême

1821

5.5. Death of Napoleon at Longwood on St. Helena

Bibliography

I

Sources and General Literature

Atlas administratif du Premier Empire. Edited by F. de Dainville and J. Tulard, Paris, 1965.

Catéchisme à l'usage de toutes les Eglises de l'Empire français. Paris, 1806.

Correspondance de Napoléon Ier. 32 Vols., Paris, 1858–1870.

Correspondance et relations de J. Fiévée avec Bonaparte pendant onze années 1802–1813. 3 Vols., Paris, 1836.

Denkwürdigkeiten des Marschalls Marmont, Herzog von Ragusa. Halle, 1857.

Deutschland unter Napoleon in Augenzeugenberichten. Edited by E. Klessmann, Munich, 1976.

Deutschland und Italien im Zeitalter Napoleons. Edited by A. von Reden-Dohna, Wiesbaden, 1979.

GOUJON, A.: *Les Bulletins officiels de la Grande-Armée.* 4 Vols., Paris, 1820–1821.

Kampf um Freiheit. Dokumente zur Zeit der nationalen Erhebung, 1789–1815. Edited by F. Donath and W. Markov, Berlin, 1954.

MELCHIOR-BONNET, B.: *Dictionnaire de la Révolution et de l'Empire.* Paris, 1965.

Mémoires de M. le comte de Montlosier sur la Révolution française, le Consulat, l'Empire, la Restauration et les principaux événements qui l'ont suivi. Paris, 1829.

Napoléon Bonaparte. Oeuvres littéraires et écrits militaires. Edited by J. Tulard, 3 Vols., Paris 1967–1968.

Ordres et apostilles de Napoléon (1799–1814). Edited by A. Chuquet, 4 Vols., Paris, 1911–1912.

PALLUEL, A.: *Dictionnaire de l'Empereur.* Paris, 1969.

THIÉBAULT, P.C.F.: *Memoiren aus der Zeit der französischen Revolution und des Kaiserreichs.* Stuttgart, 1902.

II

Napoleon Bonaparte

ANNAULT, A.V.: *Napoleons Leben.* Frankfurt/Main, 1826.

BOURRIENNE, L.A.: *Memoiren über Napoleon, das Directorium, das Consulat, das Kaiserreich und die Restauration.* Leipzig, 1829–1830.

CHANDLER, D.: *Napoleon.* London, 1973.

CRONIN, V.: *Napoleon. Eine Biographie.* (Glasgow, 1971) Hamburg, Düsseldorf, 1973.

GARROS, L.: *Quel roman que ma vie! Itinéraire de Napoléon Bonaparte.* Paris, 1947.

GODECHOT, J.: *Napoléon.* Paris, 1969.

GOTTHART, H.: *Vive l'Empereur! Eine Napoleon-Chronik.* Hamburg, 1967.

GRAND-CARTERET, J.: *Napoleon in der Caricatur.* Leipzig, no date.

HEROLD, C.: *Der korsische Degen. Napoleon und seine Zeit.* Munich, 1966.

KEMBLE, K.: *Napoleon immortal. The Medical History and Private Life of Napoleon Bonaparte.* London, 1959.

LEFEBVRE, G.: *Napoléon.* Paris, 2nd edition 1951 and new editions.

MANFRED, A.Z.: *Napoleon Bonaparte.* (Moscow, 1971) Berlin, 1978.

MARKOV, W.: *Napoleone.* Milan, 1967.

MASSON, F.: *Napoléon et sa famille.* 13 Vols., Paris, 1897–1919.

MISTLER, J.: *Napoléon et l'Empire.* Paris, 1968.

NAPOLEON: *Ich, der Kaiser. Eine Autobiographie.* Edited by K. Klinger, Munich, 1978.

Napoleon und Europa. Edited by H.O. Sieburg, Cologne/Berlin (West), 1971.

TARLÉ, E.V.: *Napoleon.* (Moscow, 1936) Berlin, 1974.

TERSEN, E.: *Napoléon.* Paris, 1959.

THIRY, J.: *Napoléon Bonaparte.* 28 Vols., Paris, 1938–1975.

THOMPSON, J.M.: *Napoleon,* London, 1952.

ZAHORSKI, A.: *Napoleon.* Warsaw, 1982.

III

Consulate and Empire

BEAUVAIS, C.T.: *Victoires et conquêtes des Français.* 28 Vols., Paris, 1817–1826.

BERGERON, L.: *L'Episode napoléonien. Aspects intérieurs, 1799–1815.* Paris, 1972.

BERGERON, L.: *Grand Notables du Premier Empire. Notices de biographie sociale.* Paris, 1978.

BERTAUD, J.P.: *Le Premier Empire, legs de la Révolution.* Paris, 1973.

CHANDLER, D.: *The Campaigns of Napoleon.* New York, 1966.

COLLAVERI. F.: *La Franc-Maçonnerie des Bonaparte.* Paris, 1982.

CONELLY, O.: *Napoleon's Satellite Kingdoms.* New York, 1965.

DAUDET, L.: *Deux idoles sanglants, la Révolution et son fils Bonaparte.* Paris, 1939.

DUMAS, M.: *Précis d'événements militaires ou essai historique sur les campagnes de 1799 à 1814.* 19 Vols., Paris, 1816–1826.

DURANT, W. and A.: *Die Französische Revolution und der Aufstieg Napoleons.* (New York, 1975) Munich, 1979.

FEHRENBACH, E.: *Vom Ancien Régime zum Wiener Kongress.* Munich, 1981.

FIEDLER, S.: *Das Zeitalter der französischen Revolution und Napoleons. Grundriss der Militär- und Kriegsgeschichte,* II. Munich, 1976.

GIESSELMANN, W.: *Die brumairianische Elite. Kontinuität und Wandel der französischen Führungsschicht zwischen Ancien Régime und Julimonarchie.* Stuttgart, 1977.

GODECHOT, J.: *Les Institutions de la France sous la Révolution et l'Empire.* Paris, 1951, 2nd edition 1969.

GODECHOT, J.: *L'Europe et l'Amérique à l'époque napoléonienne.* Paris, 1967.

HAUTECOURT, E.: *L'Art sous la Révolution et l'Empire en France.* Paris, 1953.

HELMERT, H., and USCZECK, H.: *Europäische Befreiungskriege 1808–1814/15. Militärischer Verlauf.* Berlin, 2nd edition 1981.

Histoire de la France contemporaine, 1789–1980, Vol. II: *1799–1855* (J.P. BERTAUD, *La France du Consulat et de l'Empire 1799–1815.* Paris, 1979.

JANNEAU, G.: *L'Empire.* Paris, 1965.

JESCHONEK, B.: *Waterloo 1815. Illustrierte historische Hefte,* No. 15, 3rd edition, Berlin, 1982.

JOMINI, H. DE: *Histoire critique et militaire des campagnes de la Révolution.* Paris, 1819–1824.

KIRCHEISEN, F.M.: *Napoleon I. und das Zeitalter der Befreiungskriege im Bilde.* Munich, Leipzig, 1914.

LATREILLE, A.: *L'ère napoléonienne.* Paris, 1974.

LÈVY-LEBOYER, M.: *Les Banques européennes et l'industrialisation de l'Europe au début du XIXe siècle.* Paris, 1964.

MADELIN, L.: *Histoire du Consulat et de l'Empire.* Paris, 1936–1954.

MASSIN, J.: *Almanach du Premier Empire. Du Neuf Thermidor à Waterloo.* Paris, 1965.

REICHARDT, J.F.: *Vertraute Briefe aus Paris, 1792.* Edited and with an introduction by Rolf Weber, Berlin, 1980.

RUDÉ, G.F.: *Europa im Umbruch. Vom Vorabend der Französischen Revolution bis zum Wiener Kongress.* Munich, 1981.

SIEBURG, F.: *Im Licht und Schatten der Freiheit. Frankreich 1789–1848.* Stuttgart, 3rd edition 1979.

SIX, G.: *Les Généraux de la Révolution et de l'Empire.* Paris, 1947.

SOBOUL, A.: *Le Premier Empire.* Paris, 1973.

SOBOUL, A.: *La Civilisation et la Révolution française,* Vol. III: *La France napoléonienne.* Paris, 1983.

STREISAND, J.: *Deutsche Geschichte 1789–1815.* Berlin, 5th edition 1981.

THIERS, A.: *Histoire du Consulat et de l'Empire.* 20 Vols., Paris, 1845–1862.

TULARD, J.: *La vie quotidienne des Français sous Napoléon.* Paris, 1978.

TULARD, J.: *Le Grand Empire.* Paris, 1982.

VILLEFOSSE, L. DE, and BOUSSOUNOUSE, J.: *L'opposition à Napoléon.* Paris, 1969.

WITTKOPP, J.F.: *Die Welt des Empire. Directoire, Empire, Klassizismus.* Munich, 1968.

Sources of Illustrations

Graphische Sammlungen Albertina, Vienna: 30

Bibliothèque de la ville de Paris: 112

Bibliothèque Nationale, Paris: 95, 206, 207, 210, 214/215, 223, 235, 237

Breitenborn, Dieter: 5, 12 right, 20 bottom, 22 bottom, 25, 31, 40, 66, 68, 78, 84, 86, 88, 111, 113, 114, 122 bottom, 130, 134, 135, 156 top, 159, 162, 164, 165, 172, 173, 194, 208, 218, 219, 235, 236, 241, 254 top, 255, 264, 266 bottom

Bulloz, Paris: 158

Deutsche Fotothek, Dresden: 12 left, 15, 17, 22 top, 41, 56, 57, 79, 82, 83, 87, 89, 91, 94, 108, 114, 116, 120, 122 top, 126, 132, 133, 140 left, 142, 156 bottom, 160, 161 left, 204, 205 top, 224, 226, 227, 258

Deutsche Staatsbibliothek, Berlin: 2, 19, 52, 98, 105, 121, 161 right, 193, 195, 196, 197, 198, 238, 253, 254, 257 bottom

Documentation photographique de la Réunion des musées nationaux, Paris: 136/137, 138, 145, 146, 147, 148/149, 150, 153, 157

École nationale supérieure des Beaux-Arts, Paris: 139

Giraudon, Paris: 155, 209

Henschelverlag, Berlin: 42, 62, 101, 109, 142, 154, 176

Kunsthalle Hamburg/Ralph Kleinhempel: 35, 129

Kunsthistorisches Museum, Vienna: 8

Musée Granet, Aix-en-Provence: 151

Musée Marmottan, Paris: 69

Museo del Prado, Madrid: 177

Museum der bildenden Künste, Leipzig: 28, 38, 53, 76, 80, 97, 106, 144, 185, 228, 265

Museum für Deutsche Geschichte, Berlin: 29, 49, 54, 64, 229, 234

Museum für Geschichte der Stadt Leipzig/Reiner Funk: 72

Joachim Petri: 32, 33, 44, 48, 216, 232 top, 261

Nationale Forschungs- und Gedenkstätten, Weimar: 65/Eberhard Renno: 211, 212, 213

National Maritime Museum, London: 253

Petri, Joachim, Leipzig: 20 top, 50, 60, 70, 73, 74, 75, 263

Schäfer, Georg, Schweinfurt: 191

Seemann-Verlag, Leipzig: 143, 152, 179, 188, 192

Staatliche Galerie Dessau, Schloss Georgium: 190

Staatliche Kunstsammlungen Dresden
Gemäldegalerie Neue Meister: 71, 186, 187
Kunstgewerbemuseum: 169

Staatliche Museen Berlin: 175
Kunstgewerbemuseum: 166, 167, 168
Kupferstichkabinett and Collection of Drawings: 4, 14, 36, 39, 67, 102, 104, 117, 119, 140 right, 199, 200, 201, 205 bottom, 221, 240, 242/243, 244, 245, 260, 266 top
Nationalgalerie: 174

Staatliche Schlösser und Gärten, Homburg vor der Höhe: 24

Staatliches Kupferstichkabinett and Collection of Drawings, Greiz: 10, 11, 26, 27/Joachim Petri: 13, 16, 18, 23 left, 23 right, 46, 47, 48, 92/93, 103, 107, 123, 203, 219 top, 225, 249 bottom, 250

Staatsgalerie Stuttgart: 184

Statens Museum for Kunst, Copenhagen: 183

Steuerlein, Asmus, Dresden: 43

Tate Gallery, London: 178, 180/181

Universitätsbibliothek Leipzig/Werner Pinkert: 127

Verlagsarchiv: 59, 118, 125, 131, 170, 171, 182, 230, 248/249, 262

Index of Names

DE GERMANIS

Brenet F.

PRIMATIAE BELLI ARMA SIGNA MILITARIA
E MANVBIIS VERTINGINS
CIVITATI DONATA.
VI ID OCT MDCCCV.

TEMPLVM JANI.

PAIX DE PRESBOURG
XXVI DÉCEMBRE
Andrieu F. MDCCCV. *Denon D.*

Brenet F. *Denon D.*
VENISE RENDUE
A L'ITALIE
XXVI DÉCEMBRE
MDCCCV.

L'EMPEREUR COMMANDE LA GRANDE ARMÉE.

Brenet F. *Denon D.*
LEVÉE DU CAMP DE BOULOGNE LE XXIV
AOUT MDCCCV
PASSAGE DU RHIN LE XIV SEP
MDCCCV.